ᵀʰᵉ BEAUTY™

VOLUME TWO

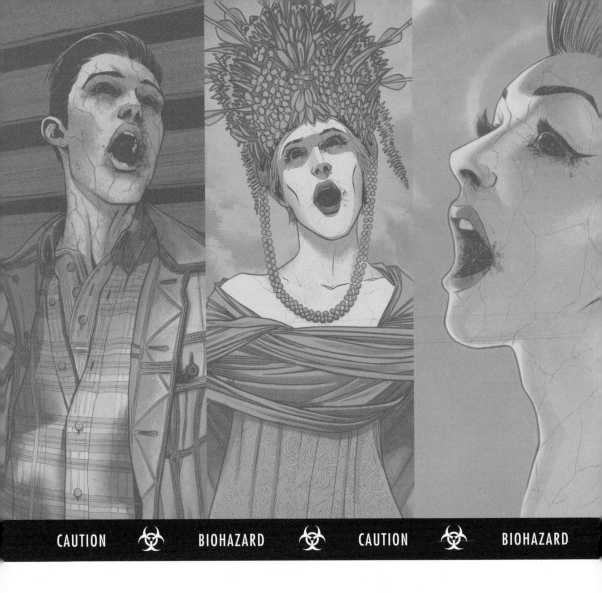

CAUTION   BIOHAZARD   CAUTION   BIOHAZARD

IMAGE COMICS, INC.

ROBERT KIRKMAN Chief Operating Officer • ERIK LARSEN Chief Financial Officer • TODD McFARLANE President
MARC SILVESTRI Chief Executive Officer • JIM VALENTINO Vice-President • ERIC STEPHENSON Publisher
COREY MURPHY Director of Sales • JEFF BOISON Director of Publishing Planning & Book Trade Sales
JEREMY SULLIVAN Director of Digital Sales • KAT SALAZAR Director of PR & Marketing
BRANWYN BIGGLESTONE Controller • DREW GILL Art Director • JONATHAN CHAN Production Manager
MEREDITH WALLACE Print Manager • BRIAH SKELLY Publicist • SASHA HEAD Sales & Marketing Production Designer
RANDY OKAMURA Digital Production Designer • DAVID BROTHERS Branding Manager • OLIVIA NGAI Content Manager
ADDISON DUKE Production Artist • VINCENT KUKUA Production Artist • TRICIA RAMOS Production Artist
JEFF STANG Direct Market Sales Representative • EMILIO BAUTISTA Digital Sales Associate
LEANNA CAUNTER Accounting Assistant • CHLOE RAMOS-PETERSON Library Market Sales Representative

www.imagecomics.com

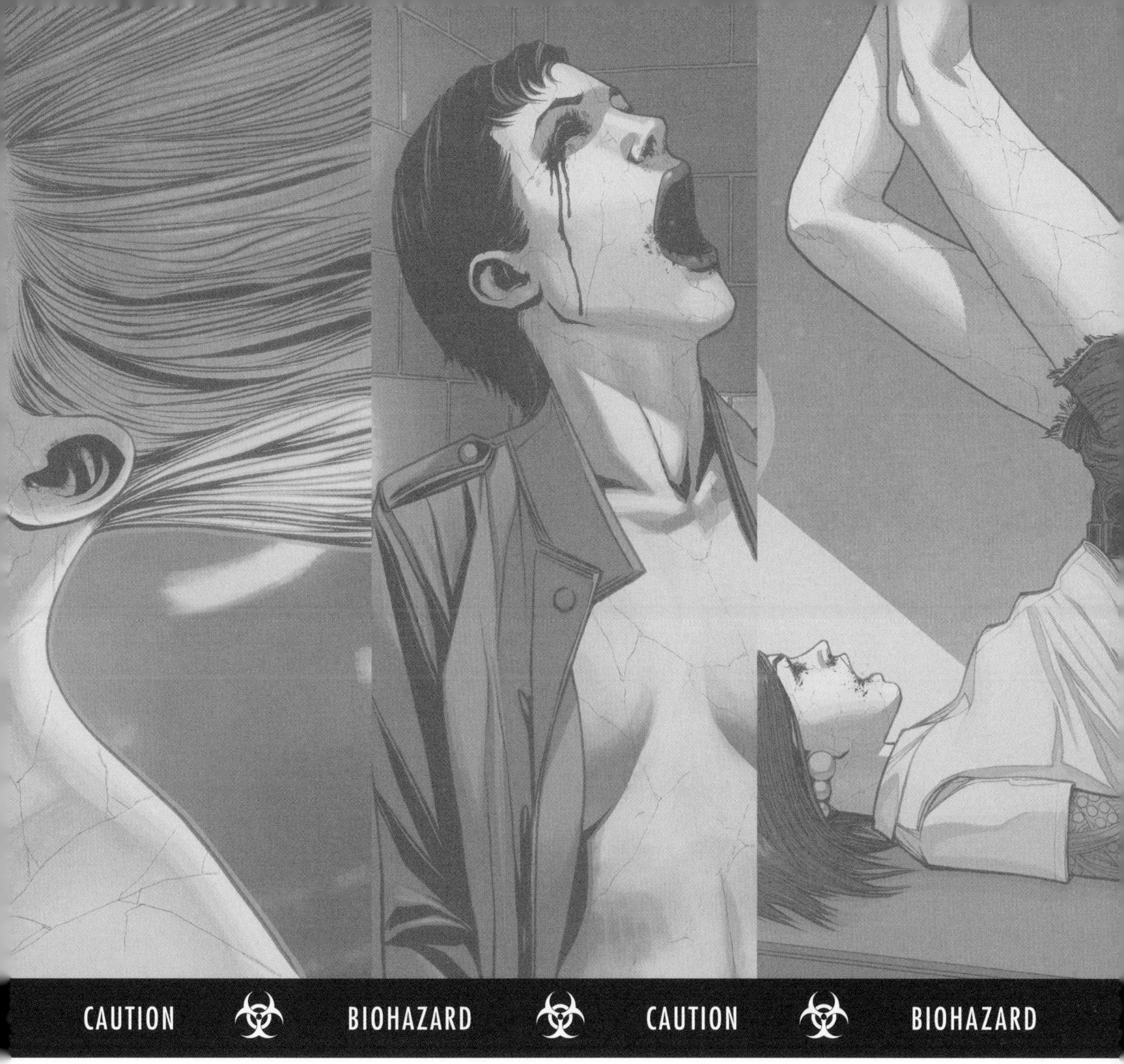
CAUTION
BIOHAZARD
CAUTION
BIOHAZARD

JEREMY HAUN & JASON A. HURLEY
story

MIKE HUDDLESTON [CHAPTER 7]
BRETT WELDELE [CHAPTERS 8—10]
STEPHEN GREEN [CHAPTER 11]
art

JOHN RAUCH [CHAPTERS 7+11]
color

FONOGRAFIKS
lettering & design

JOEL ENOS
editor

CHAPTER

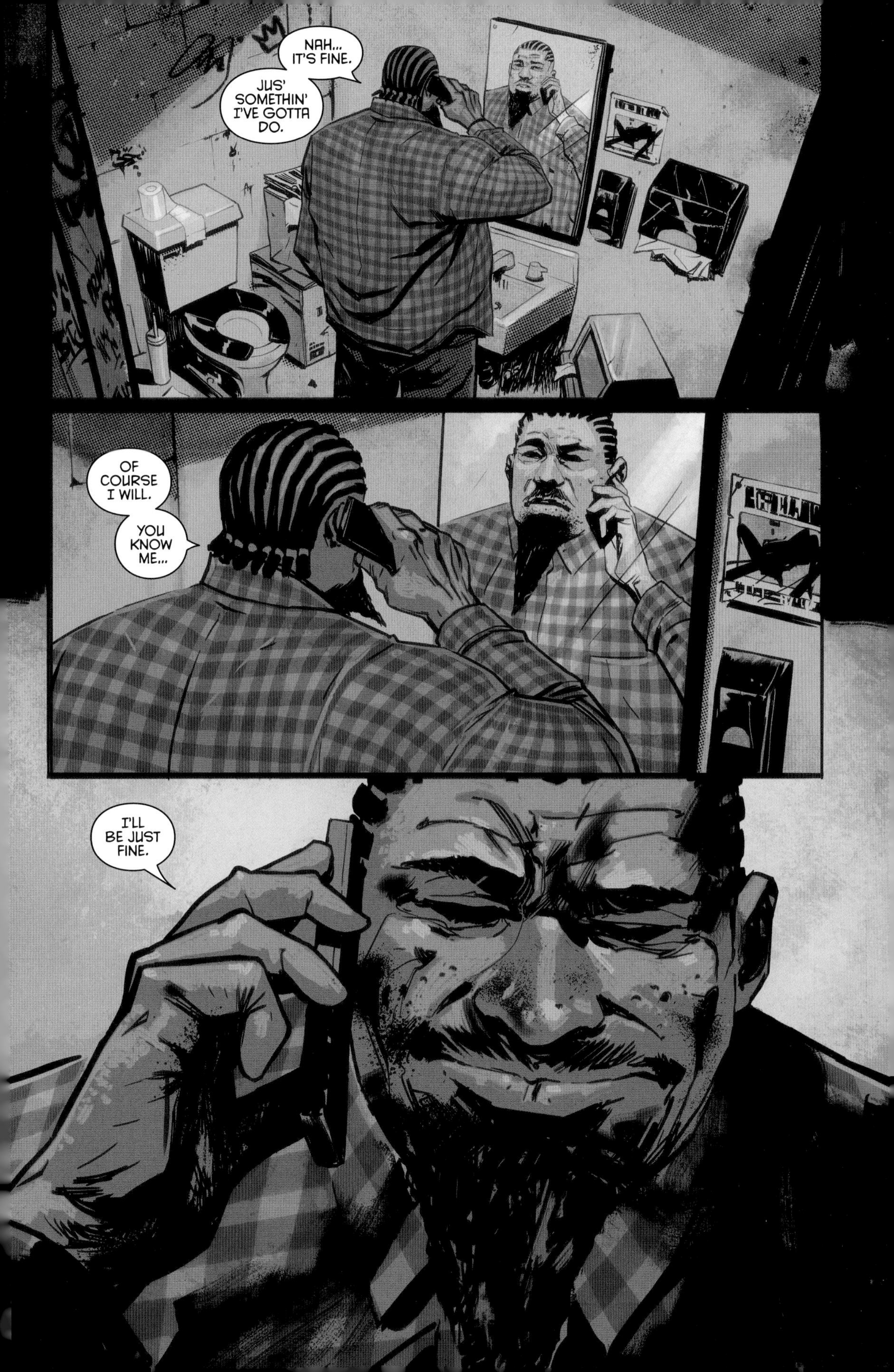
NAH... IT'S FINE.
JUS' SOMETHIN' I'VE GOTTA DO.
OF COURSE I WILL.
YOU KNOW ME...
I'LL BE JUST FINE.

I'LL DROP YOU A LINE AS SOON AS I CAN. MIGHT BE A FEW DAYS -- WEEK AT THE MOST, BUT I'LL HIT YOU UP.

ALRIGHT.

YEAH. YEAH.

TALK TO YOU SOON, BONITA.

My granddad had this little shop in the garage behind our house. Everybody in the neighborhood would bring him things to fix -- a toaster, a carburetor, whatever.

He'd fix it all.

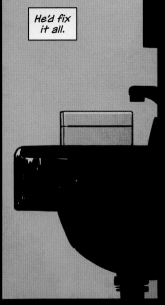

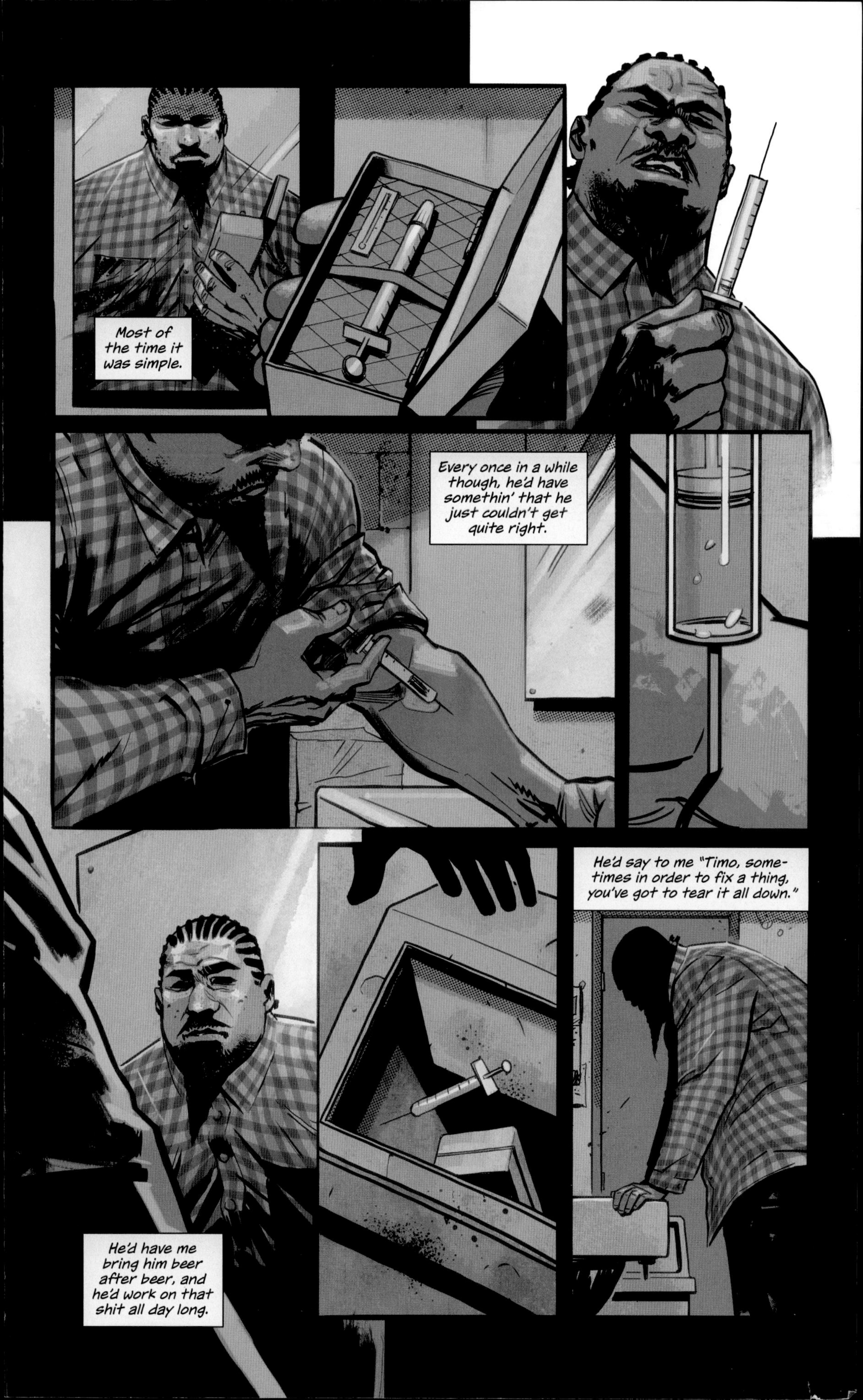
Most of the time it was simple.
Every once in a while though, he'd have somethin' that he just couldn't get quite right.
He'd have me bring him beer after beer, and he'd work on that shit all day long.
He'd say to me "Timo, sometimes in order to fix a thing, you've got to tear it all down."

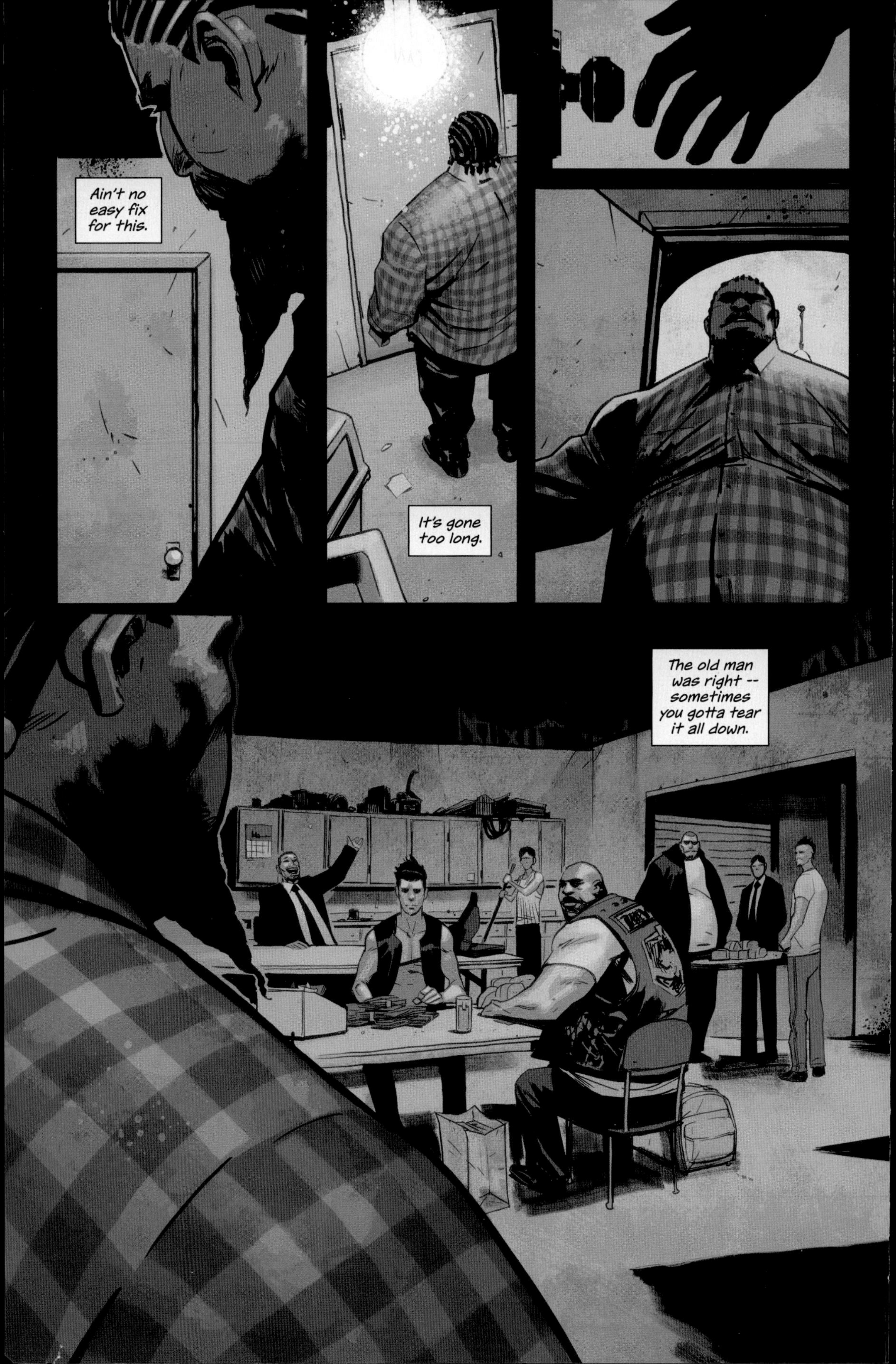
Ain't no easy fix for this.
It's gone too long.
The old man was right -- sometimes you gotta tear it all down.

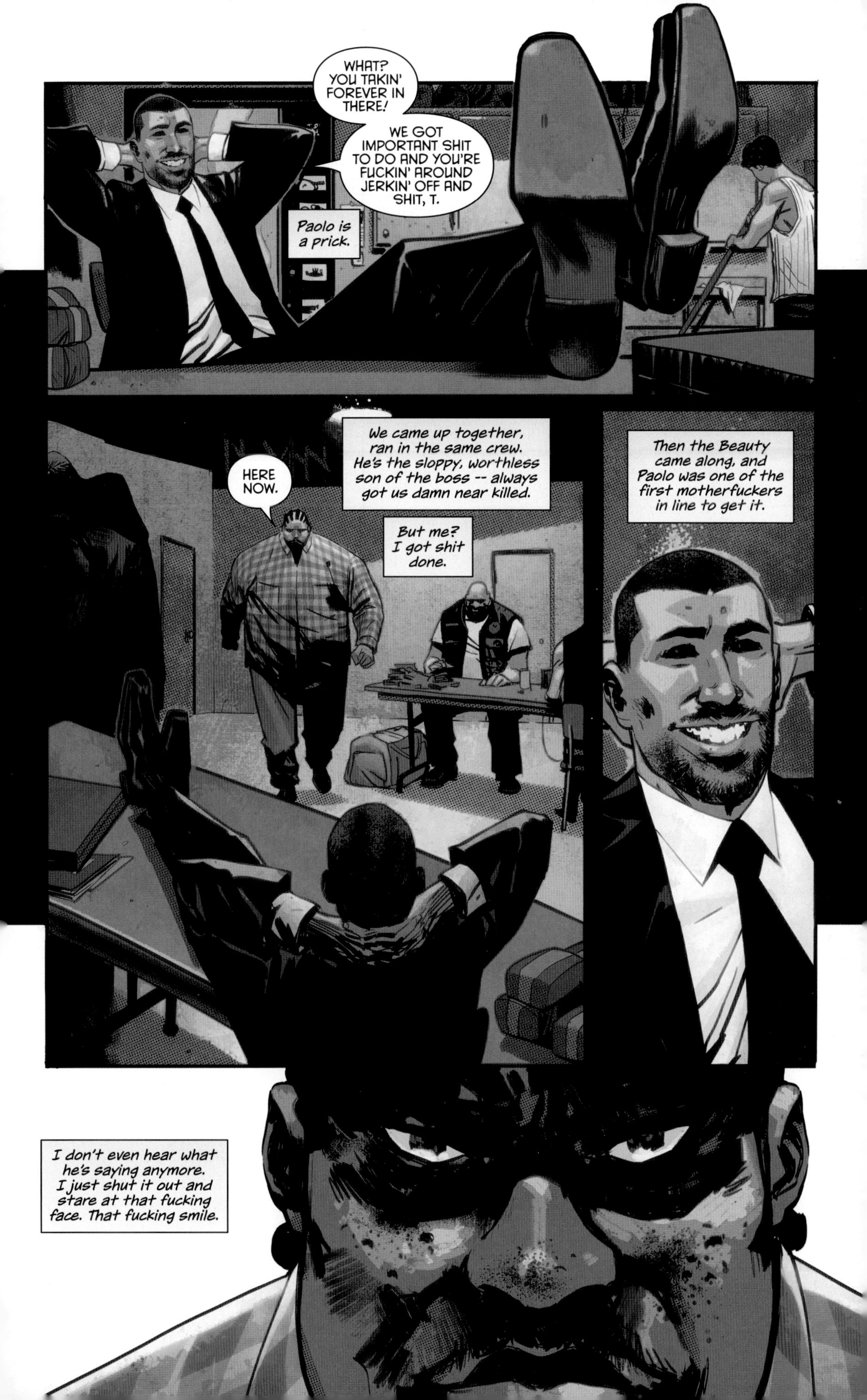
WHAT? YOU TAKIN' FOREVER IN THERE!
WE GOT IMPORTANT SHIT TO DO AND YOU'RE FUCKIN' AROUND JERKIN' OFF AND SHIT, T.
Paolo is a prick.
HERE NOW.
We came up together, ran in the same crew. He's the sloppy, worthless son of the boss -- always got us damn near killed.
But me? I got shit done.
Then the Beauty came along, and Paolo was one of the first motherfuckers in line to get it.
I don't even hear what he's saying anymore. I just shut it out and stare at that fucking face. That fucking smile.

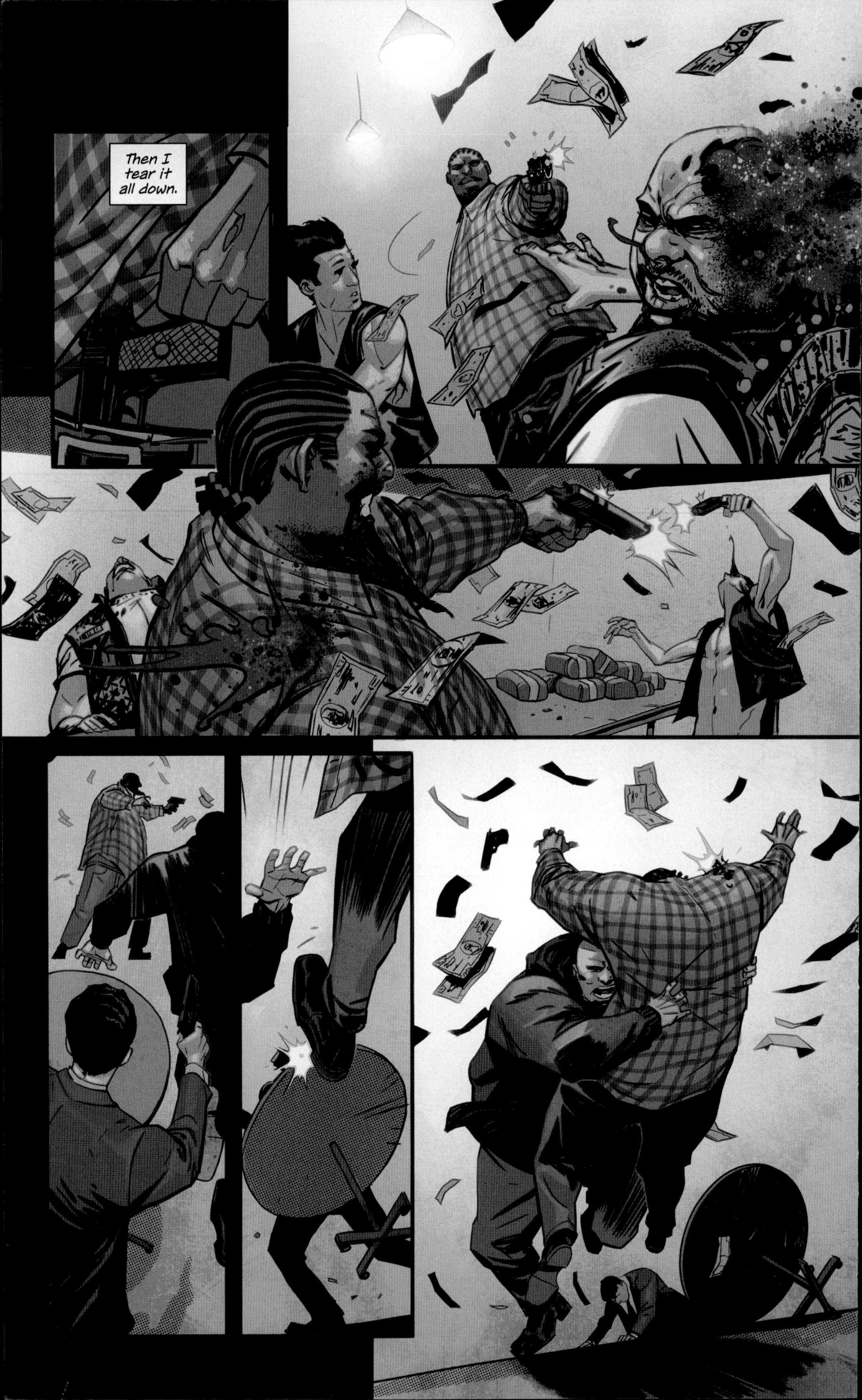
Then I tear it all down.

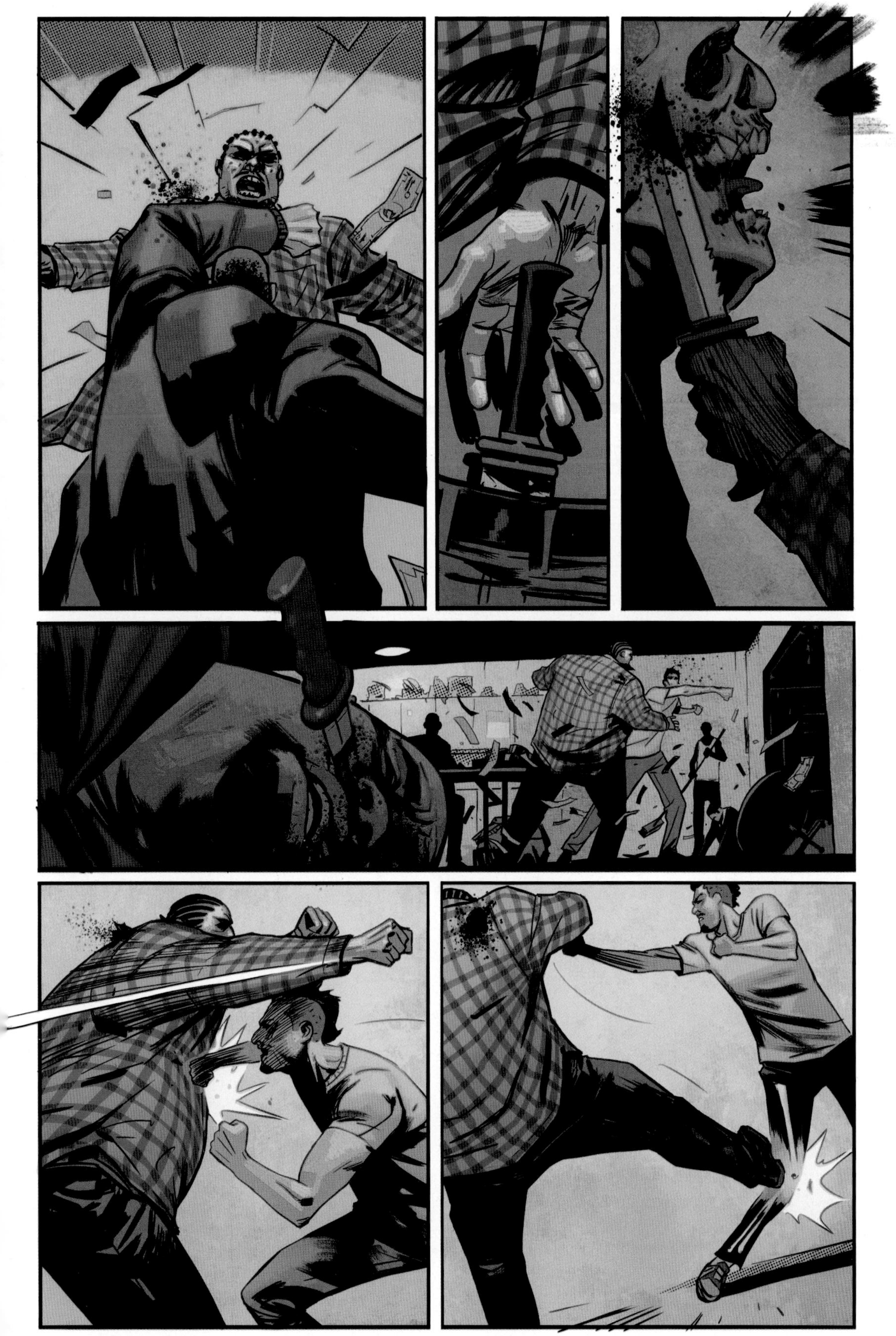

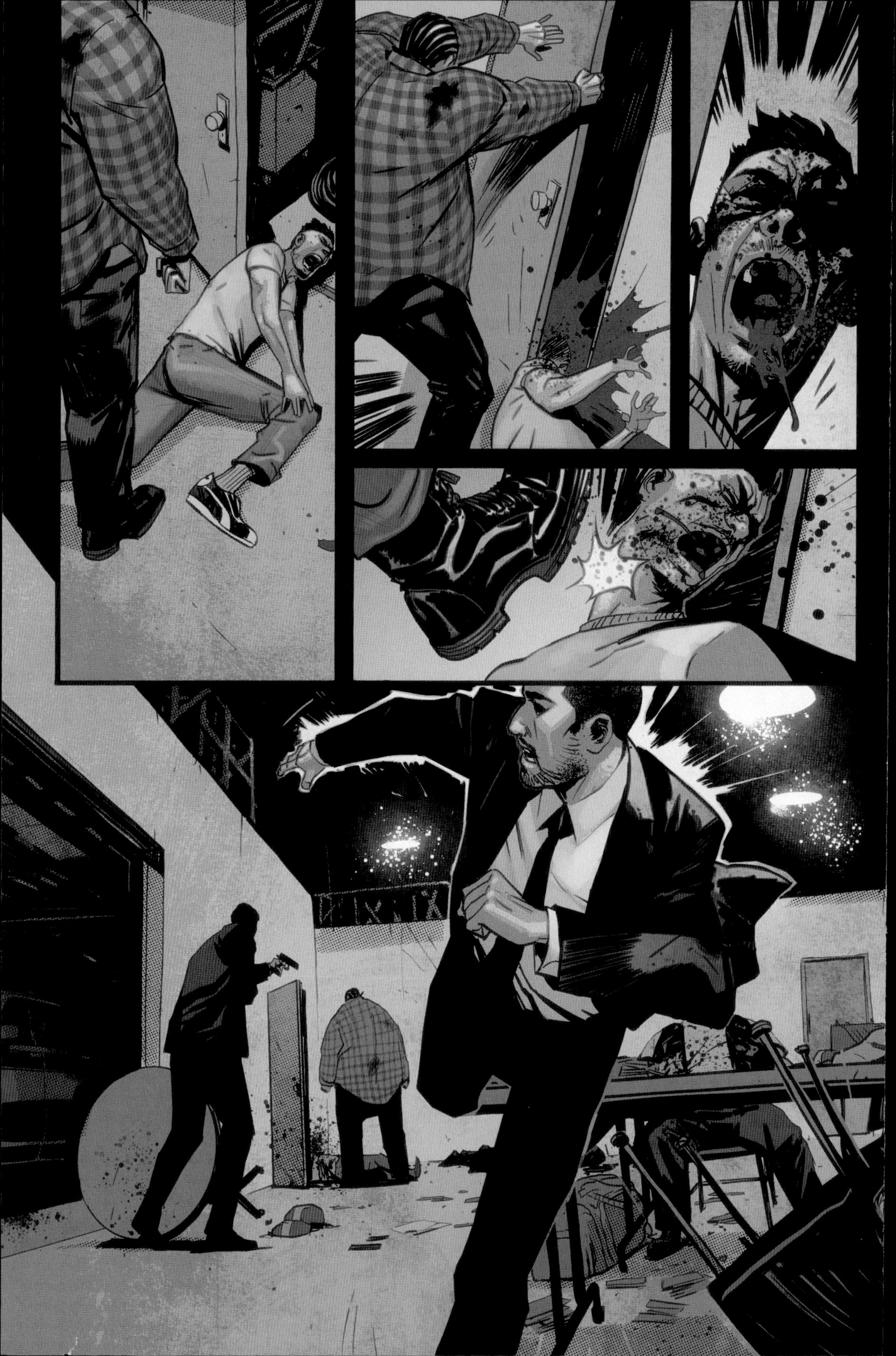

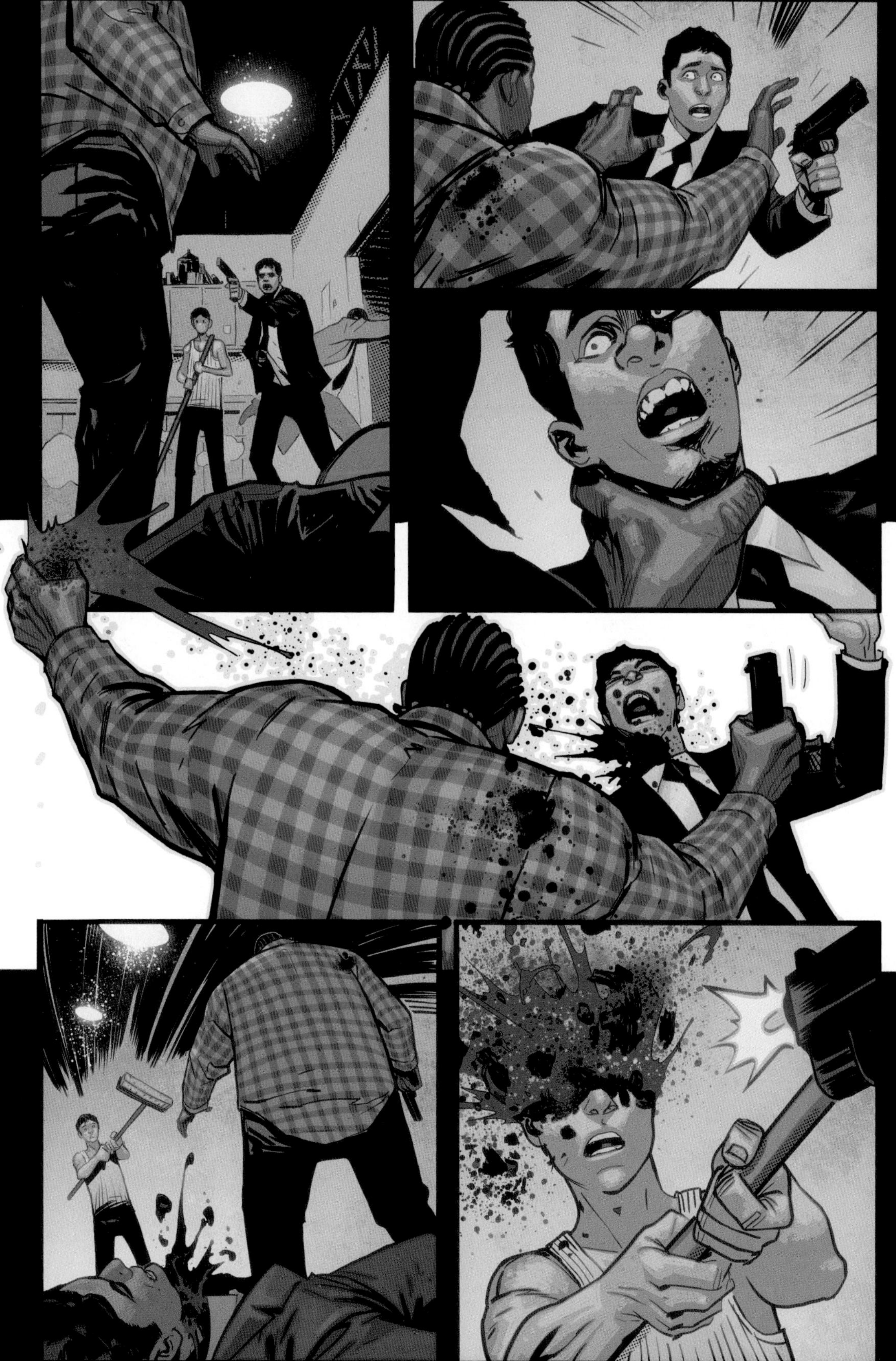

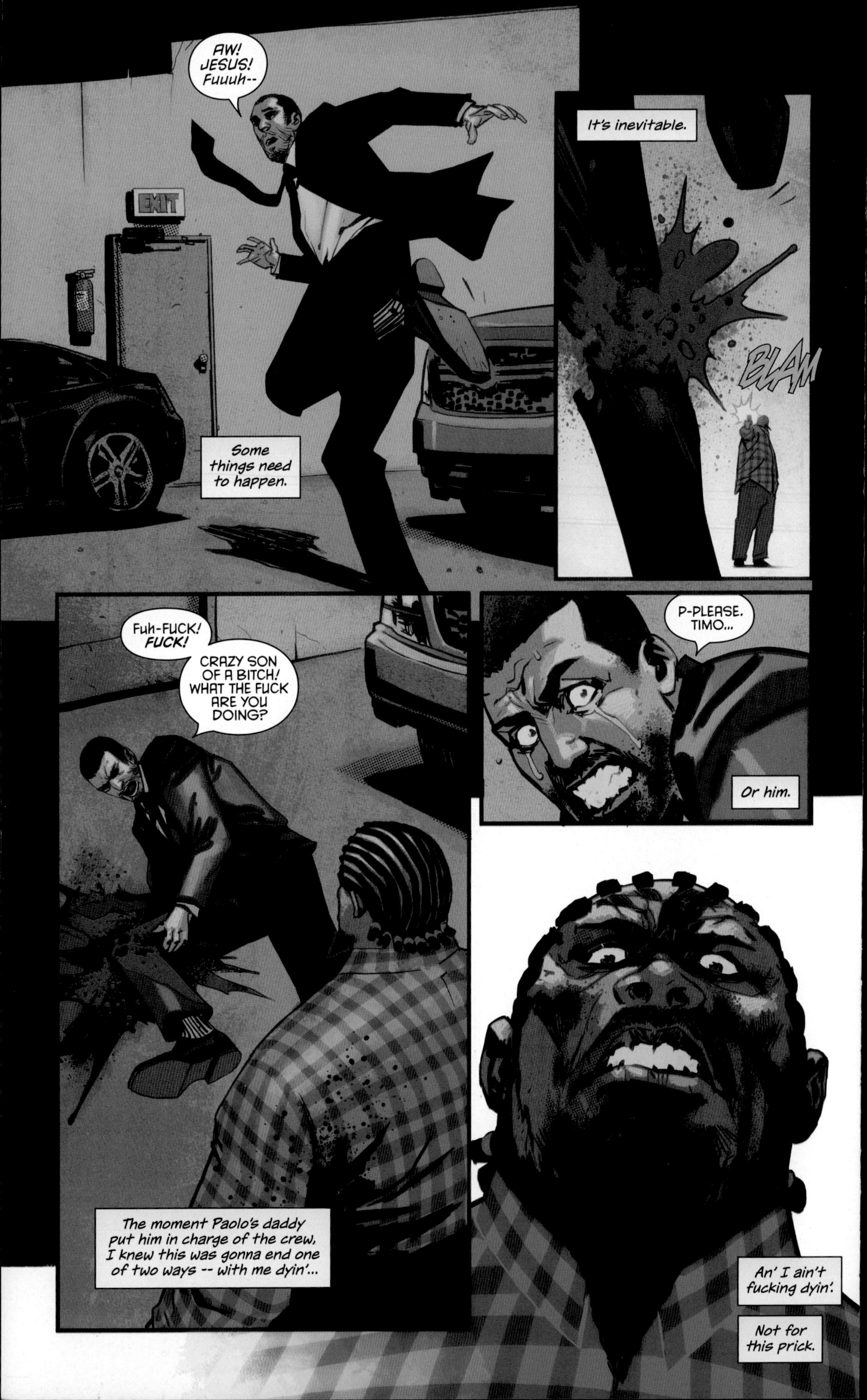
AW! JESUS! Fuuuh--
Some things need to happen.
It's inevitable.
BLAM
Fuh-FUCK! FUCK!
CRAZY SON OF A BITCH! WHAT THE FUCK ARE YOU DOING?
The moment Paolo's daddy put him in charge of the crew, I knew this was gonna end one of two ways -- with me dyin'...
P-PLEASE. TIMO...
Or him.
An' I ain't fucking dyin'.
Not for this prick.

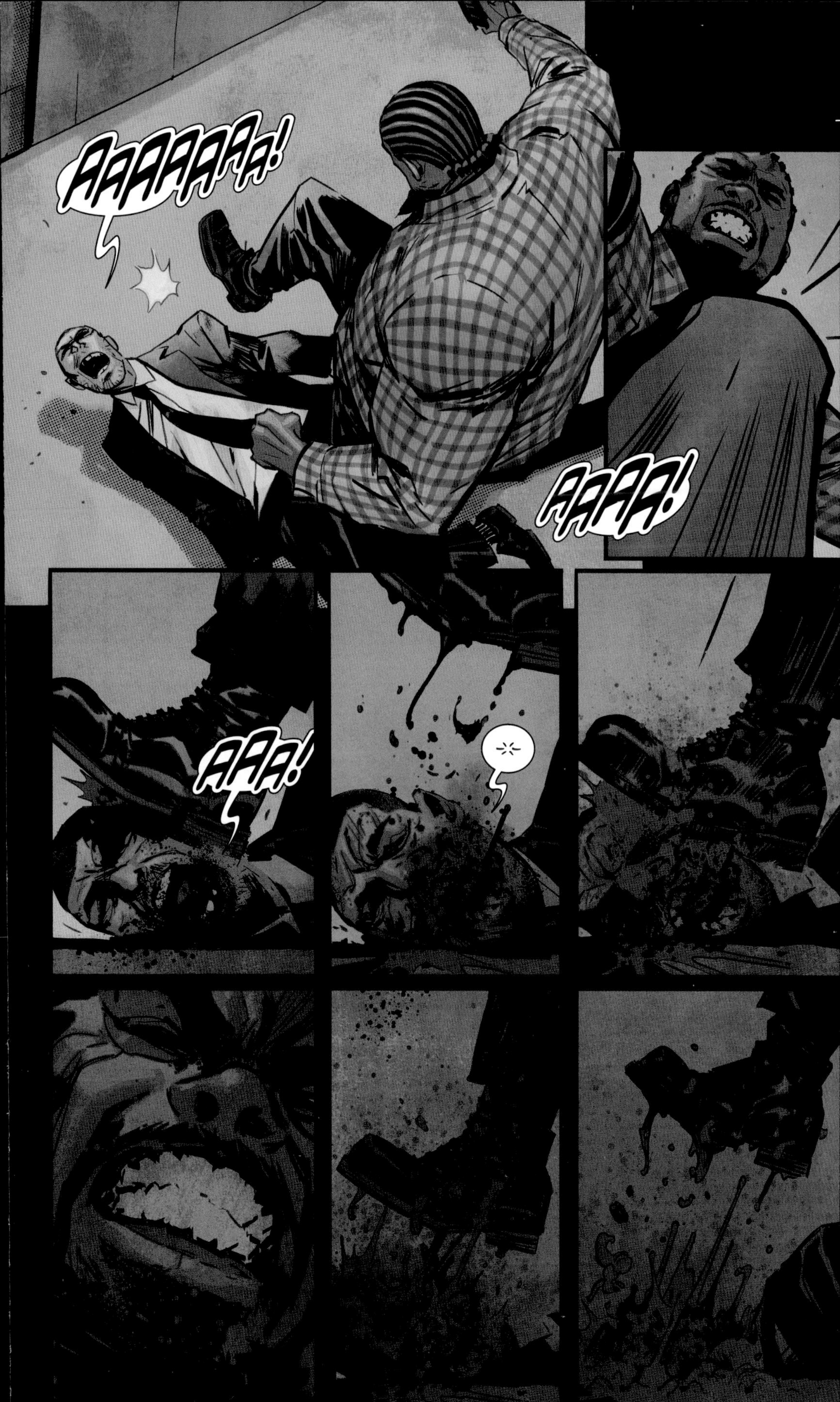
AAAAAAAA!
AAAA!
AAA!

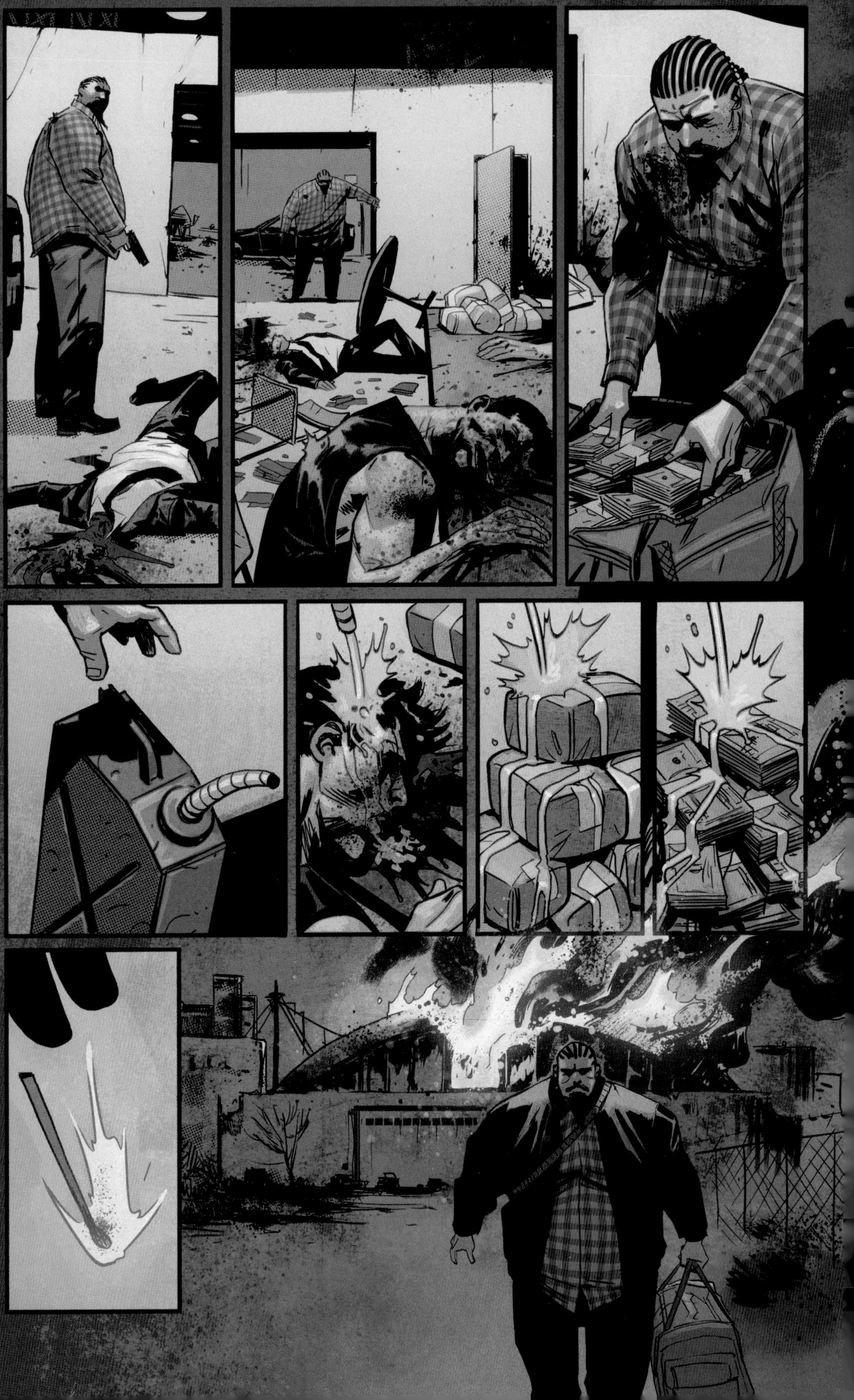

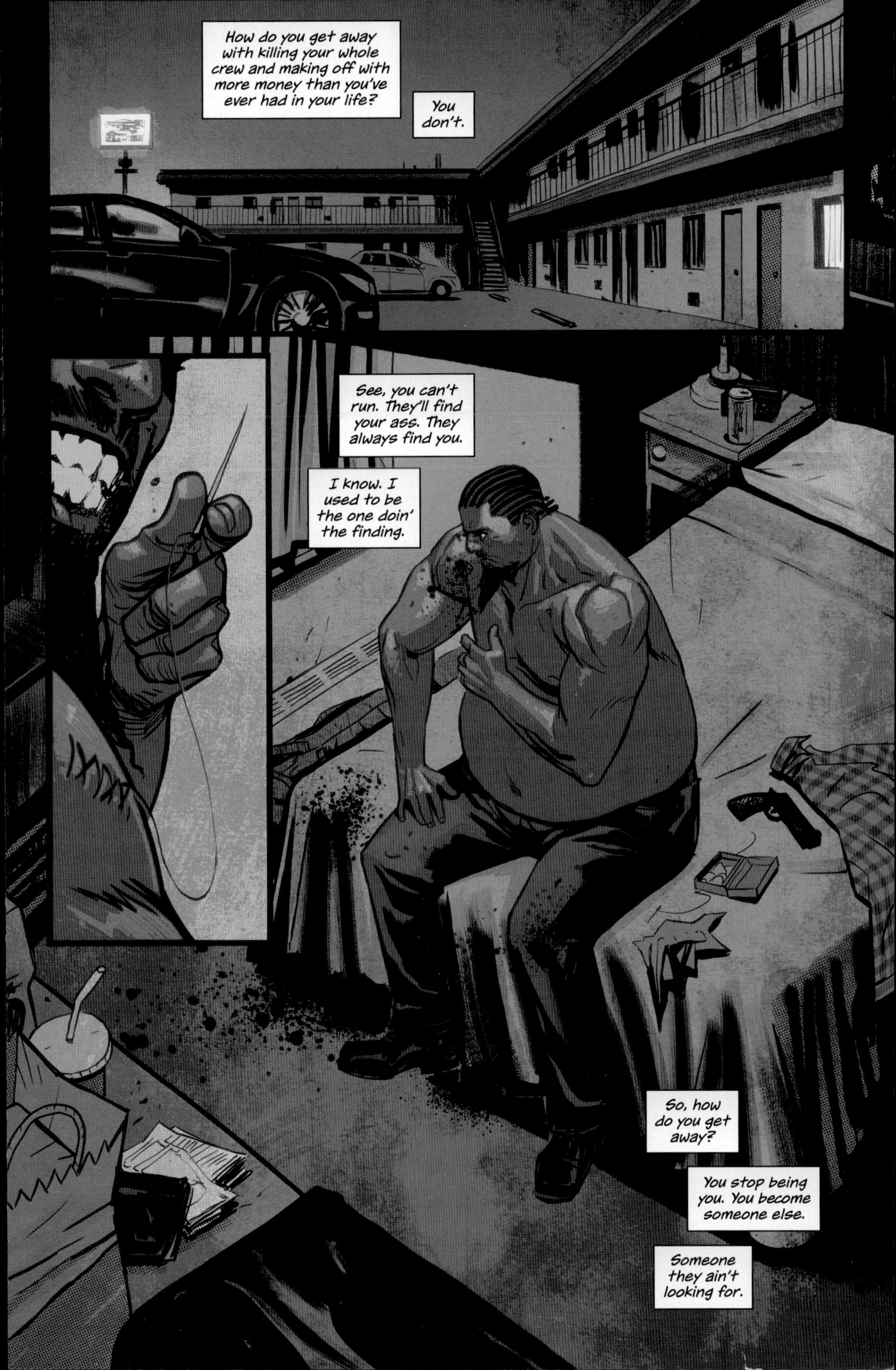
How do you get away with killing your whole crew and making off with more money than you've ever had in your life?
You don't.
See, you can't run. They'll find your ass. They always find you.
I know. I used to be the one doin' the finding.
So, how do you get away?
You stop being you. You become someone else.
Someone they ain't looking for.

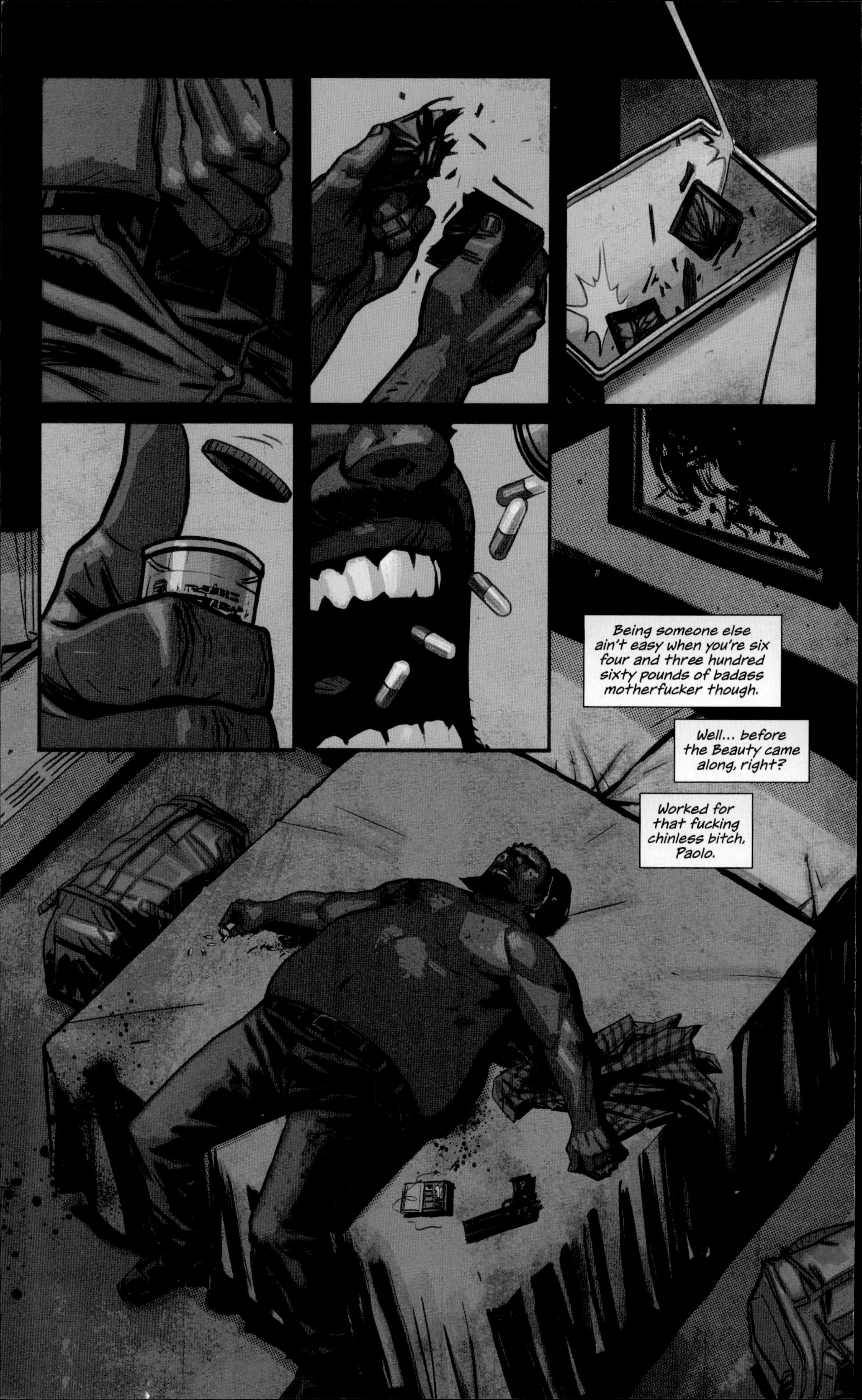
Being someone else ain't easy when you're six four and three hundred sixty pounds of badass motherfucker though.
Well... before the Beauty came along, right?
Worked for that fucking chinless bitch, Paolo.

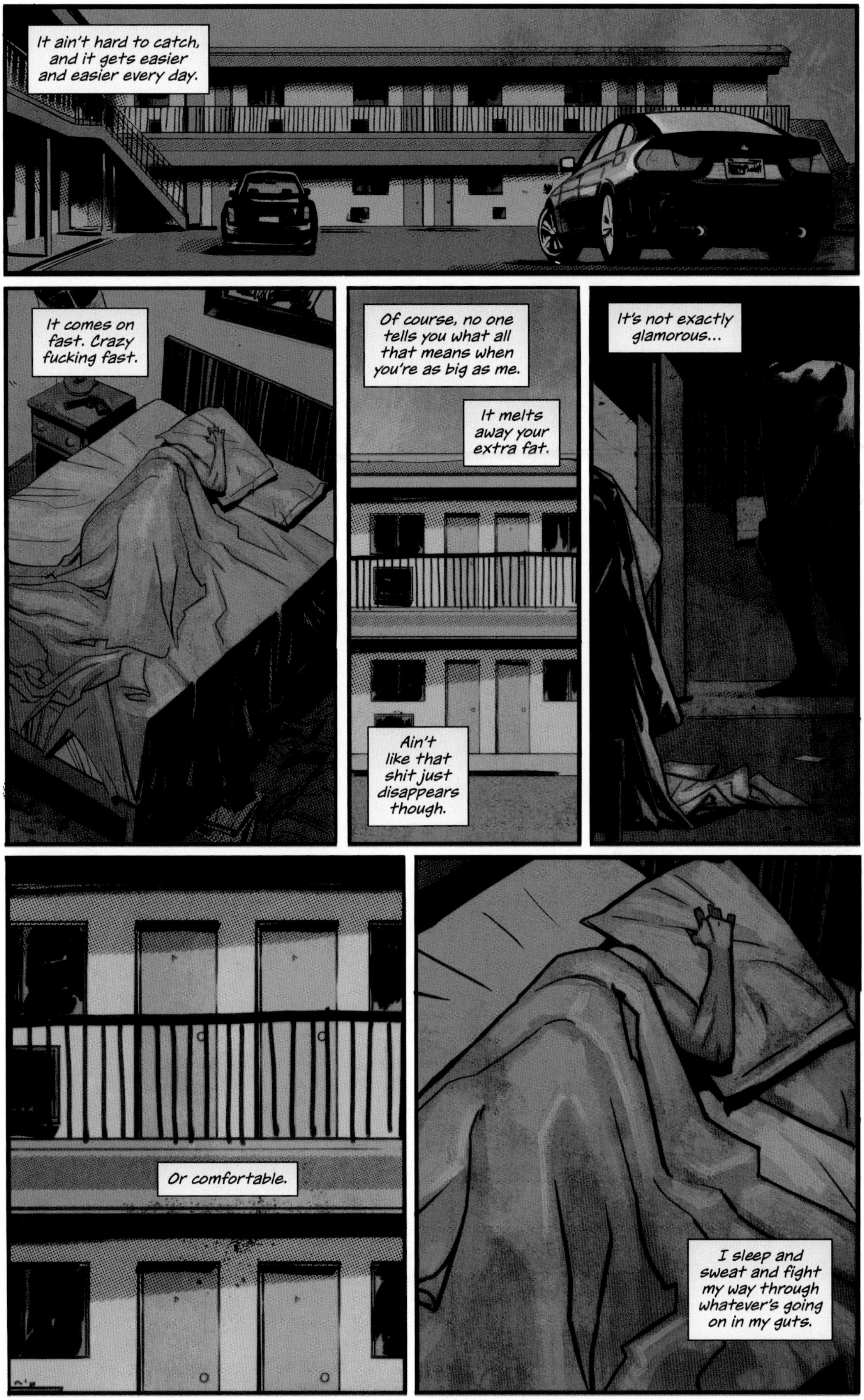
It ain't hard to catch, and it gets easier and easier every day.
It comes on fast. Crazy fucking fast.
Of course, no one tells you what all that means when you're as big as me.
It melts away your extra fat.
Ain't like that shit just disappears though.
It's not exactly glamorous...
Or comfortable.
I sleep and sweat and fight my way through whatever's going on in my guts.

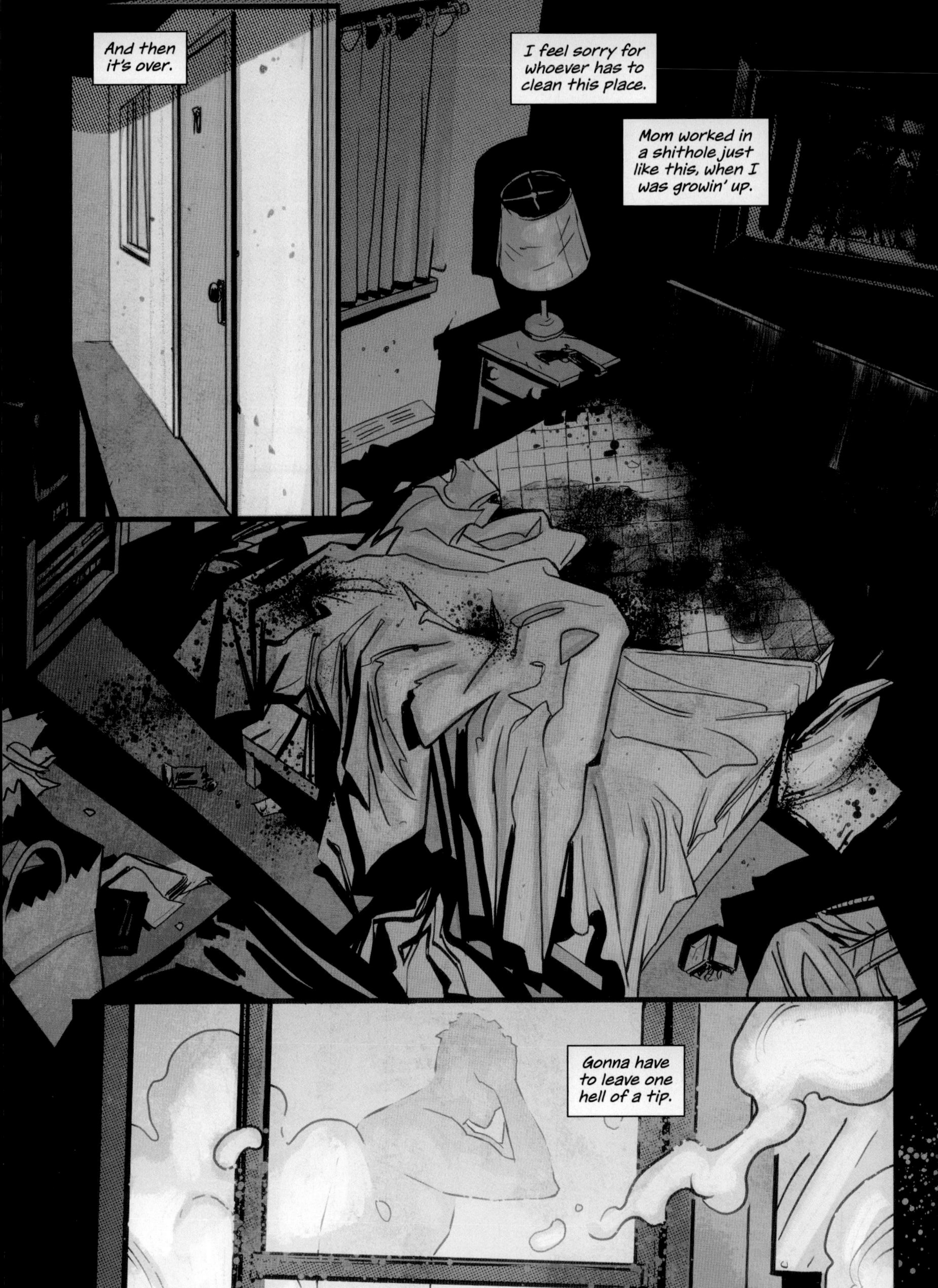
And then it's over.
I feel sorry for whoever has to clean this place.
Mom worked in a shithole just like this, when I was growin' up.
Gonna have to leave one hell of a tip.

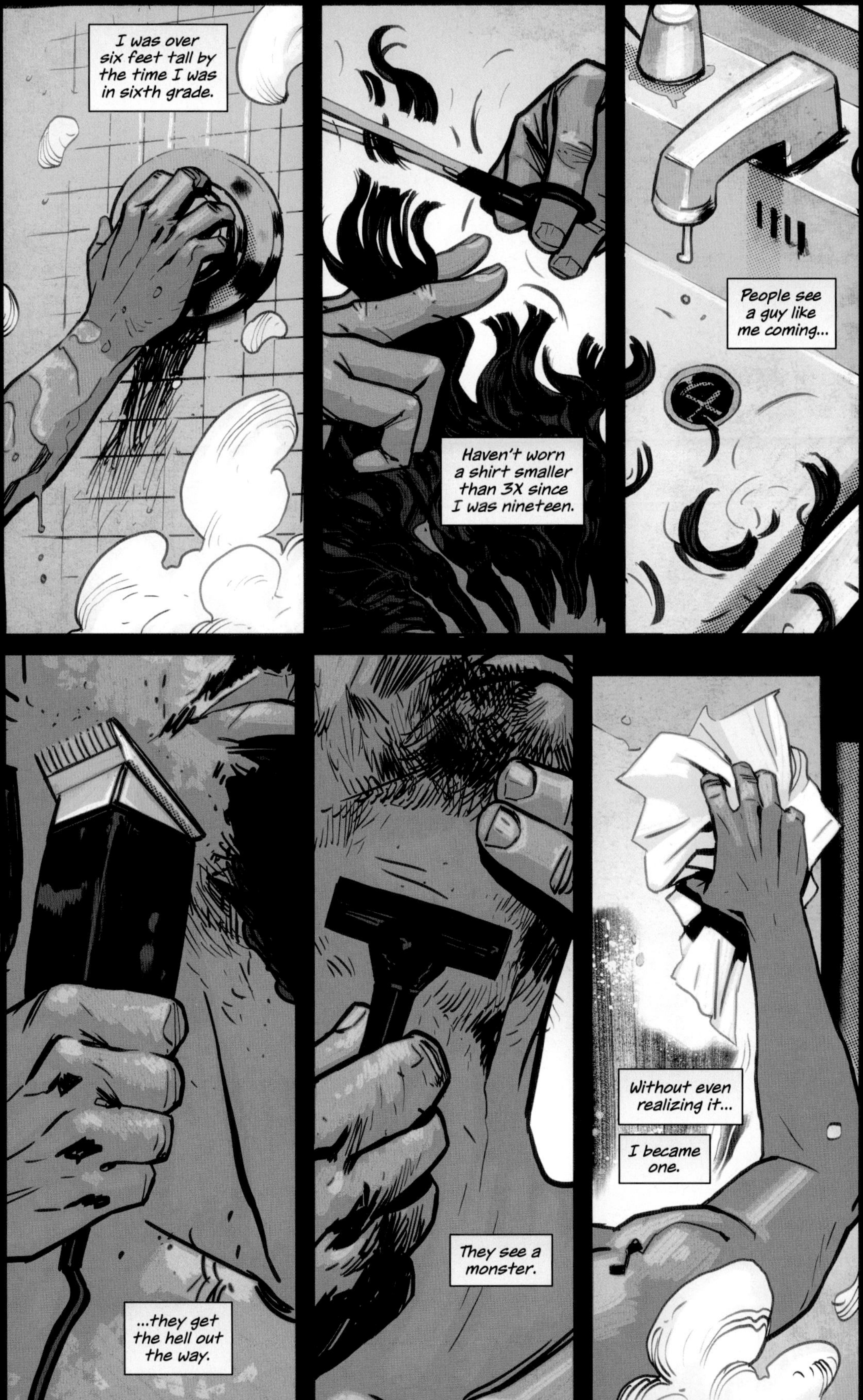
I was over six feet tall by the time I was in sixth grade.
Haven't worn a shirt smaller than 3X since I was nineteen.
People see a guy like me coming...
...they get the hell out the way.
They see a monster.
Without even realizing it...
I became one.

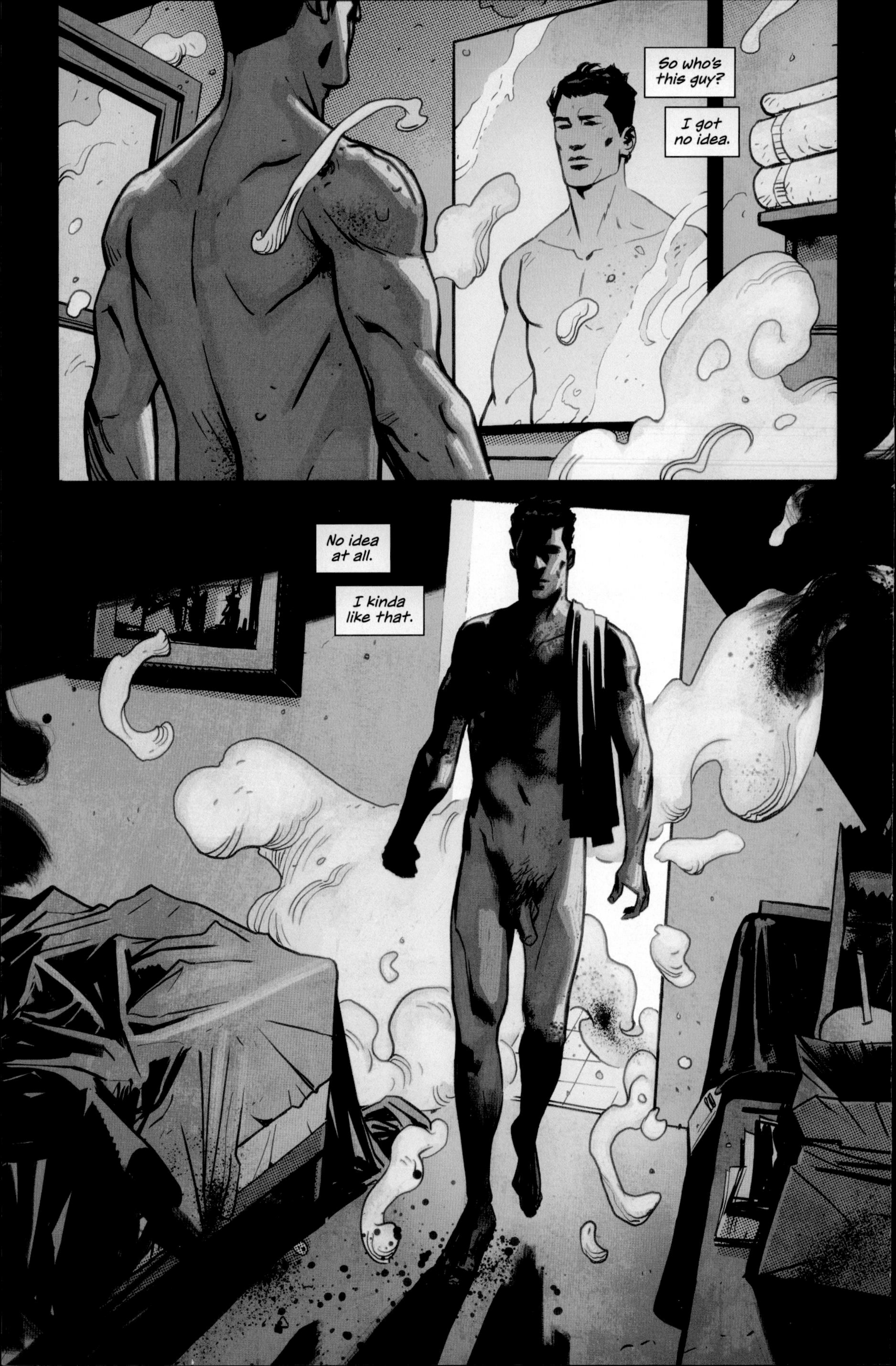
So who's this guy?
I got no idea.
No idea at all.
I kinda like that.

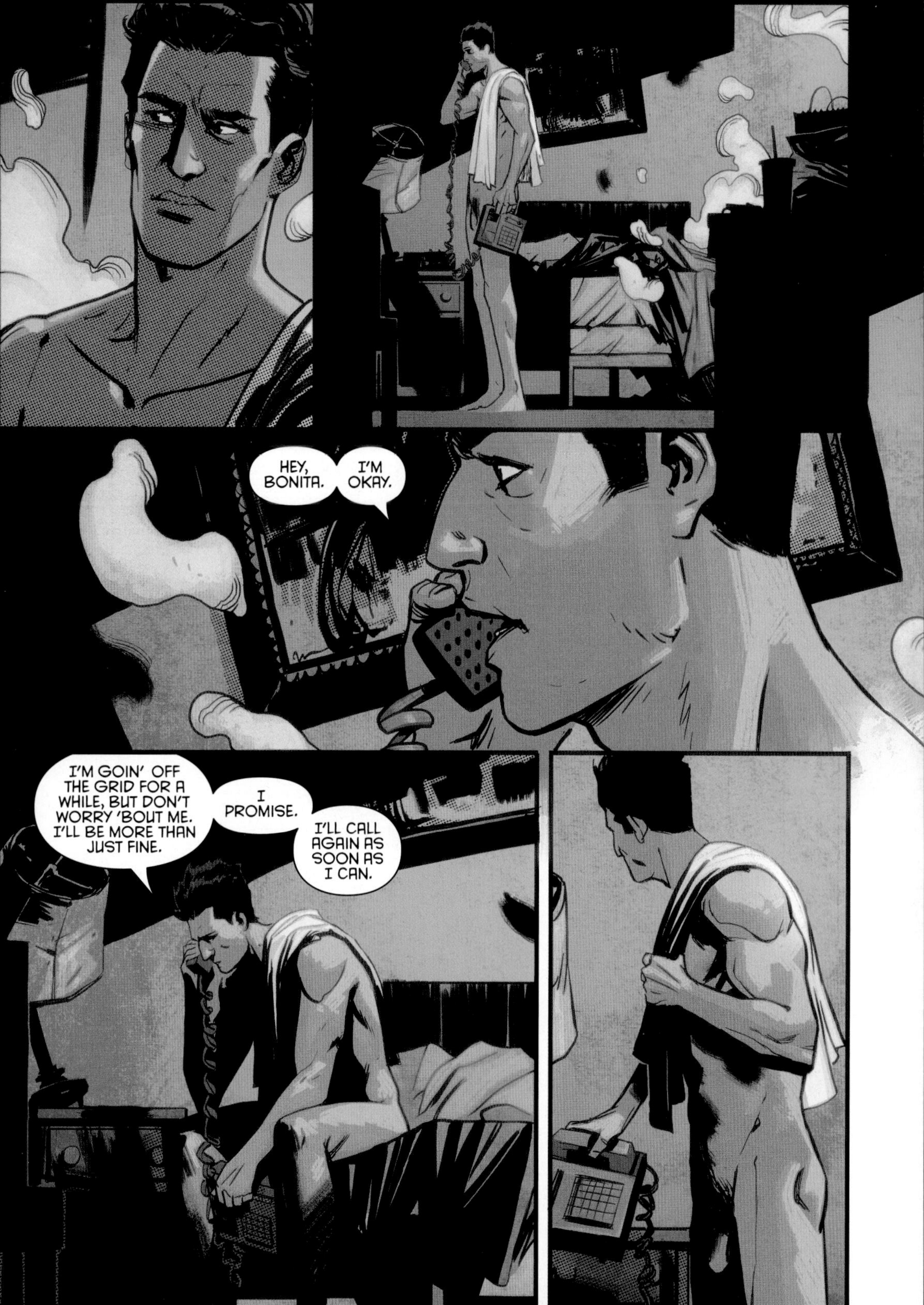
HEY, BONITA.
I'M OKAY.
I'M GOIN' OFF THE GRID FOR A WHILE, BUT DON'T WORRY 'BOUT ME. I'LL BE MORE THAN JUST FINE.
I PROMISE.
I'LL CALL AGAIN AS SOON AS I CAN.

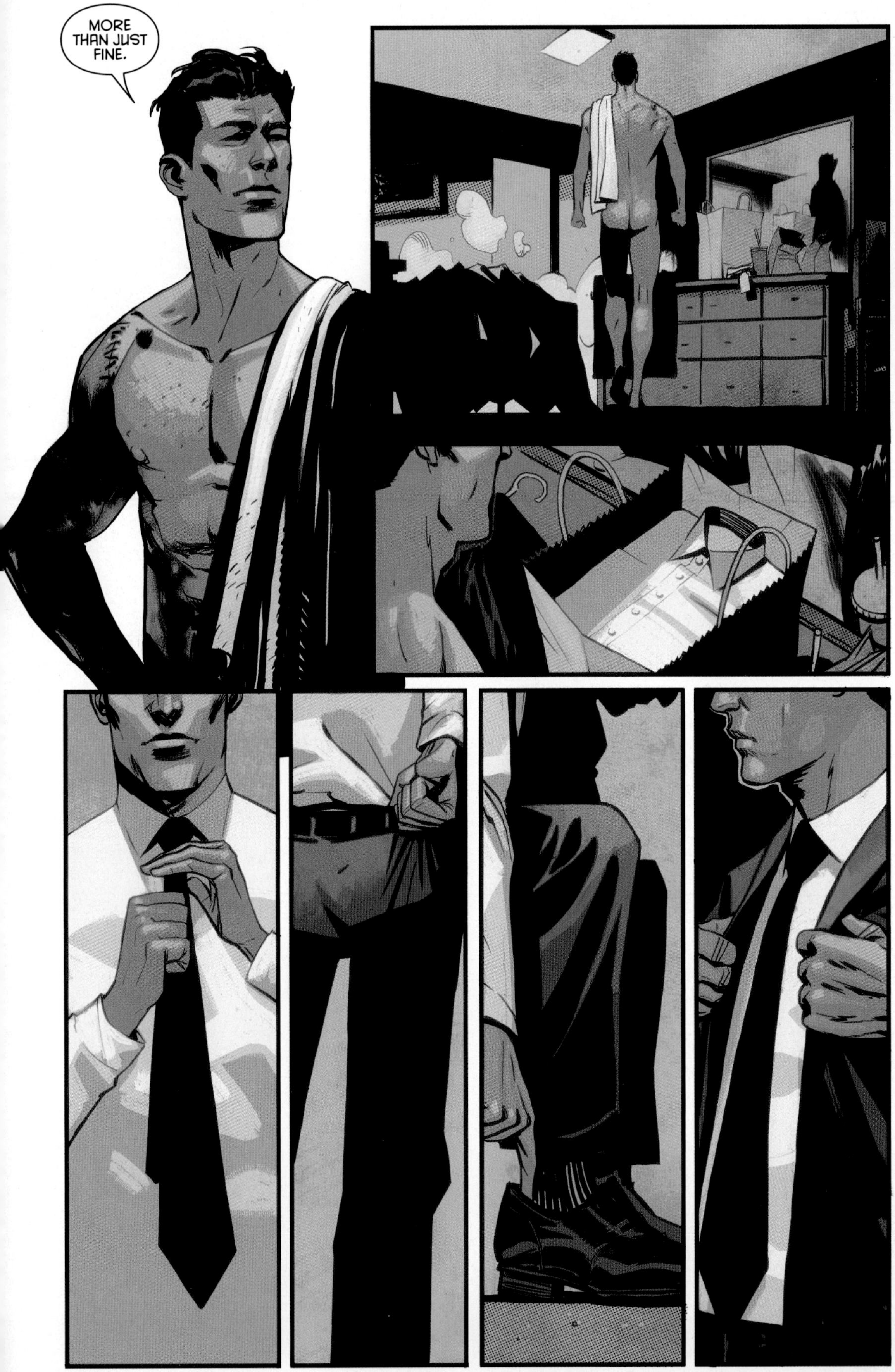
MORE THAN JUST FINE.

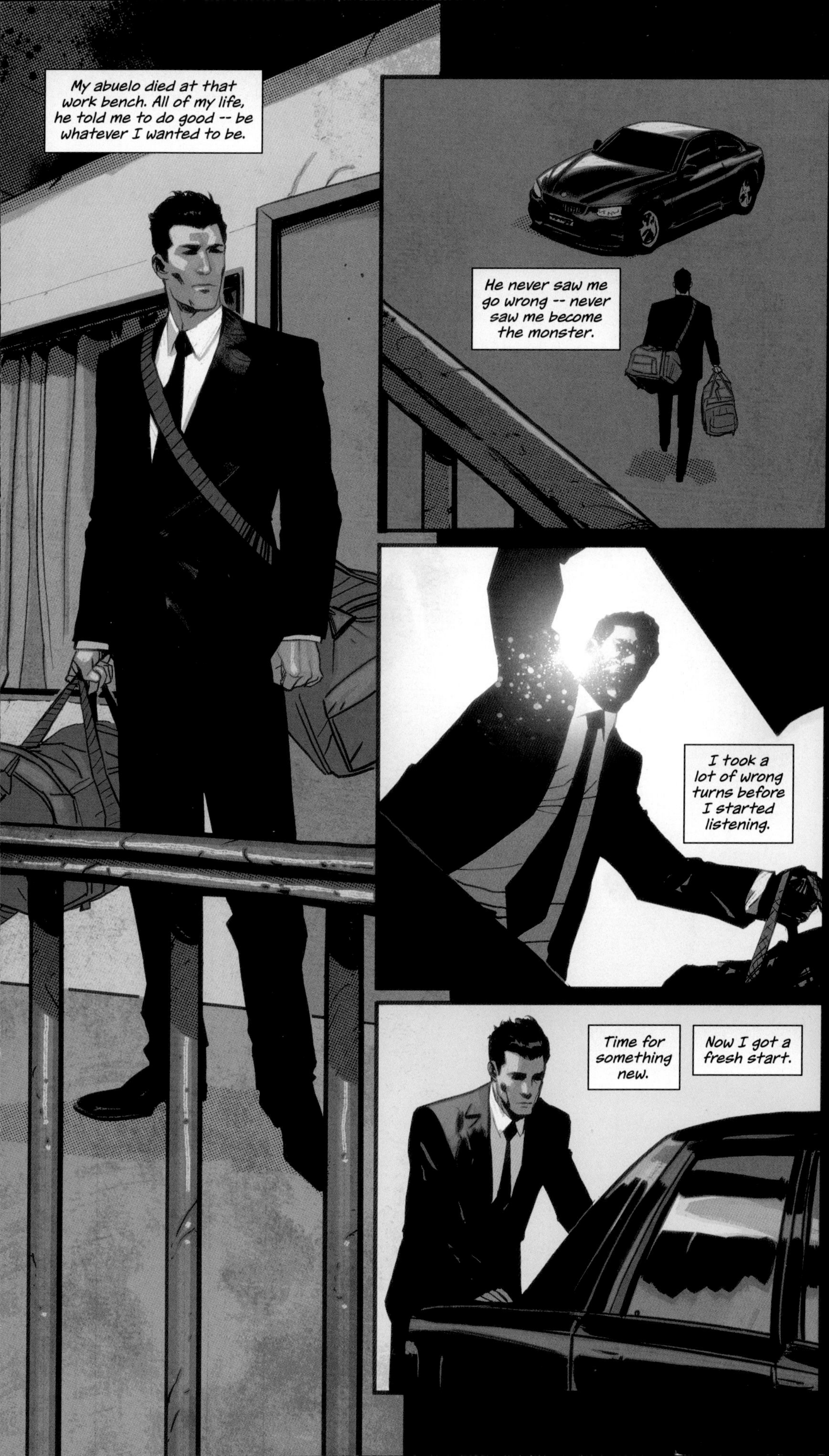

My abuelo died at that work bench. All of my life, he told me to do good -- be whatever I wanted to be.
He never saw me go wrong -- never saw me become the monster.
I took a lot of wrong turns before I started listening.
Time for something new.
Now I got a fresh start.

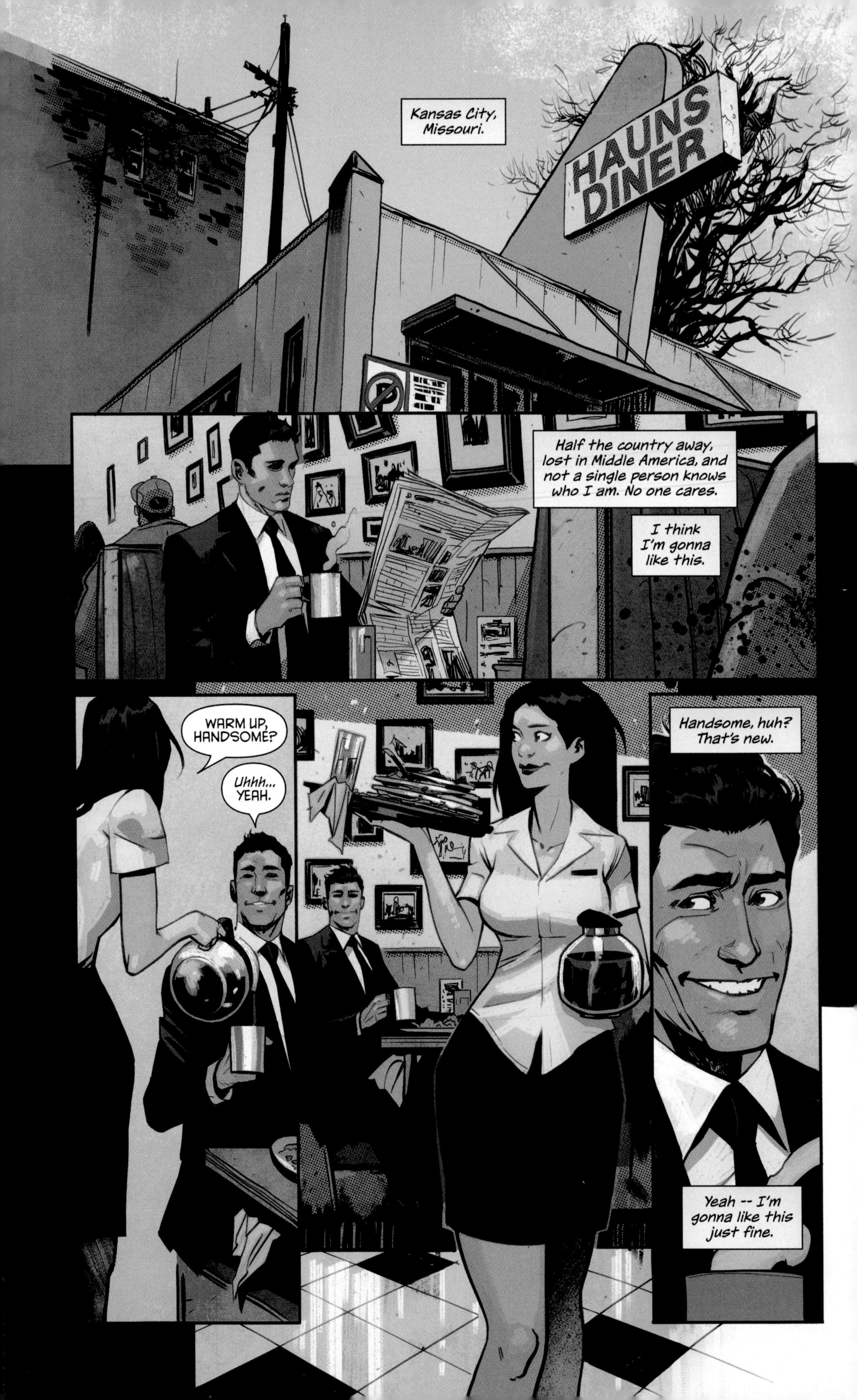

HAUNS DINER
Kansas City, Missouri.
Half the country away, lost in Middle America, and not a single person knows who I am. No one cares.
I think I'm gonna like this.
WARM UP, HANDSOME?
Uhhh... YEAH.
Handsome, huh? That's new.
Yeah -- I'm gonna like this just fine.

CHAPTER

8

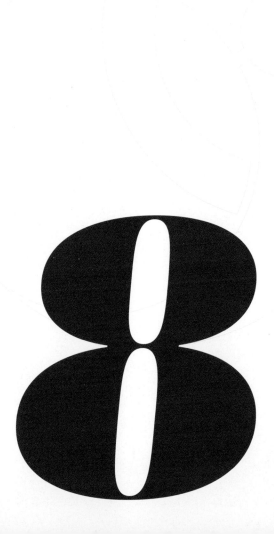

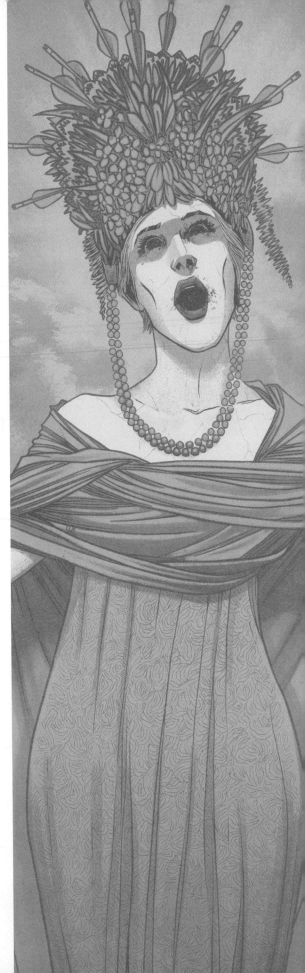

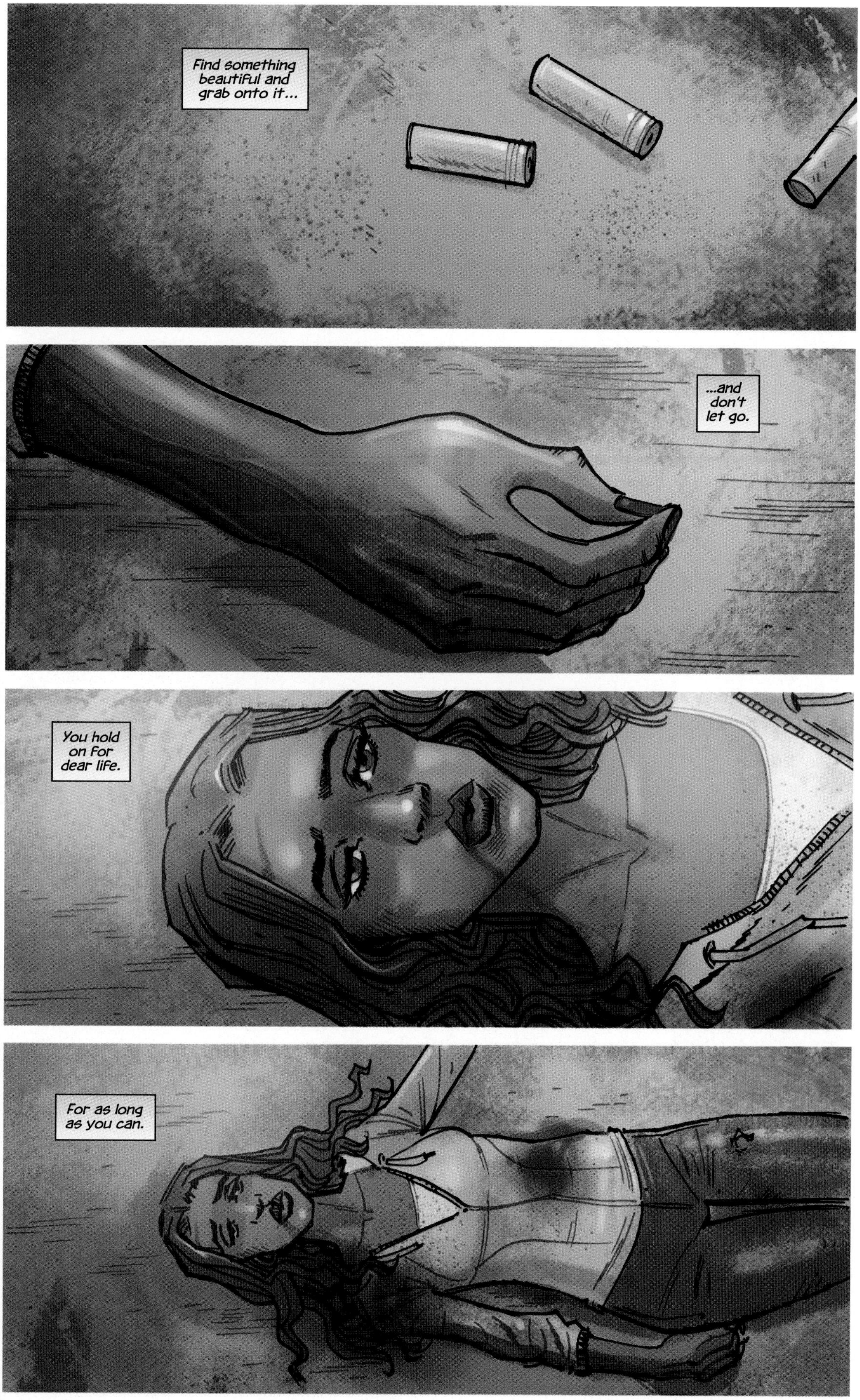
Find something beautiful and grab onto it...
...and don't let go.
You hold on for dear life.
For as long as you can.

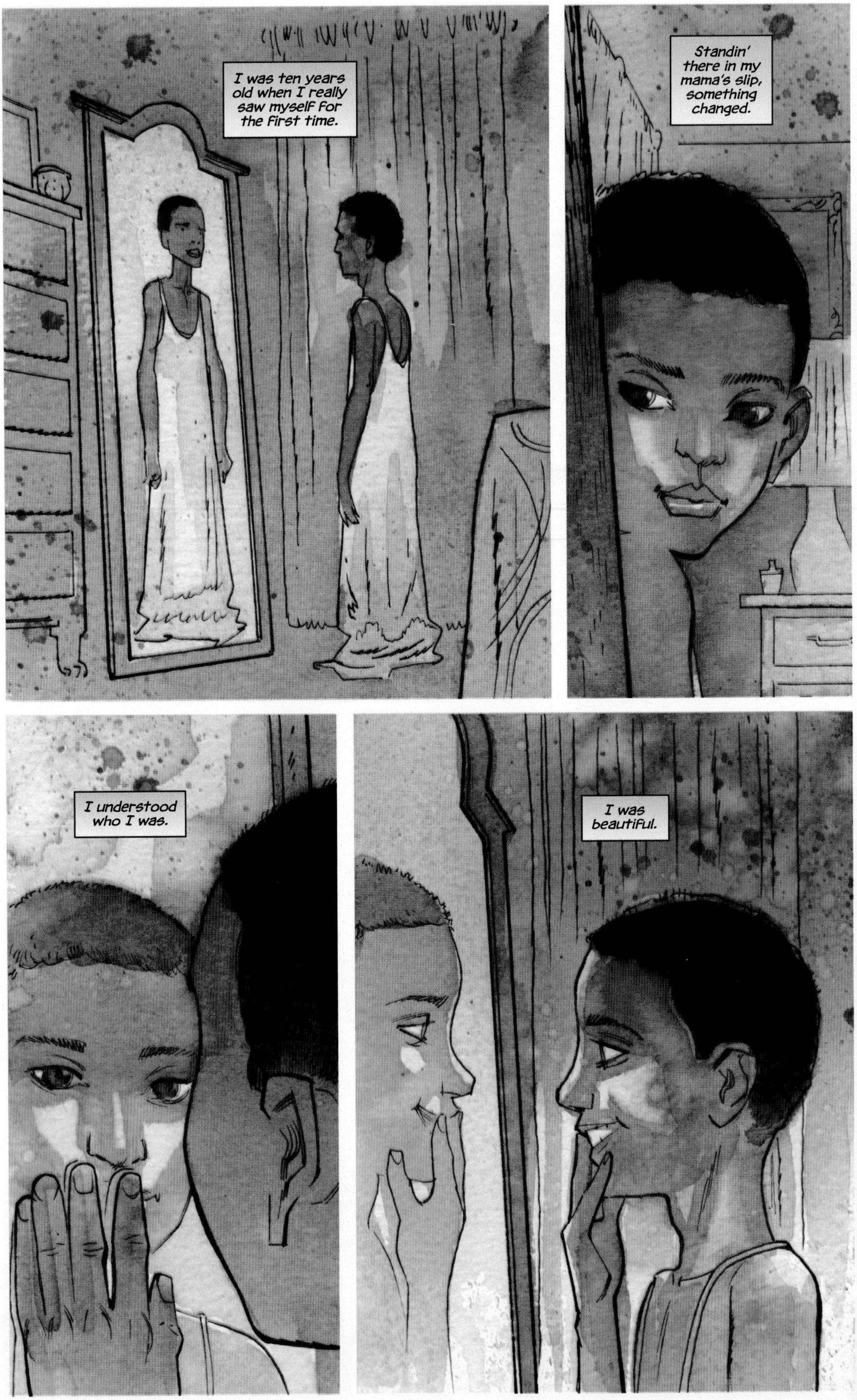
I was ten years old when I really saw myself for the first time.
Standin' there in my mama's slip, something changed.
I understood who I was.
I was beautiful.

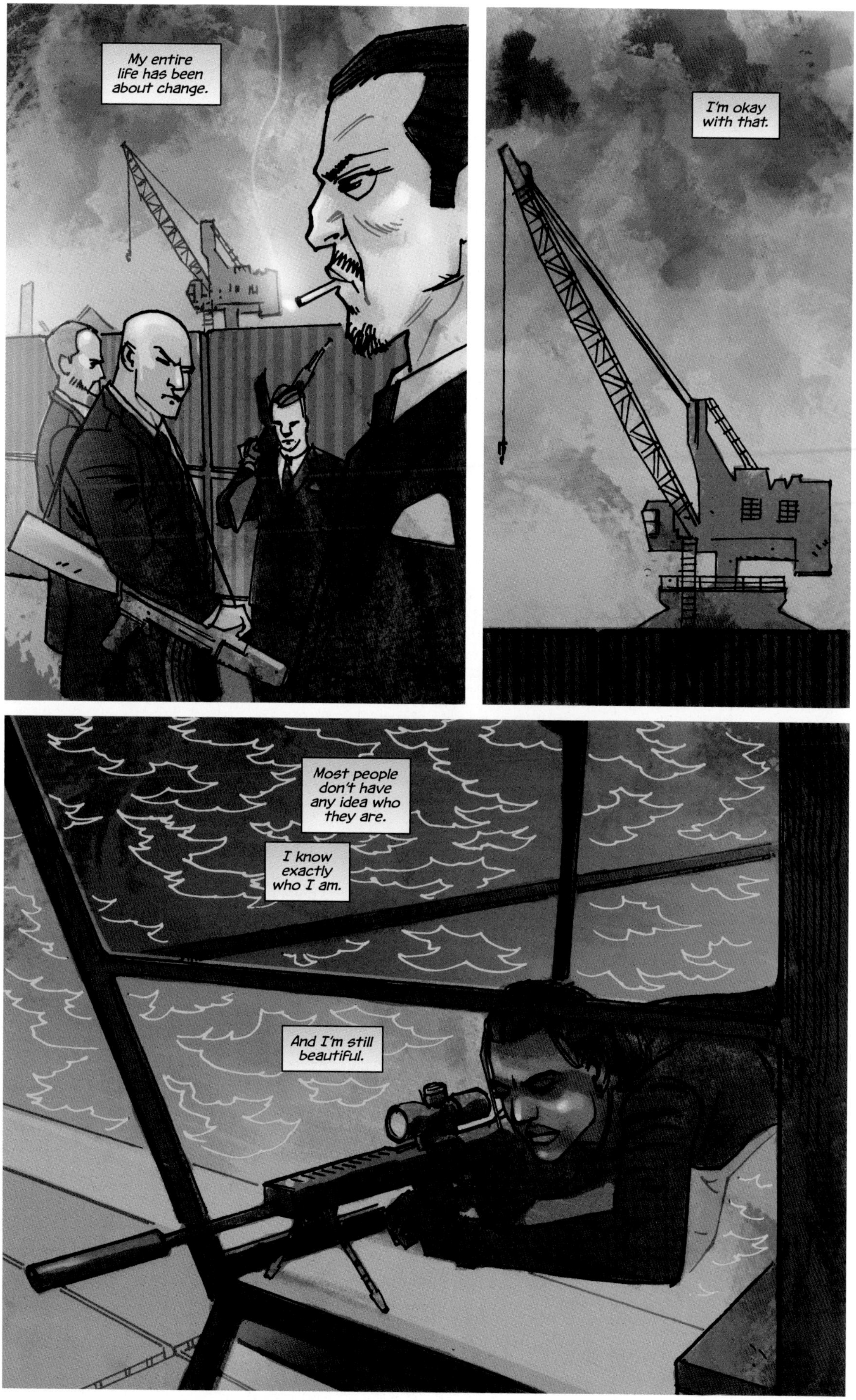
My entire life has been about change.
I'm okay with that.
Most people don't have any idea who they are.
I know exactly who I am.
And I'm still beautiful.

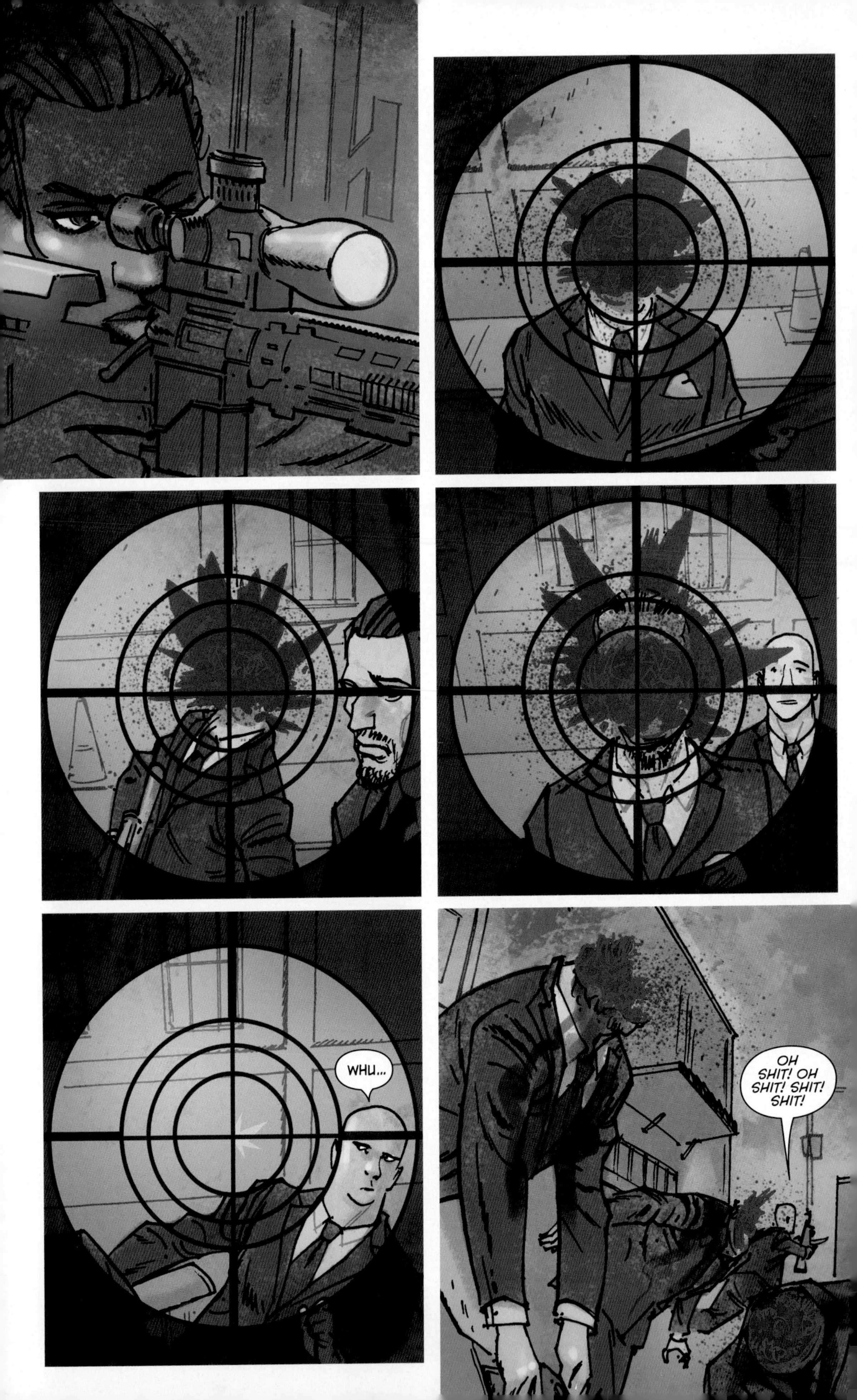
WHU...
OH SHIT! OH SHIT! SHIT! SHIT!

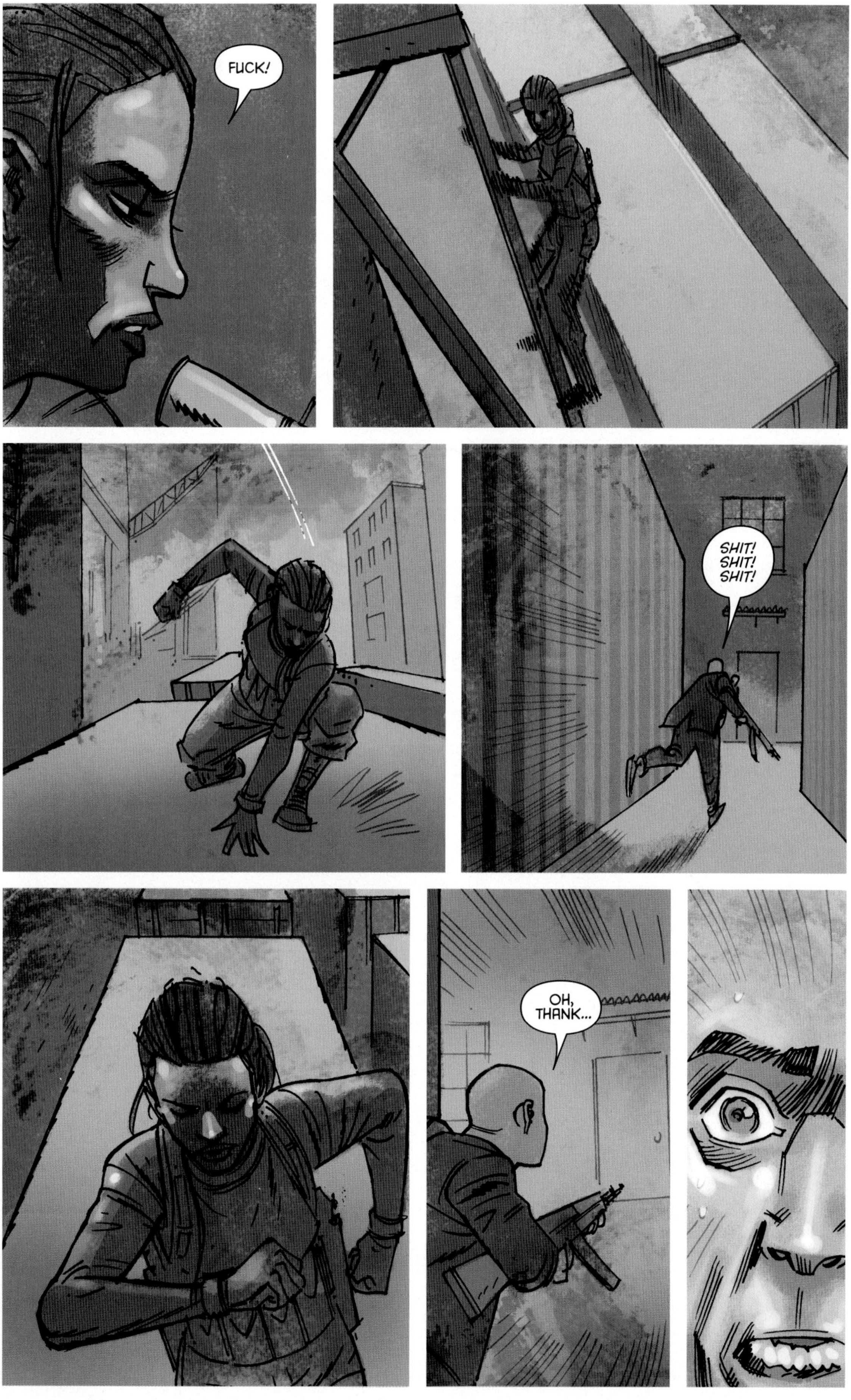
FUCK!
SHIT! SHIT! SHIT!
OH, THANK...

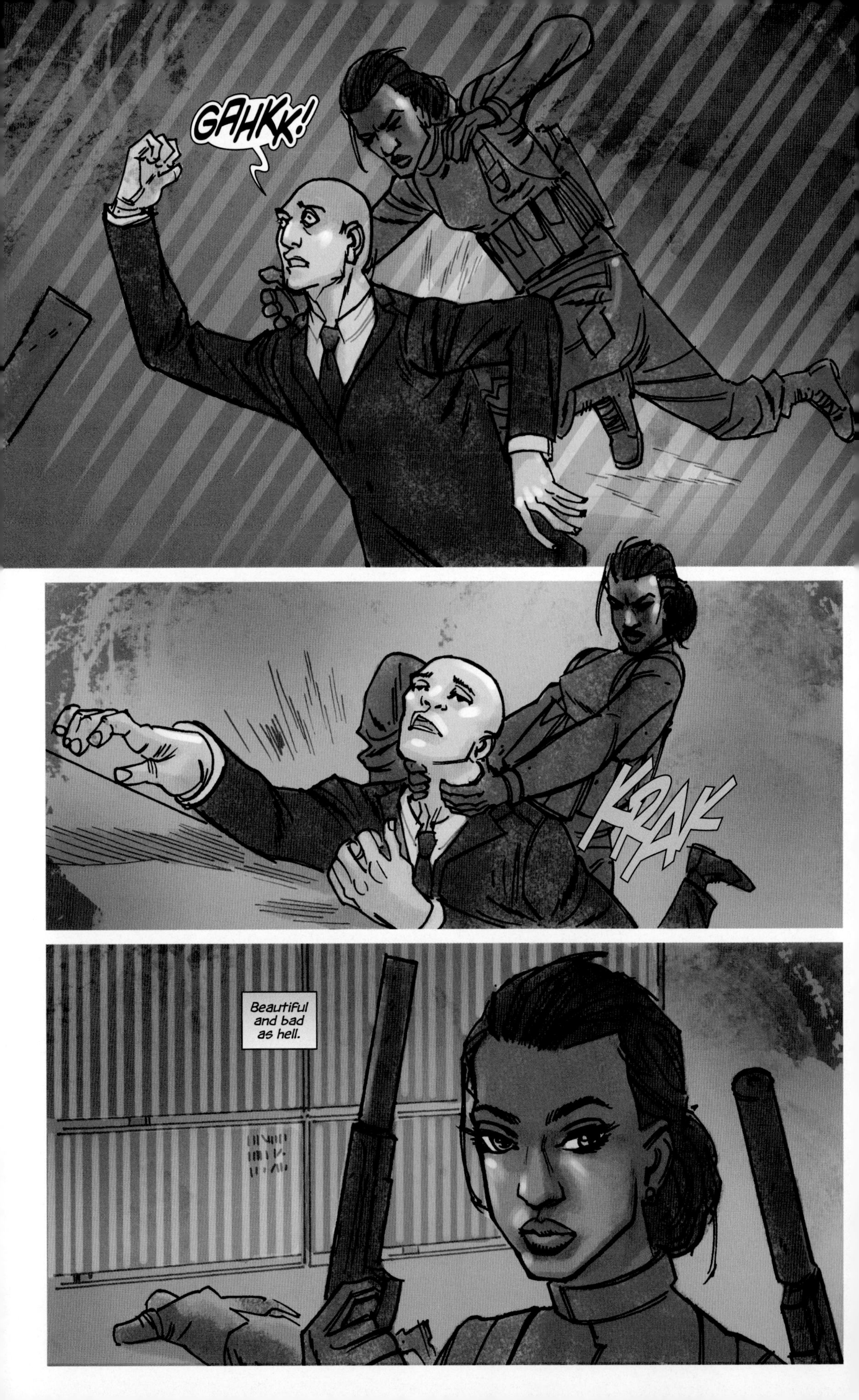
GAHKK!
KRAK
Beautiful and bad as hell.

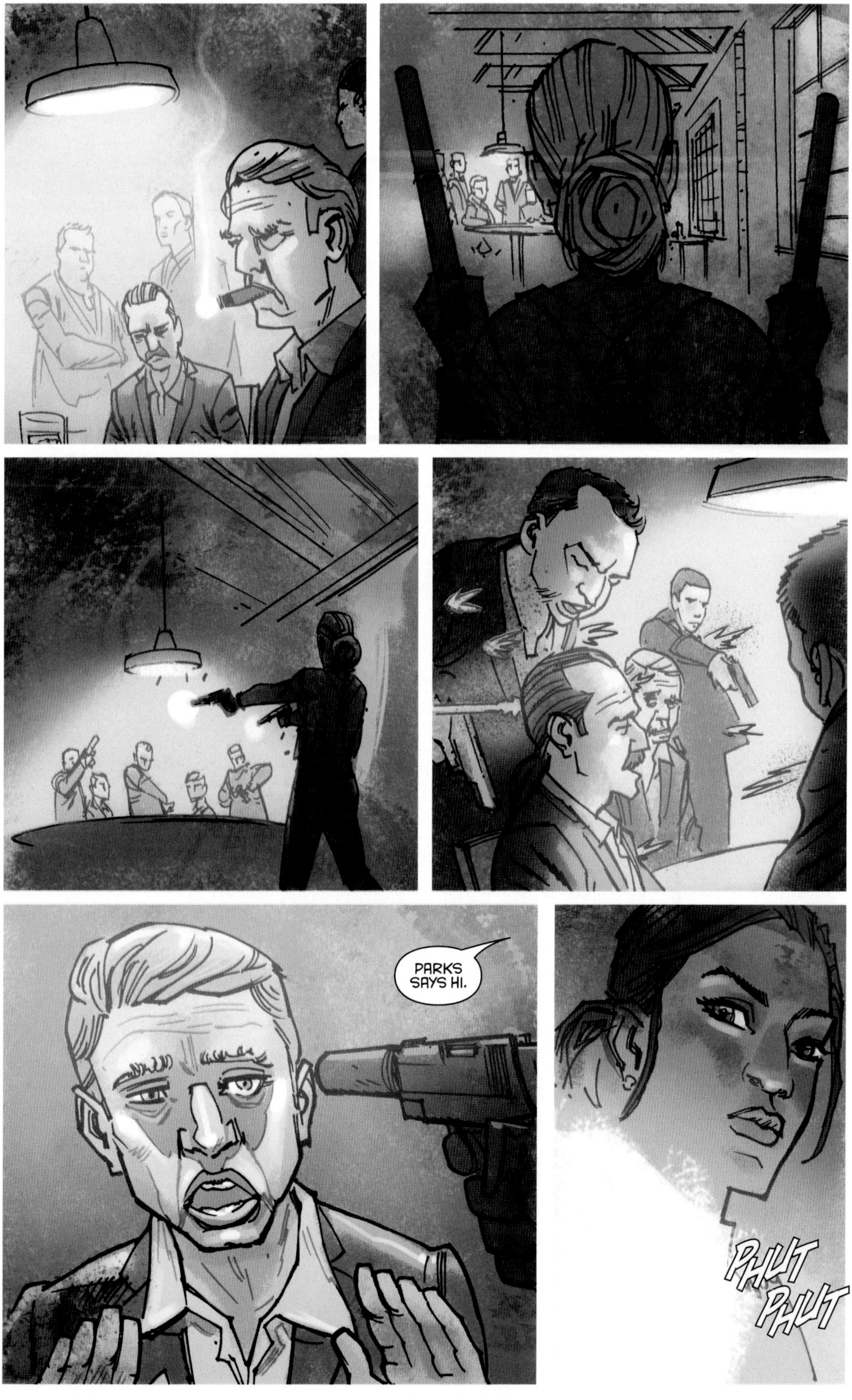
PARKS SAYS HI.
PHUT PHUT

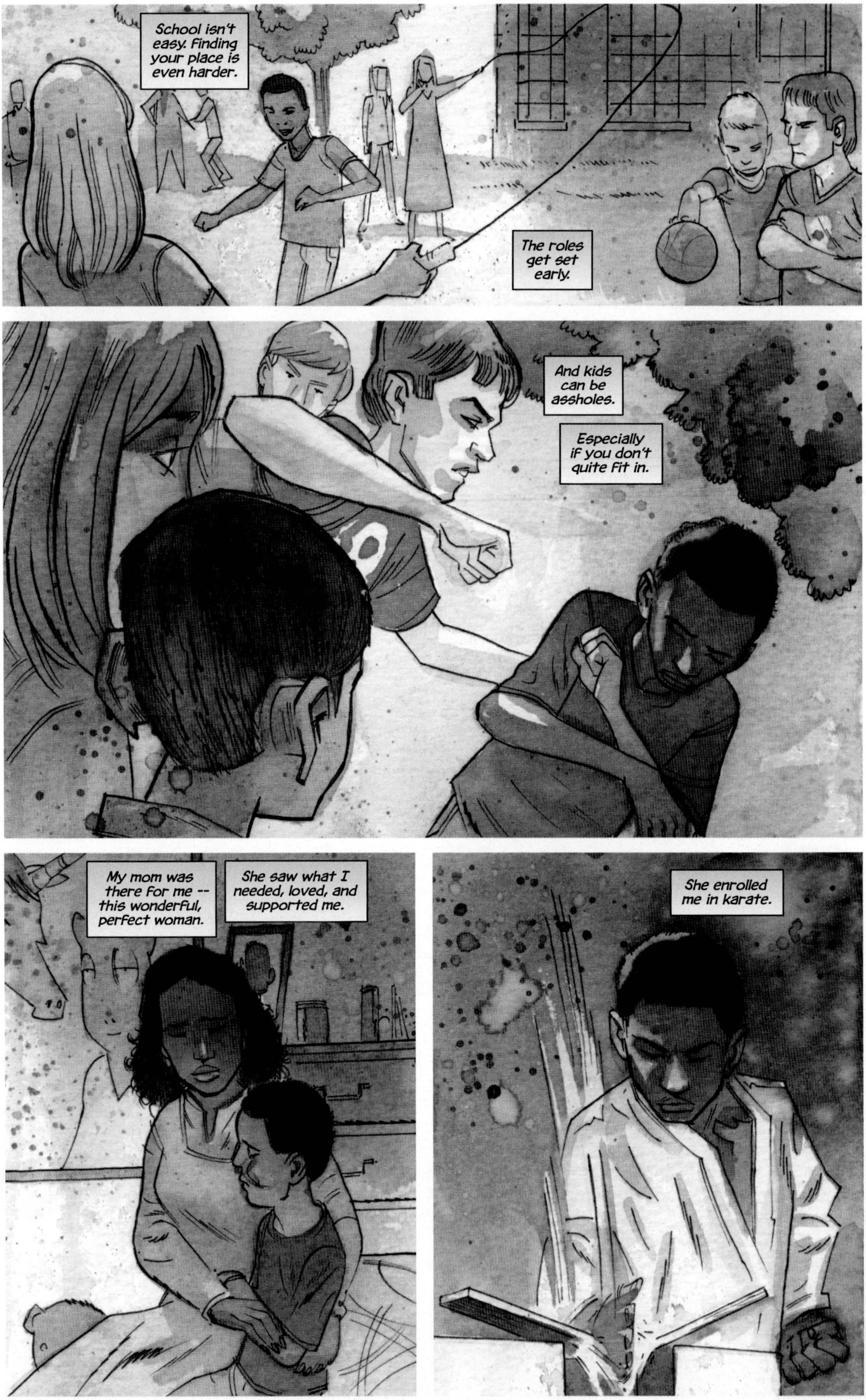

School isn't easy. Finding your place is even harder.
The roles get set early.
And kids can be assholes.
Especially if you don't quite fit in.
My mom was there for me -- this wonderful, perfect woman.
She saw what I needed, loved, and supported me.
She enrolled me in karate.

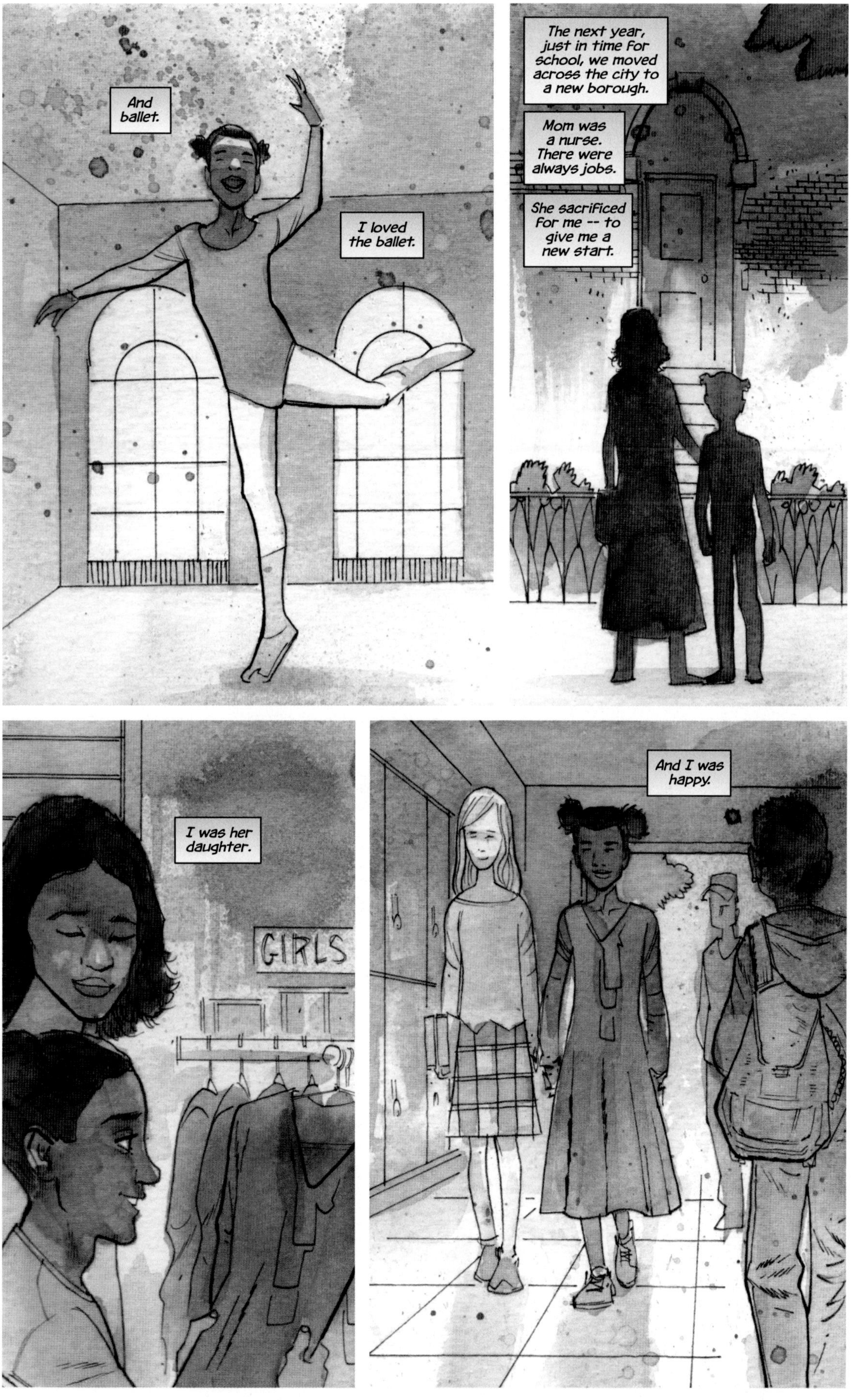
And ballet.
I loved the ballet.
The next year, just in time for school, we moved across the city to a new borough.
Mom was a nurse. There were always jobs.
She sacrificed for me -- to give me a new start.
I was her daughter.
GIRLS
And I was happy.

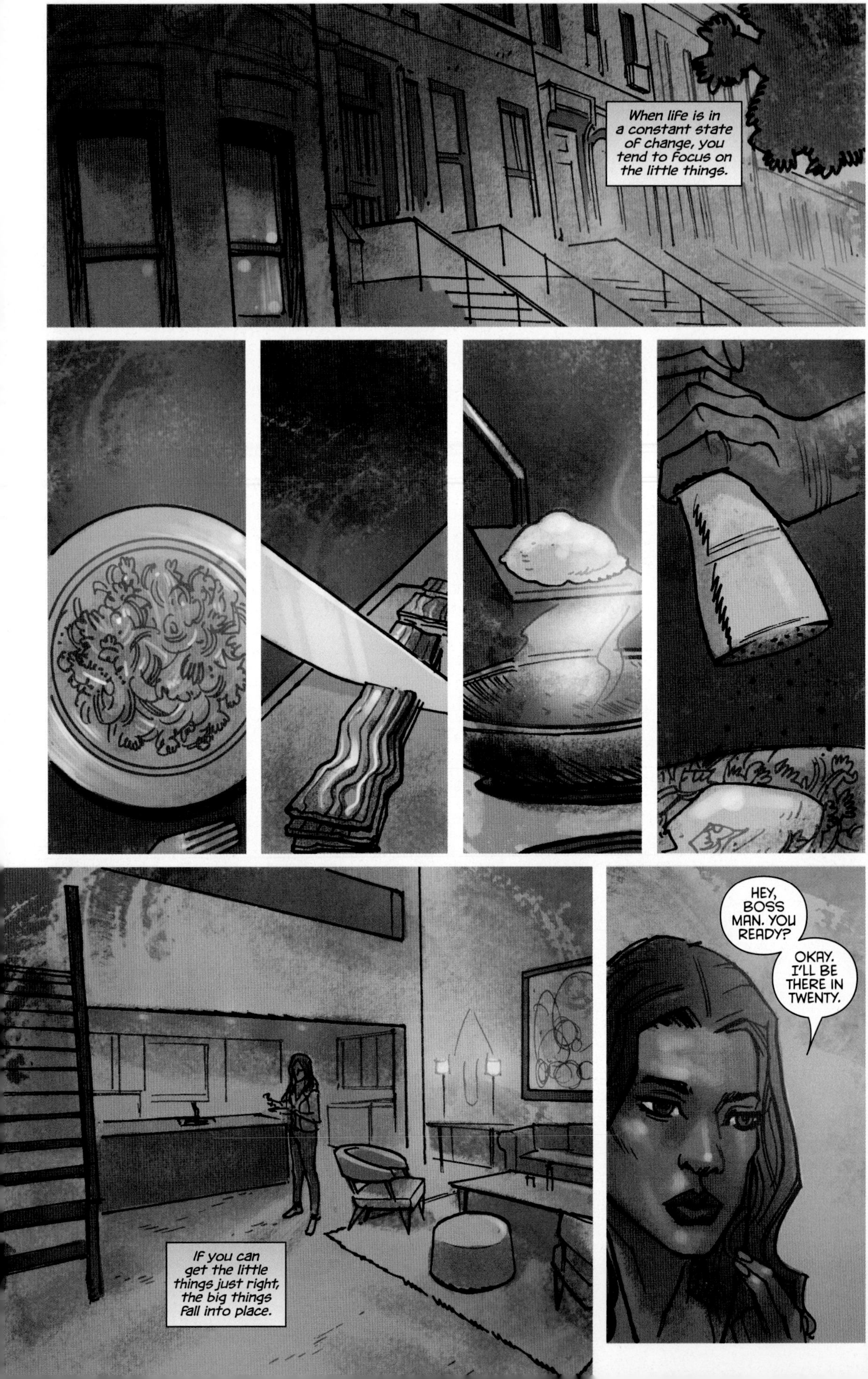

When life is in a constant state of change, you tend to focus on the little things.
If you can get the little things just right, the big things fall into place.
HEY, BOSS MAN. YOU READY?
OKAY. I'LL BE THERE IN TWENTY.

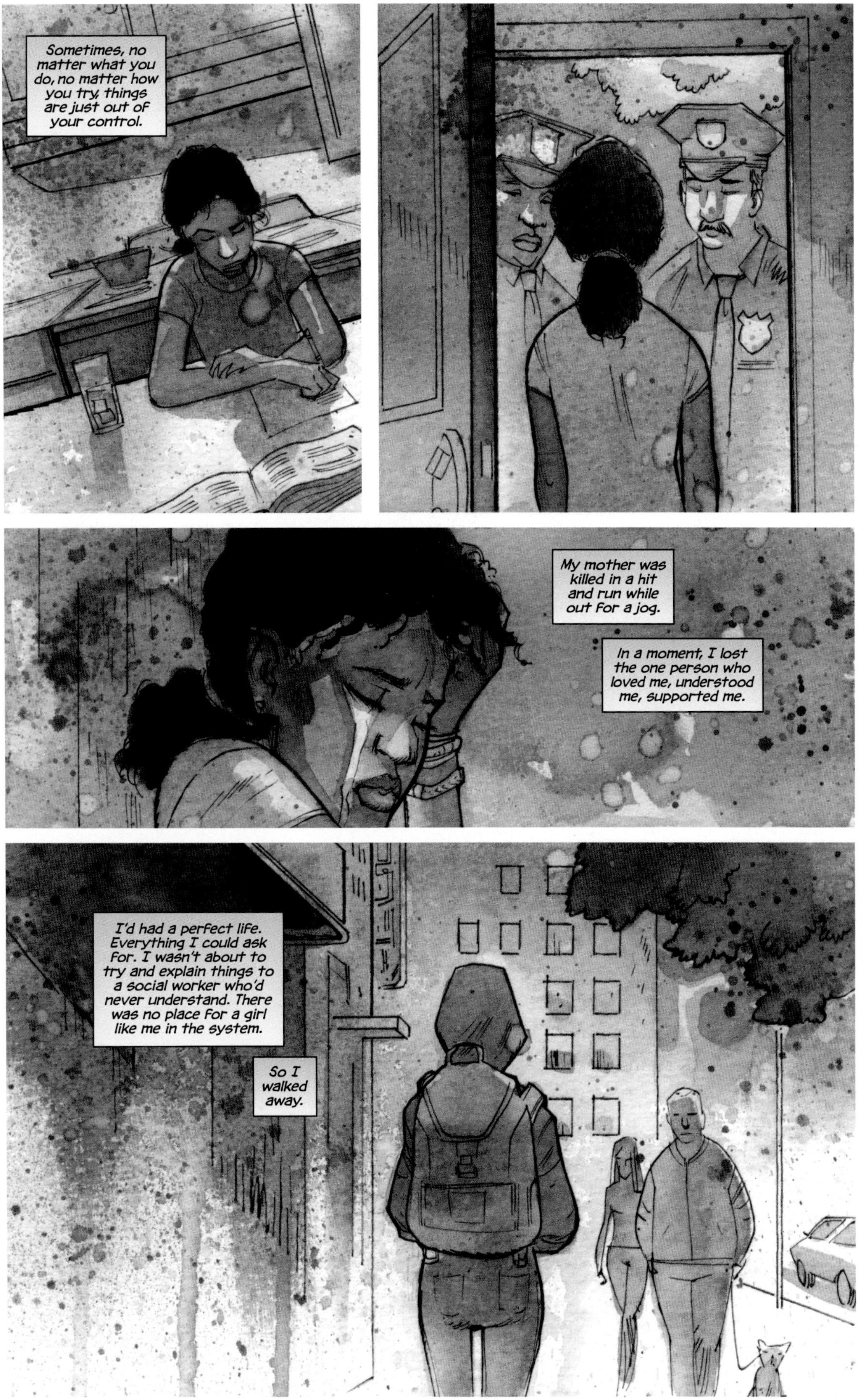
Sometimes, no matter what you do, no matter how you try, things are just out of your control.
My mother was killed in a hit and run while out for a jog.
In a moment, I lost the one person who loved me, understood me, supported me.
I'd had a perfect life. Everything I could ask for. I wasn't about to try and explain things to a social worker who'd never understand. There was no place for a girl like me in the system.
So I walked away.

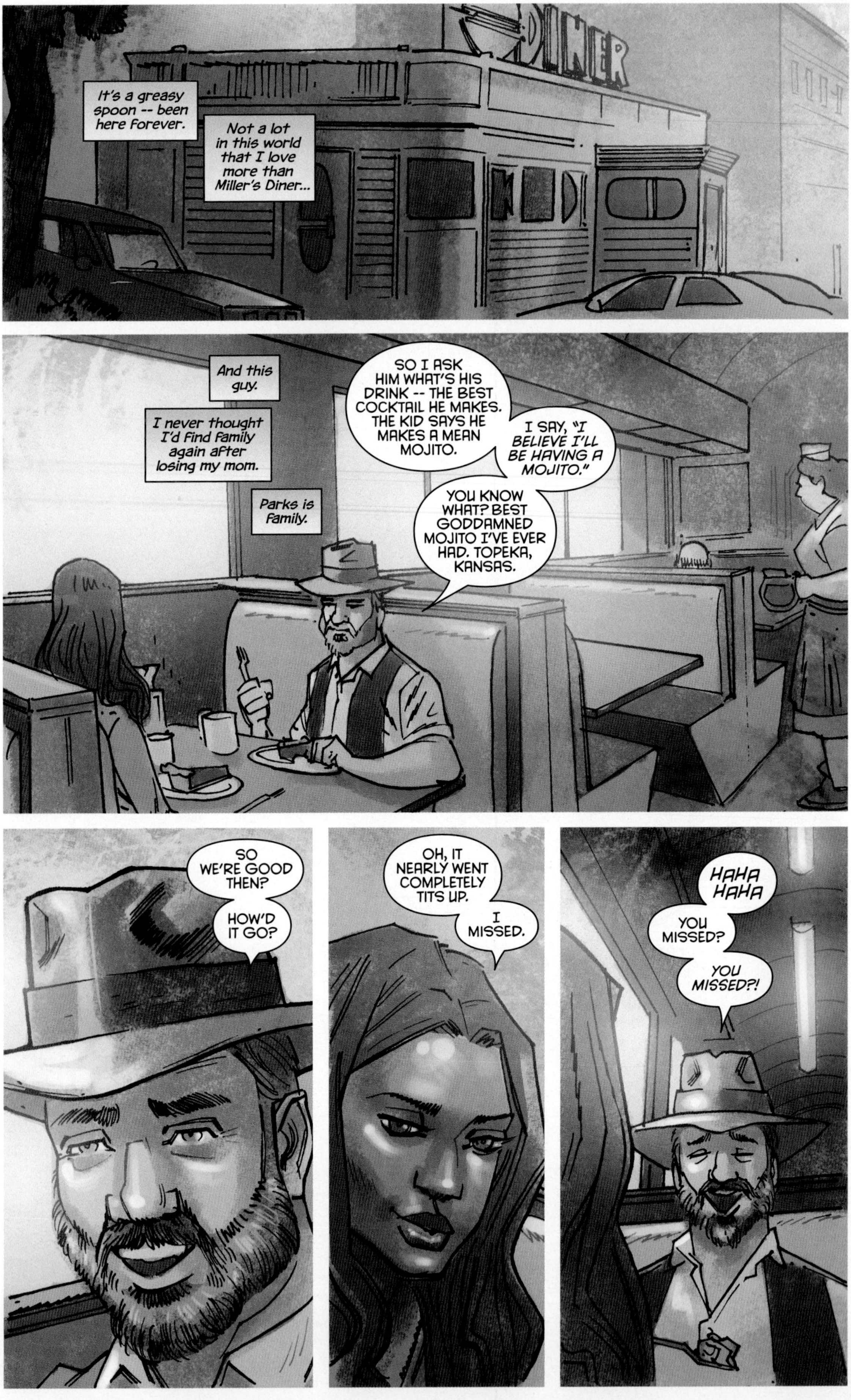

DINER
It's a greasy spoon -- been here forever.
Not a lot in this world that I love more than Miller's Diner...
And this guy.
I never thought I'd find family again after losing my mom.
Parks is family.
SO I ASK HIM WHAT'S HIS DRINK -- THE BEST COCKTAIL HE MAKES. THE KID SAYS HE MAKES A MEAN MOJITO.
I SAY, "I BELIEVE I'LL BE HAVING A MOJITO."
YOU KNOW WHAT? BEST GODDAMNED MOJITO I'VE EVER HAD. TOPEKA, KANSAS.
SO WE'RE GOOD THEN?
HOW'D IT GO?
OH, IT NEARLY WENT COMPLETELY TITS UP.
I MISSED.
HAHA HAHA
YOU MISSED?
YOU MISSED?!

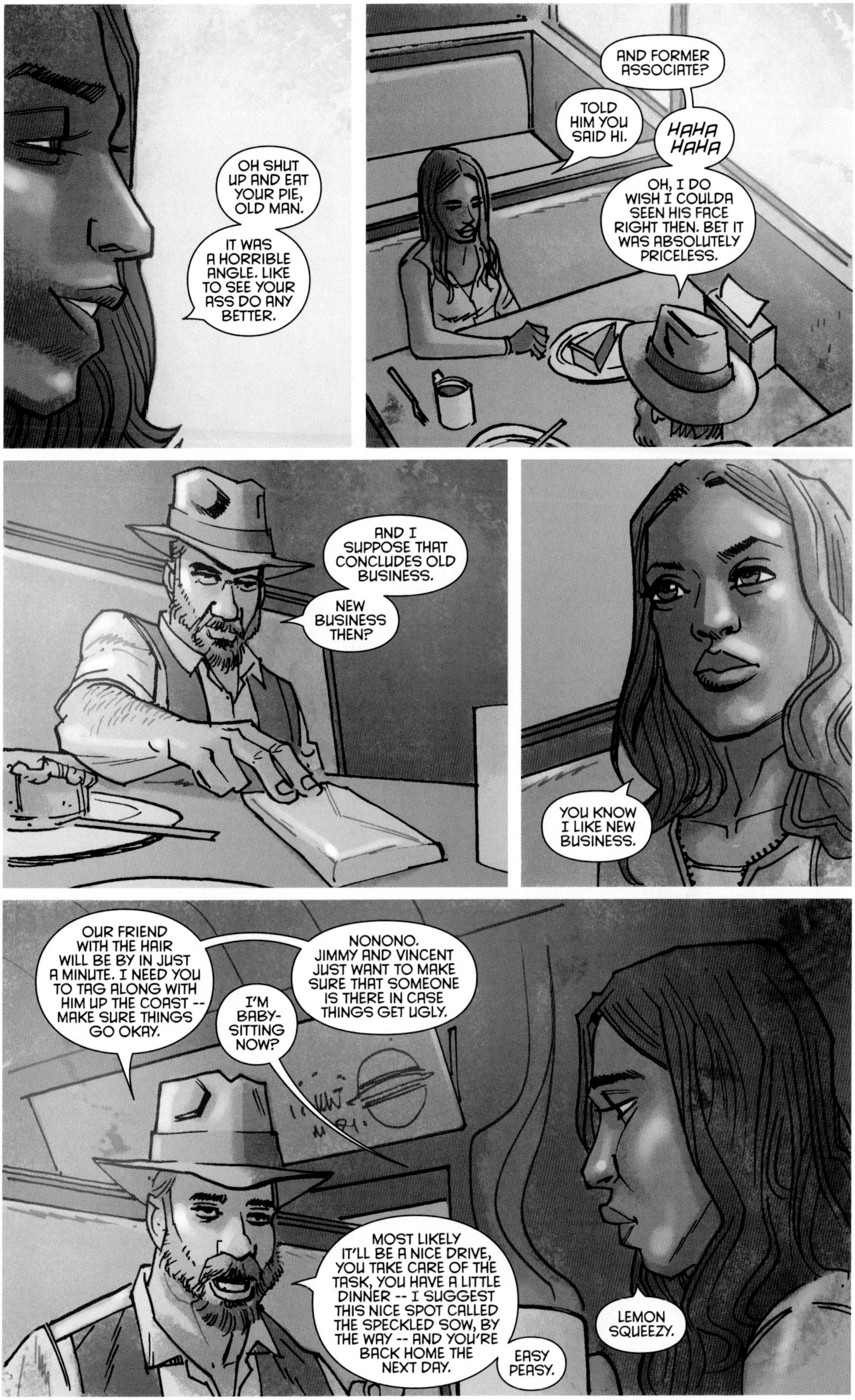
OH SHUT UP AND EAT YOUR PIE, OLD MAN.
IT WAS A HORRIBLE ANGLE. LIKE TO SEE YOUR ASS DO ANY BETTER.
AND FORMER ASSOCIATE?
TOLD HIM YOU SAID HI.
HAHA HAHA
OH, I DO WISH I COULDA SEEN HIS FACE RIGHT THEN. BET IT WAS ABSOLUTELY PRICELESS.
AND I SUPPOSE THAT CONCLUDES OLD BUSINESS.
NEW BUSINESS THEN?
YOU KNOW I LIKE NEW BUSINESS.
OUR FRIEND WITH THE HAIR WILL BE BY IN JUST A MINUTE. I NEED YOU TO TAG ALONG WITH HIM UP THE COAST -- MAKE SURE THINGS GO OKAY.
I'M BABY-SITTING NOW?
NONONO. JIMMY AND VINCENT JUST WANT TO MAKE SURE THAT SOMEONE IS THERE IN CASE THINGS GET UGLY.
MOST LIKELY IT'LL BE A NICE DRIVE, YOU TAKE CARE OF THE TASK, YOU HAVE A LITTLE DINNER -- I SUGGEST THIS NICE SPOT CALLED THE SPECKLED SOW, BY THE WAY -- AND YOU'RE BACK HOME THE NEXT DAY.
EASY PEASY.
LEMON SQUEEZY.

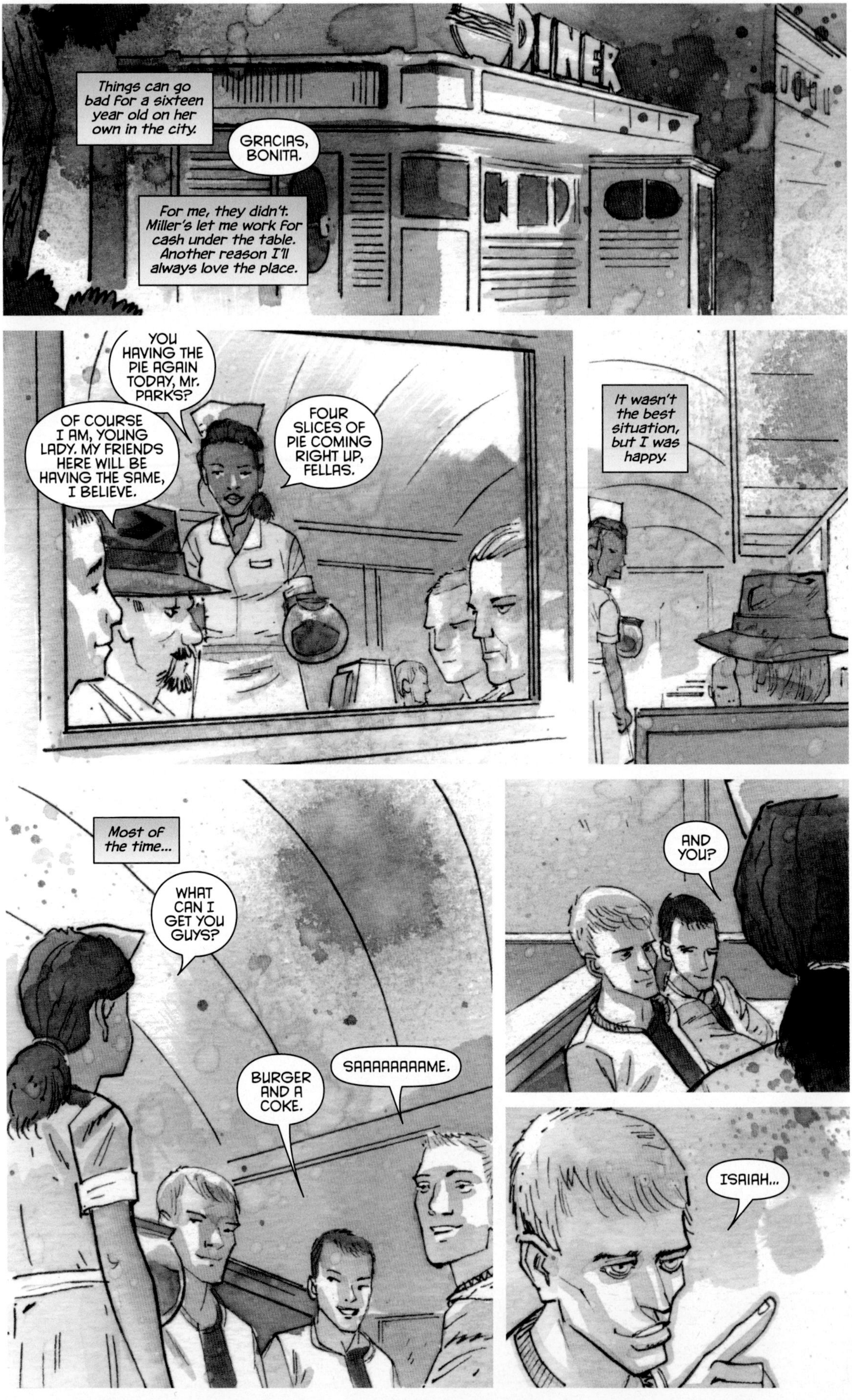
DINER
Things can go bad for a sixteen year old on her own in the city.
GRACIAS, BONITA.
For me, they didn't. Miller's let me work for cash under the table. Another reason I'll always love the place.
YOU HAVING THE PIE AGAIN TODAY, Mr. PARKS?
OF COURSE I AM, YOUNG LADY. MY FRIENDS HERE WILL BE HAVING THE SAME, I BELIEVE.
FOUR SLICES OF PIE COMING RIGHT UP, FELLAS.
It wasn't the best situation, but I was happy.
Most of the time...
WHAT CAN I GET YOU GUYS?
BURGER AND A COKE.
SAAAAAAAAME.
AND YOU?
ISAIAH...

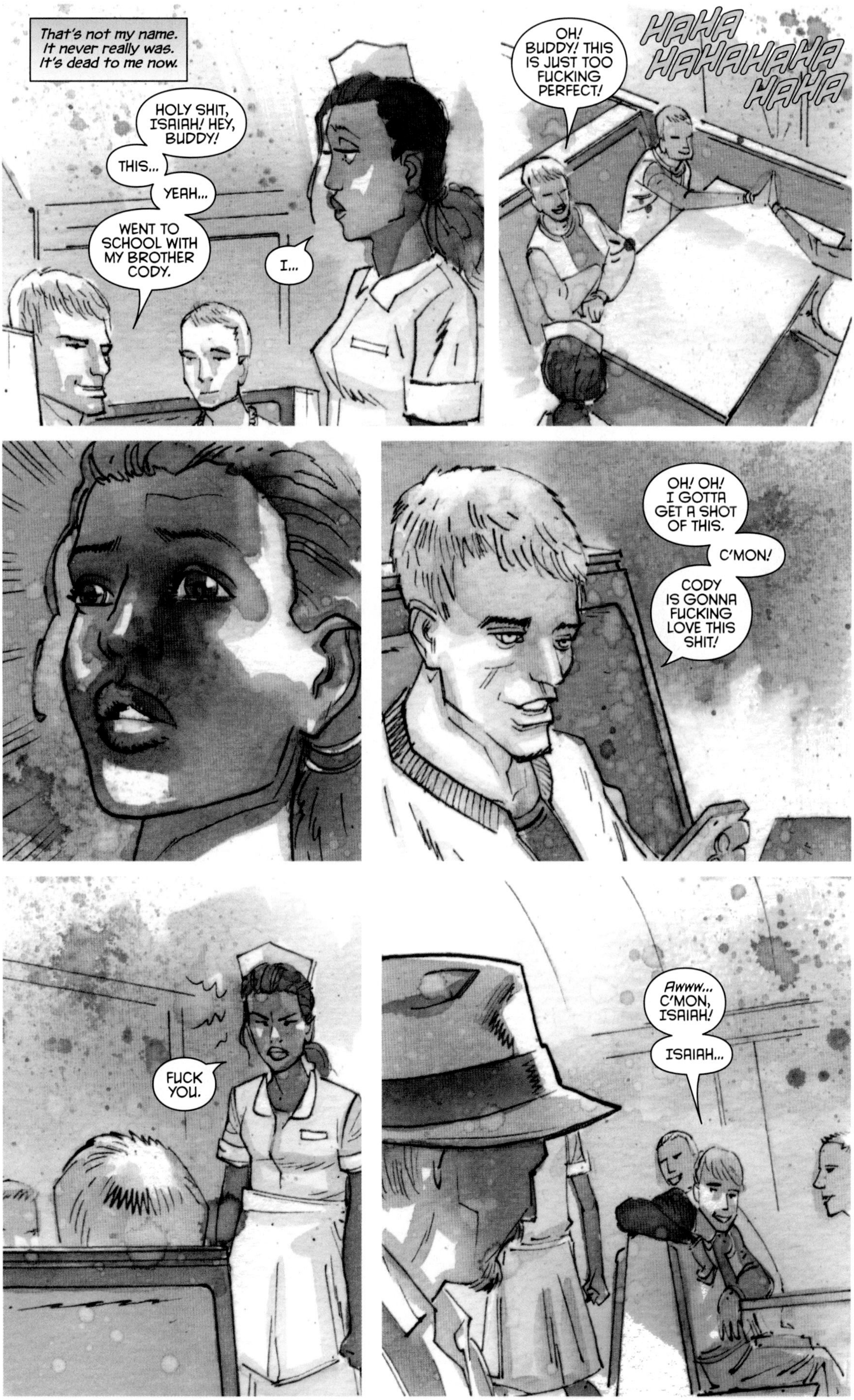
That's not my name. It never really was. It's dead to me now.
HOLY SHIT, ISAIAH! HEY, BUDDY!
THIS...
YEAH...
WENT TO SCHOOL WITH MY BROTHER CODY.
I...
OH! BUDDY! THIS IS JUST TOO FUCKING PERFECT!
HAHA HAHAHAHAHA HAHA
OH! OH! I GOTTA GET A SHOT OF THIS.
C'MON!
CODY IS GONNA FUCKING LOVE THIS SHIT!
FUCK YOU.
Awww... C'MON, ISAIAH!
ISAIAH...

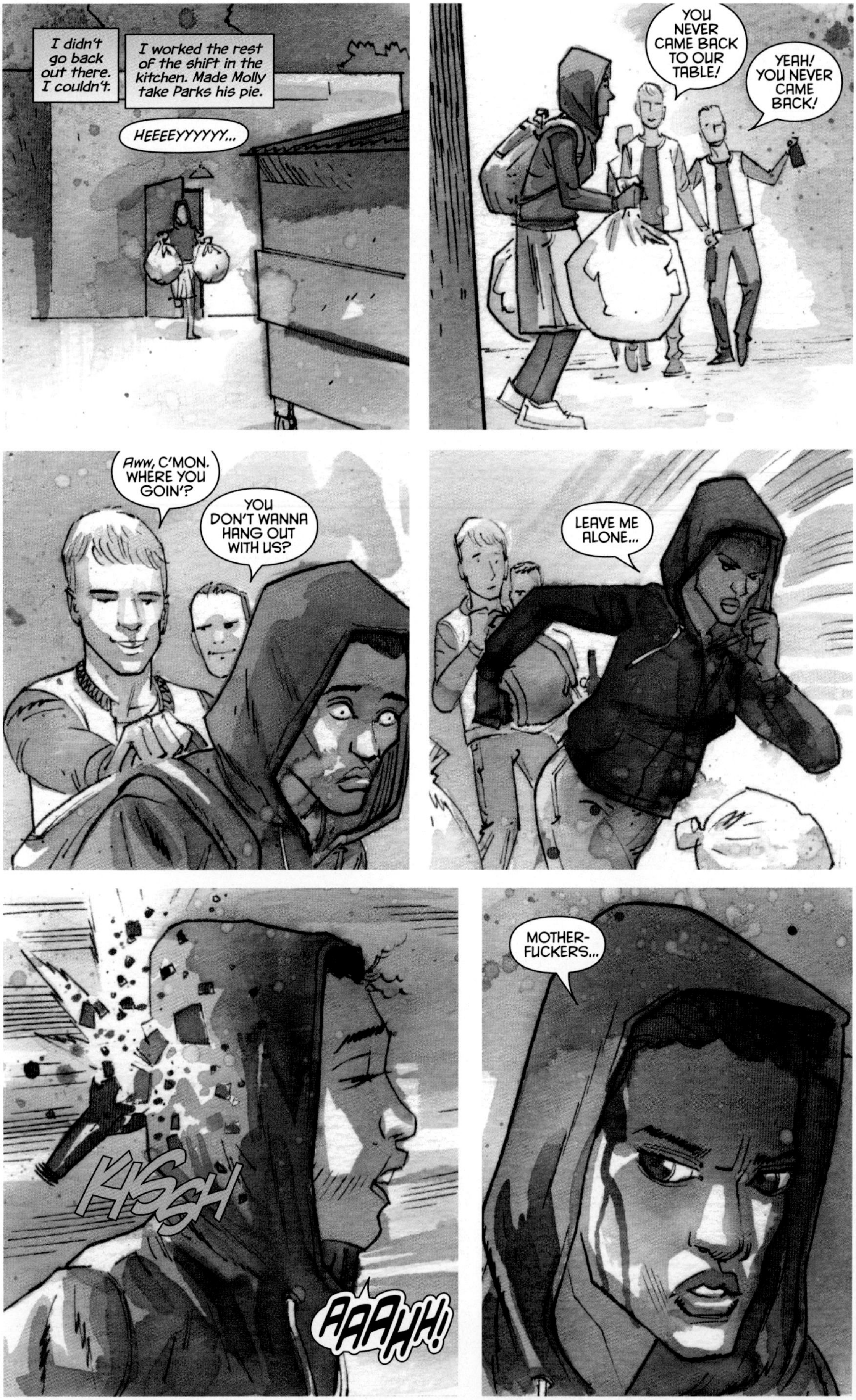
I didn't go back out there. I couldn't.
I worked the rest of the shift in the kitchen. Made Molly take Parks his pie.
HEEEEYYYYYY...
YOU NEVER CAME BACK TO OUR TABLE!
YEAH! YOU NEVER CAME BACK!
AWW, C'MON. WHERE YOU GOIN'?
YOU DON'T WANNA HANG OUT WITH US?
LEAVE ME ALONE...
KSSH
AAAHH!
MOTHER-FUCKERS...

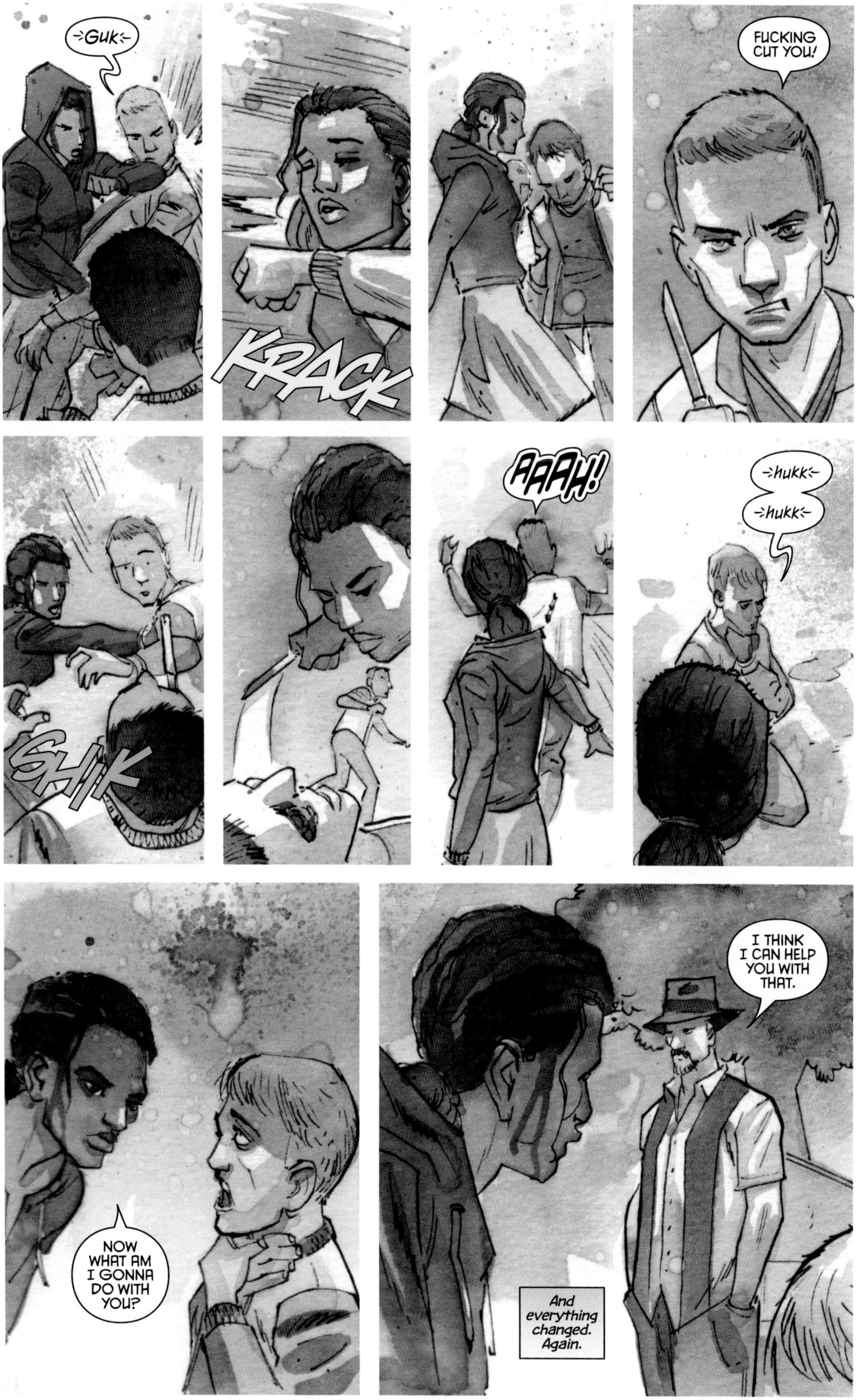
GUK
FUCKING CUT YOU!
KRACK
SHIK
AAAH!
hukk
hukk
NOW WHAT AM I GONNA DO WITH YOU?
I THINK I CAN HELP YOU WITH THAT.
And everything changed. Again.

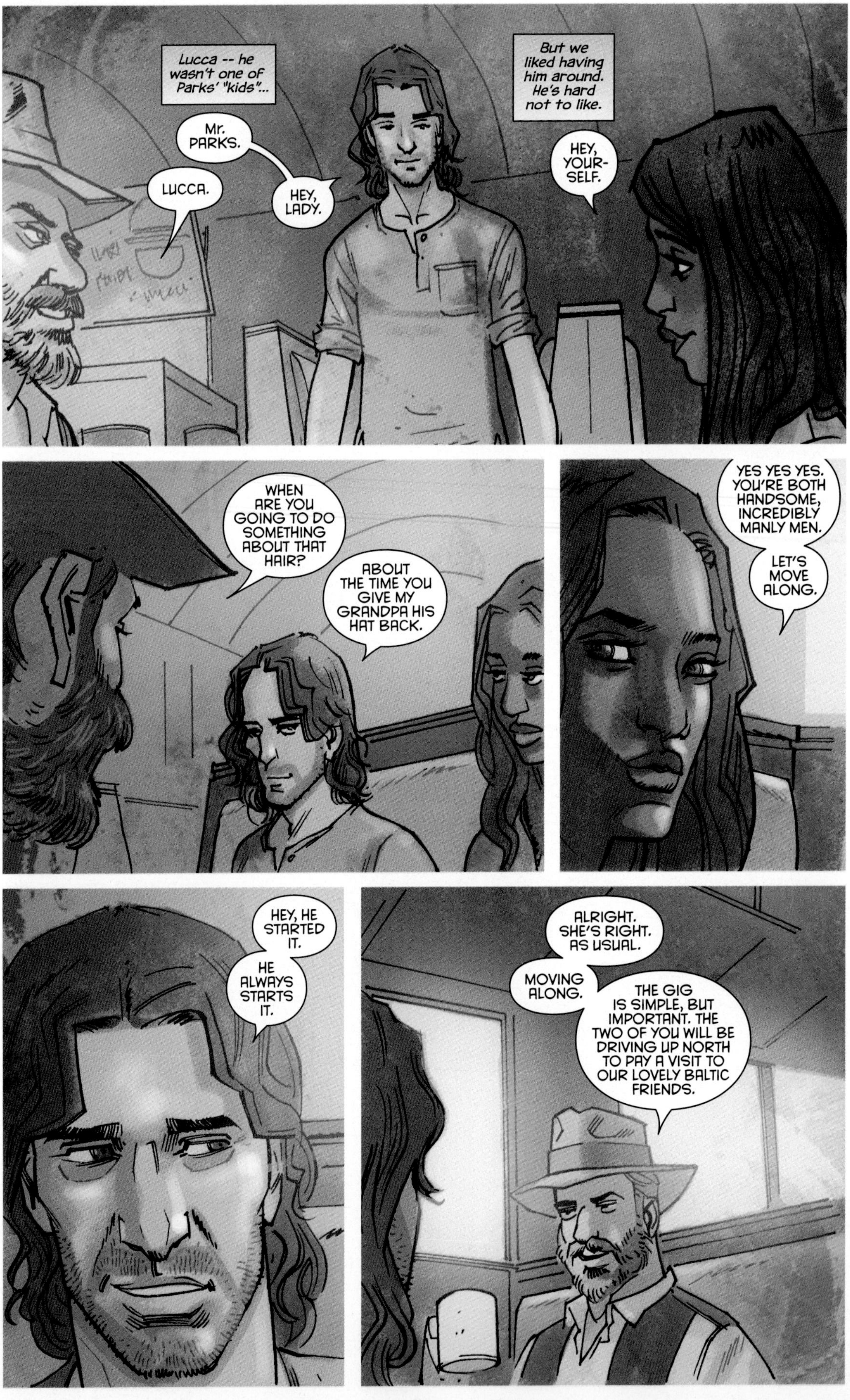
Lucca -- he wasn't one of Parks' "kids"...
Mr. PARKS.
LUCCA.
HEY, LADY.
But we liked having him around. He's hard not to like.
HEY, YOURSELF.
WHEN ARE YOU GOING TO DO SOMETHING ABOUT THAT HAIR?
ABOUT THE TIME YOU GIVE MY GRANDPA HIS HAT BACK.
YES YES YES. YOU'RE BOTH HANDSOME, INCREDIBLY MANLY MEN.
LET'S MOVE ALONG.
HEY, HE STARTED IT.
HE ALWAYS STARTS IT.
ALRIGHT. SHE'S RIGHT. AS USUAL.
MOVING ALONG.
THE GIG IS SIMPLE, BUT IMPORTANT. THE TWO OF YOU WILL BE DRIVING UP NORTH TO PAY A VISIT TO OUR LOVELY BALTIC FRIENDS.

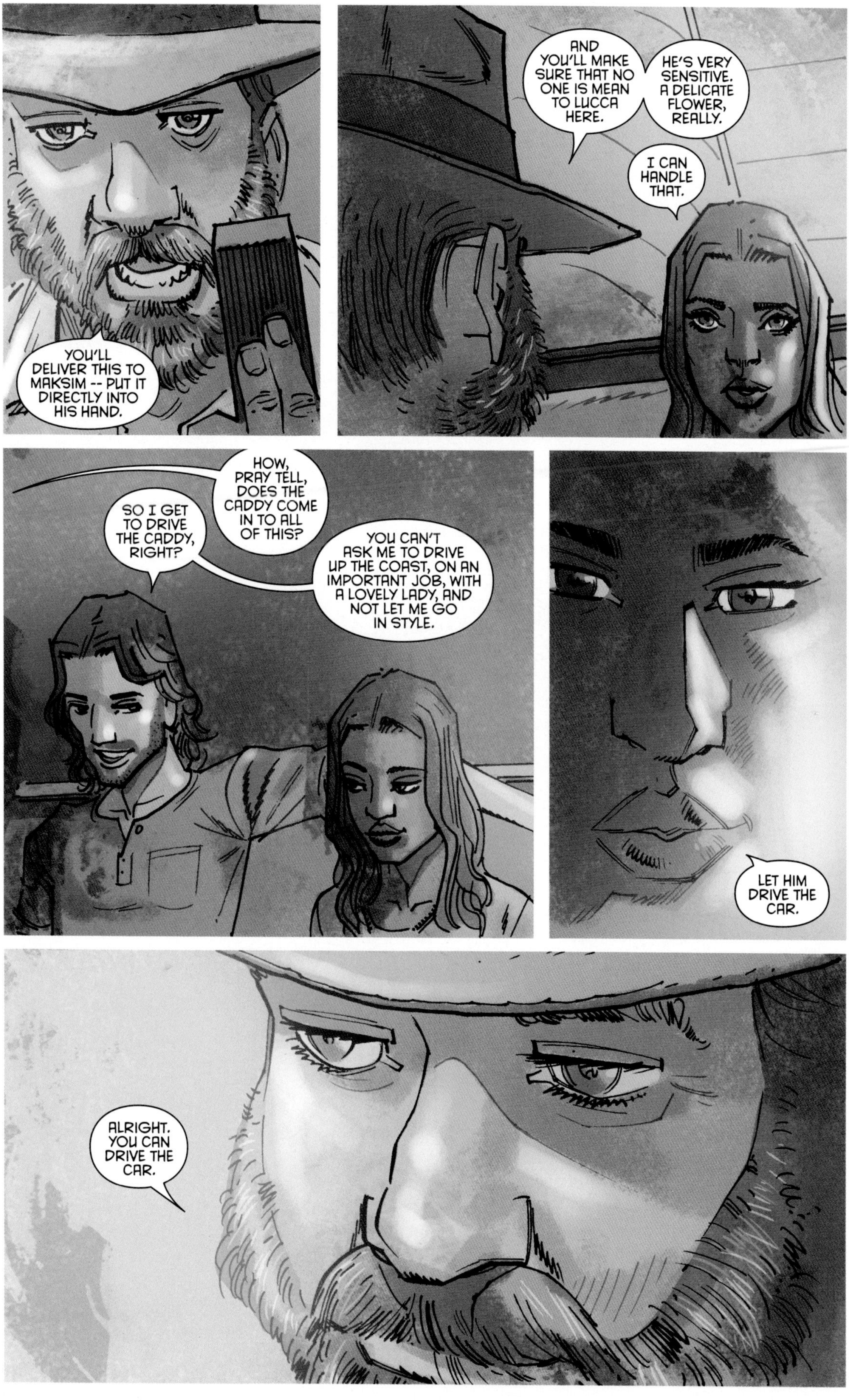
YOU'LL DELIVER THIS TO MAKSIM -- PUT IT DIRECTLY INTO HIS HAND.
AND YOU'LL MAKE SURE THAT NO ONE IS MEAN TO LUCCA HERE.
HE'S VERY SENSITIVE. A DELICATE FLOWER, REALLY.
I CAN HANDLE THAT.
SO I GET TO DRIVE THE CADDY, RIGHT?
HOW, PRAY TELL, DOES THE CADDY COME IN TO ALL OF THIS?
YOU CAN'T ASK ME TO DRIVE UP THE COAST, ON AN IMPORTANT JOB, WITH A LOVELY LADY, AND NOT LET ME GO IN STYLE.
LET HIM DRIVE THE CAR.
ALRIGHT. YOU CAN DRIVE THE CAR.

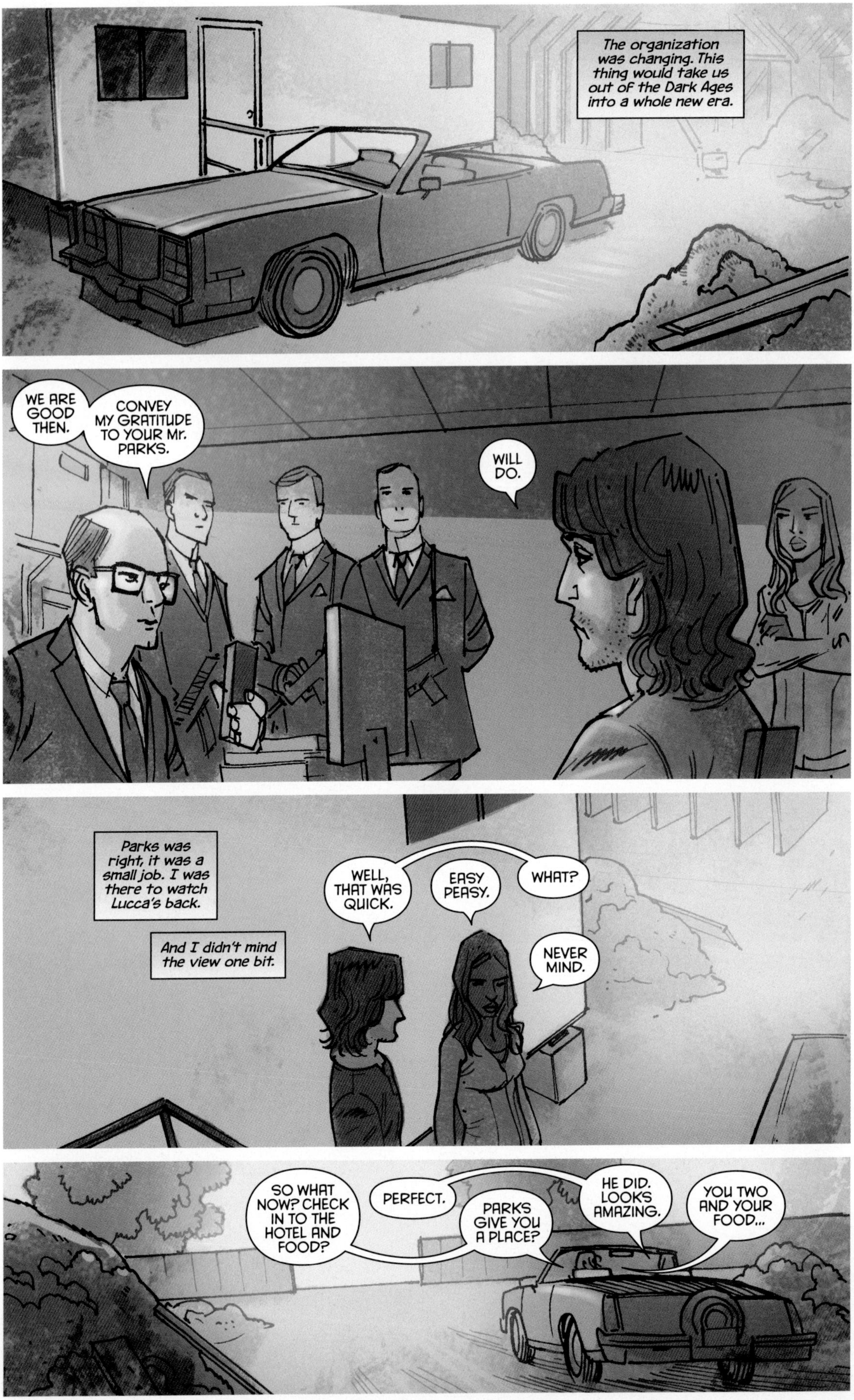
The organization was changing. This thing would take us out of the Dark Ages into a whole new era.
WE ARE GOOD THEN.
CONVEY MY GRATITUDE TO YOUR Mr. PARKS.
WILL DO.
Parks was right, it was a small job. I was there to watch Lucca's back.
And I didn't mind the view one bit.
WELL, THAT WAS QUICK.
EASY PEASY.
WHAT?
NEVER MIND.
SO WHAT NOW? CHECK IN TO THE HOTEL AND FOOD?
PERFECT.
PARKS GIVE YOU A PLACE?
HE DID. LOOKS AMAZING.
YOU TWO AND YOUR FOOD...

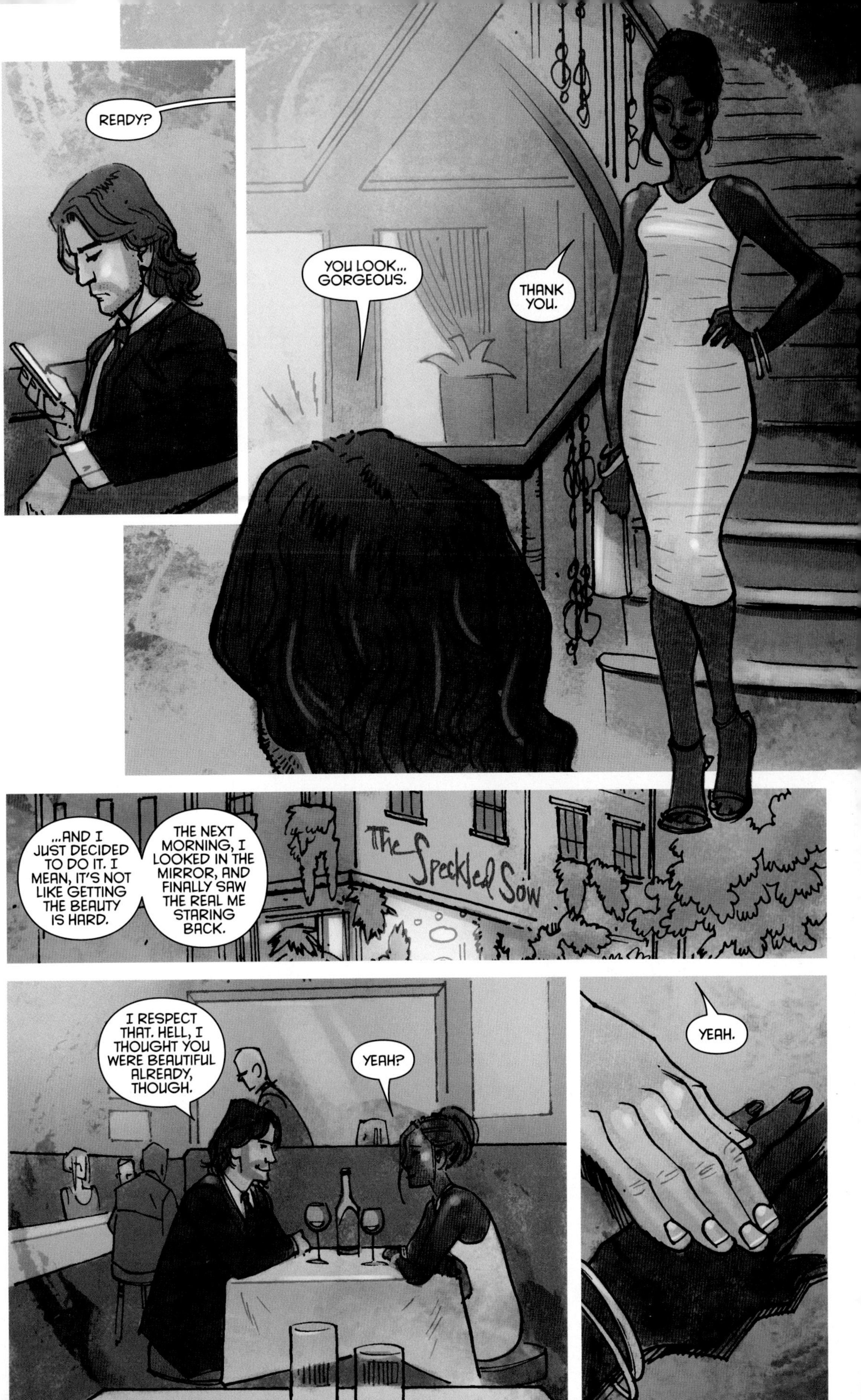
READY?
YOU LOOK... GORGEOUS.
THANK YOU.
...AND I JUST DECIDED TO DO IT. I MEAN, IT'S NOT LIKE GETTING THE BEAUTY IS HARD.
THE NEXT MORNING, I LOOKED IN THE MIRROR, AND FINALLY SAW THE REAL ME STARING BACK.
The Speckled Sow
I RESPECT THAT. HELL, I THOUGHT YOU WERE BEAUTIFUL ALREADY, THOUGH.
YEAH?
YEAH.

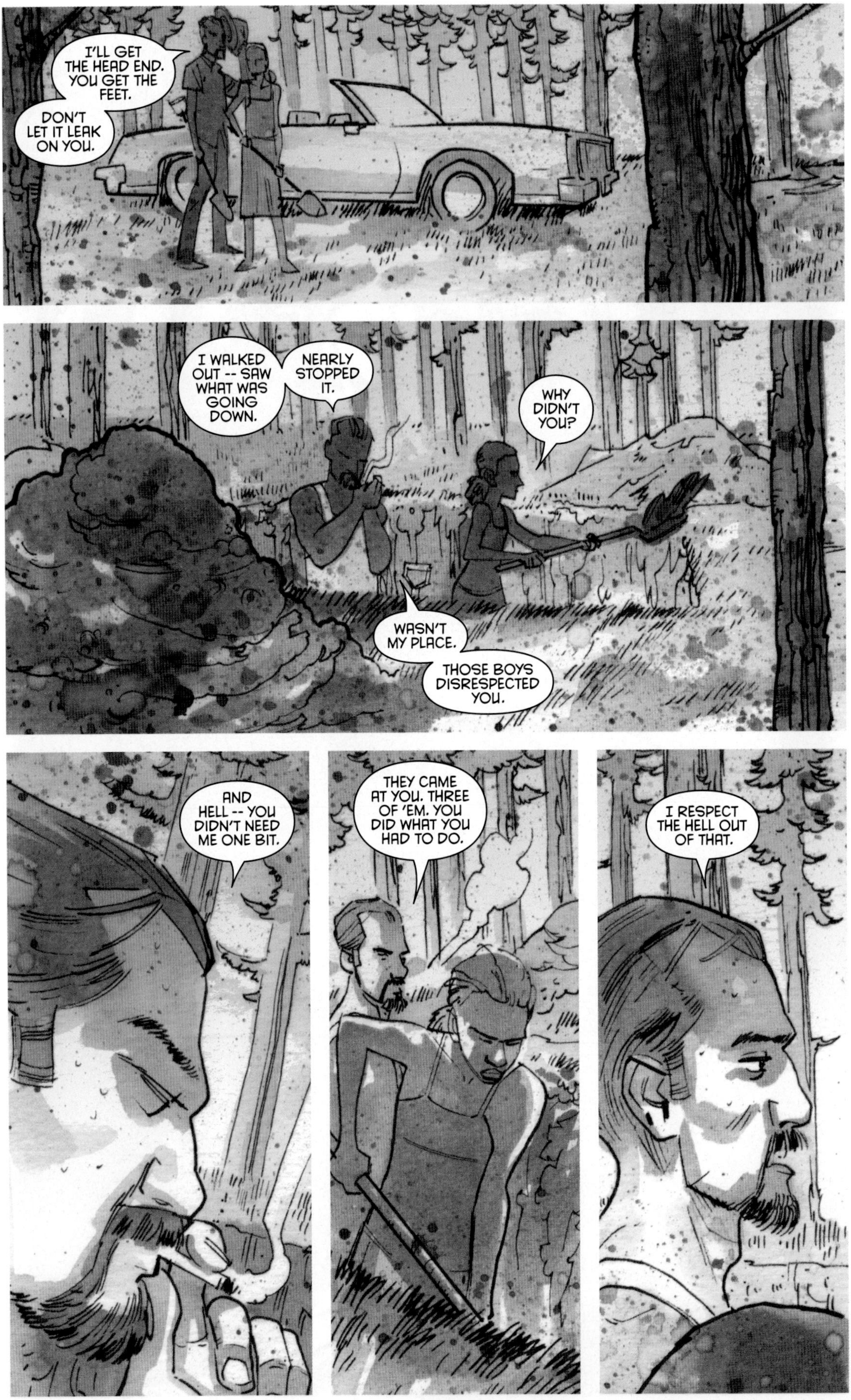
I'LL GET THE HEAD END. YOU GET THE FEET.
DON'T LET IT LEAK ON YOU.
I WALKED OUT -- SAW WHAT WAS GOING DOWN.
NEARLY STOPPED IT.
WHY DIDN'T YOU?
WASN'T MY PLACE.
THOSE BOYS DISRESPECTED YOU.
AND HELL -- YOU DIDN'T NEED ME ONE BIT.
THEY CAME AT YOU. THREE OF 'EM. YOU DID WHAT YOU HAD TO DO.
I RESPECT THE HELL OUT OF THAT.

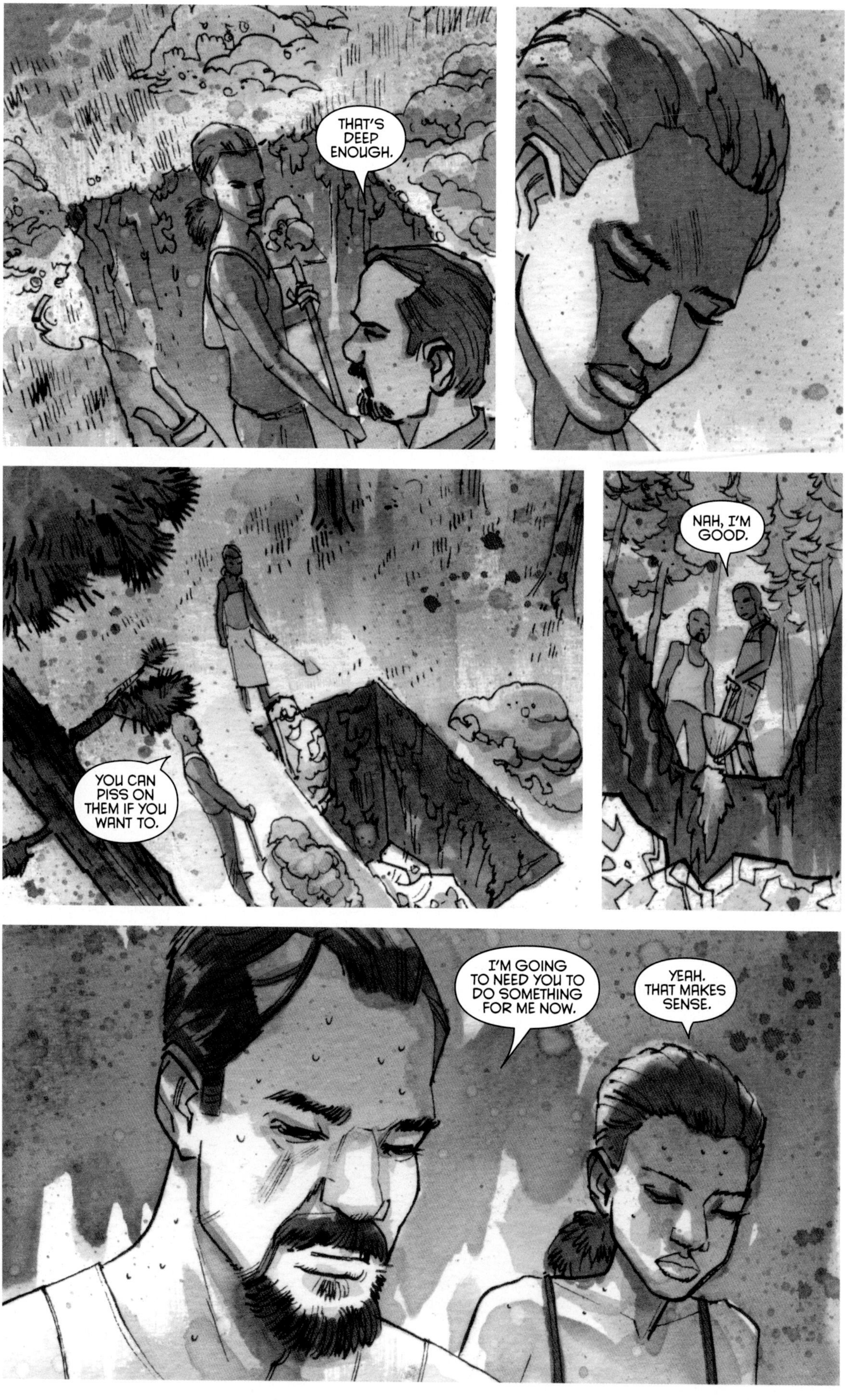
THAT'S DEEP ENOUGH.
NAH, I'M GOOD.
YOU CAN PISS ON THEM IF YOU WANT TO.
I'M GOING TO NEED YOU TO DO SOMETHING FOR ME NOW.
YEAH. THAT MAKES SENSE.

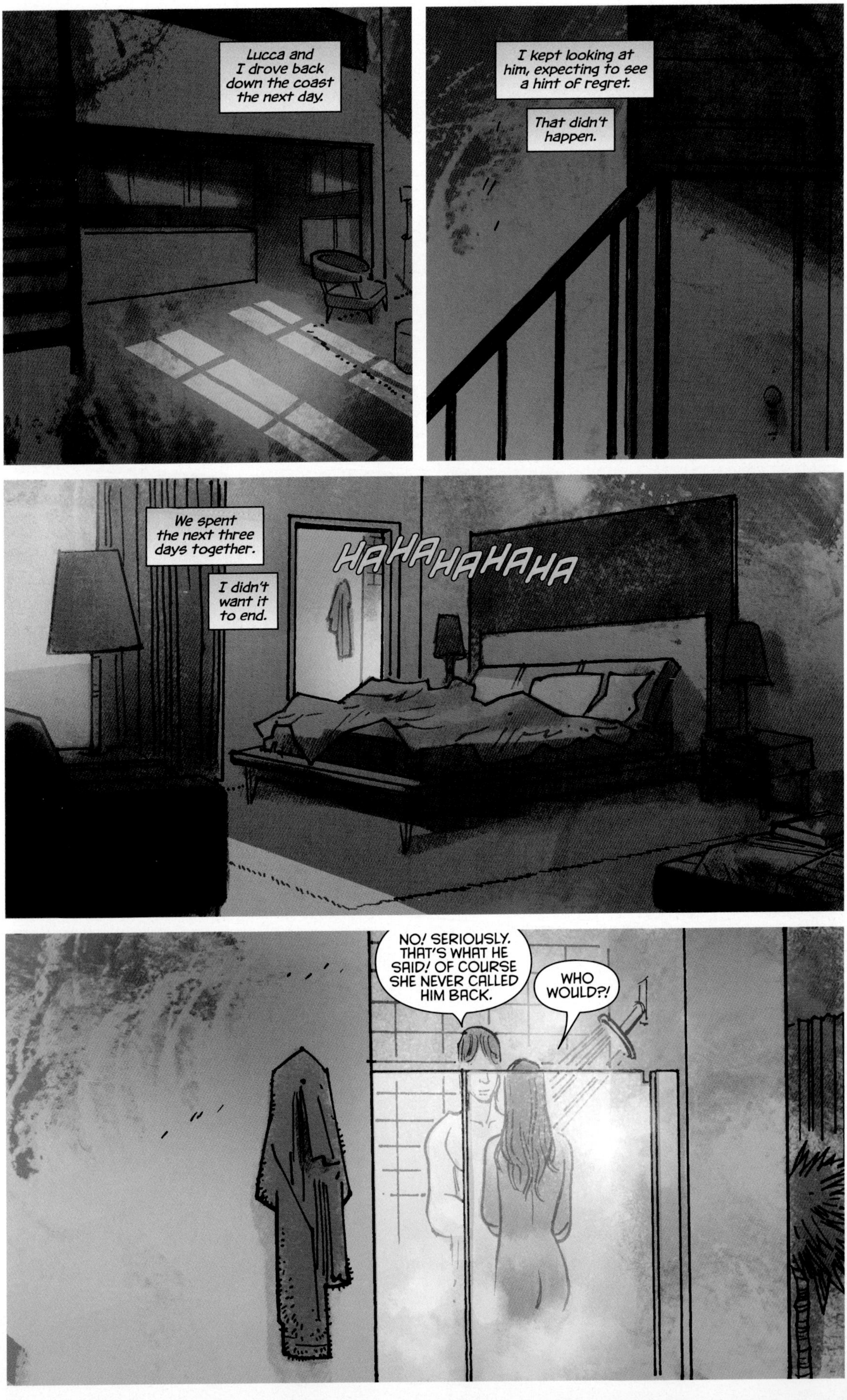
Lucca and I drove back down the coast the next day.
I kept looking at him, expecting to see a hint of regret.
That didn't happen.
We spent the next three days together.
I didn't want it to end.
HAHAHAHAHAHA
NO! SERIOUSLY. THAT'S WHAT HE SAID! OF COURSE SHE NEVER CALLED HIM BACK.
WHO WOULD?!

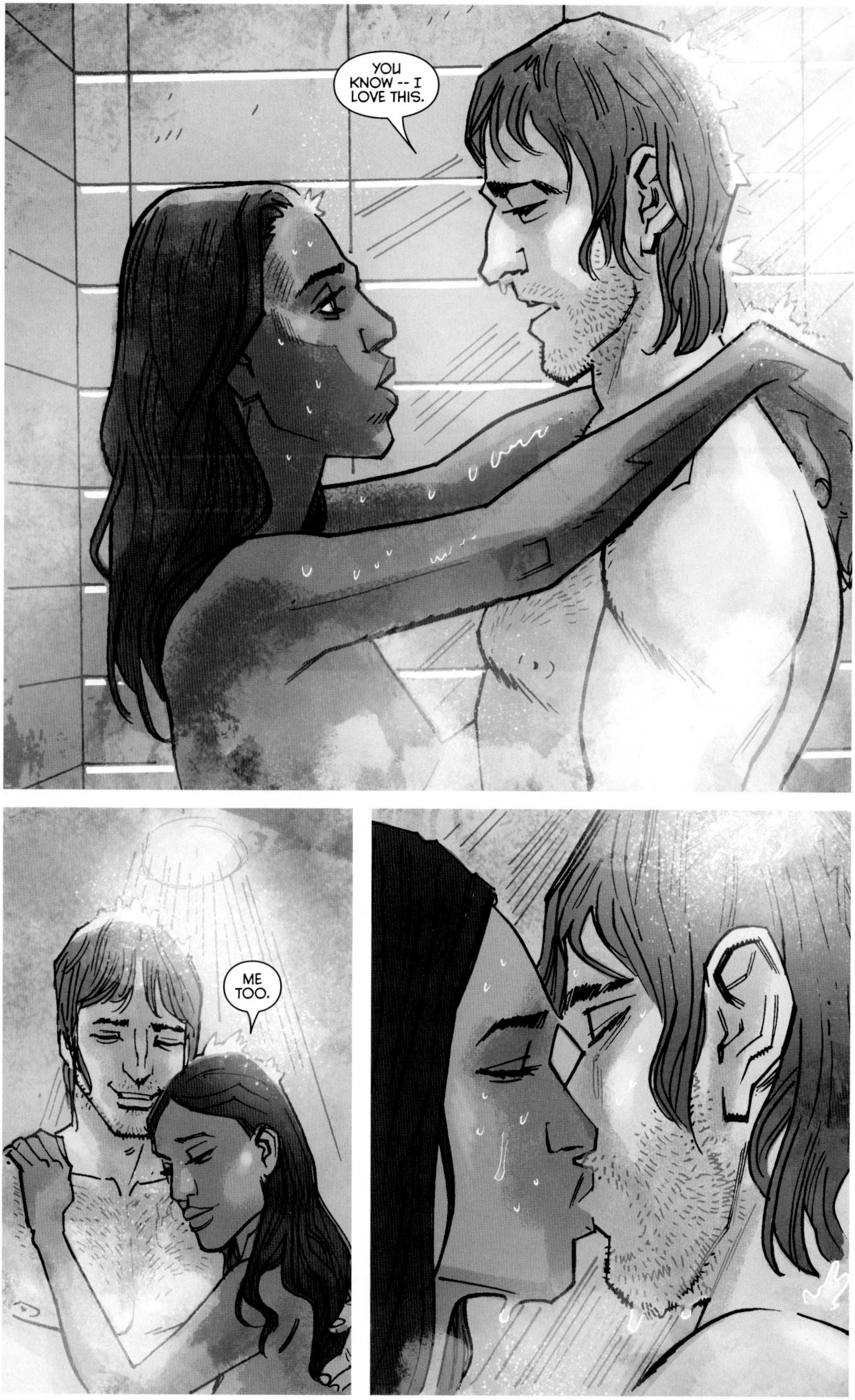
YOU KNOW -- I LOVE THIS.
ME TOO.

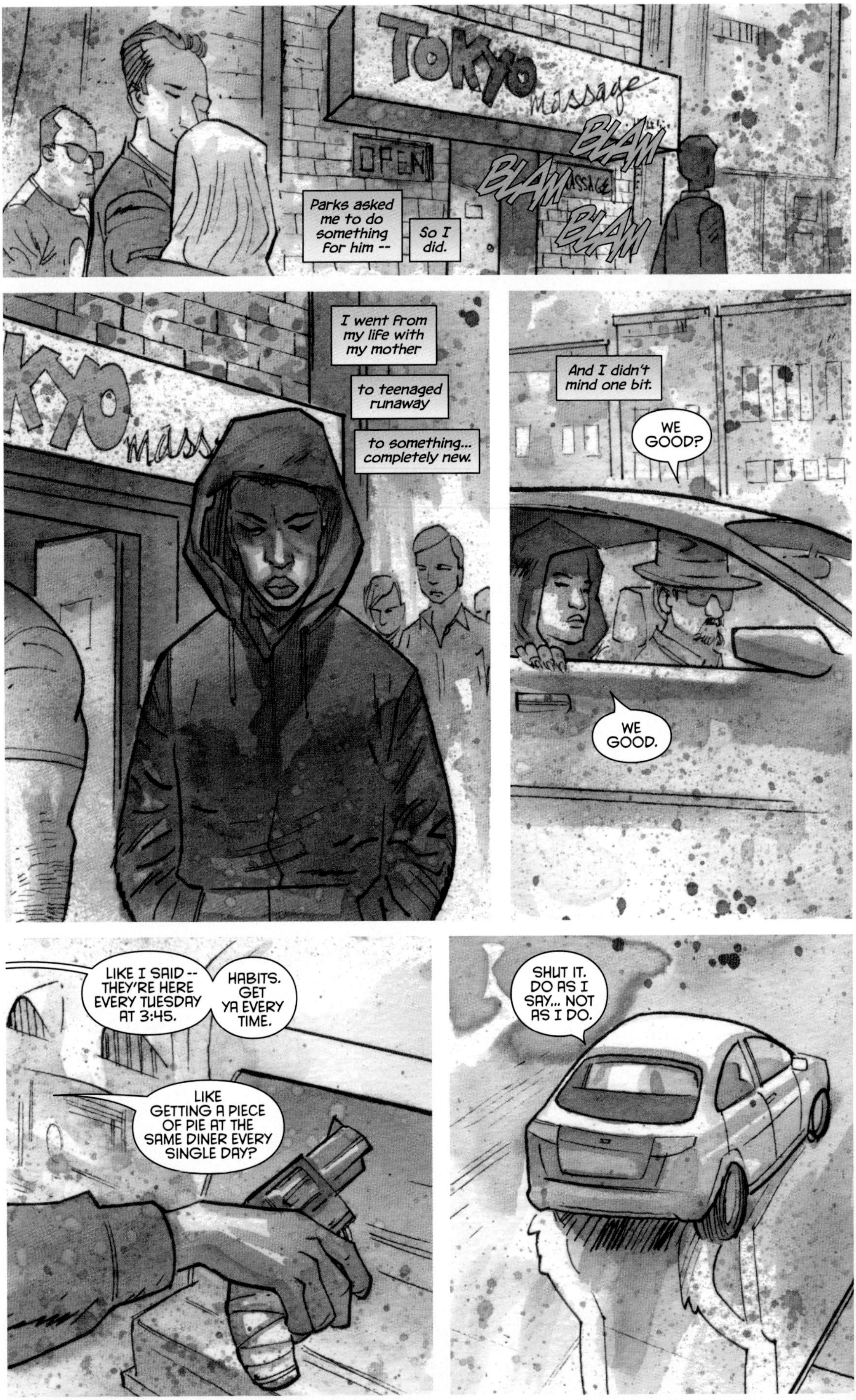
TOKYO massage
OPEN
MASSAGE
Parks asked me to do something for him --
So I did.
BLAM
BLAM
BLAM
I went from my life with my mother
to teenaged runaway
to something... completely new.
And I didn't mind one bit.
WE GOOD?
WE GOOD.
LIKE I SAID -- THEY'RE HERE EVERY TUESDAY AT 3:45.
HABITS. GET YA EVERY TIME.
LIKE GETTING A PIECE OF PIE AT THE SAME DINER EVERY SINGLE DAY?
SHUT IT. DO AS I SAY... NOT AS I DO.

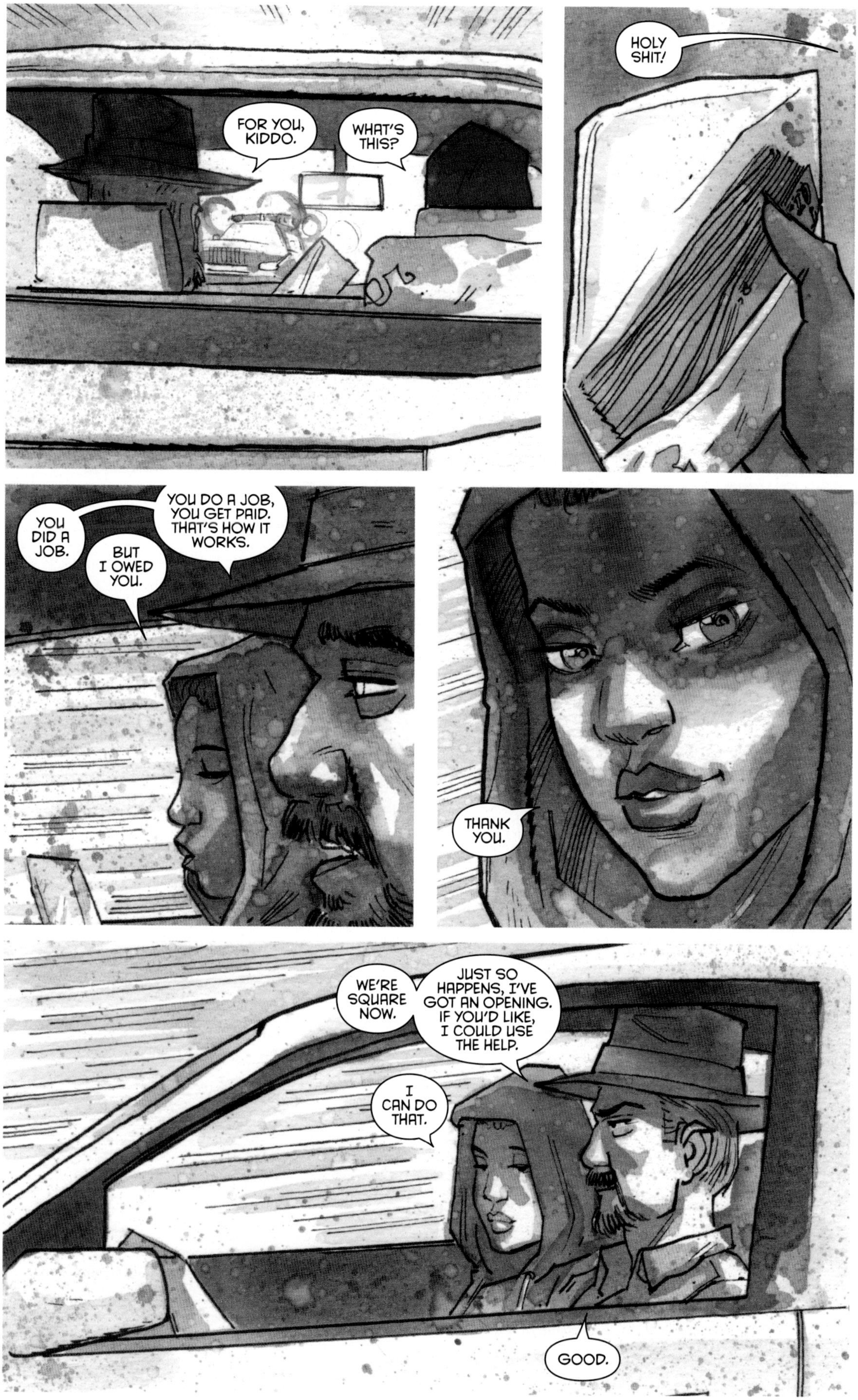
FOR YOU, KIDDO.
WHAT'S THIS?
HOLY SHIT!
YOU DID A JOB.
YOU DO A JOB, YOU GET PAID. THAT'S HOW IT WORKS.
BUT I OWED YOU.
THANK YOU.
WE'RE SQUARE NOW.
JUST SO HAPPENS, I'VE GOT AN OPENING. IF YOU'D LIKE, I COULD USE THE HELP.
I CAN DO THAT.
GOOD.

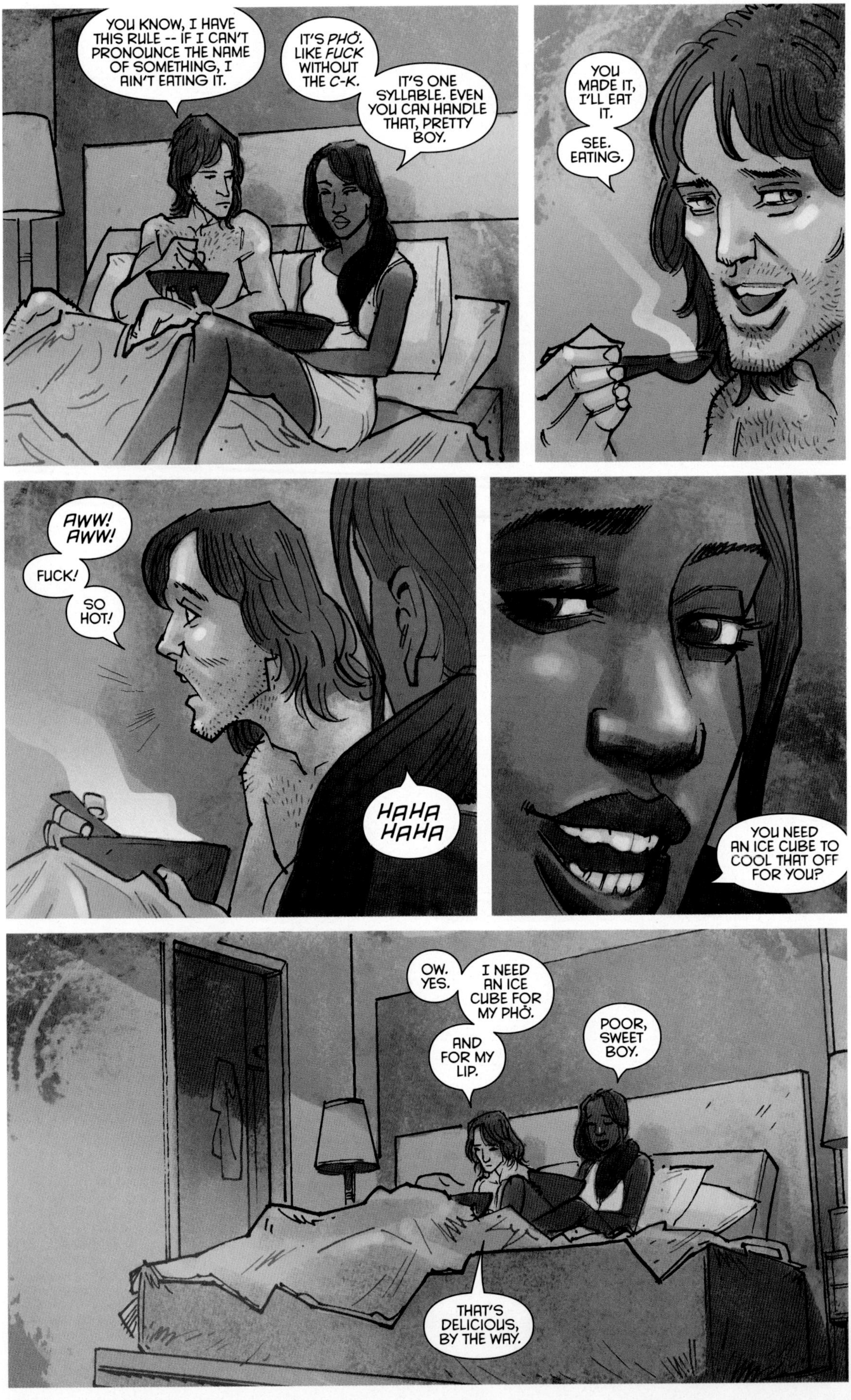
YOU KNOW, I HAVE THIS RULE -- IF I CAN'T PRONOUNCE THE NAME OF SOMETHING, I AIN'T EATING IT.
IT'S *PHỞ*. LIKE *FUCK* WITHOUT THE *C-K*.
IT'S ONE SYLLABLE. EVEN YOU CAN HANDLE THAT, PRETTY BOY.
YOU MADE IT, I'LL EAT IT.
SEE. EATING.
AWW! AWW!
FUCK!
SO HOT!
HAHA HAHA
YOU NEED AN ICE CUBE TO COOL THAT OFF FOR YOU?
OW. YES.
I NEED AN ICE CUBE FOR MY PHỞ.
AND FOR MY LIP.
POOR, SWEET BOY.
THAT'S DELICIOUS, BY THE WAY.

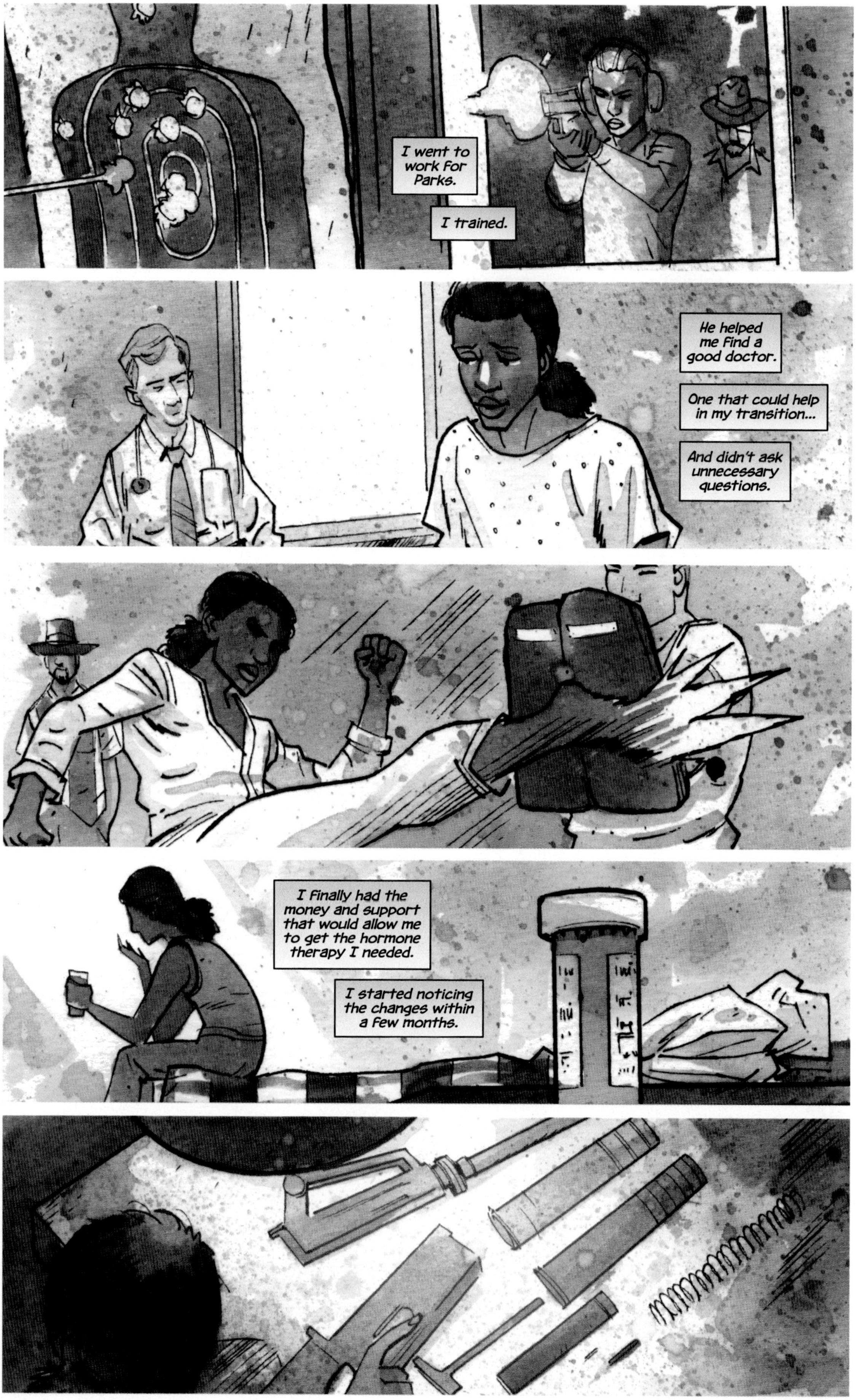
I went to work for Parks.
I trained.
He helped me find a good doctor.
One that could help in my transition...
And didn't ask unnecessary questions.
I finally had the money and support that would allow me to get the hormone therapy I needed.
I started noticing the changes within a few months.

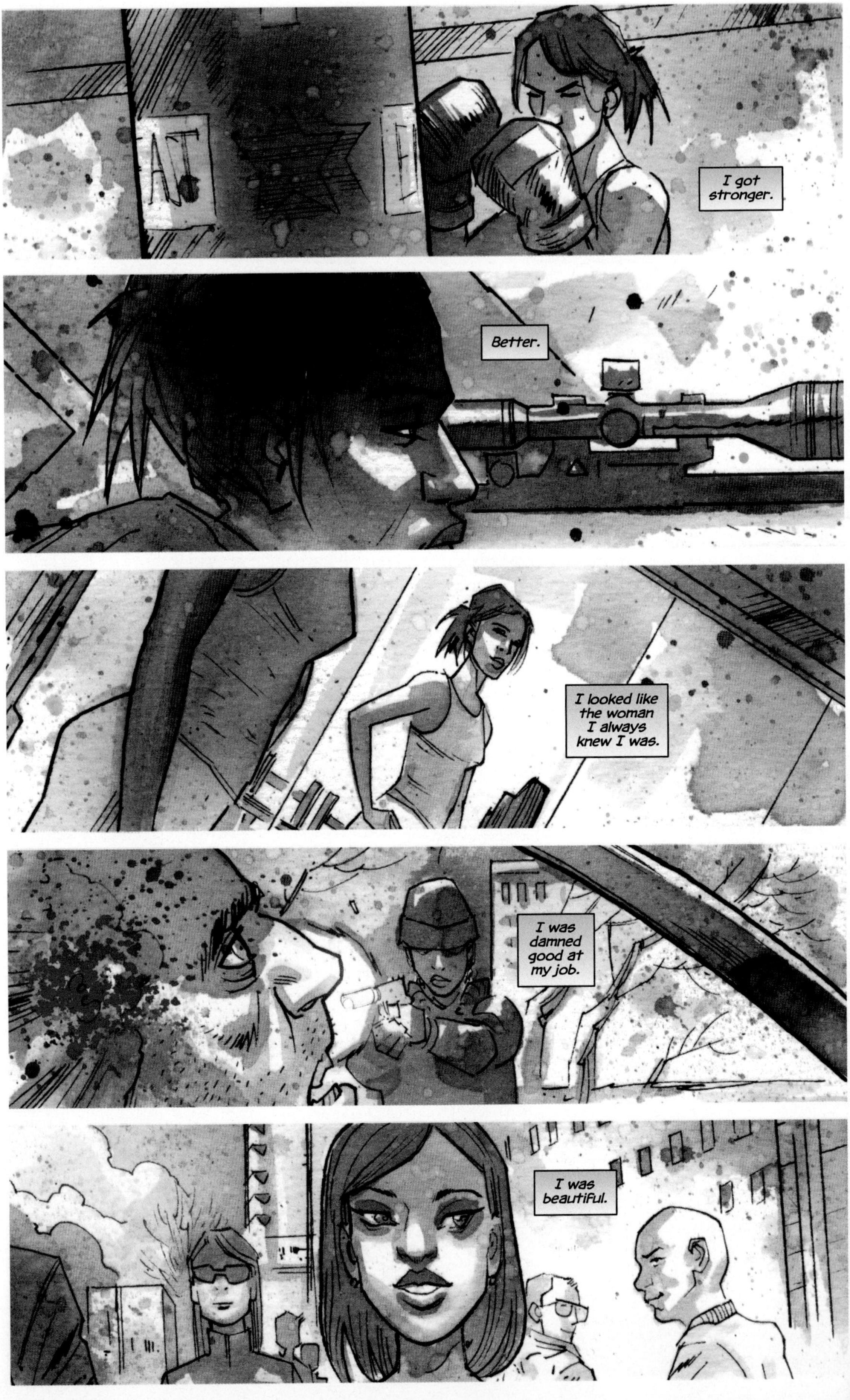
I got stronger.
Better.
I looked like the woman I always knew I was.
I was damned good at my job.
I was beautiful.

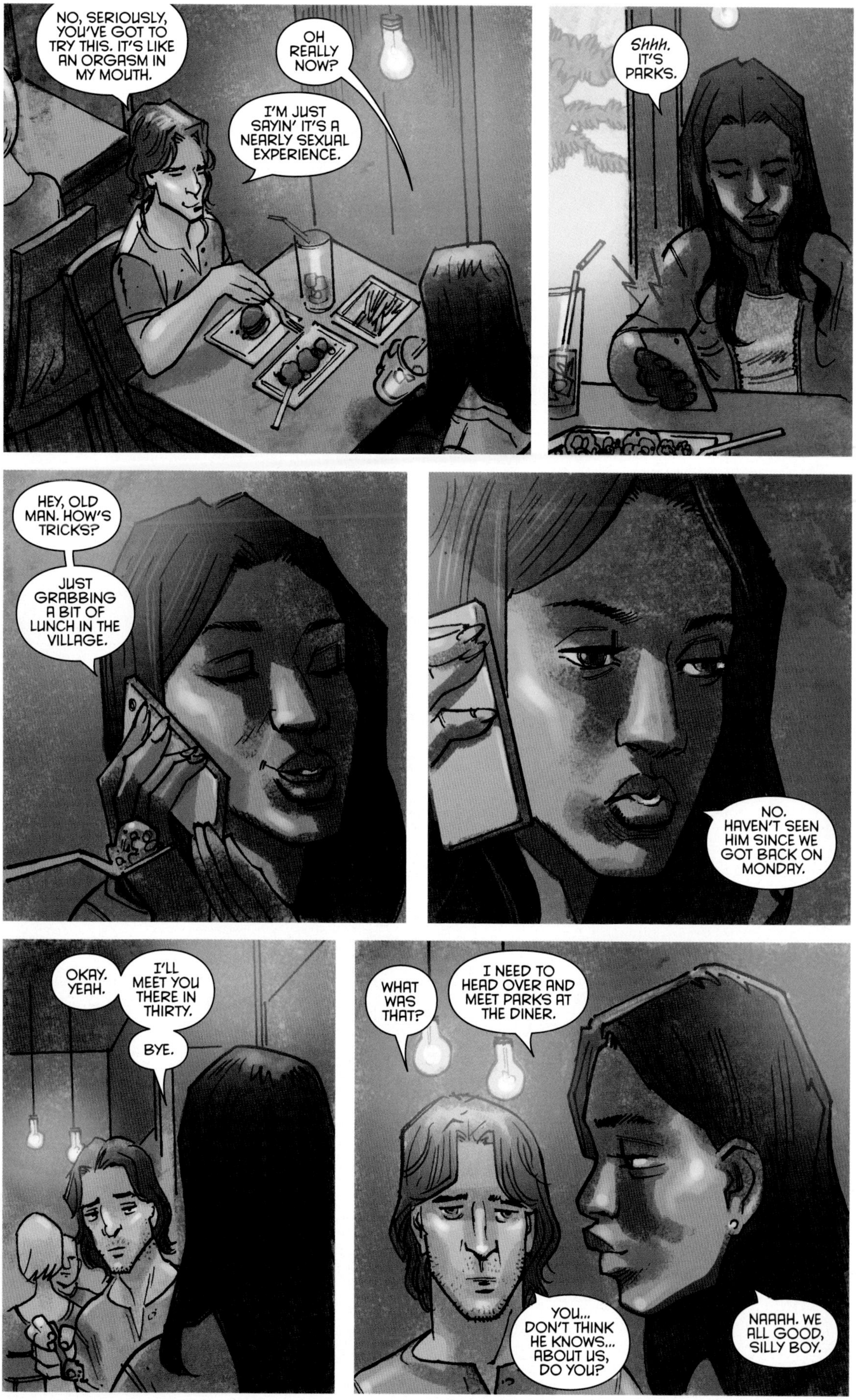
NO, SERIOUSLY, YOU'VE GOT TO TRY THIS. IT'S LIKE AN ORGASM IN MY MOUTH.
OH REALLY NOW?
I'M JUST SAYIN' IT'S A NEARLY SEXUAL EXPERIENCE.
Shhh. IT'S PARKS.
HEY, OLD MAN. HOW'S TRICKS?
JUST GRABBING A BIT OF LUNCH IN THE VILLAGE.
NO. HAVEN'T SEEN HIM SINCE WE GOT BACK ON MONDAY.
OKAY. YEAH.
I'LL MEET YOU THERE IN THIRTY.
BYE.
WHAT WAS THAT?
I NEED TO HEAD OVER AND MEET PARKS AT THE DINER.
YOU... DON'T THINK HE KNOWS... ABOUT US, DO YOU?
NAAAH. WE ALL GOOD, SILLY BOY.

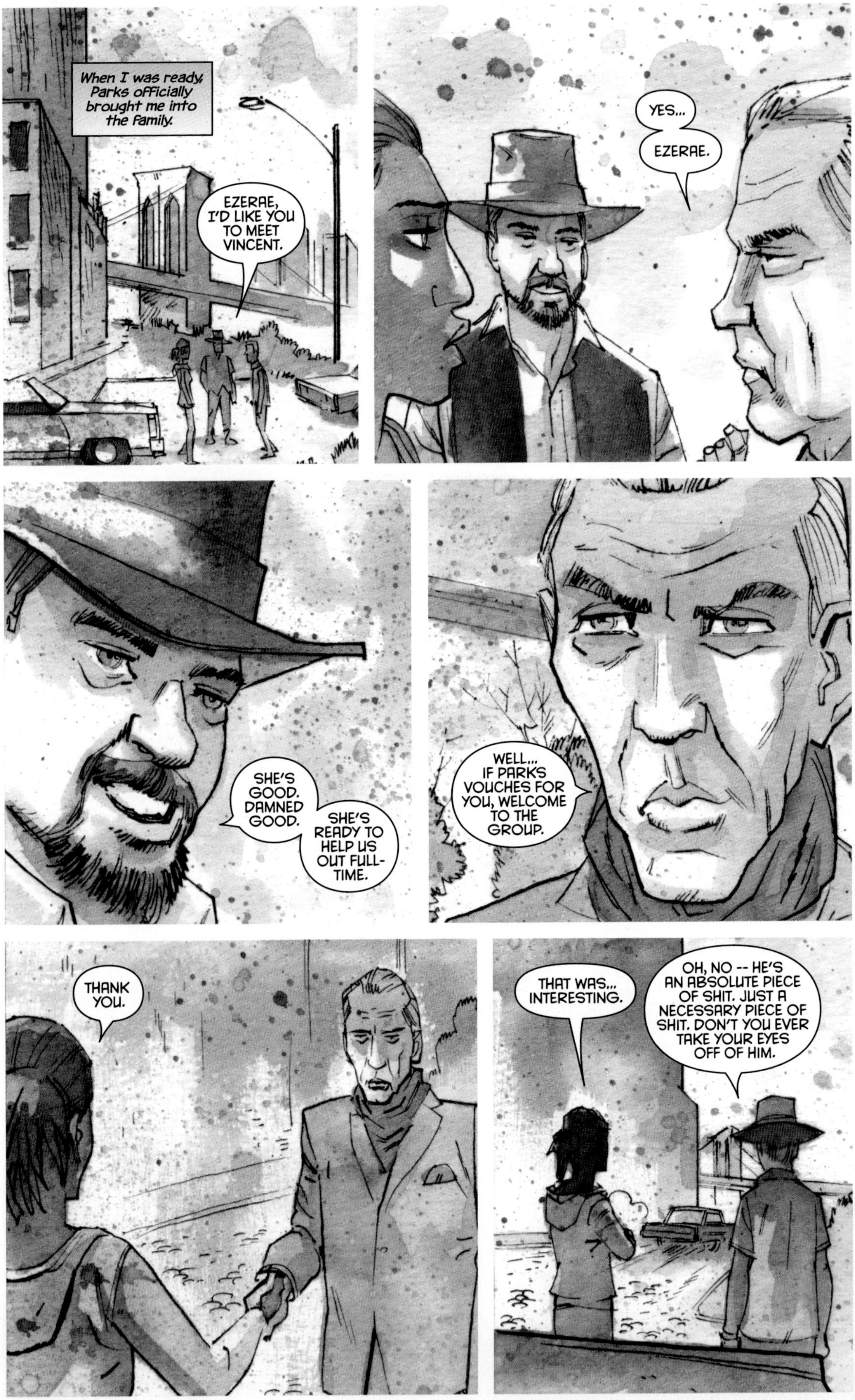
When I was ready, Parks officially brought me into the family.
EZERAE, I'D LIKE YOU TO MEET VINCENT.
YES...
EZERAE.
SHE'S GOOD. DAMNED GOOD.
SHE'S READY TO HELP US OUT FULL-TIME.
WELL... IF PARKS VOUCHES FOR YOU, WELCOME TO THE GROUP.
THANK YOU.
THAT WAS... INTERESTING.
OH, NO -- HE'S AN ABSOLUTE PIECE OF SHIT. JUST A NECESSARY PIECE OF SHIT. DON'T YOU EVER TAKE YOUR EYES OFF OF HIM.

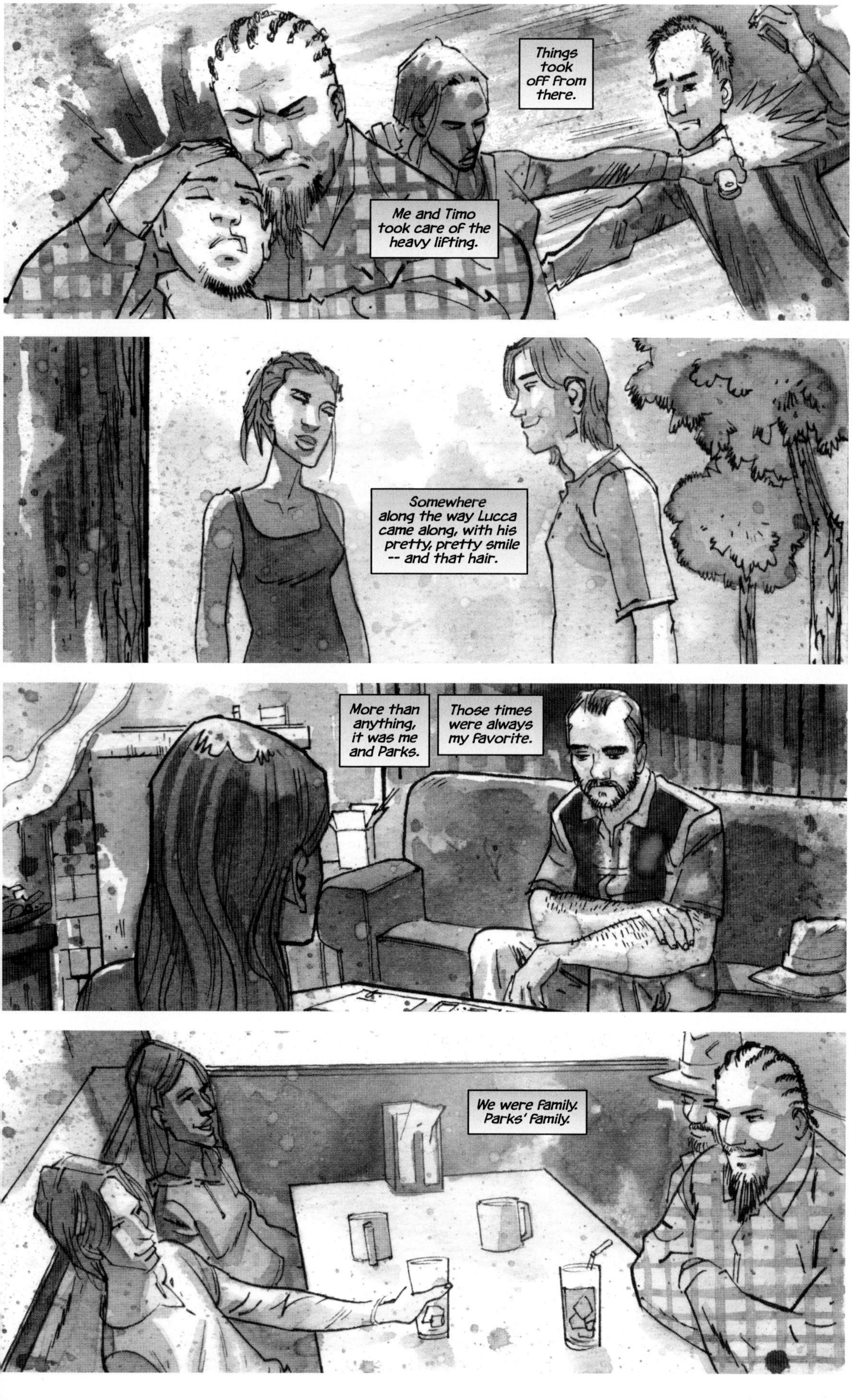
Things took off from there.
Me and Timo took care of the heavy lifting.
Somewhere along the way Lucca came along, with his pretty, pretty smile -- and that hair.
More than anything, it was me and Parks.
Those times were always my favorite.
We were family. Parks' family.

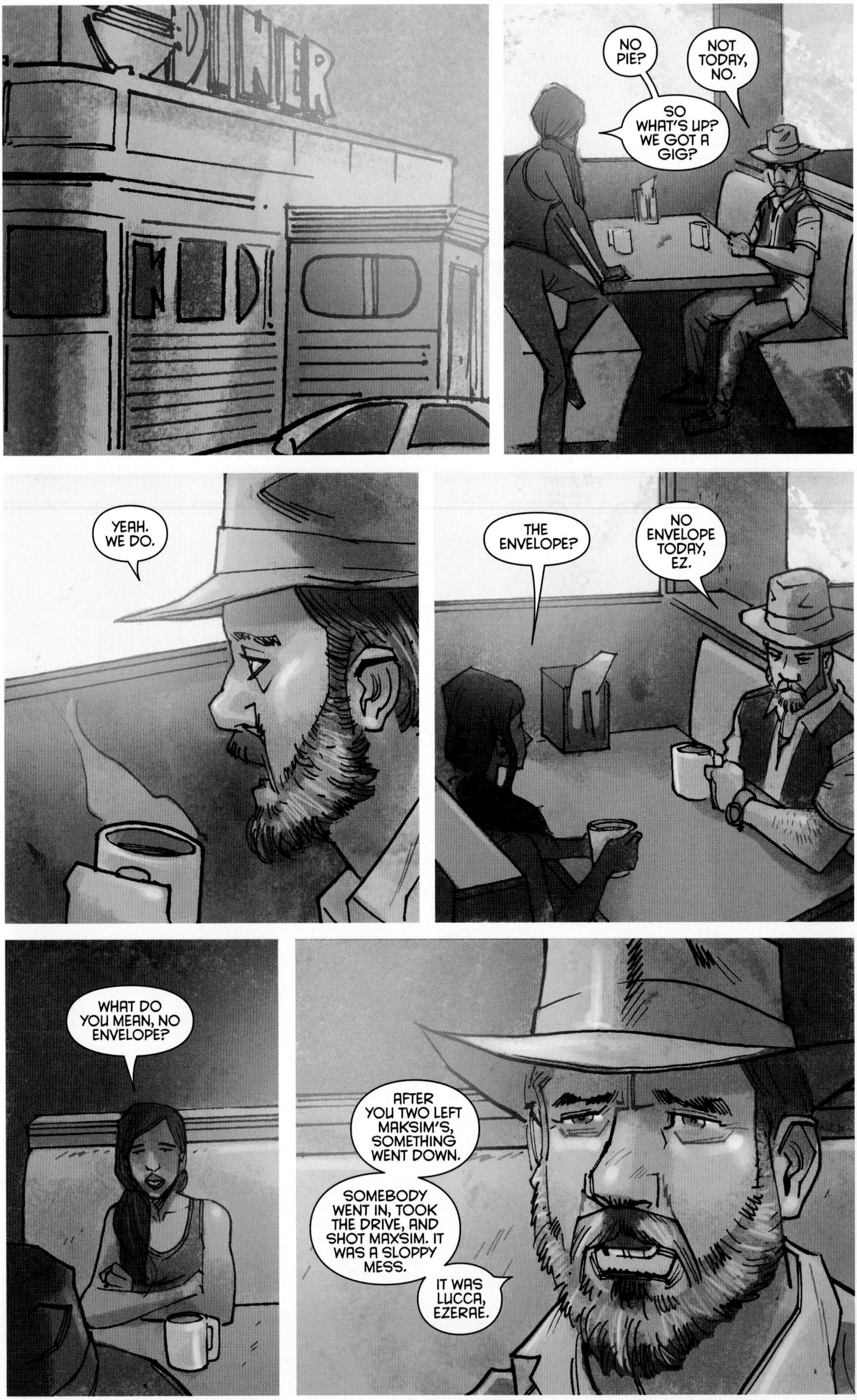
NO PIE?
NOT TODAY, NO.
SO WHAT'S UP? WE GOT A GIG?
YEAH. WE DO.
THE ENVELOPE?
NO ENVELOPE TODAY, EZ.
WHAT DO YOU MEAN, NO ENVELOPE?
AFTER YOU TWO LEFT MAKSIM'S, SOMETHING WENT DOWN.
SOMEBODY WENT IN, TOOK THE DRIVE, AND SHOT MAXSIM. IT WAS A SLOPPY MESS.
IT WAS LUCCA, EZERAE.

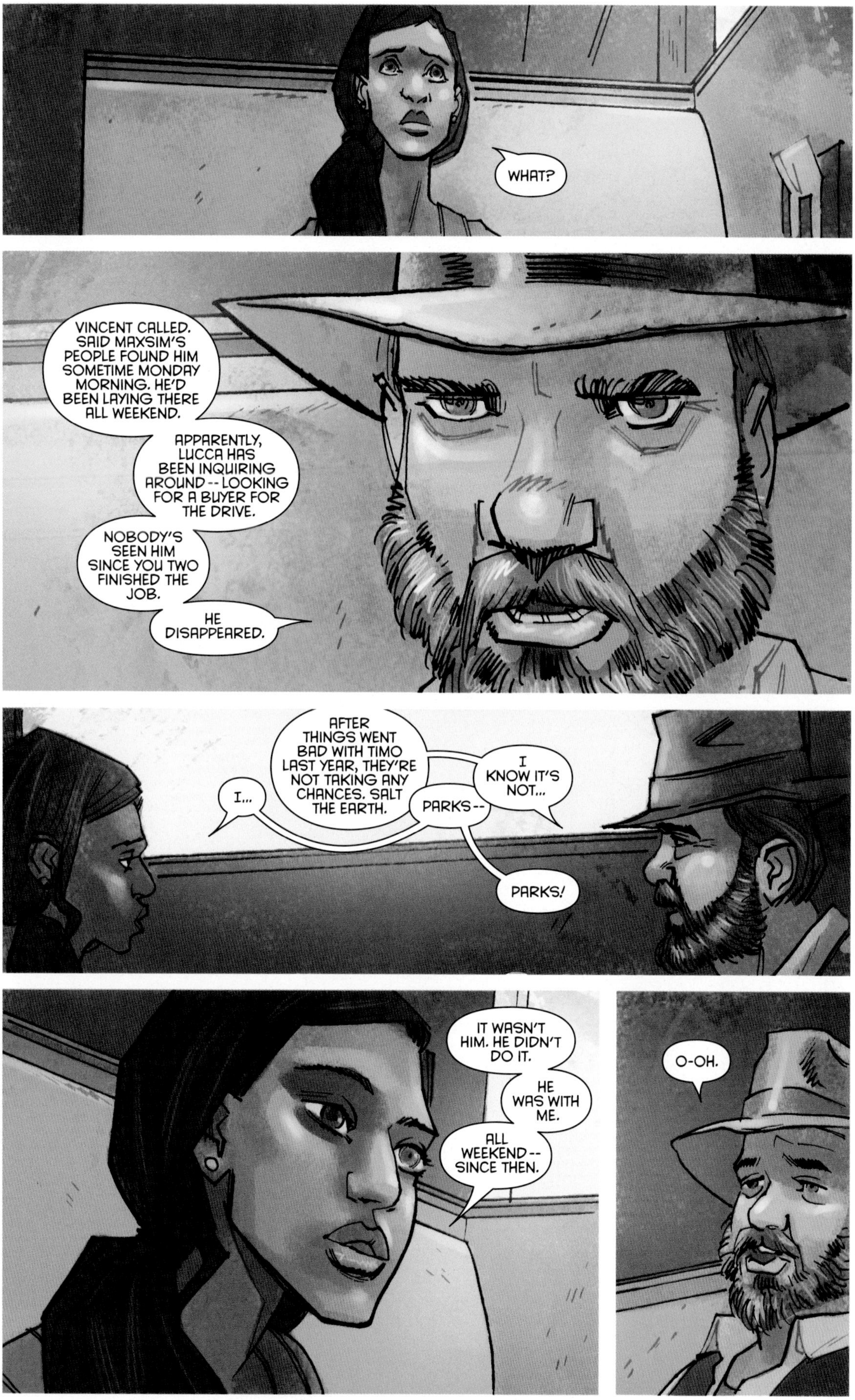
WHAT?
VINCENT CALLED. SAID MAXSIM'S PEOPLE FOUND HIM SOMETIME MONDAY MORNING. HE'D BEEN LAYING THERE ALL WEEKEND.
APPARENTLY, LUCCA HAS BEEN INQUIRING AROUND -- LOOKING FOR A BUYER FOR THE DRIVE.
NOBODY'S SEEN HIM SINCE YOU TWO FINISHED THE JOB.
HE DISAPPEARED.
AFTER THINGS WENT BAD WITH TIMO LAST YEAR, THEY'RE NOT TAKING ANY CHANCES. SALT THE EARTH.
I KNOW IT'S NOT...
I...
PARKS--
PARKS!
IT WASN'T HIM. HE DIDN'T DO IT.
HE WAS WITH ME.
ALL WEEKEND-- SINCE THEN.
O-OH.

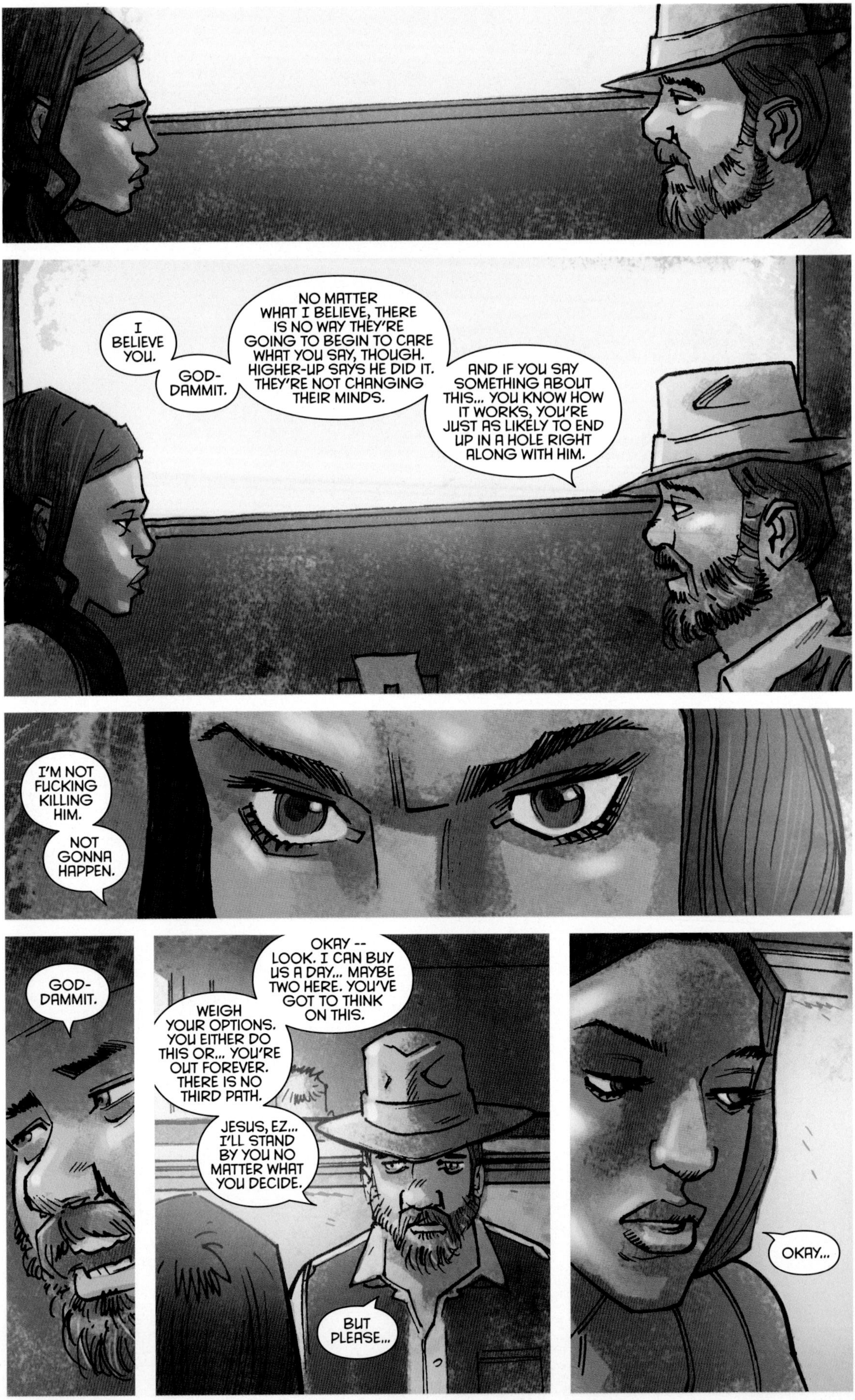
I BELIEVE YOU.
GOD-DAMMIT.
NO MATTER WHAT I BELIEVE, THERE IS NO WAY THEY'RE GOING TO BEGIN TO CARE WHAT YOU SAY, THOUGH. HIGHER-UP SAYS HE DID IT. THEY'RE NOT CHANGING THEIR MINDS.
AND IF YOU SAY SOMETHING ABOUT THIS... YOU KNOW HOW IT WORKS, YOU'RE JUST AS LIKELY TO END UP IN A HOLE RIGHT ALONG WITH HIM.
I'M NOT FUCKING KILLING HIM.
NOT GONNA HAPPEN.
GOD-DAMMIT.
OKAY -- LOOK. I CAN BUY US A DAY... MAYBE TWO HERE. YOU'VE GOT TO THINK ON THIS.
WEIGH YOUR OPTIONS. YOU EITHER DO THIS OR... YOU'RE OUT FOREVER. THERE IS NO THIRD PATH.
JESUS, EZ... I'LL STAND BY YOU NO MATTER WHAT YOU DECIDE.
BUT PLEASE...
OKAY...

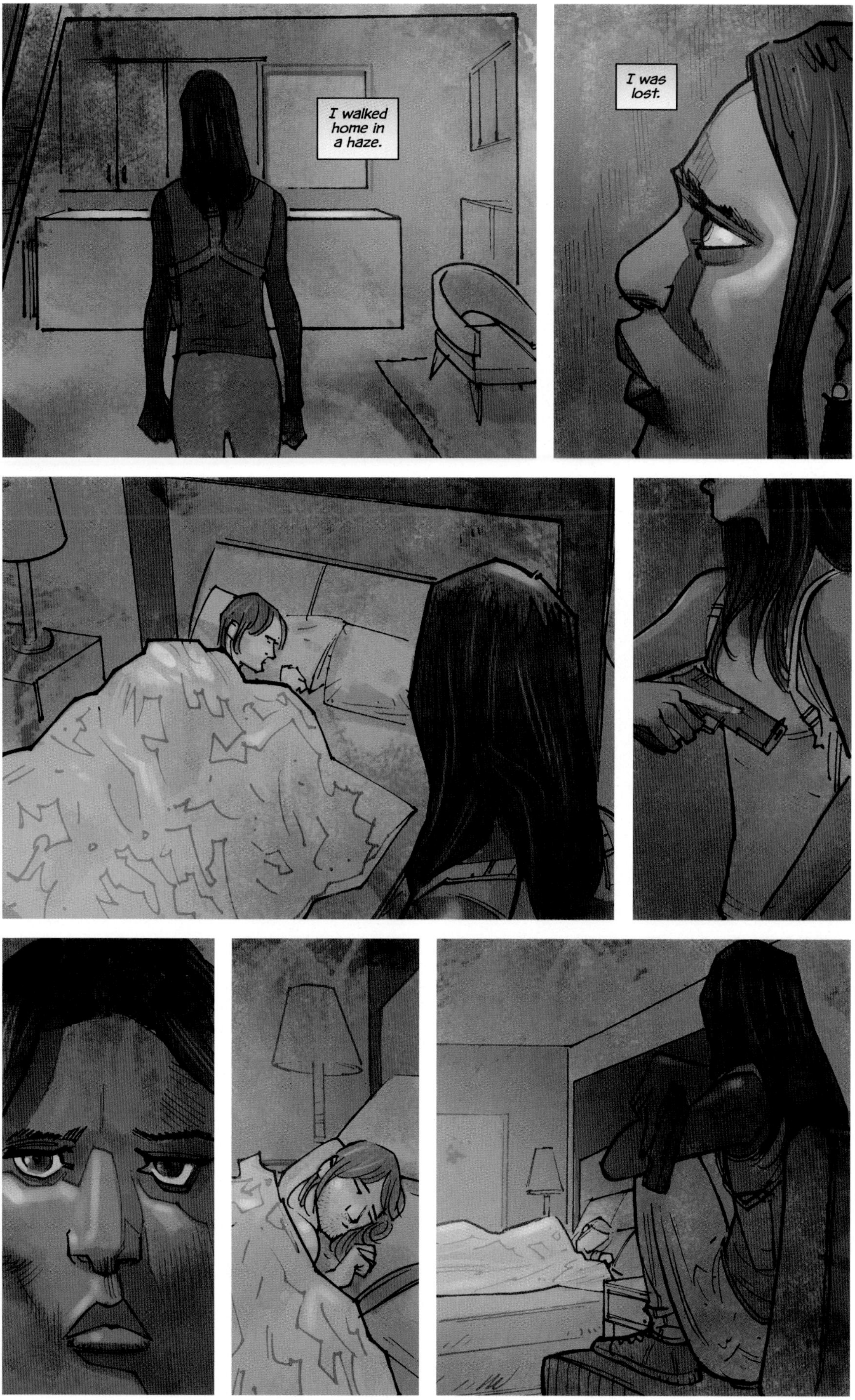
I walked home in a haze.
I was lost.

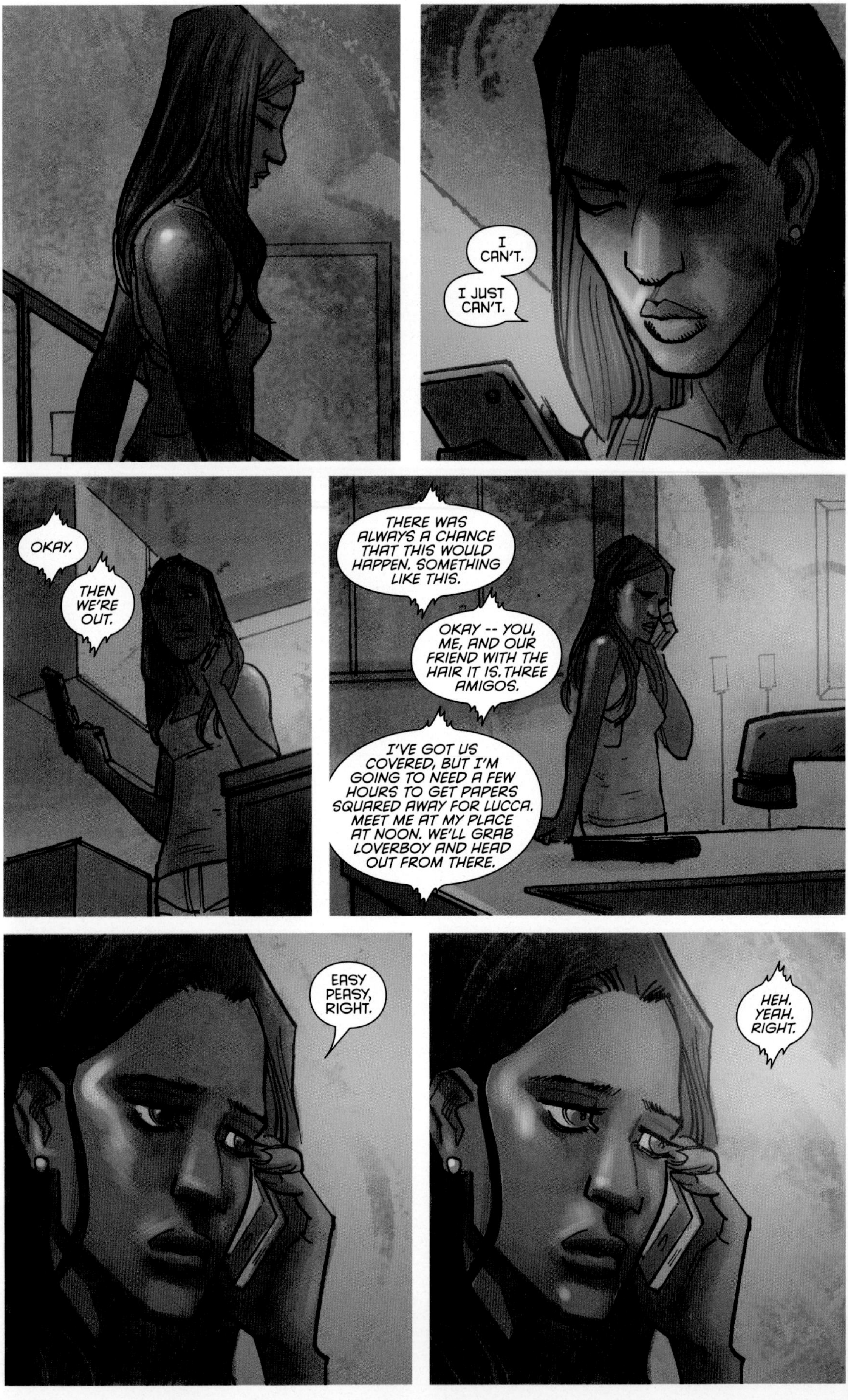
I CAN'T.
I JUST CAN'T.
OKAY.
THEN WE'RE OUT.
THERE WAS ALWAYS A CHANCE THAT THIS WOULD HAPPEN. SOMETHING LIKE THIS.
OKAY -- YOU, ME, AND OUR FRIEND WITH THE HAIR IT IS. THREE AMIGOS.
I'VE GOT US COVERED, BUT I'M GOING TO NEED A FEW HOURS TO GET PAPERS SQUARED AWAY FOR LUCCA. MEET ME AT MY PLACE AT NOON. WE'LL GRAB LOVERBOY AND HEAD OUT FROM THERE.
EASY PEASY, RIGHT.
HEH. YEAH. RIGHT.

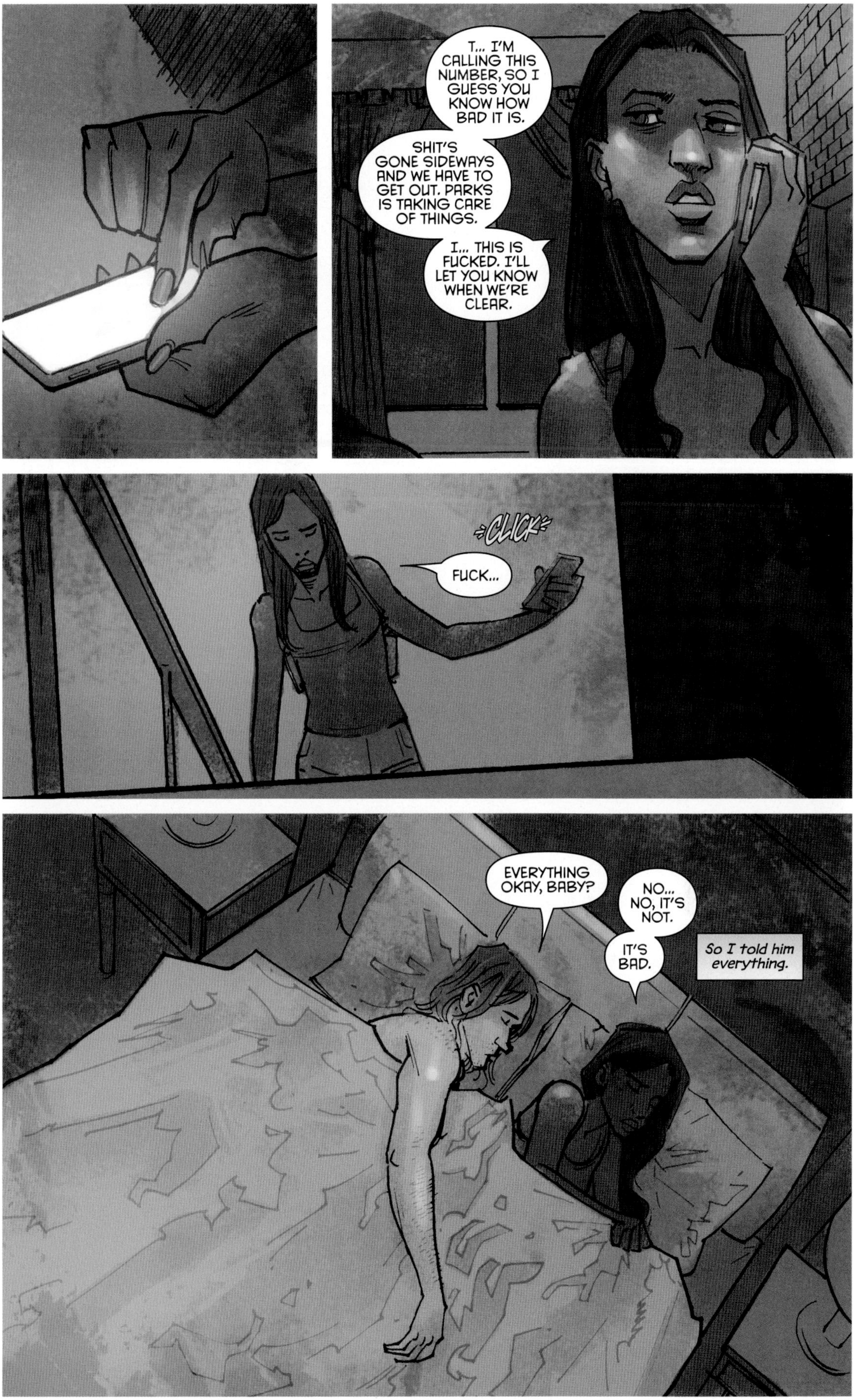
T... I'M CALLING THIS NUMBER, SO I GUESS YOU KNOW HOW BAD IT IS.
SHIT'S GONE SIDEWAYS AND WE HAVE TO GET OUT. PARKS IS TAKING CARE OF THINGS.
I... THIS IS FUCKED. I'LL LET YOU KNOW WHEN WE'RE CLEAR.
CLICK
FUCK...
EVERYTHING OKAY, BABY?
NO... NO, IT'S NOT.
IT'S BAD.
So I told him everything.

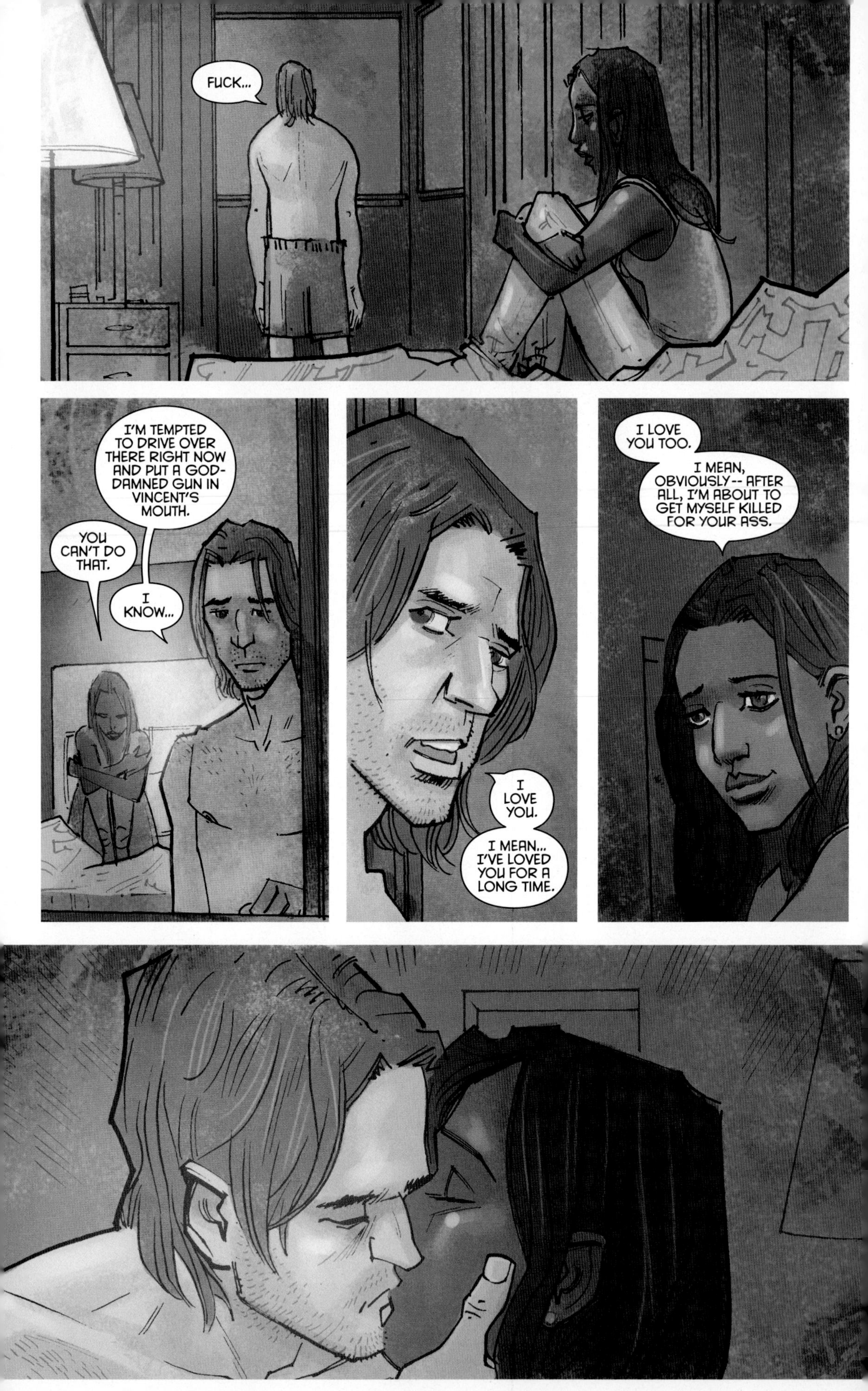
FUCK...
I'M TEMPTED TO DRIVE OVER THERE RIGHT NOW AND PUT A GOD-DAMNED GUN IN VINCENT'S MOUTH.
YOU CAN'T DO THAT.
I KNOW...
I LOVE YOU.
I MEAN... I'VE LOVED YOU FOR A LONG TIME.
I LOVE YOU TOO.
I MEAN, OBVIOUSLY-- AFTER ALL, I'M ABOUT TO GET MYSELF KILLED FOR YOUR ASS.

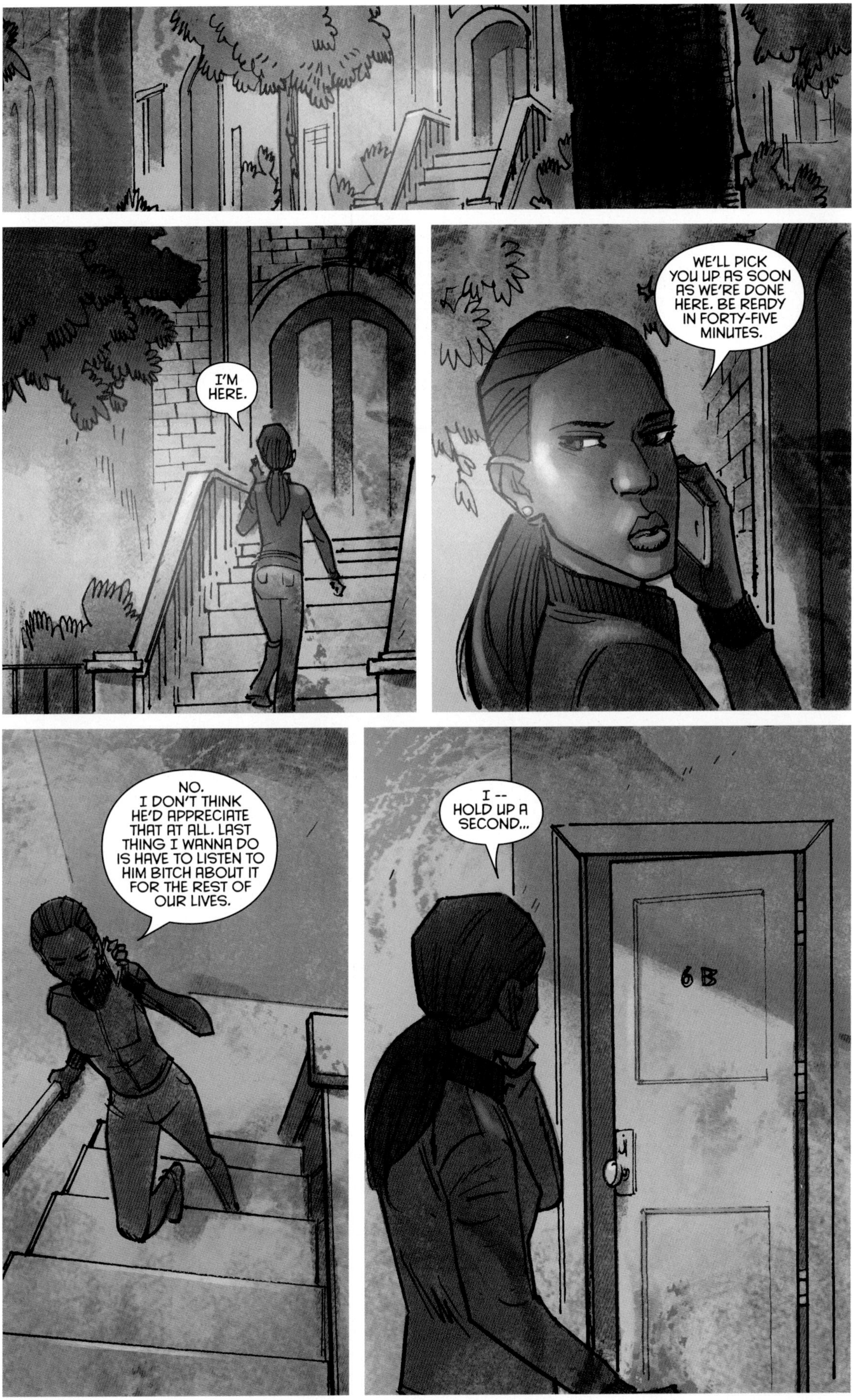
I'M HERE.
WE'LL PICK YOU UP AS SOON AS WE'RE DONE HERE. BE READY IN FORTY-FIVE MINUTES.
NO. I DON'T THINK HE'D APPRECIATE THAT AT ALL. LAST THING I WANNA DO IS HAVE TO LISTEN TO HIM BITCH ABOUT IT FOR THE REST OF OUR LIVES.
I -- HOLD UP A SECOND...
6 B

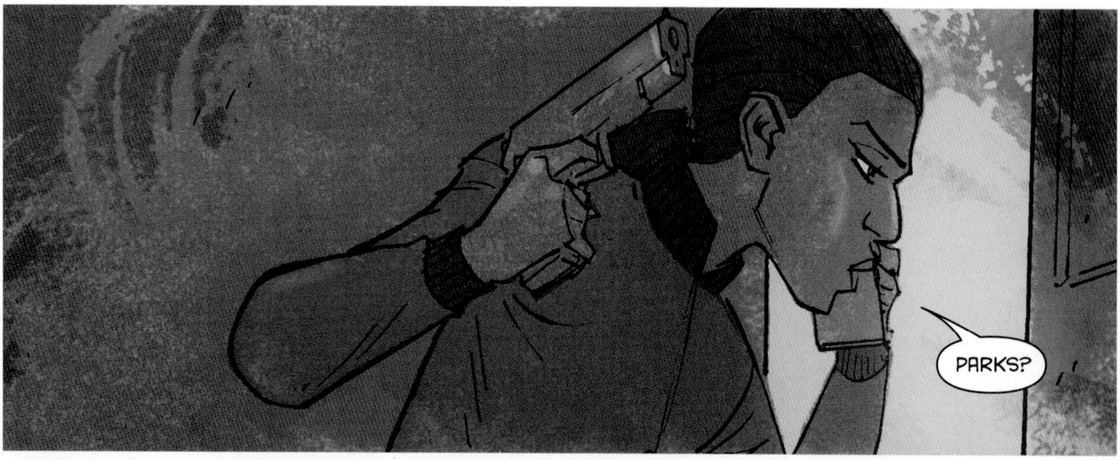
PARKS?

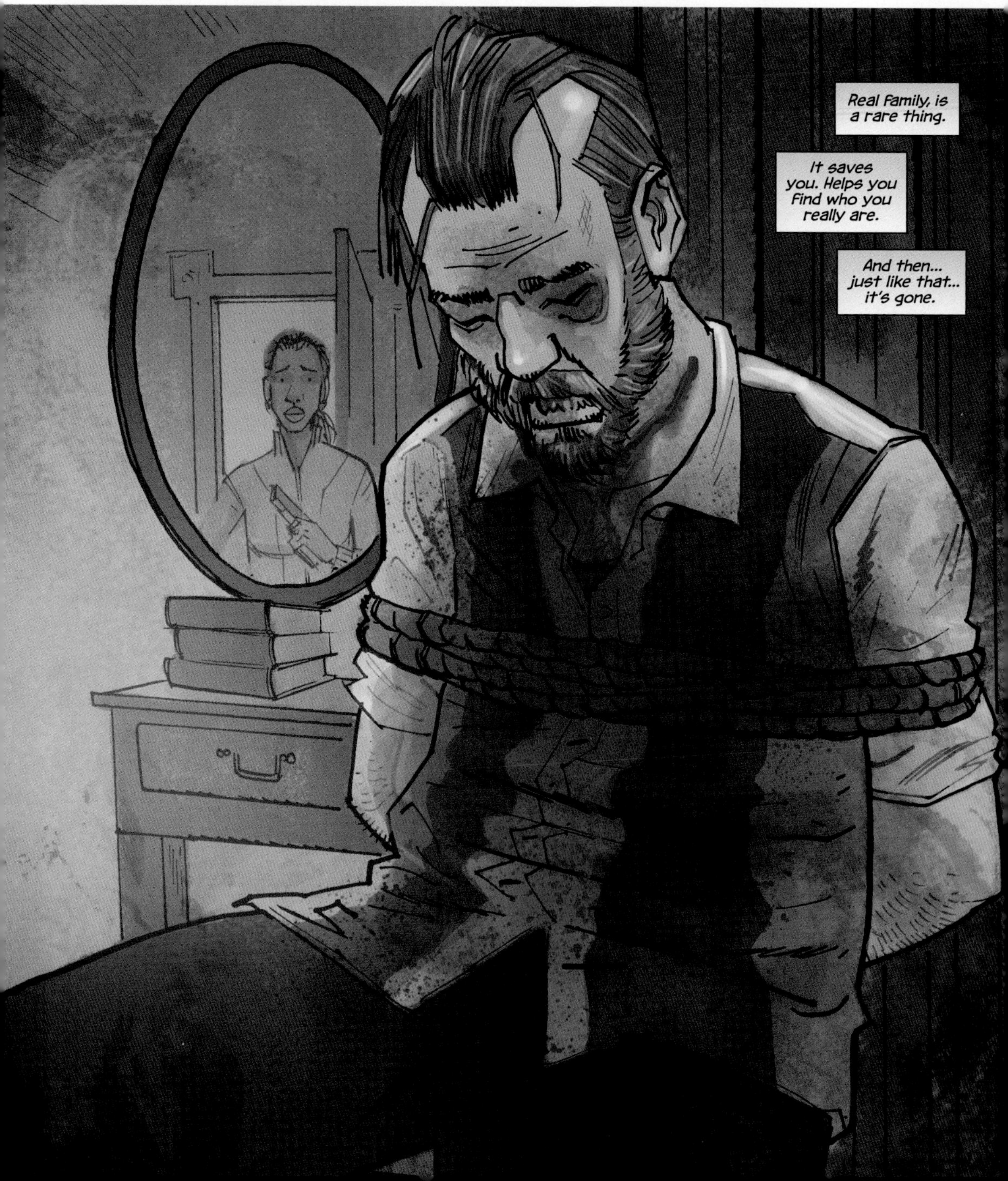
Real family, is a rare thing.
It saves you. Helps you find who you really are.
And then... just like that... it's gone.

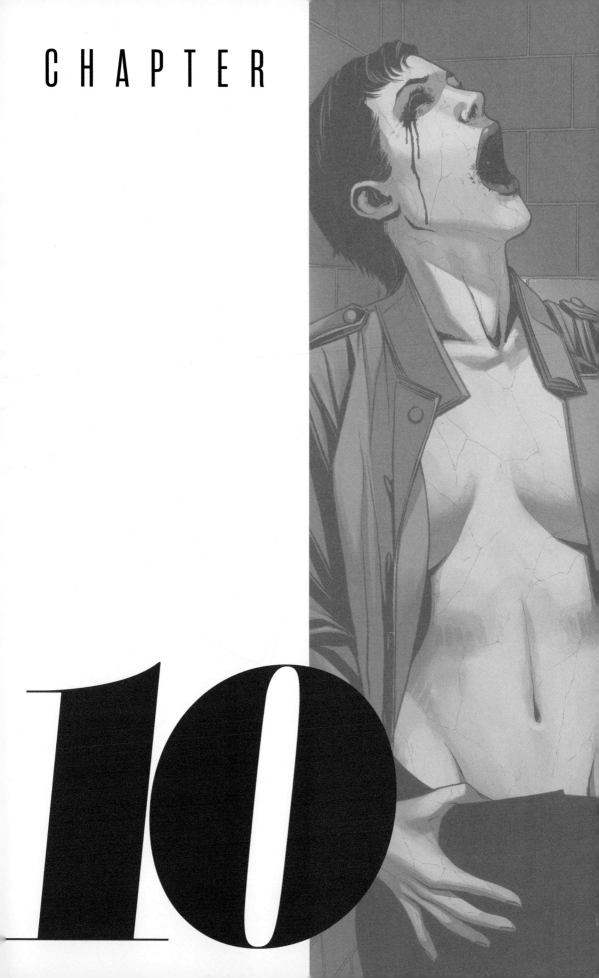

CHAPTER

10

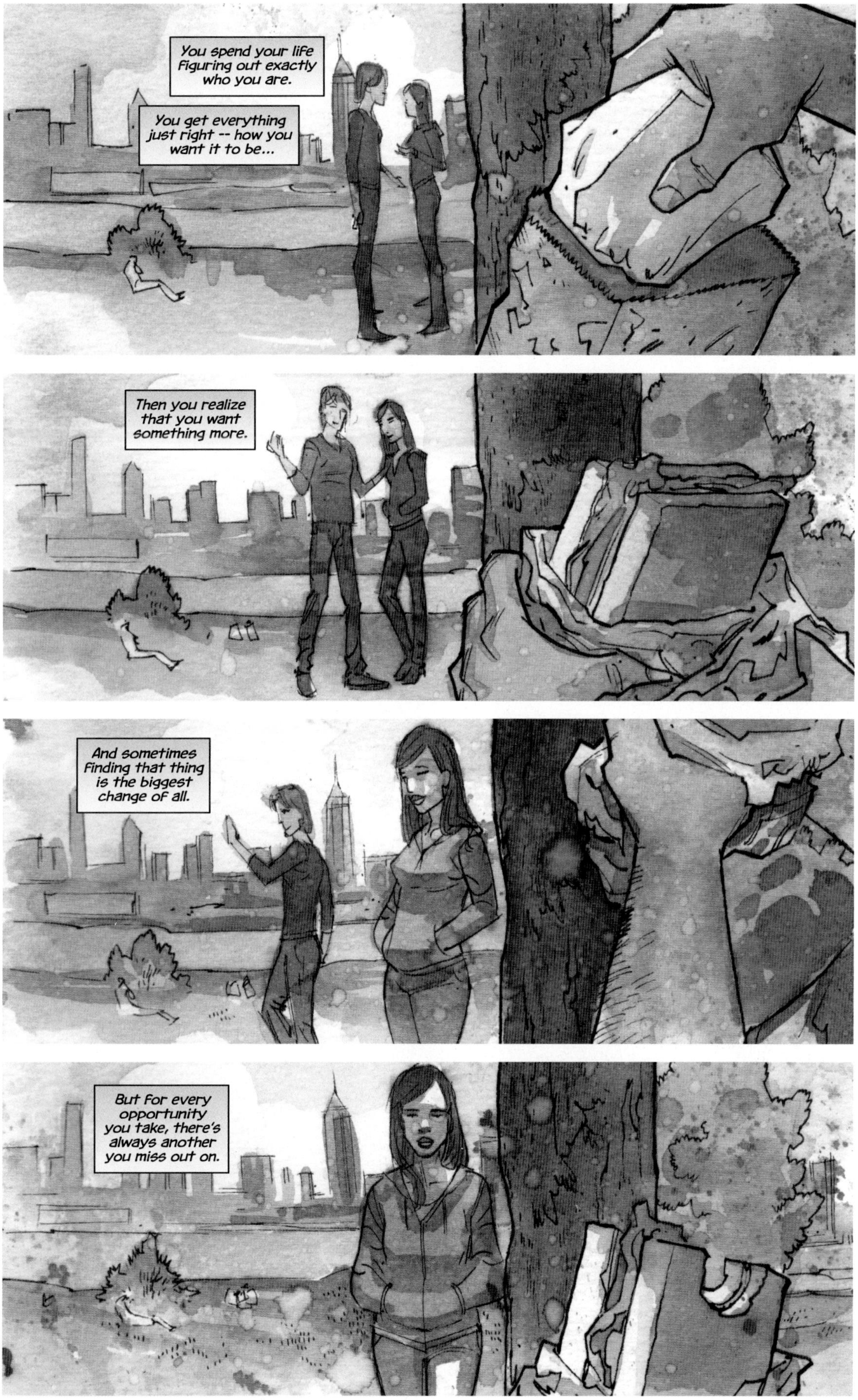
You spend your life figuring out exactly who you are.
You get everything just right -- how you want it to be...
Then you realize that you want something more.
And sometimes finding that thing is the biggest change of all.
But for every opportunity you take, there's always another you miss out on.

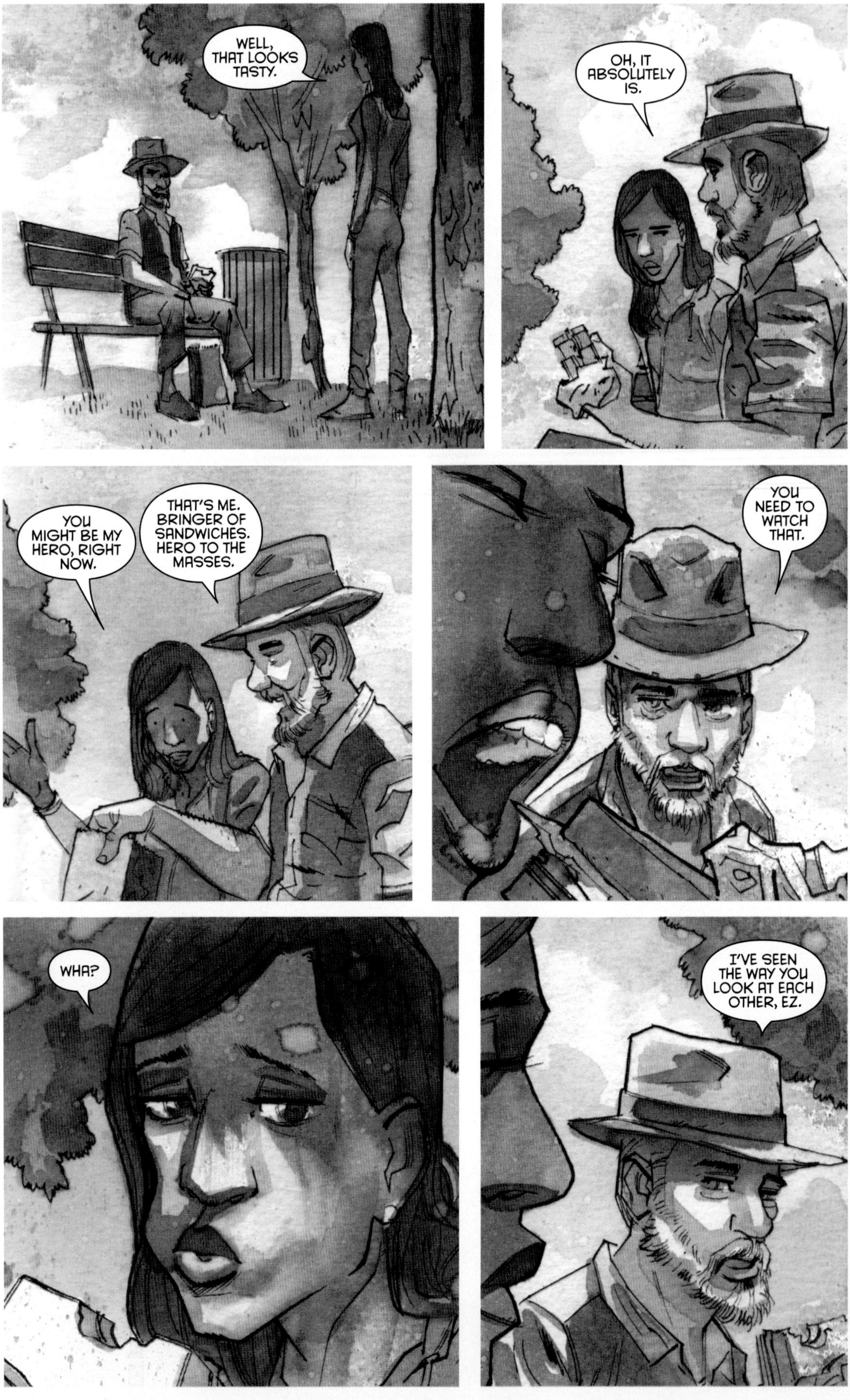
WELL, THAT LOOKS TASTY.
OH, IT ABSOLUTELY IS.
YOU MIGHT BE MY HERO, RIGHT NOW.
THAT'S ME. BRINGER OF SANDWICHES. HERO TO THE MASSES.
YOU NEED TO WATCH THAT.
WHA?
I'VE SEEN THE WAY YOU LOOK AT EACH OTHER, EZ.

WHO?

Aw-- LUCCA? NAH...

WE'RE JUST FRIENDS.

OKAY. I GET THAT.

BUT HERE'S THE THING -- STUFF HAPPENS. YOU GET CLOSE TO PEOPLE.

FRIENDS BECOME MORE THAN FRIENDS.

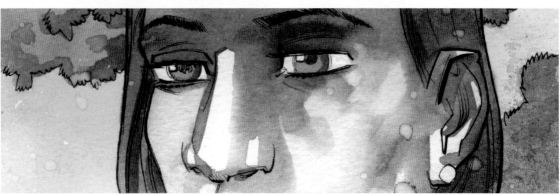

MIGHT NOT EVER BE A THING, BUT I NEEDED TO SAY IT.

IT'S MY JOB TO TAKE CARE OF YOU.

MIXING BUSINESS AND PLEASURE IS NEVER A GOOD IDEA.

BUT WITH WHAT WE DO, IT COULD GET SOMEBODY KILLED.

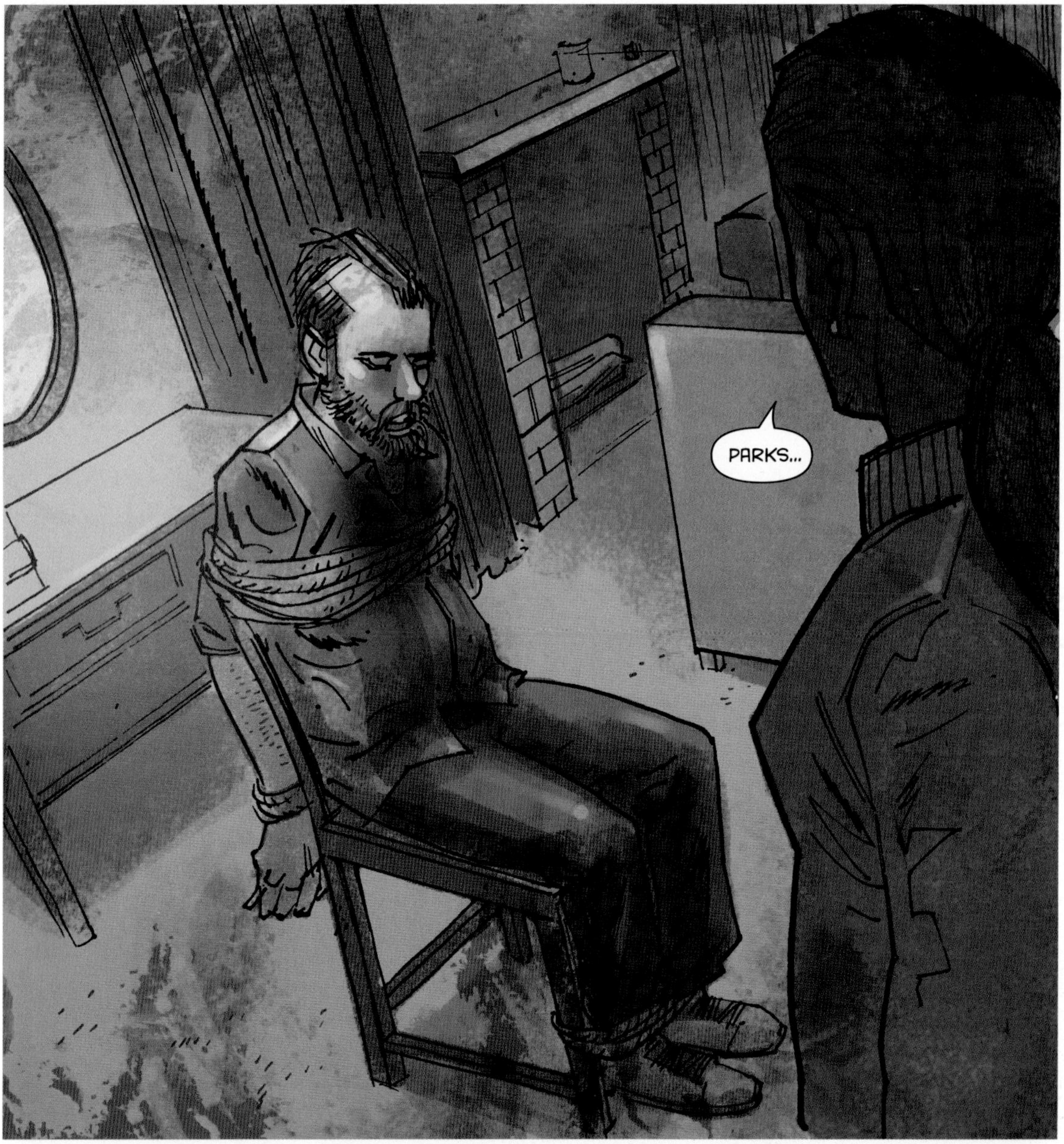
PARKS...

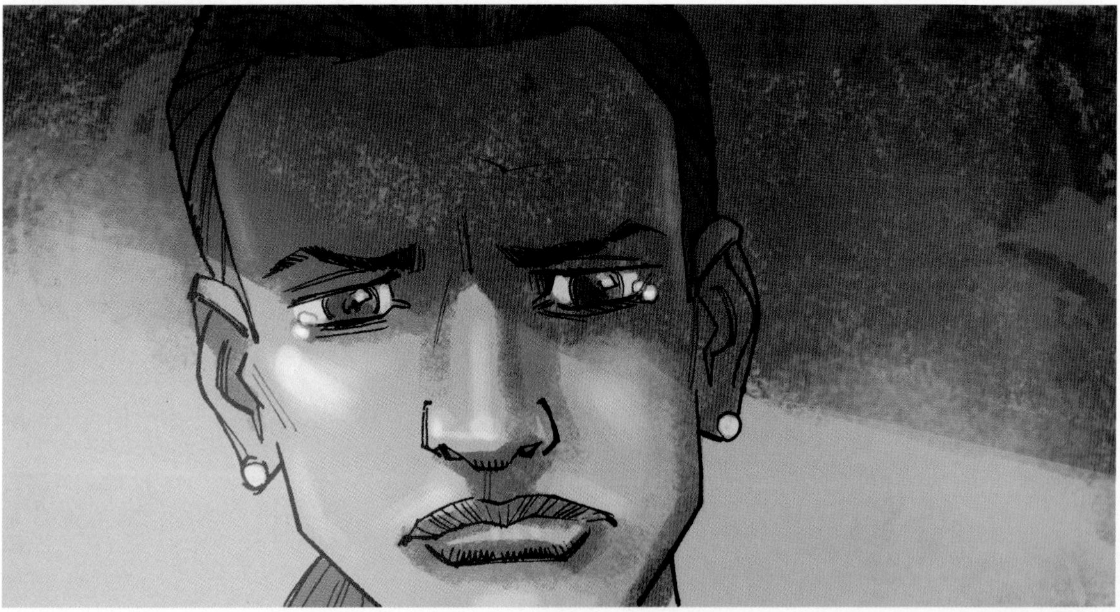

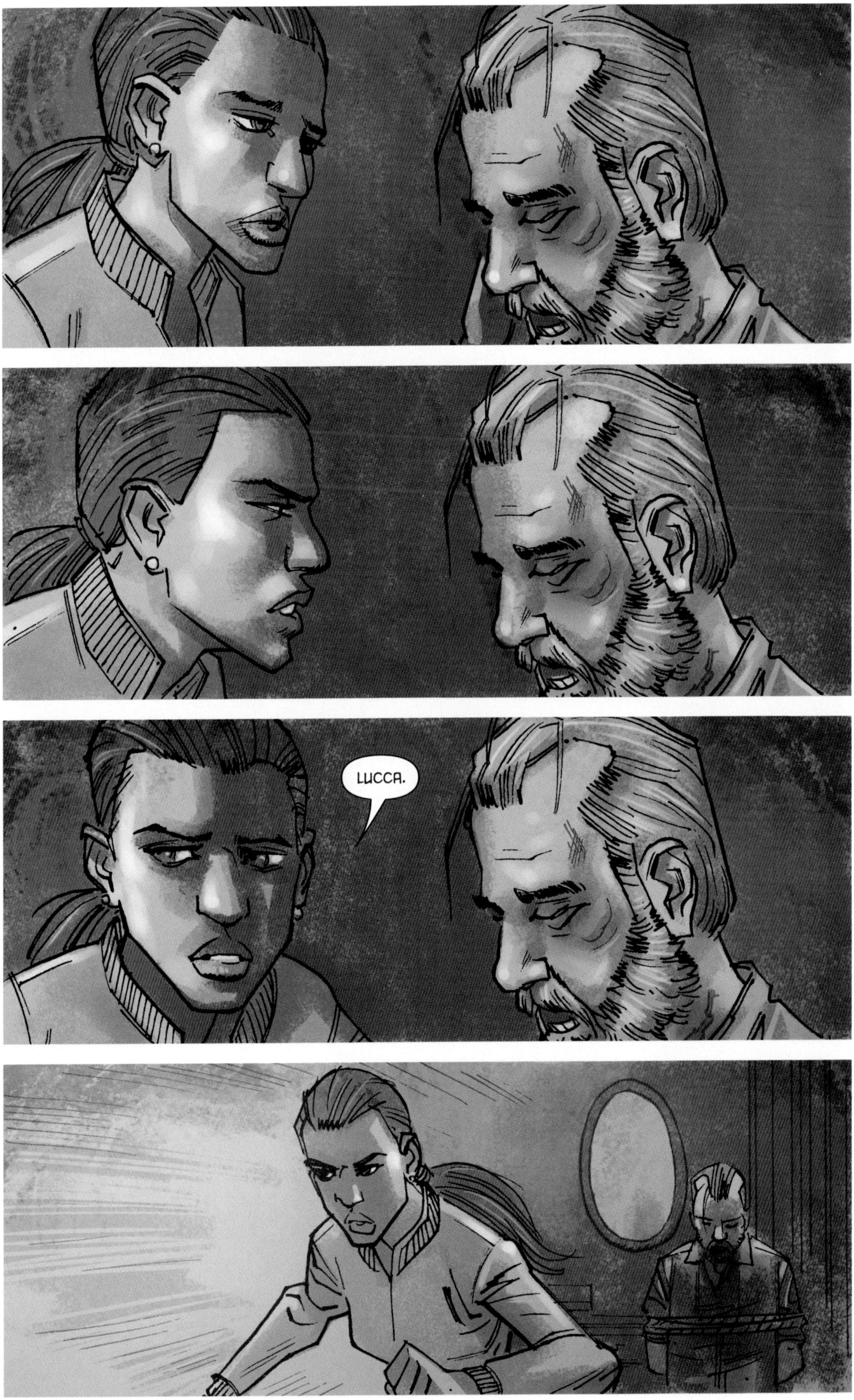
LUCCA.

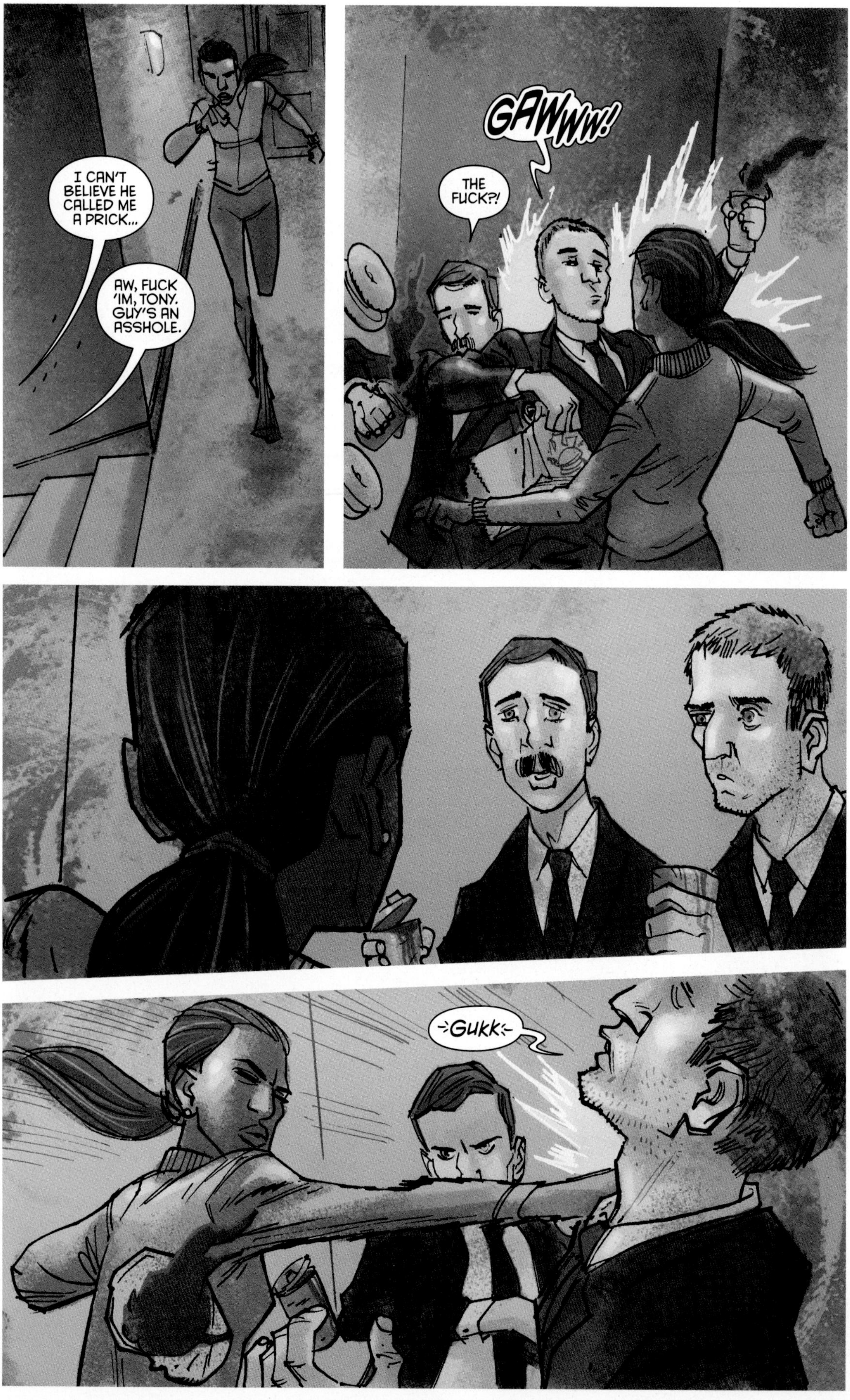
I CAN'T BELIEVE HE CALLED ME A PRICK...
AW, FUCK 'IM, TONY. GUY'S AN ASSHOLE.
GAWWW!
THE FUCK?!
GUKK

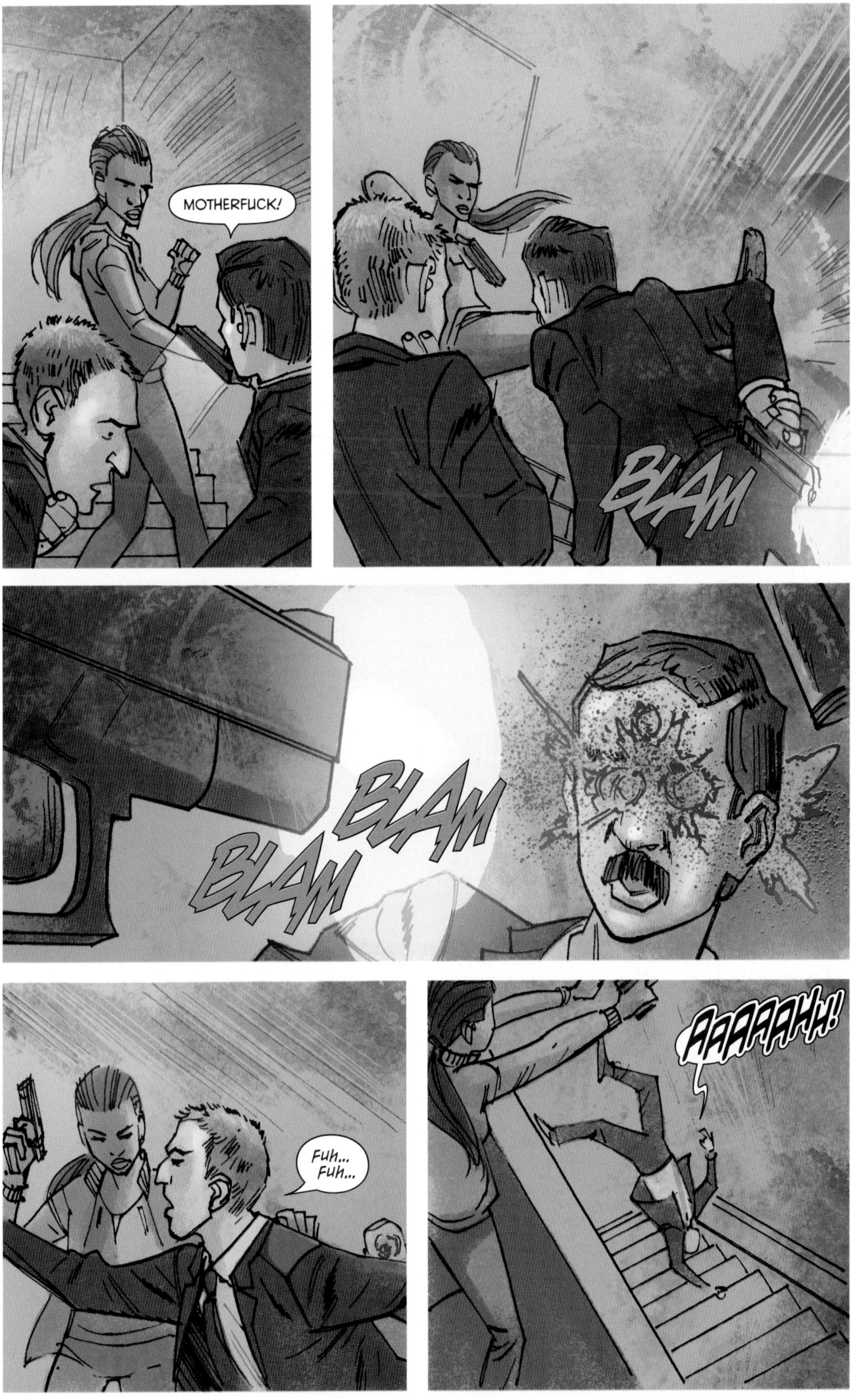
MOTHERFUCK!
BLAM
BLAM
BLAM
Fuh...
Fuh...
AAAAAHH!

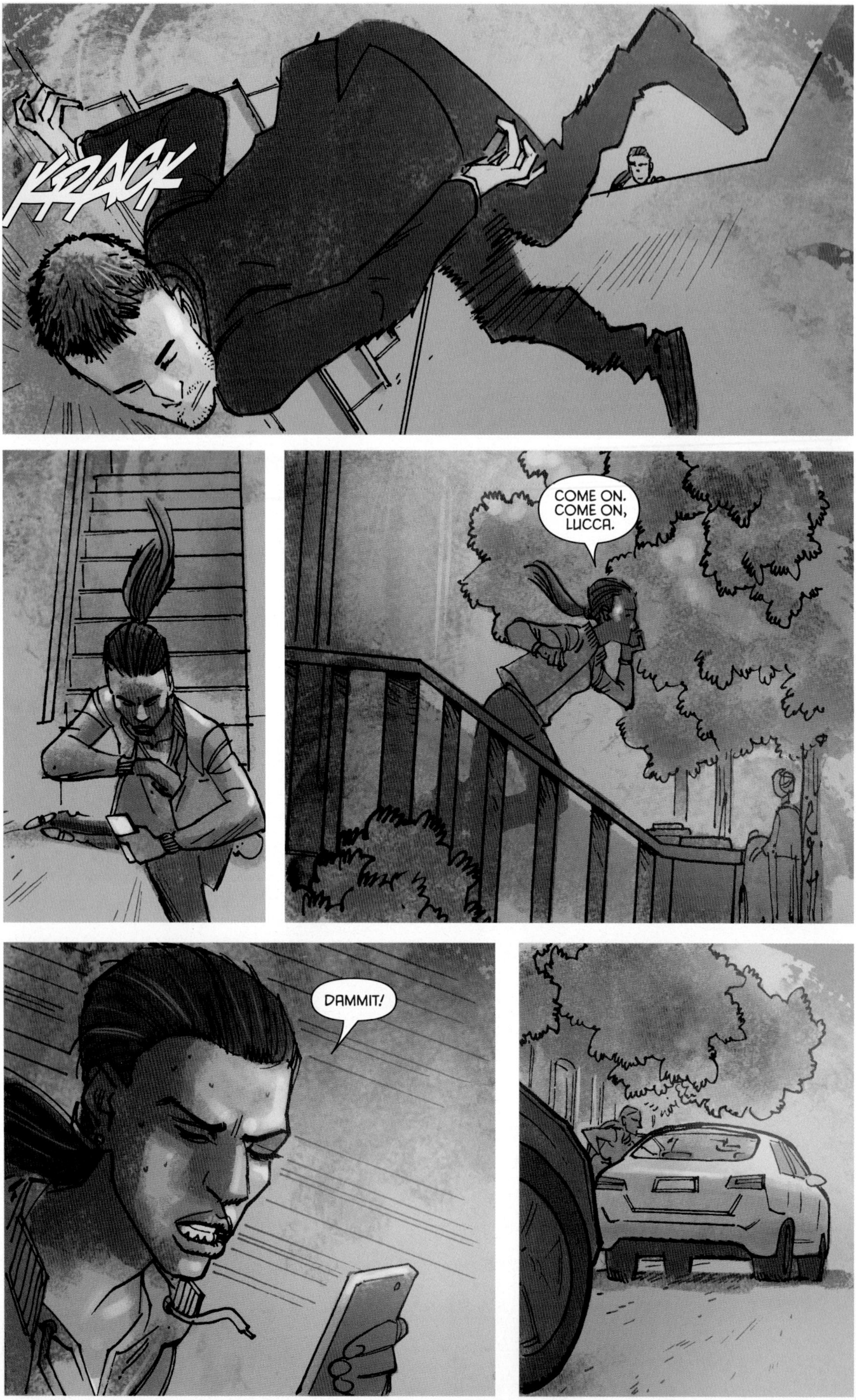
KRACK
COME ON. COME ON, LUCCA.
DAMMIT!

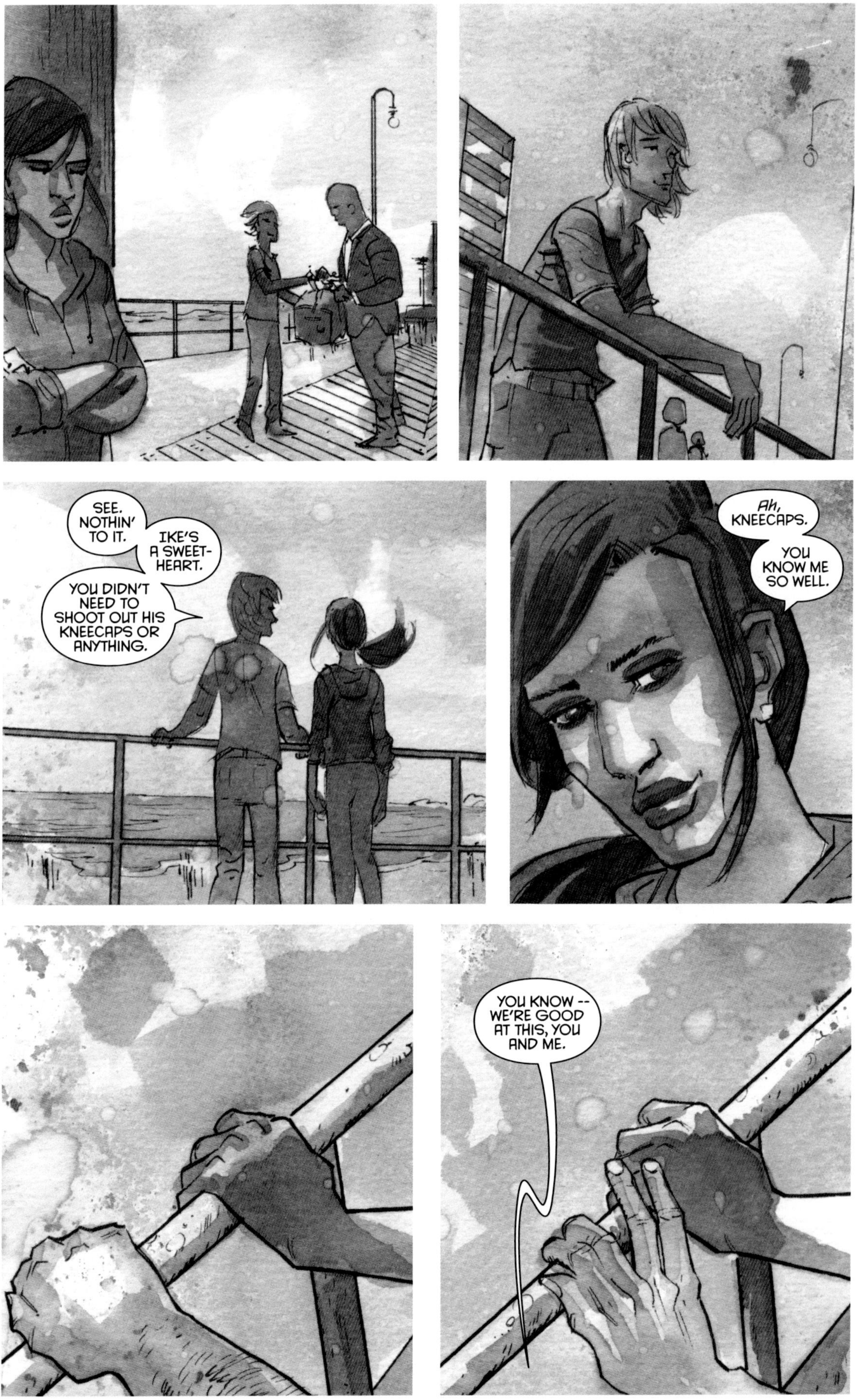
SEE. NOTHIN' TO IT.
IKE'S A SWEET-HEART.
YOU DIDN'T NEED TO SHOOT OUT HIS KNEECAPS OR ANYTHING.
Ah, KNEECAPS.
YOU KNOW ME SO WELL.
YOU KNOW -- WE'RE GOOD AT THIS, YOU AND ME.

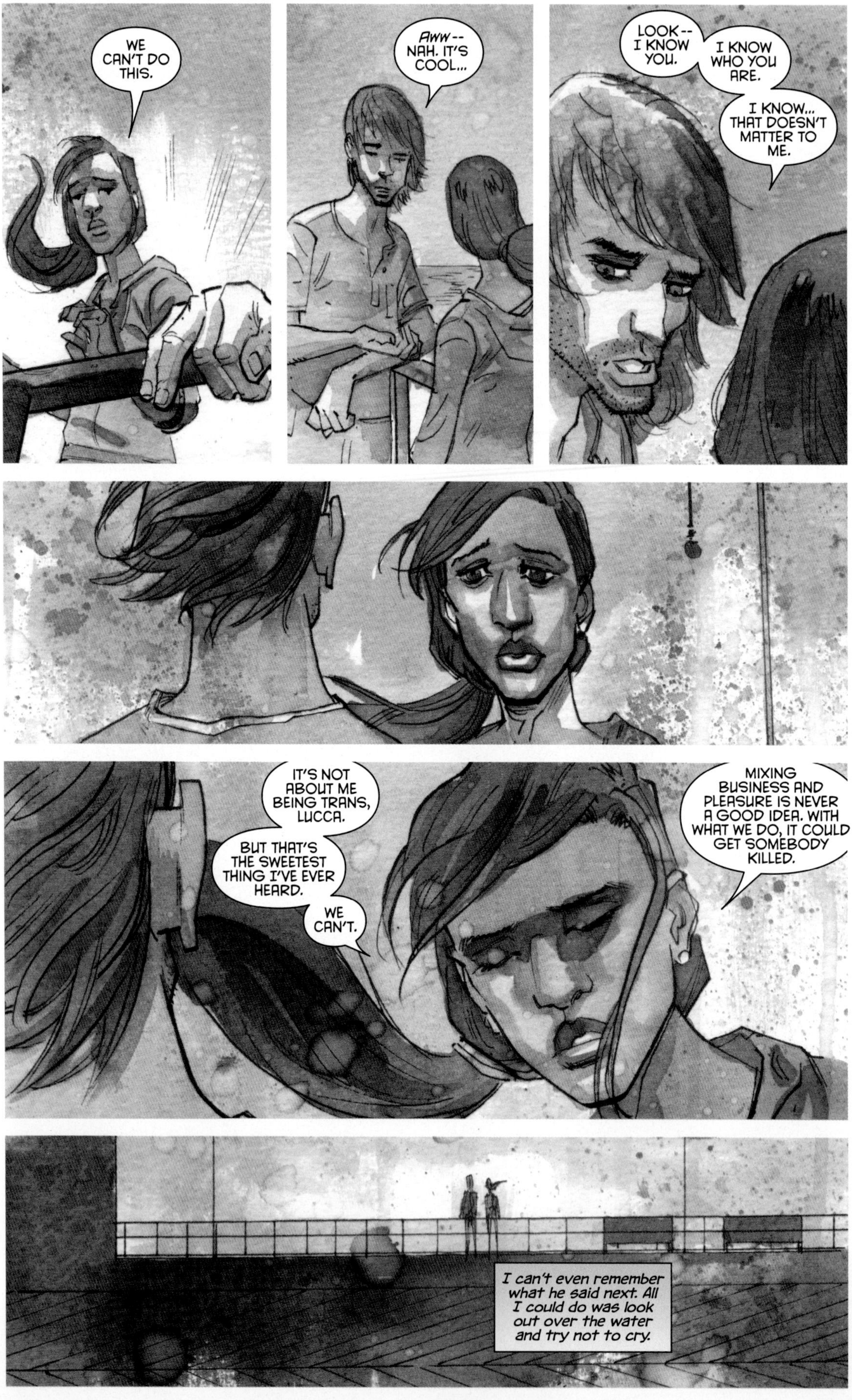
WE CAN'T DO THIS.
AWW -- NAH. IT'S COOL...
LOOK -- I KNOW YOU.
I KNOW WHO YOU ARE.
I KNOW... THAT DOESN'T MATTER TO ME.
IT'S NOT ABOUT ME BEING TRANS, LUCCA.
BUT THAT'S THE SWEETEST THING I'VE EVER HEARD.
WE CAN'T.
MIXING BUSINESS AND PLEASURE IS NEVER A GOOD IDEA. WITH WHAT WE DO, IT COULD GET SOMEBODY KILLED.
I can't even remember what he said next. All I could do was look out over the water and try not to cry.

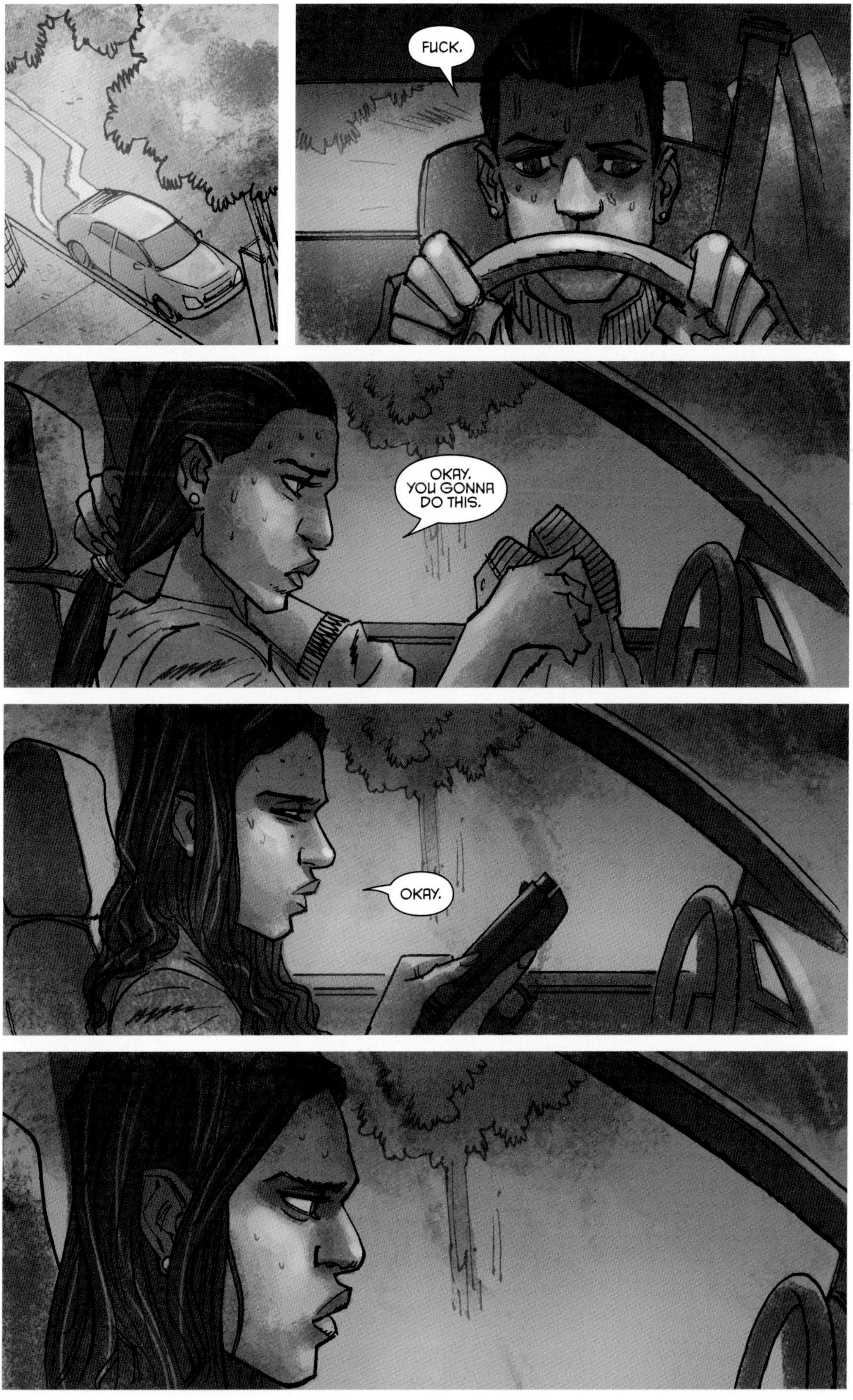
FUCK.
OKAY. YOU GONNA DO THIS.
OKAY.

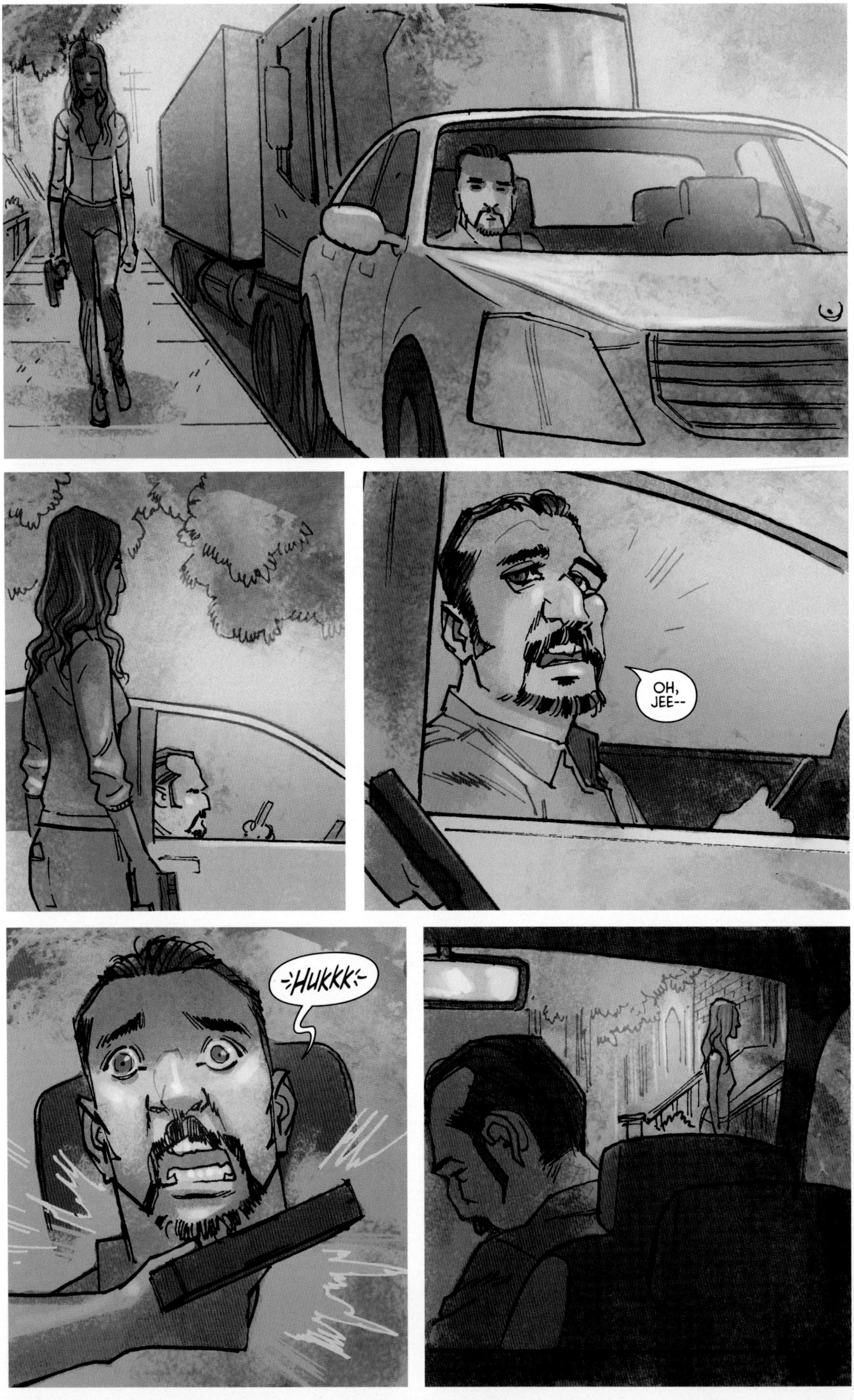
OH, JEE--
HUKKK

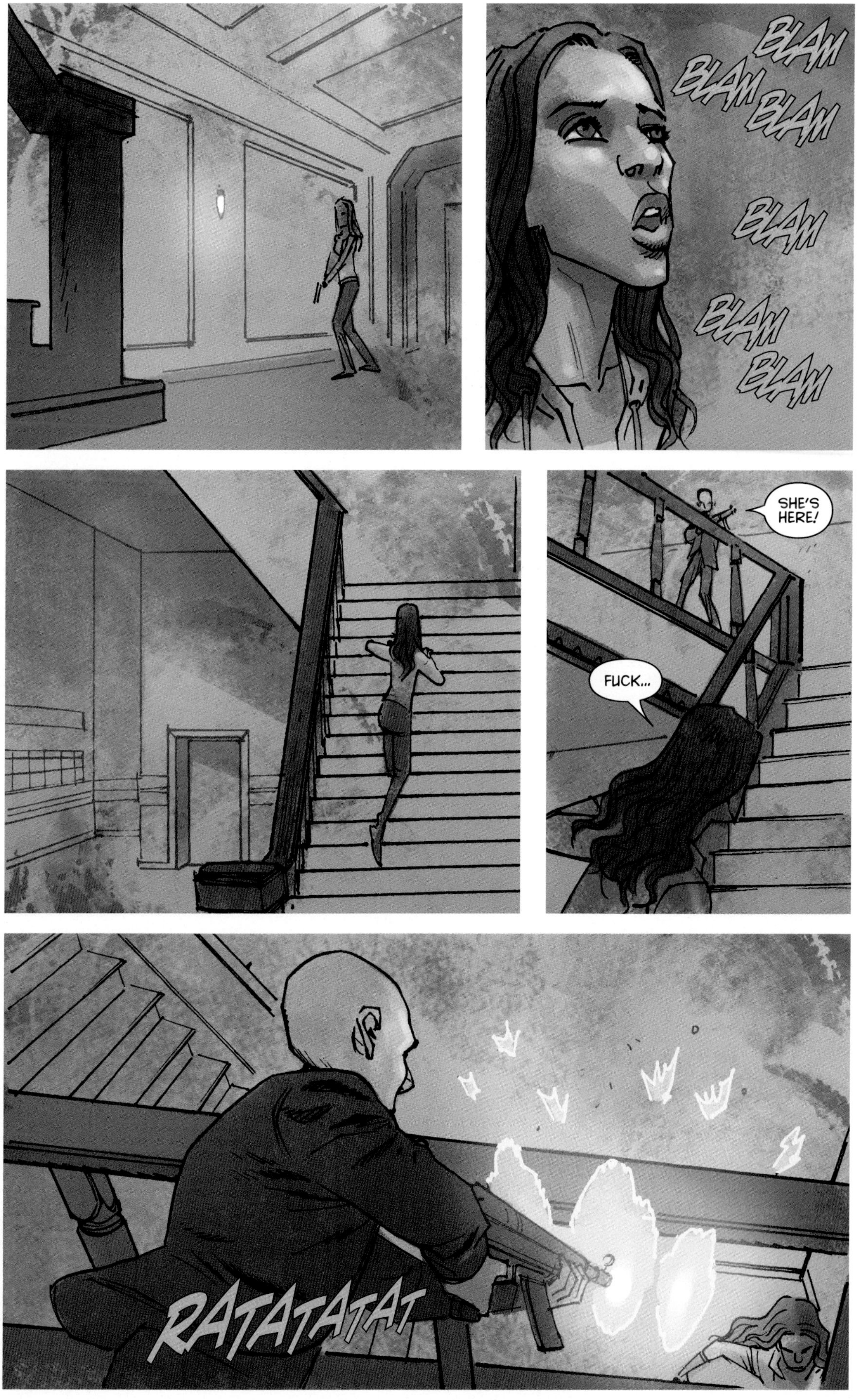
BLAM
BLAM BLAM
BLAM
BLAM
BLAM
BLAM
SHE'S HERE!
FUCK...
RATATATAT

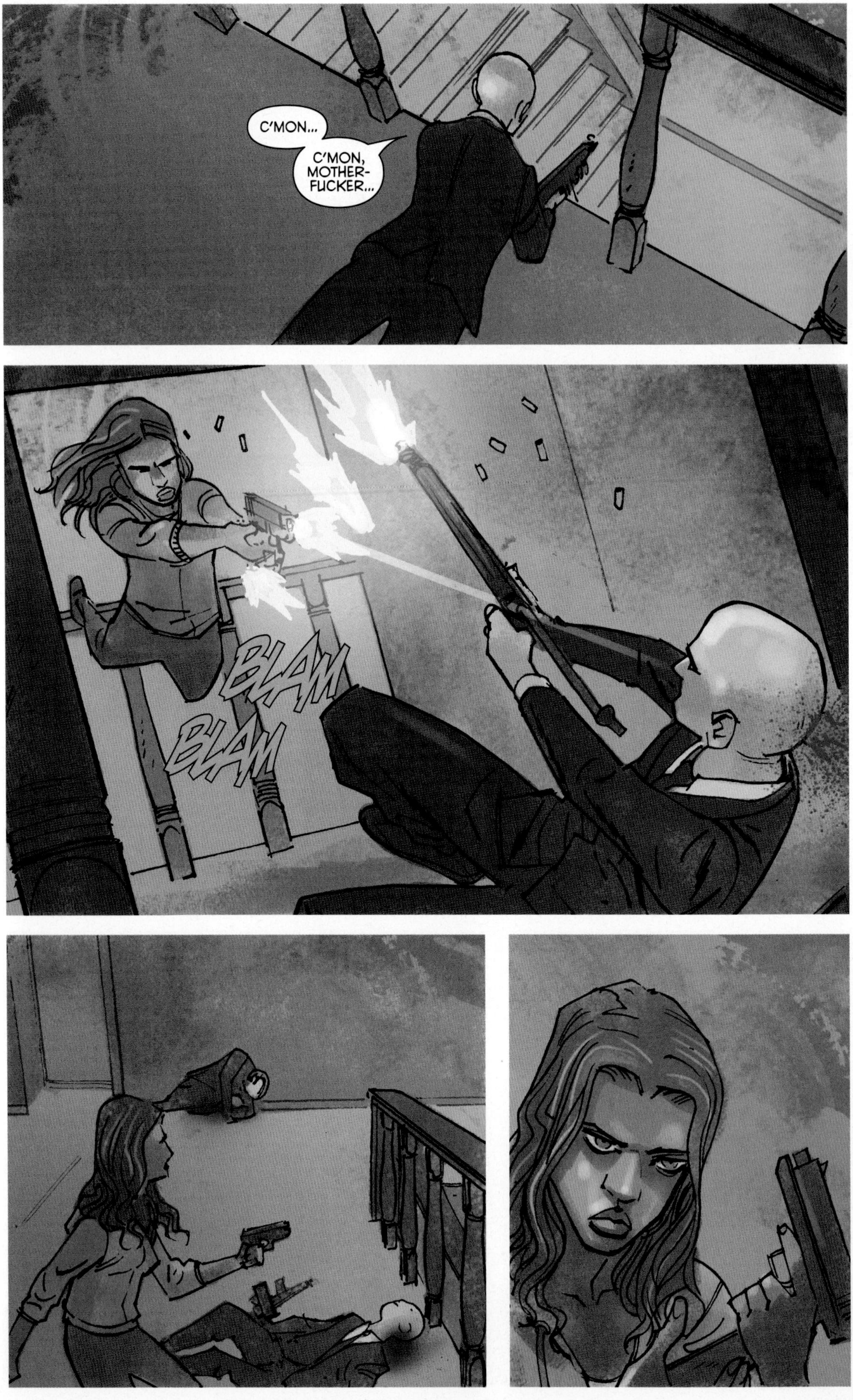
C'MON...
C'MON, MOTHER-FUCKER...
BLAM
BLAM

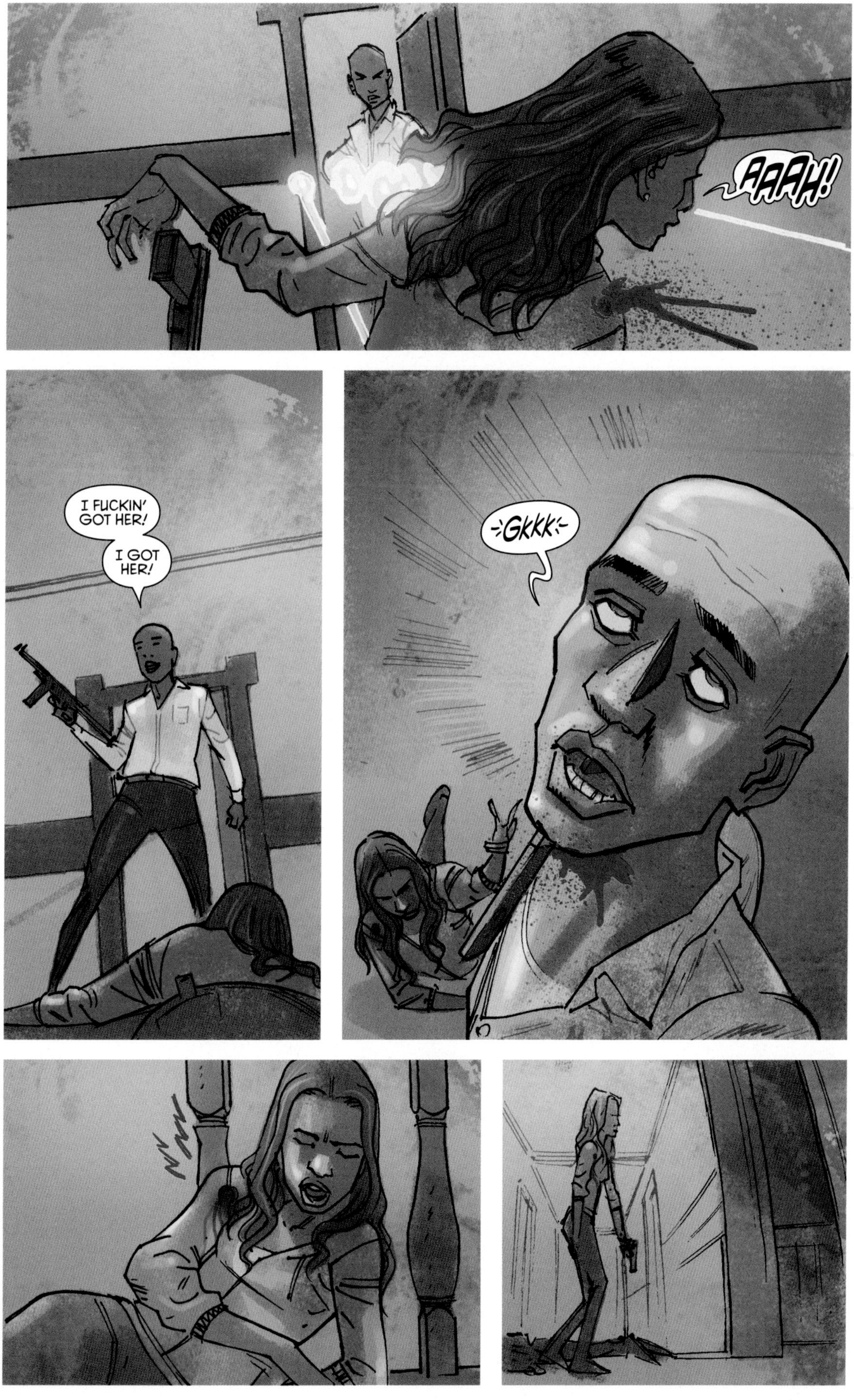
AAAH!
I FUCKIN' GOT HER!
I GOT HER!
GKKK

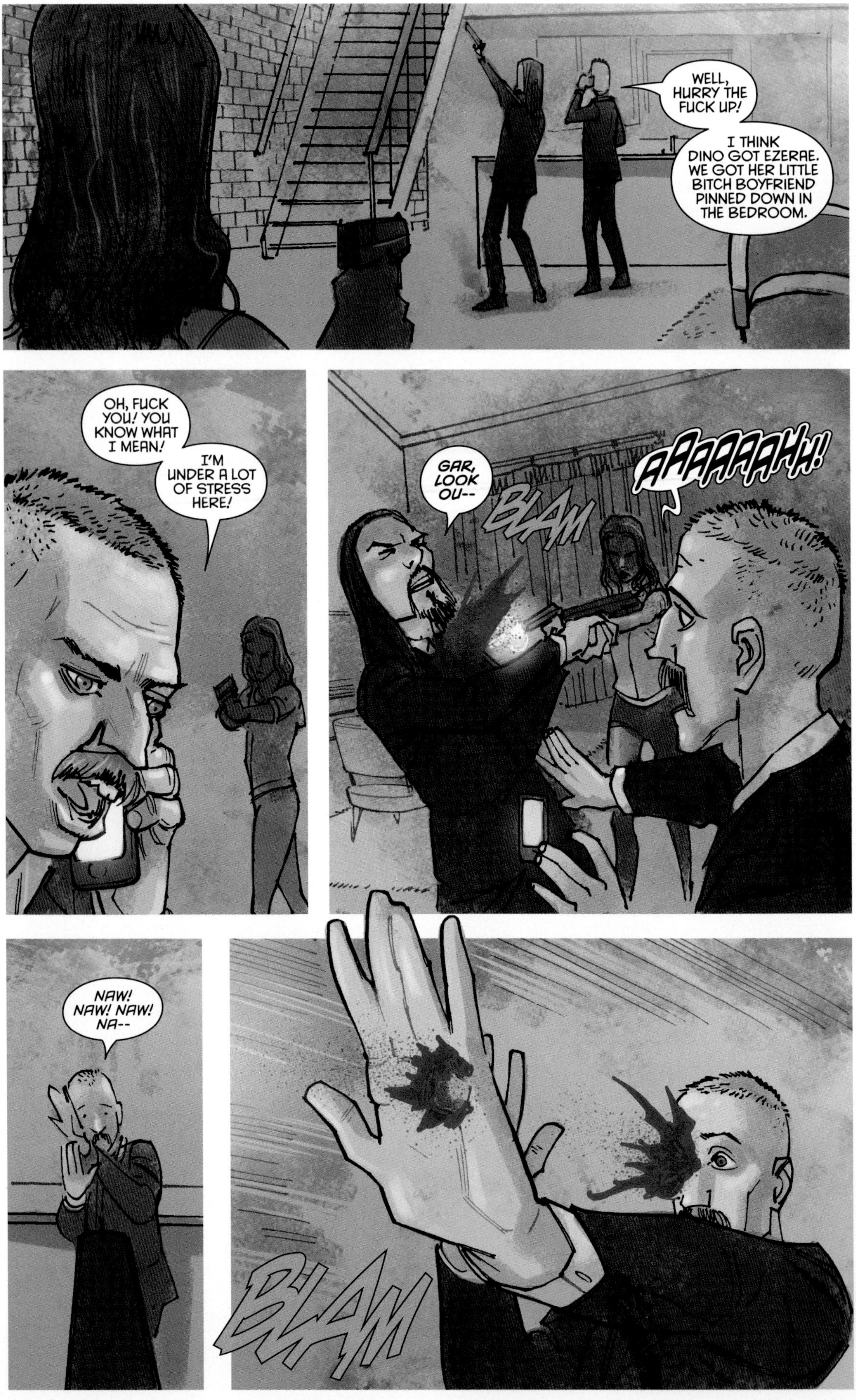
WELL, HURRY THE FUCK UP!
I THINK DINO GOT EZERAE. WE GOT HER LITTLE BITCH BOYFRIEND PINNED DOWN IN THE BEDROOM.
OH, FUCK YOU! YOU KNOW WHAT I MEAN!
I'M UNDER A LOT OF STRESS HERE!
GAR, LOOK OU--
BLAM
AAAAAAHH!
NAW! NAW! NAW! NA--
BLAM

BABY, IT'S ME!

EZ?

YOU CAN COME OUT. I GOT 'EM ALL.

JESUS CHRIST...

THEY SHOWED UP AND KICKED IN THE DOOR.

BARELY GOT TO YOUR ROOM BEFORE THEY OPENED UP.

AW, HELL -- YOU OKAY?

LUCCA!

m'okay. m'okay...

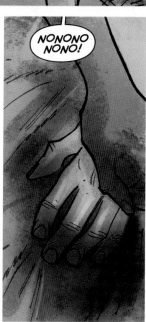

NONONO NONO!

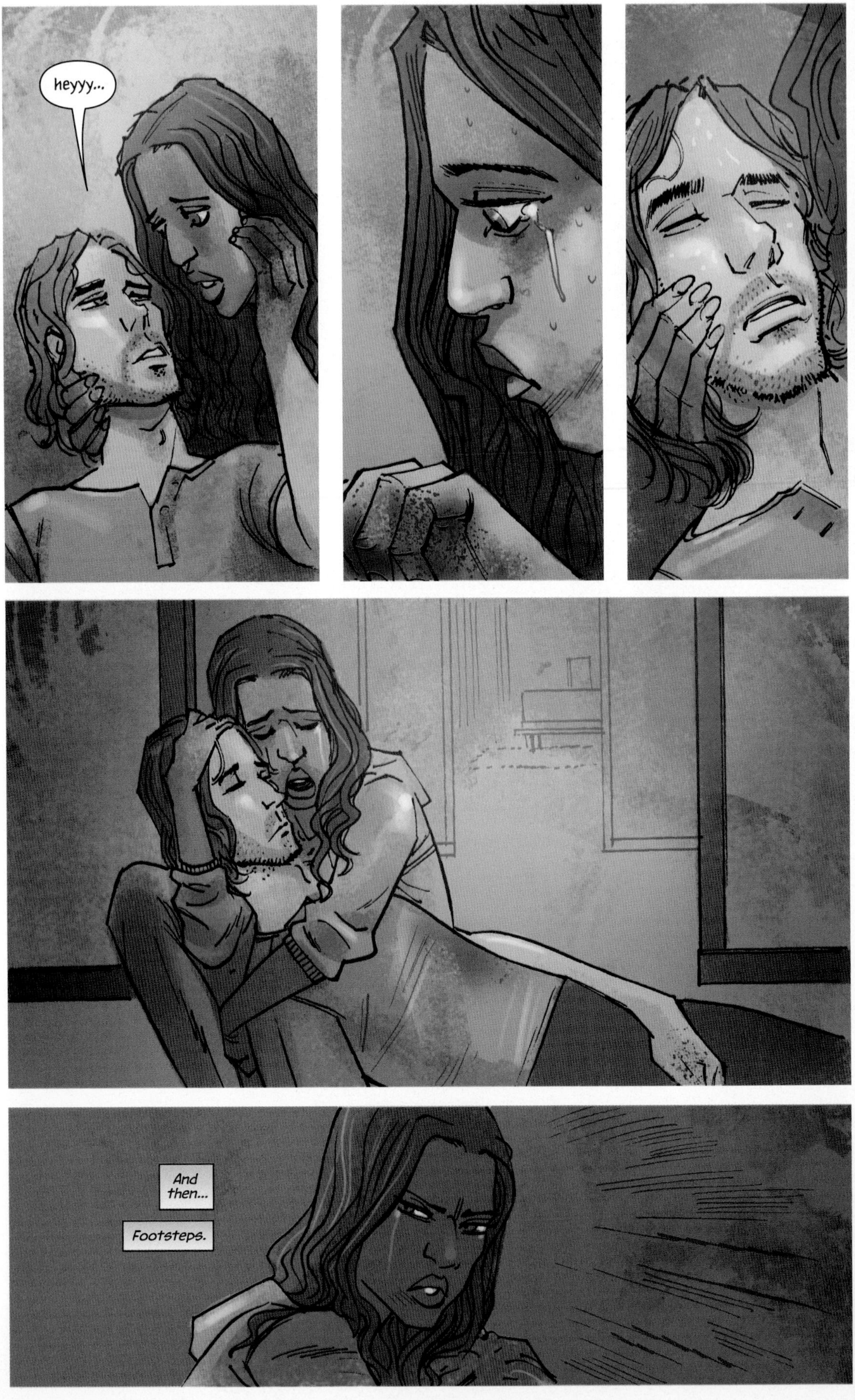
heyyy...
And then...
Footsteps.

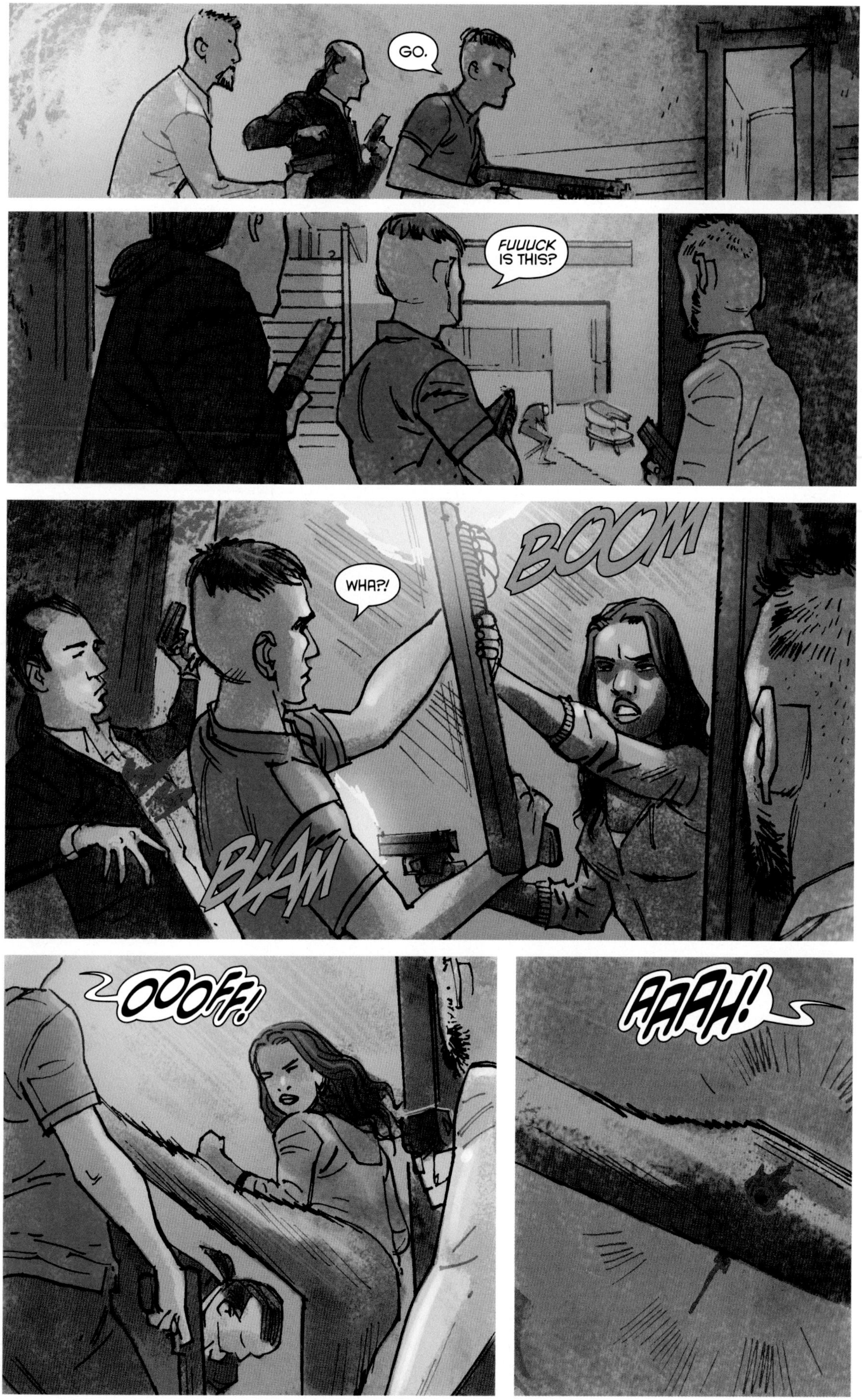
GO.
FUUUCK IS THIS?
WHA?!
BOOM
BLAM
OOOFF!
AAAH!

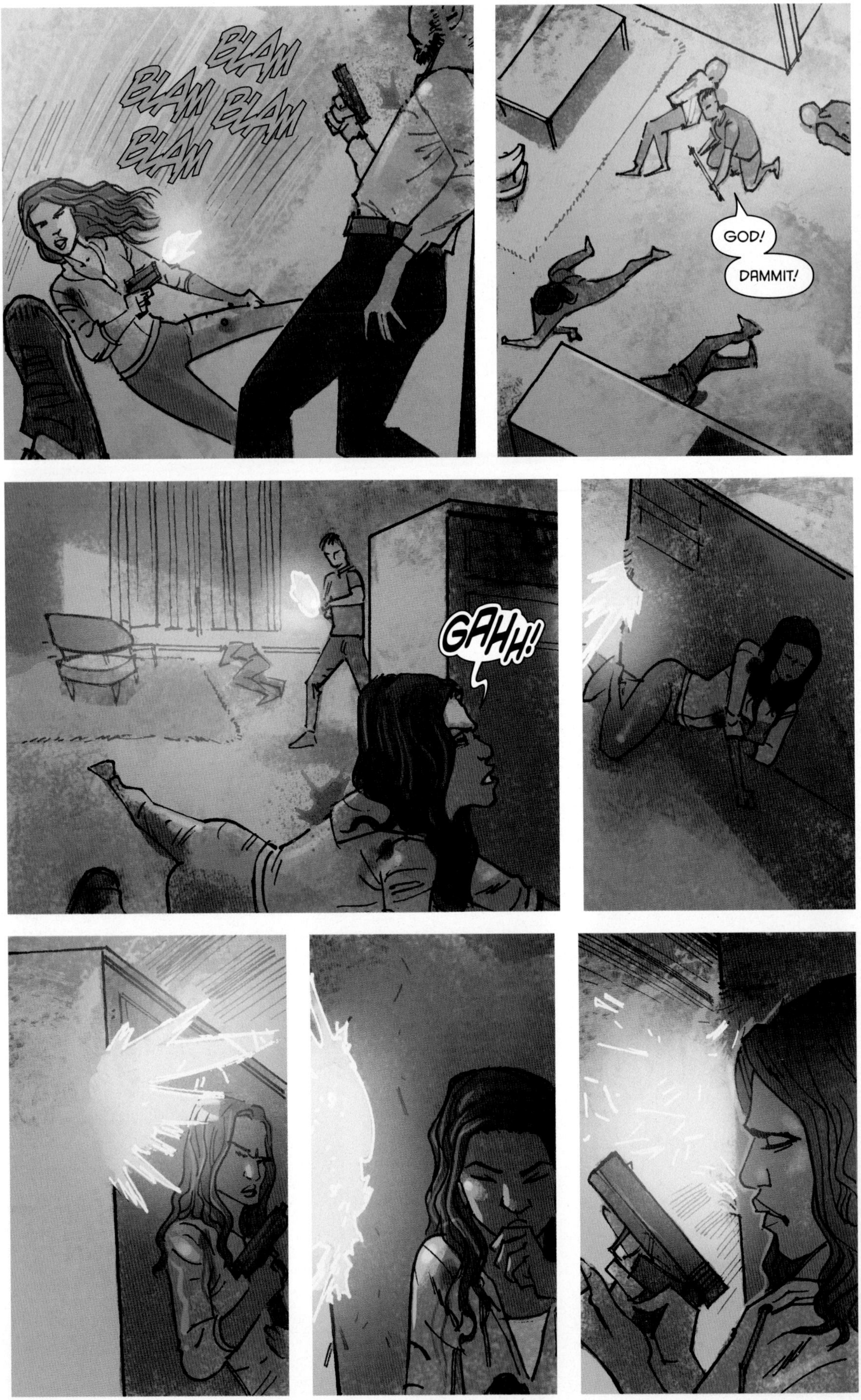
BLAM
BLAM BLAM
BLAM
GOD!
DAMMIT!
GAHH!

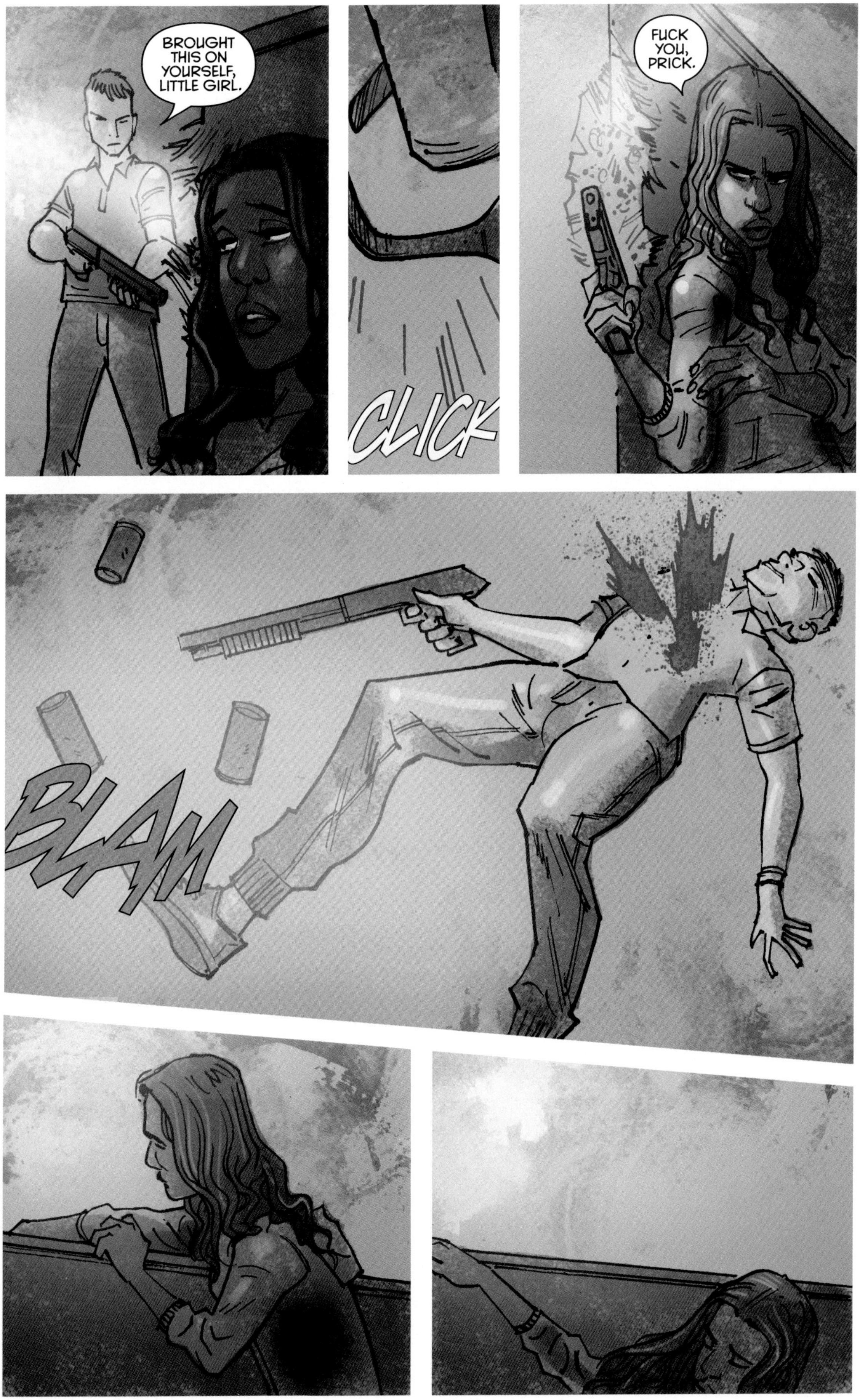
BROUGHT THIS ON YOURSELF, LITTLE GIRL.
CLICK
FUCK YOU, PRICK.
BLAM

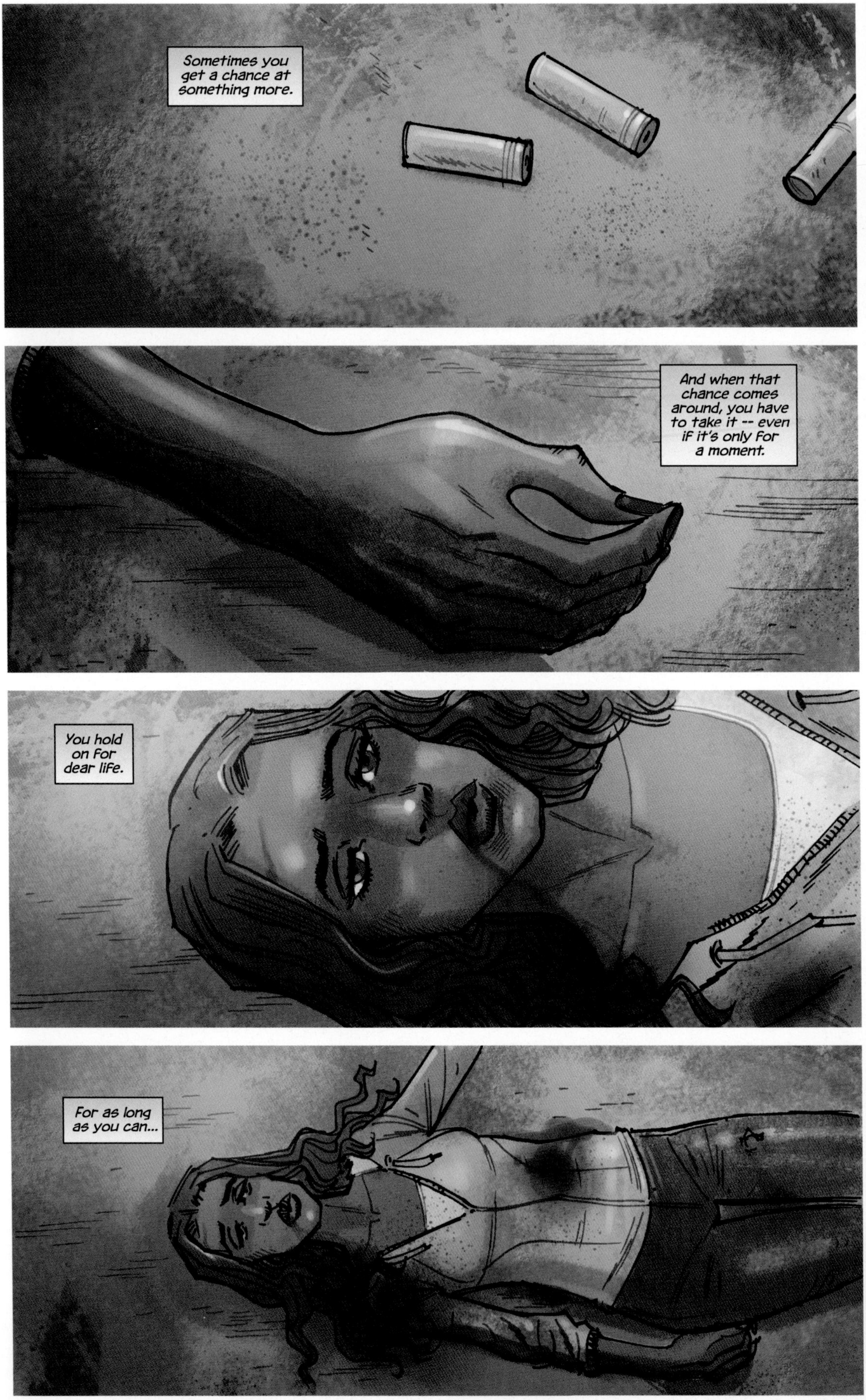
Sometimes you get a chance at something more.
And when that chance comes around, you have to take it -- even if it's only for a moment.
You hold on for dear life.
For as long as you can...

CHAPTER

11

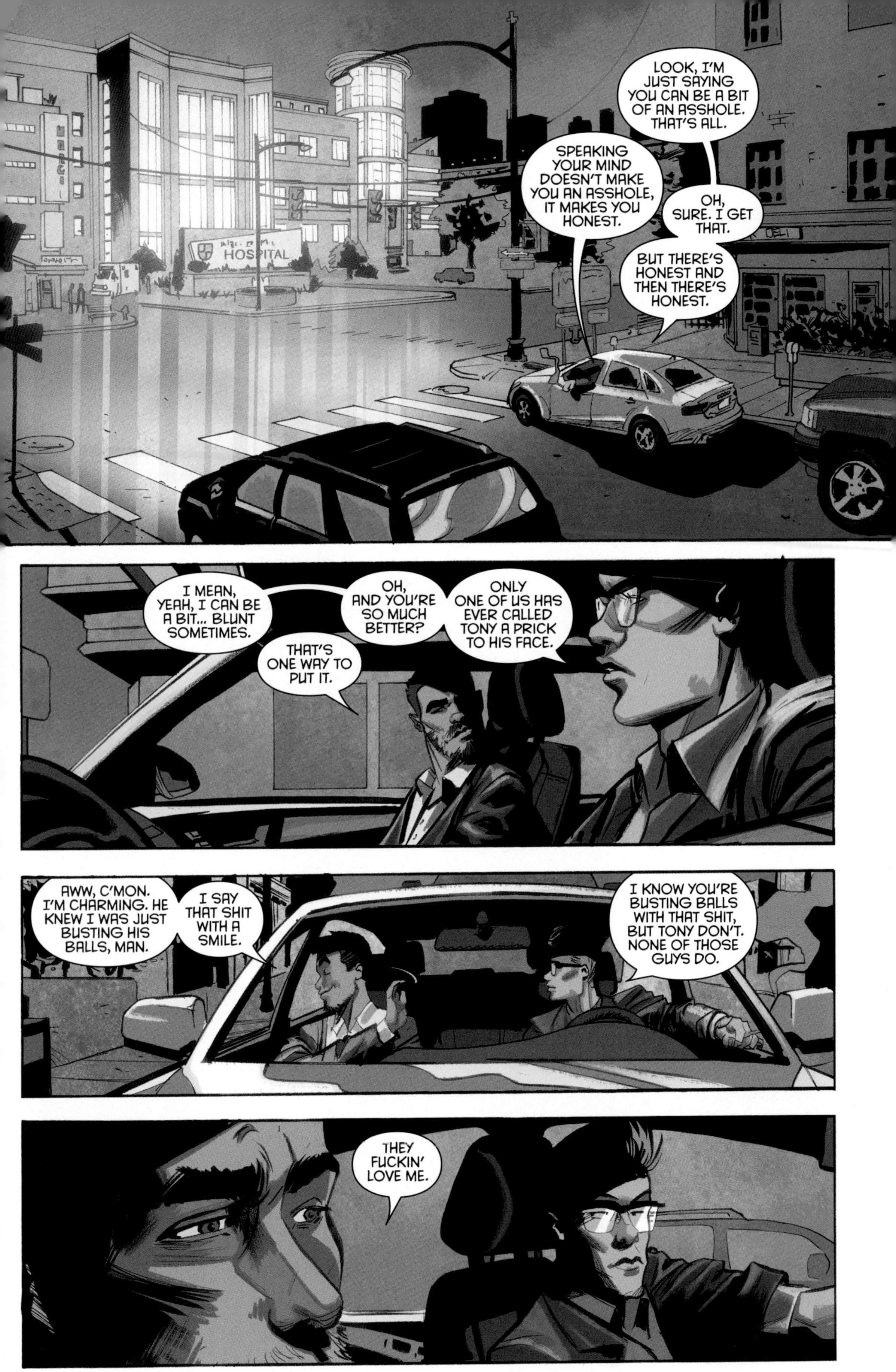
HOSPITAL
LOOK, I'M JUST SAYING YOU CAN BE A BIT OF AN ASSHOLE. THAT'S ALL.
SPEAKING YOUR MIND DOESN'T MAKE YOU AN ASSHOLE, IT MAKES YOU HONEST.
OH, SURE. I GET THAT.
BUT THERE'S HONEST AND THEN THERE'S HONEST.
I MEAN, YEAH, I CAN BE A BIT... BLUNT SOMETIMES.
THAT'S ONE WAY TO PUT IT.
OH, AND YOU'RE SO MUCH BETTER?
ONLY ONE OF US HAS EVER CALLED TONY A PRICK TO HIS FACE.
AWW, C'MON. I'M CHARMING. HE KNEW I WAS JUST BUSTING HIS BALLS, MAN.
I SAY THAT SHIT WITH A SMILE.
I KNOW YOU'RE BUSTING BALLS WITH THAT SHIT, BUT TONY DON'T. NONE OF THOSE GUYS DO.
THEY FUCKIN' LOVE ME.

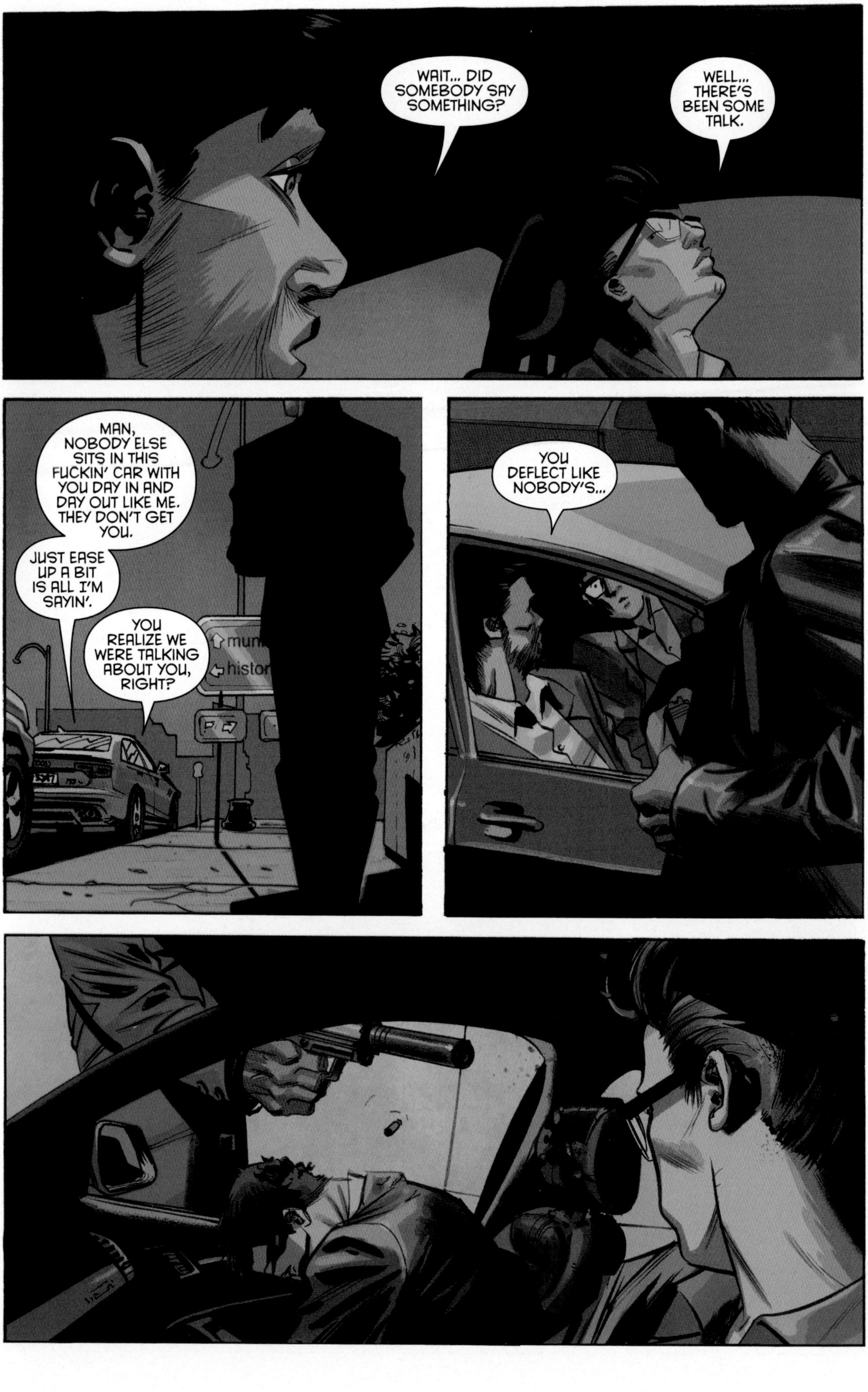
WAIT... DID SOMEBODY SAY SOMETHING?
WELL... THERE'S BEEN SOME TALK.
MAN, NOBODY ELSE SITS IN THIS FUCKIN' CAR WITH YOU DAY IN AND DAY OUT LIKE ME. THEY DON'T GET YOU.
JUST EASE UP A BIT IS ALL I'M SAYIN'.
YOU REALIZE WE WERE TALKING ABOUT YOU, RIGHT?
YOU DEFLECT LIKE NOBODY'S...

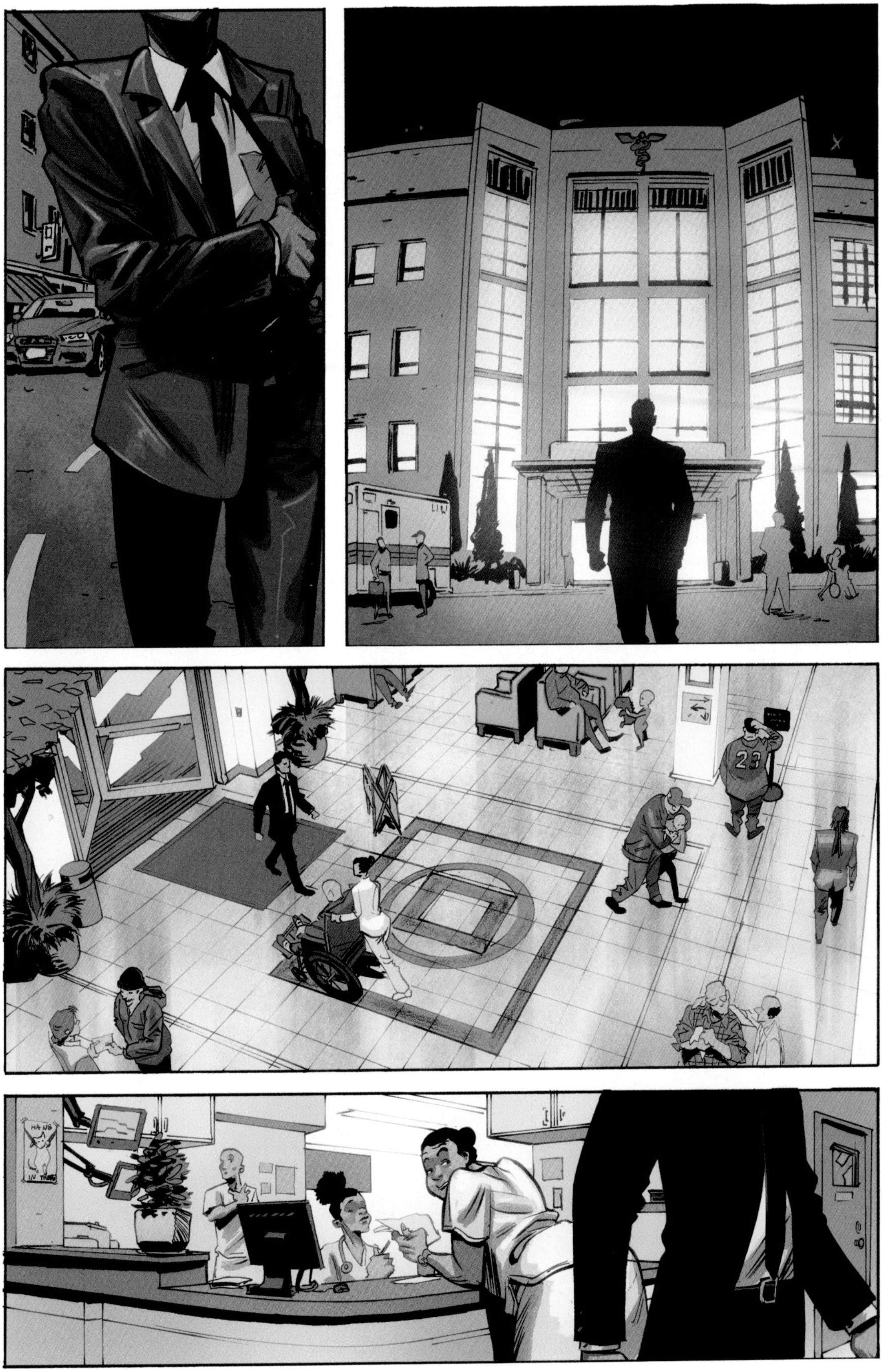

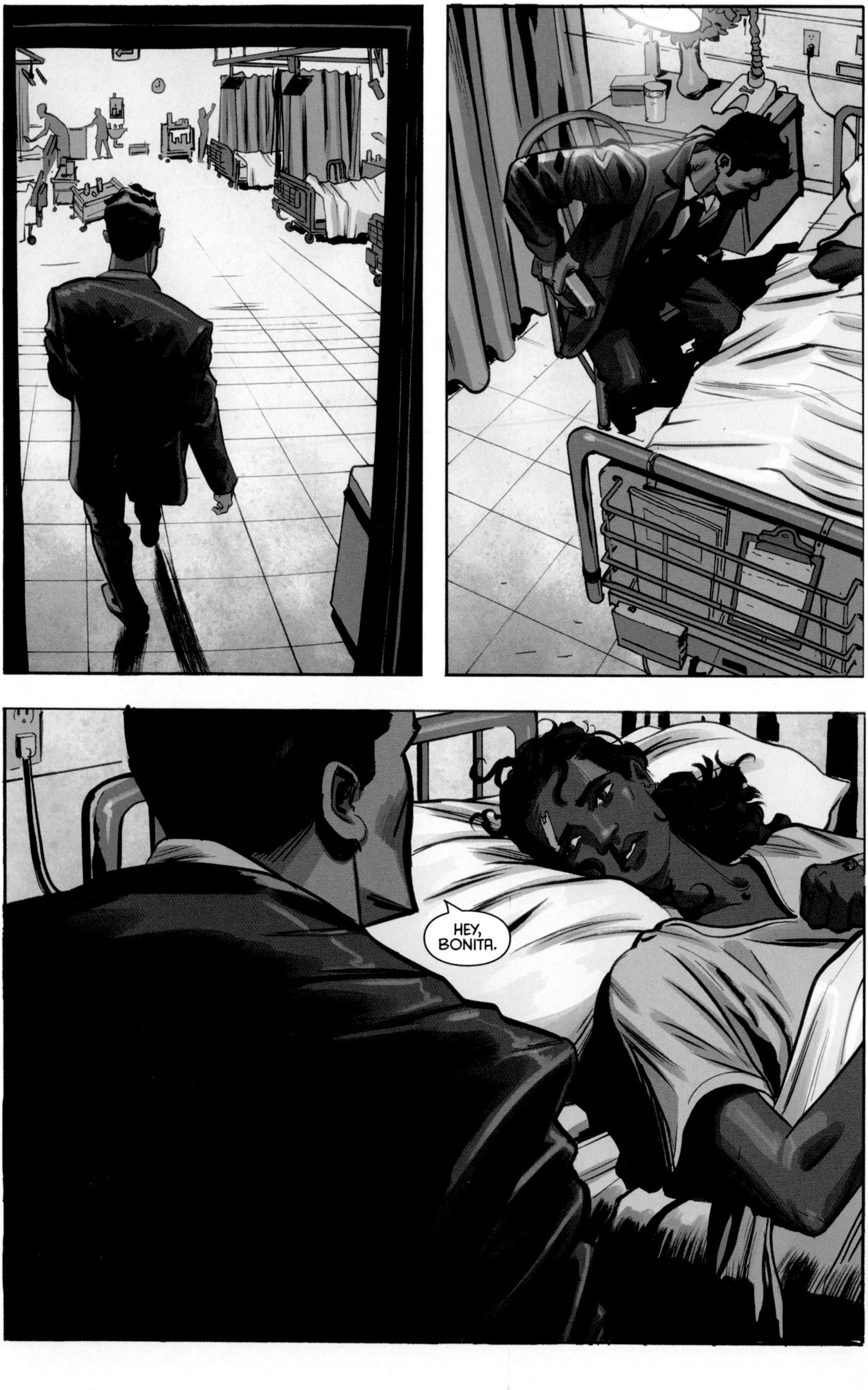
HEY, BONITA.

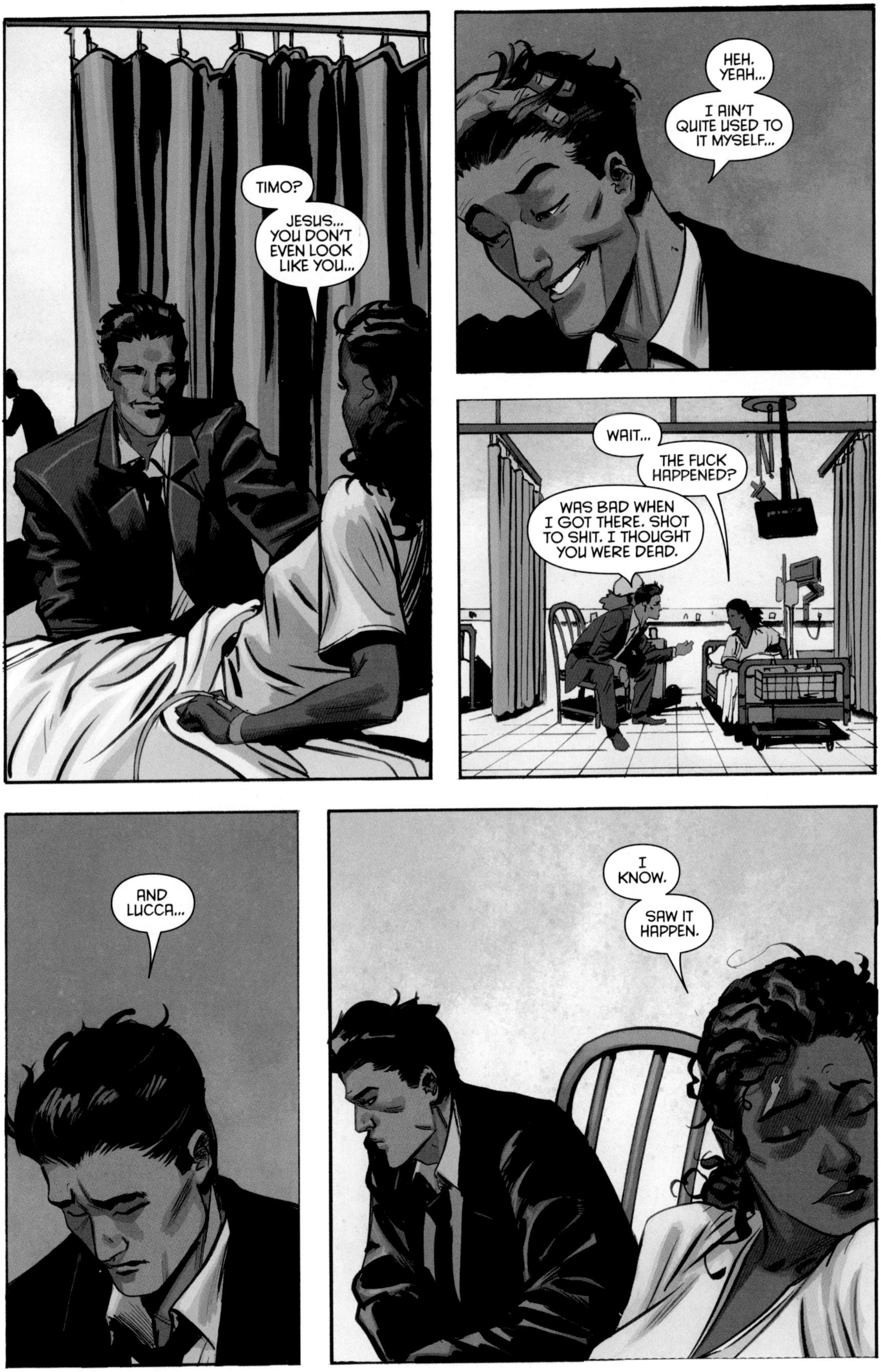
TIMO?
JESUS... YOU DON'T EVEN LOOK LIKE YOU...
HEH. YEAH...
I AIN'T QUITE USED TO IT MYSELF...
WAIT...
THE FUCK HAPPENED?
WAS BAD WHEN I GOT THERE. SHOT TO SHIT. I THOUGHT YOU WERE DEAD.
AND LUCCA...
I KNOW.
SAW IT HAPPEN.

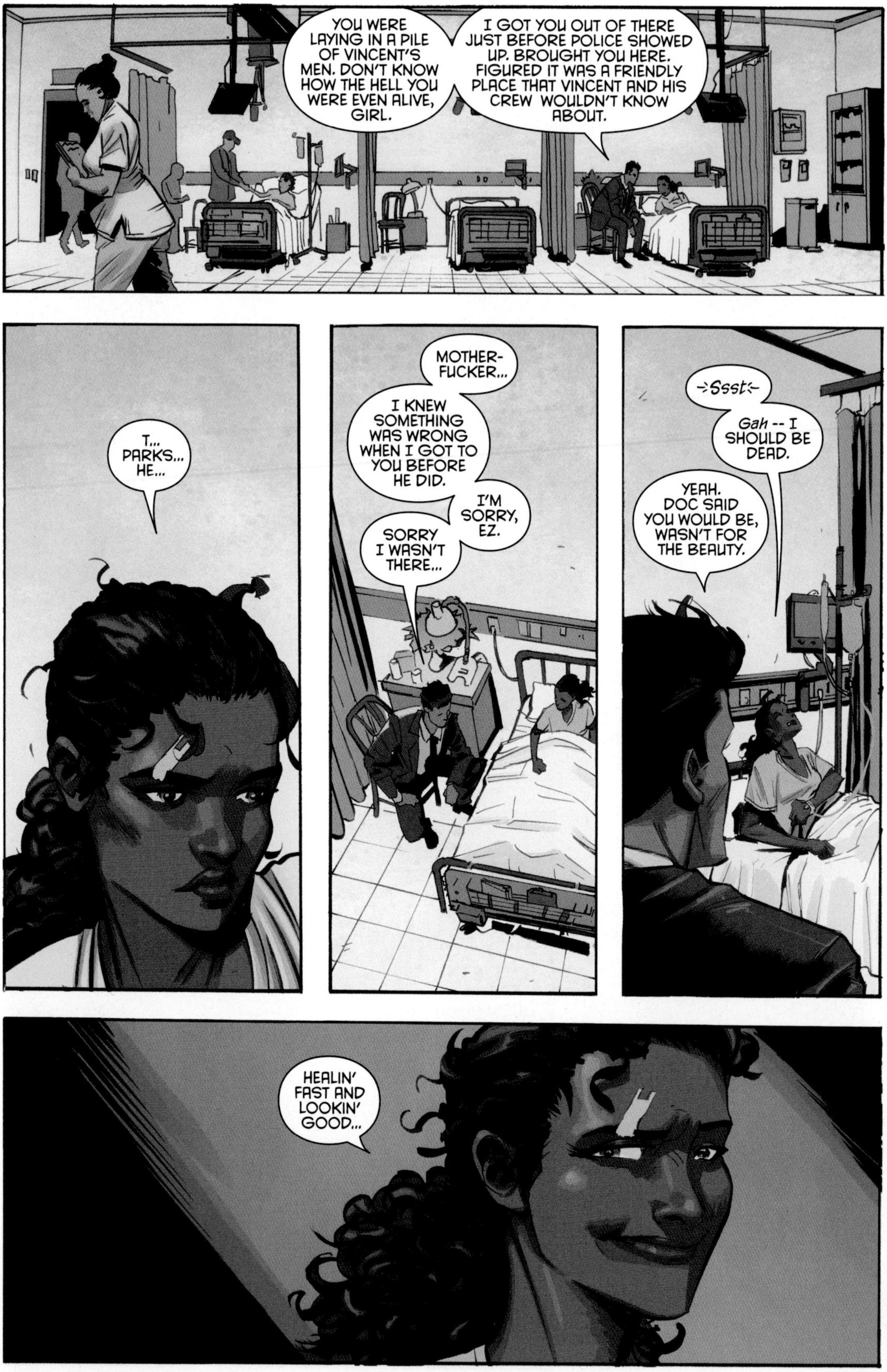
YOU WERE LAYING IN A PILE OF VINCENT'S MEN. DON'T KNOW HOW THE HELL YOU WERE EVEN ALIVE, GIRL.
I GOT YOU OUT OF THERE JUST BEFORE POLICE SHOWED UP. BROUGHT YOU HERE. FIGURED IT WAS A FRIENDLY PLACE THAT VINCENT AND HIS CREW WOULDN'T KNOW ABOUT.
T... PARKS... HE...
MOTHER-FUCKER...
I KNEW SOMETHING WAS WRONG WHEN I GOT TO YOU BEFORE HE DID.
I'M SORRY, EZ.
SORRY I WASN'T THERE...
Ssst
Gah -- I SHOULD BE DEAD.
YEAH. DOC SAID YOU WOULD BE, WASN'T FOR THE BEAUTY.
HEALIN' FAST AND LOOKIN' GOOD...

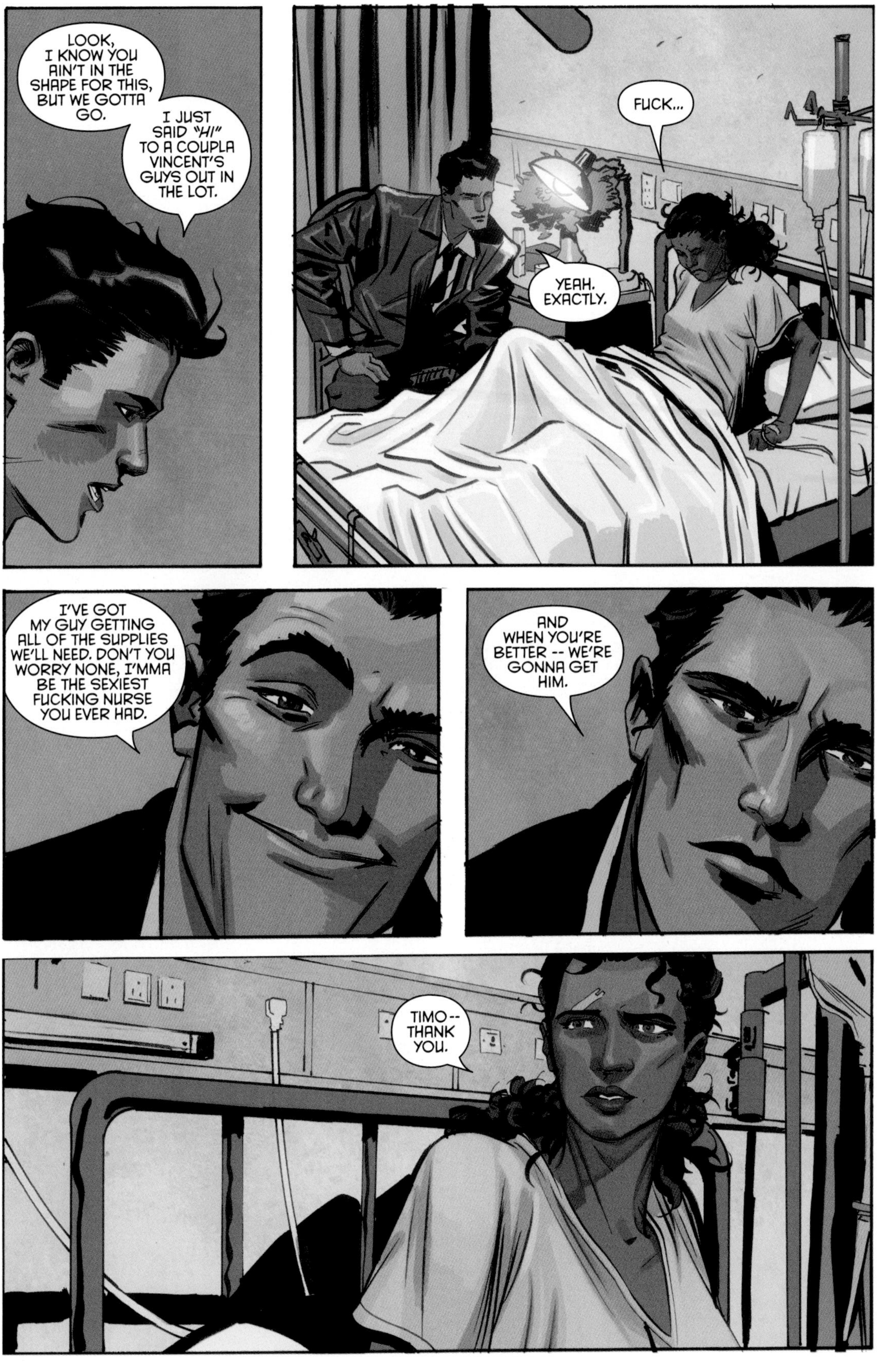
LOOK, I KNOW YOU AIN'T IN THE SHAPE FOR THIS, BUT WE GOTTA GO.
I JUST SAID "HI" TO A COUPLA VINCENT'S GUYS OUT IN THE LOT.
FUCK...
YEAH. EXACTLY.
I'VE GOT MY GUY GETTING ALL OF THE SUPPLIES WE'LL NEED. DON'T YOU WORRY NONE, I'MMA BE THE SEXIEST FUCKING NURSE YOU EVER HAD.
AND WHEN YOU'RE BETTER -- WE'RE GONNA GET HIM.
TIMO -- THANK YOU.

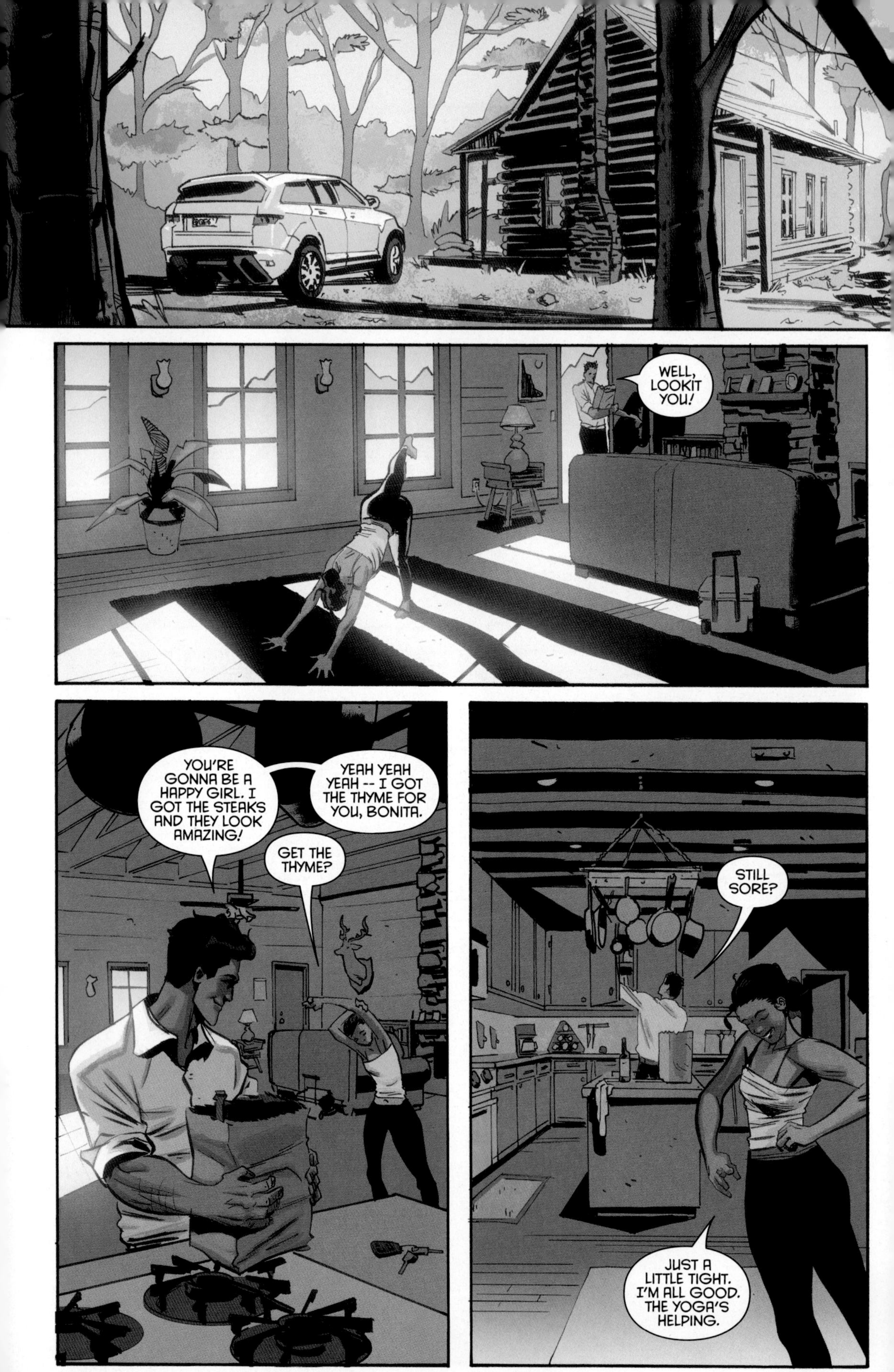
WELL, LOOKIT YOU!
YOU'RE GONNA BE A HAPPY GIRL. I GOT THE STEAKS AND THEY LOOK AMAZING!
YEAH YEAH YEAH -- I GOT THE THYME FOR YOU, BONITA.
GET THE THYME?
STILL SORE?
JUST A LITTLE TIGHT. I'M ALL GOOD. THE YOGA'S HELPING.

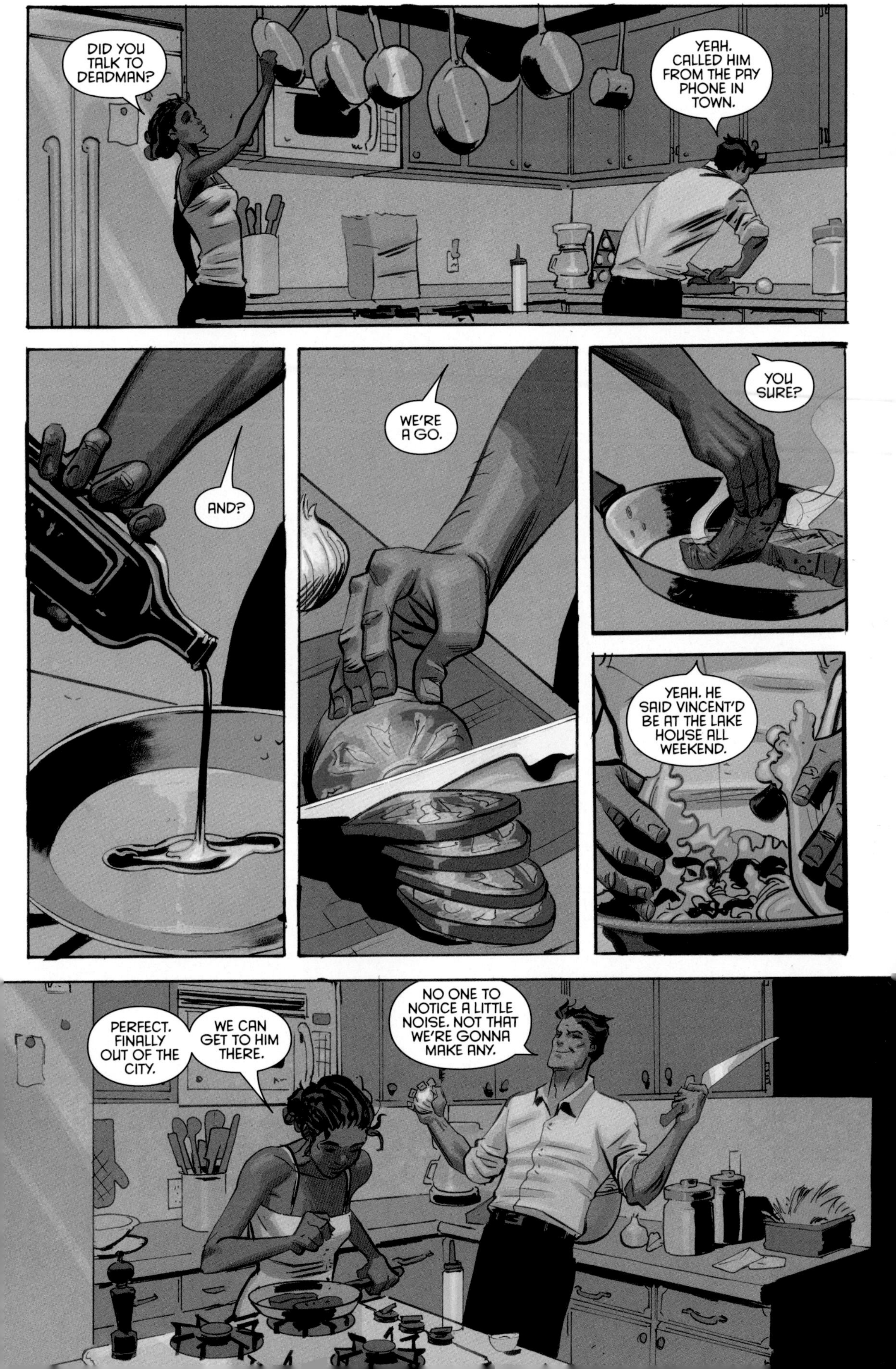
DID YOU TALK TO DEADMAN?
YEAH. CALLED HIM FROM THE PAY PHONE IN TOWN.
AND?
WE'RE A GO.
YOU SURE?
YEAH. HE SAID VINCENT'D BE AT THE LAKE HOUSE ALL WEEKEND.
PERFECT. FINALLY OUT OF THE CITY.
WE CAN GET TO HIM THERE.
NO ONE TO NOTICE A LITTLE NOISE. NOT THAT WE'RE GONNA MAKE ANY.

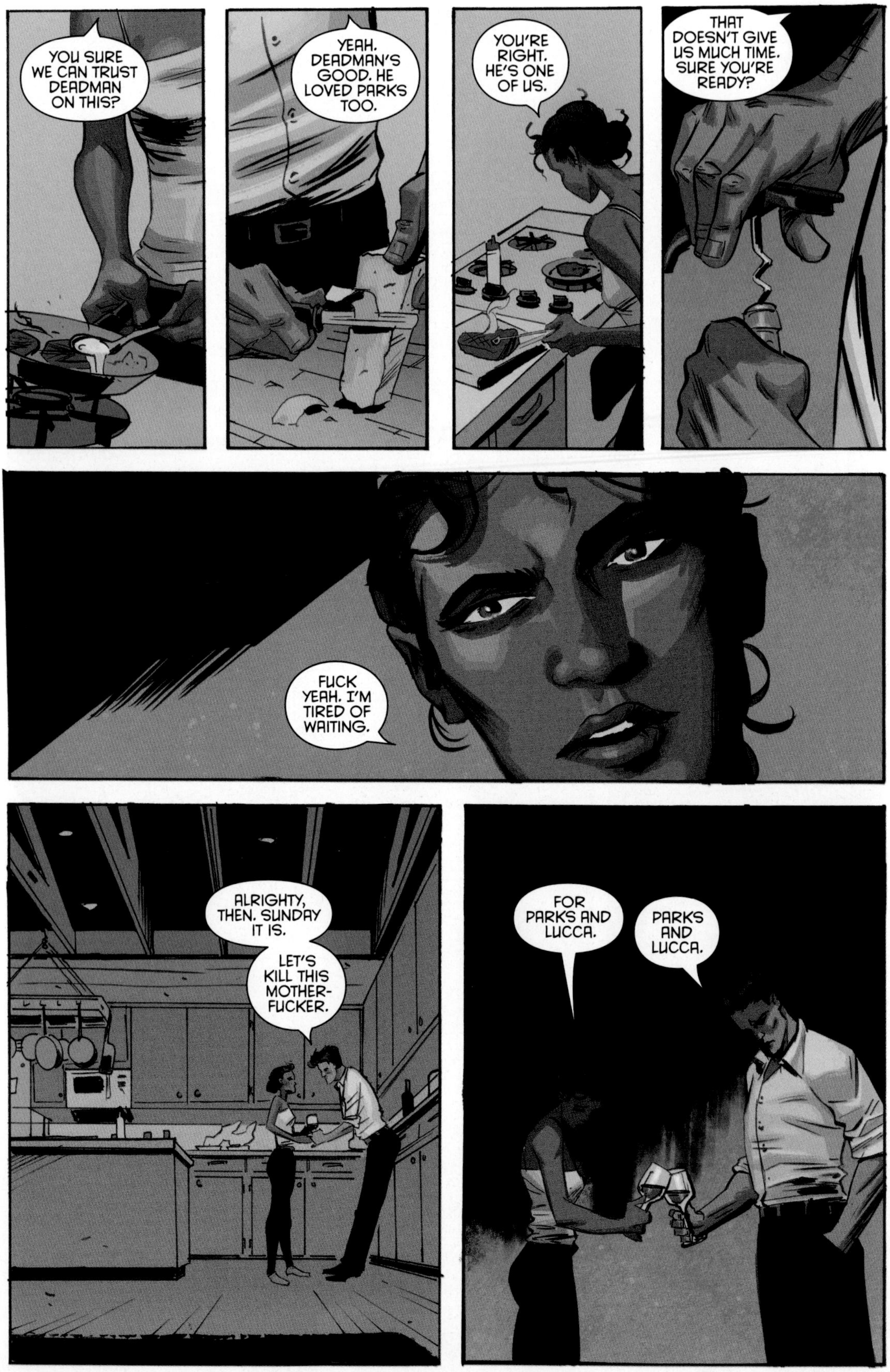
YOU SURE WE CAN TRUST DEADMAN ON THIS?
YEAH. DEADMAN'S GOOD. HE LOVED PARKS TOO.
YOU'RE RIGHT. HE'S ONE OF US.
THAT DOESN'T GIVE US MUCH TIME. SURE YOU'RE READY?
FUCK YEAH. I'M TIRED OF WAITING.
ALRIGHTY, THEN. SUNDAY IT IS.
LET'S KILL THIS MOTHER-FUCKER.
FOR PARKS AND LUCCA.
PARKS AND LUCCA.

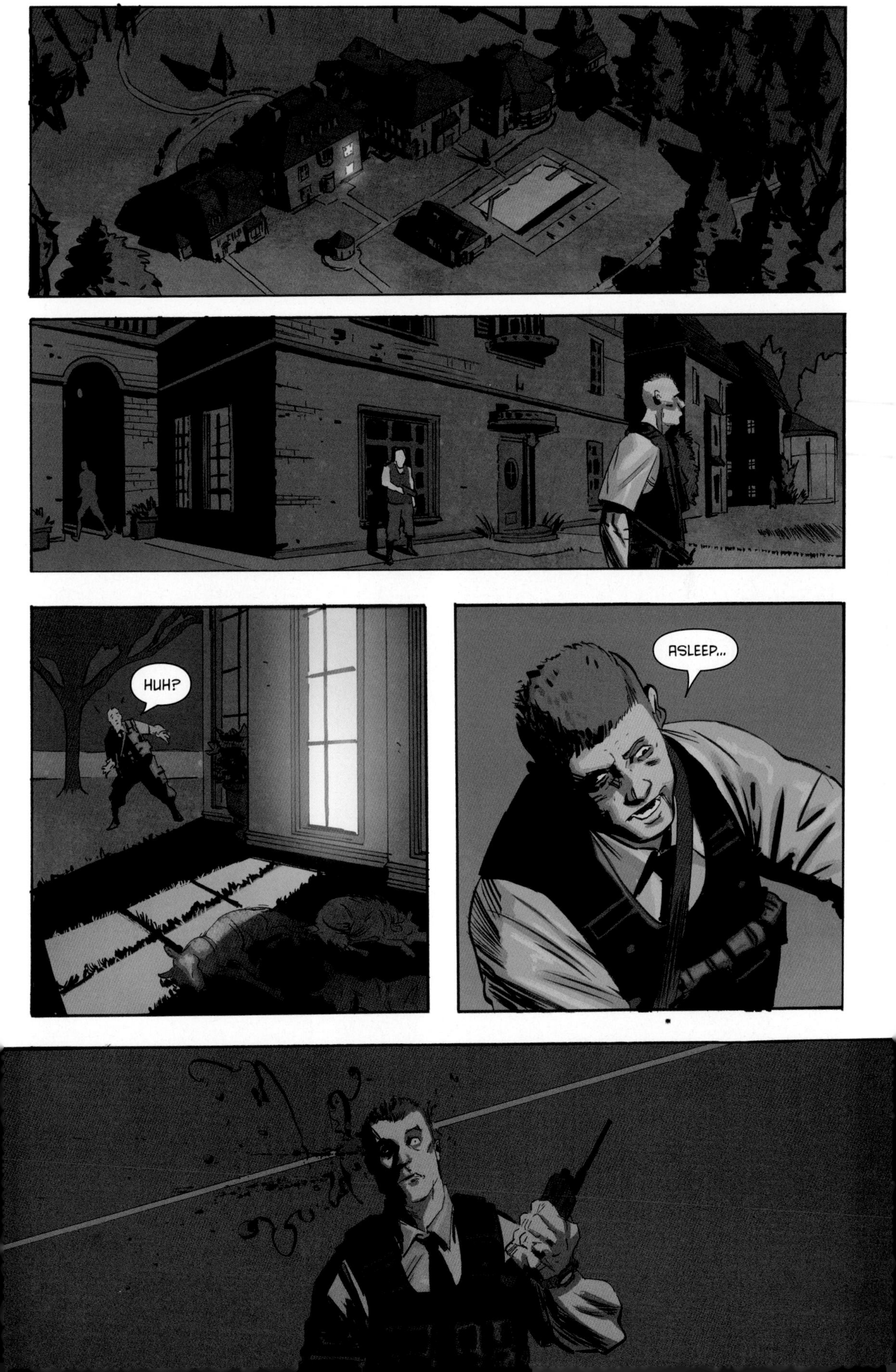
HUH?
ASLEEP...

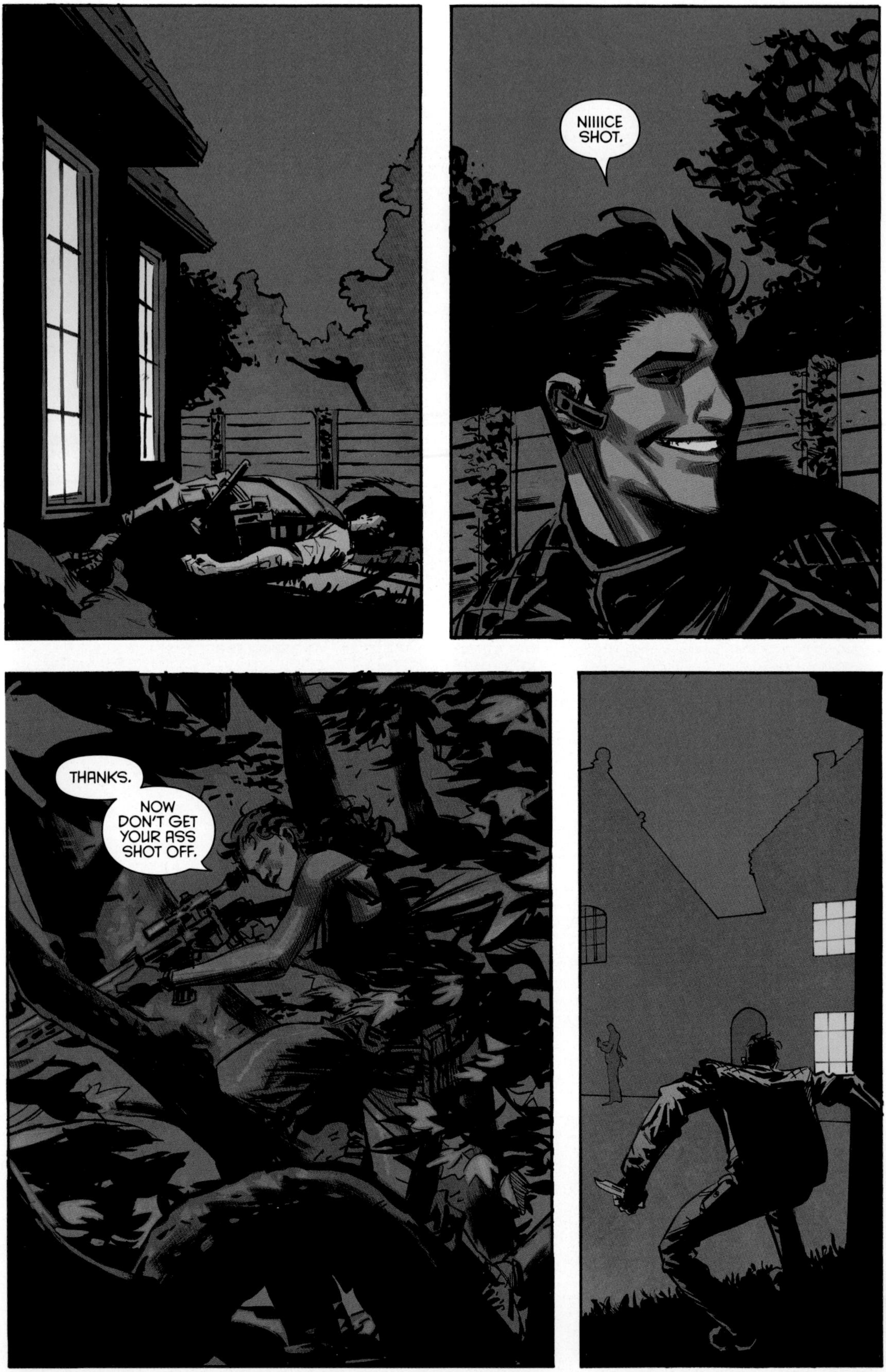
NIIIICE SHOT.
THANKS.
NOW DON'T GET YOUR ASS SHOT OFF.

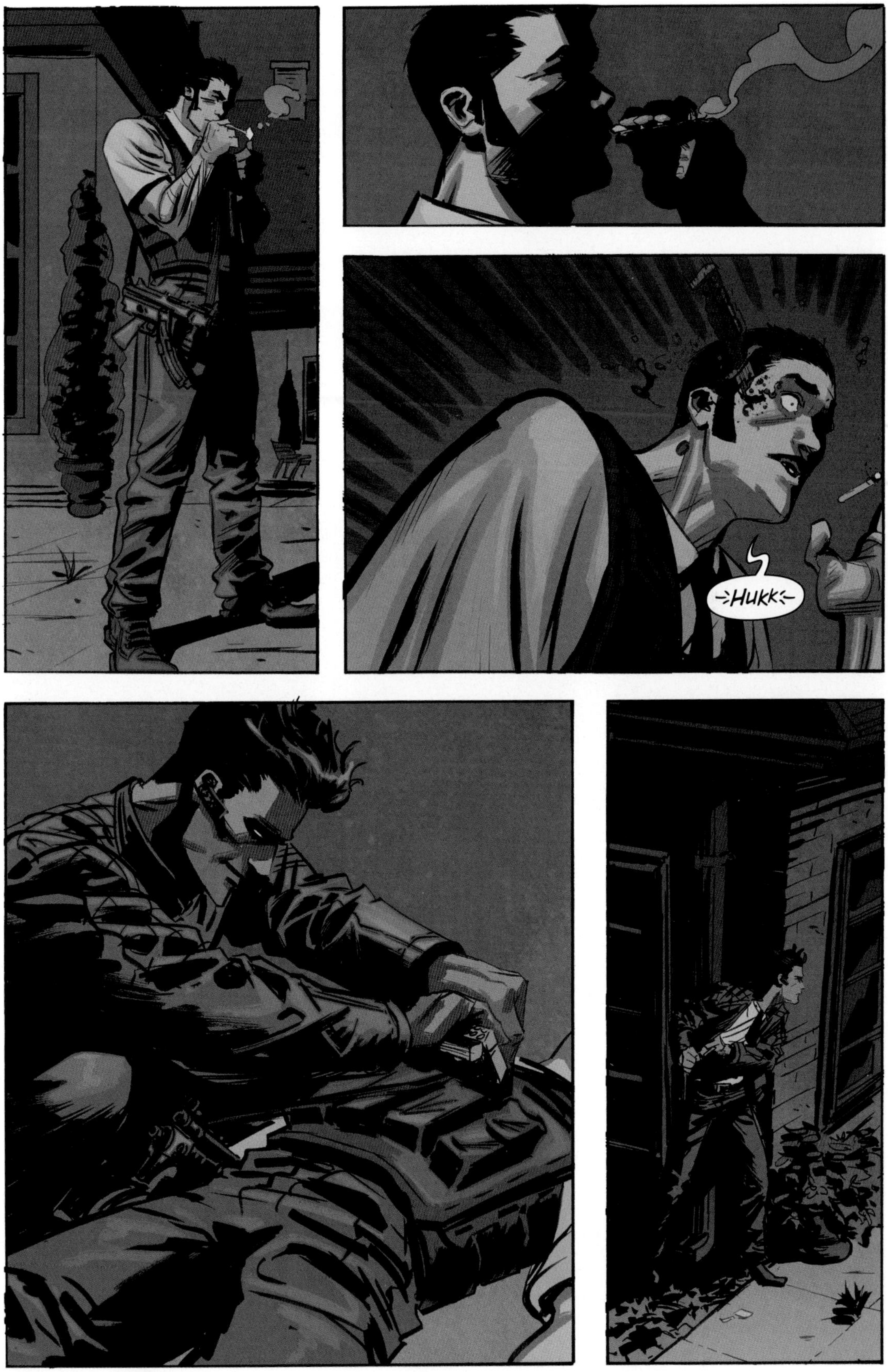
HUKK

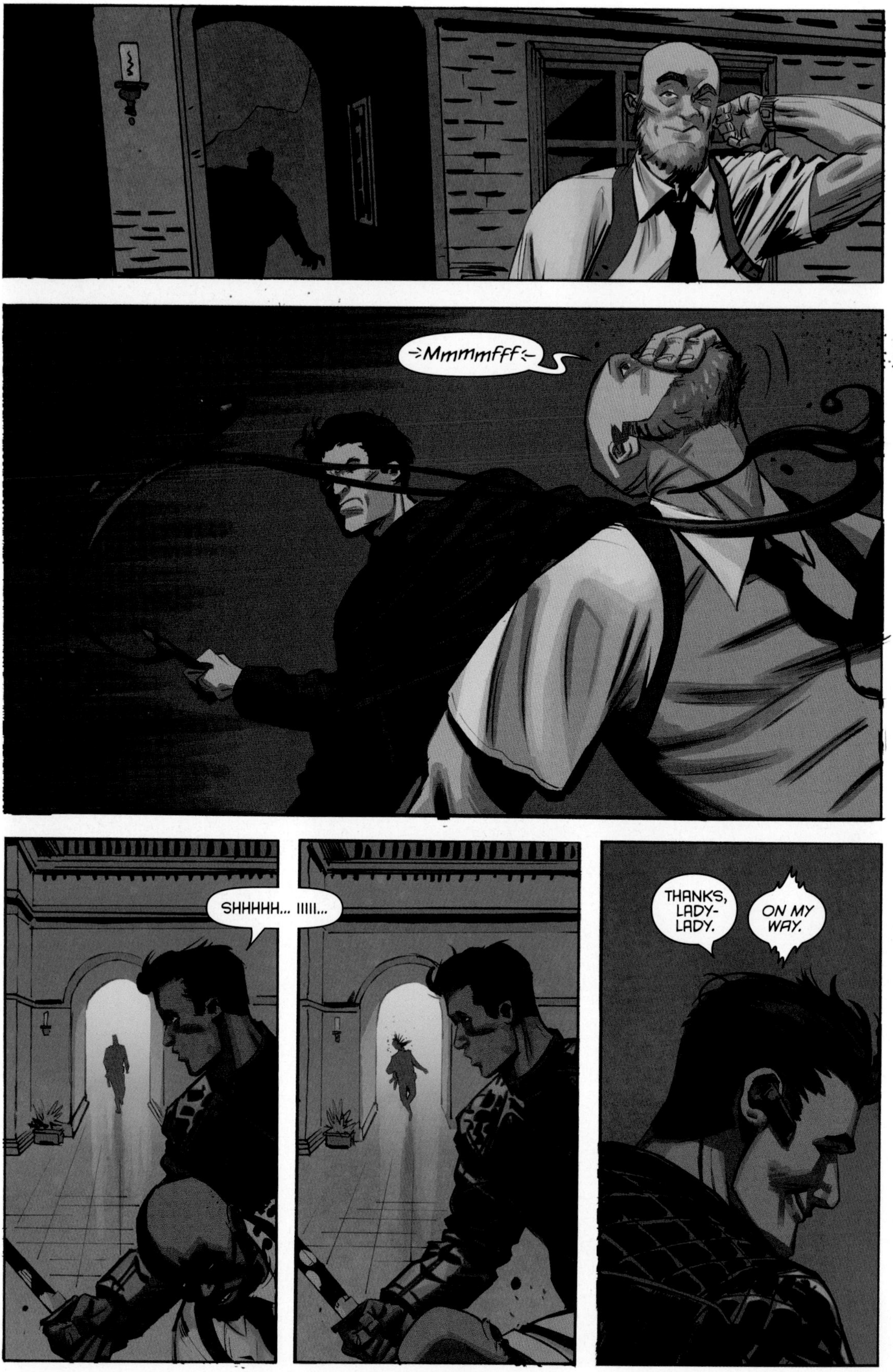
-Mmmmfff-
SHHHHH... IIIII...
THANKS, LADY-LADY.
ON MY WAY.

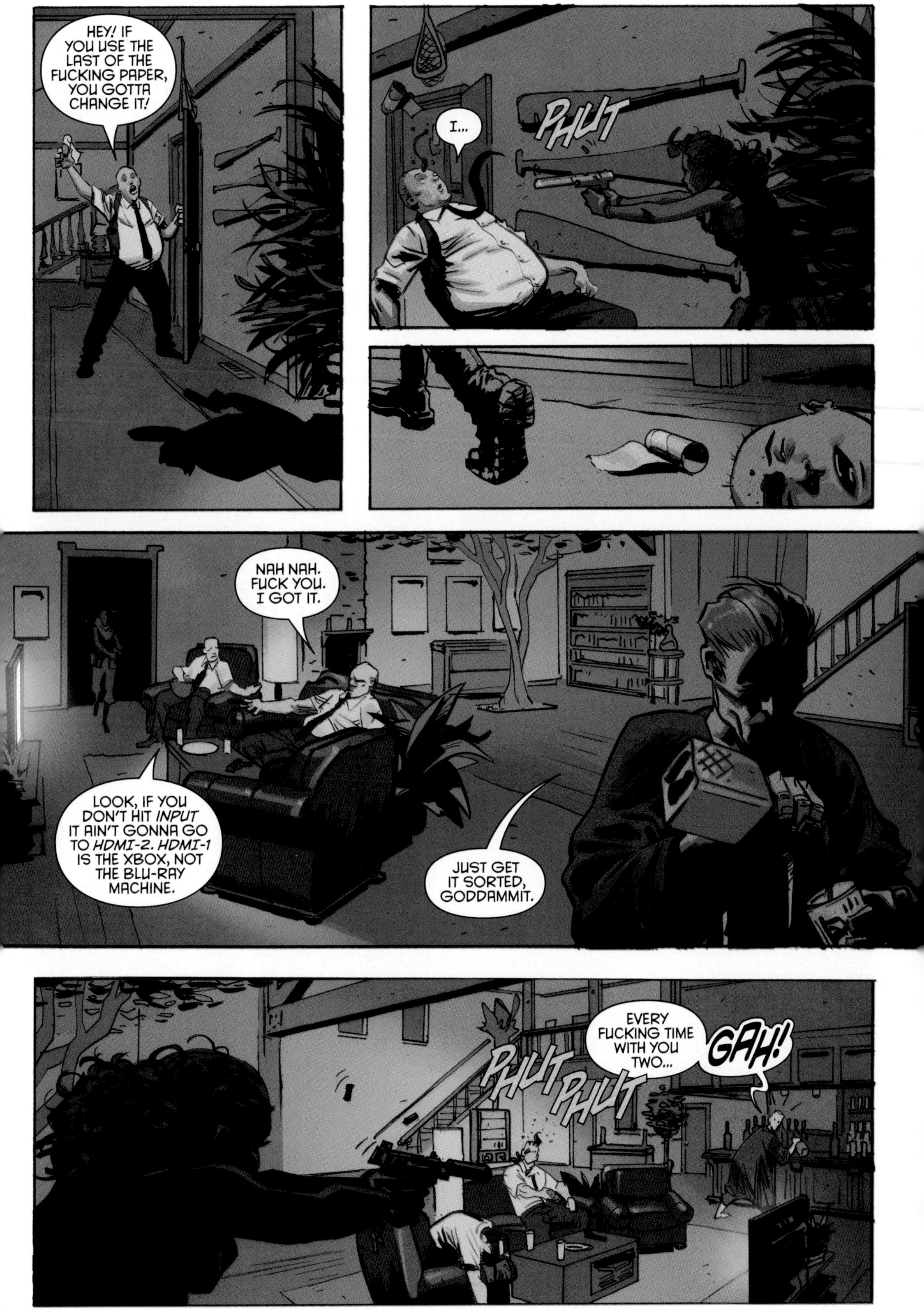
HEY! IF YOU USE THE LAST OF THE FUCKING PAPER, YOU GOTTA CHANGE IT!
I...
PHUT
NAH NAH. FUCK YOU. I GOT IT.
LOOK, IF YOU DON'T HIT INPUT IT AIN'T GONNA GO TO HDMI-2. HDMI-1 IS THE XBOX, NOT THE BLU-RAY MACHINE.
JUST GET IT SORTED, GODDAMMIT.
PHUT PHUT
EVERY FUCKING TIME WITH YOU TWO...
GAH!

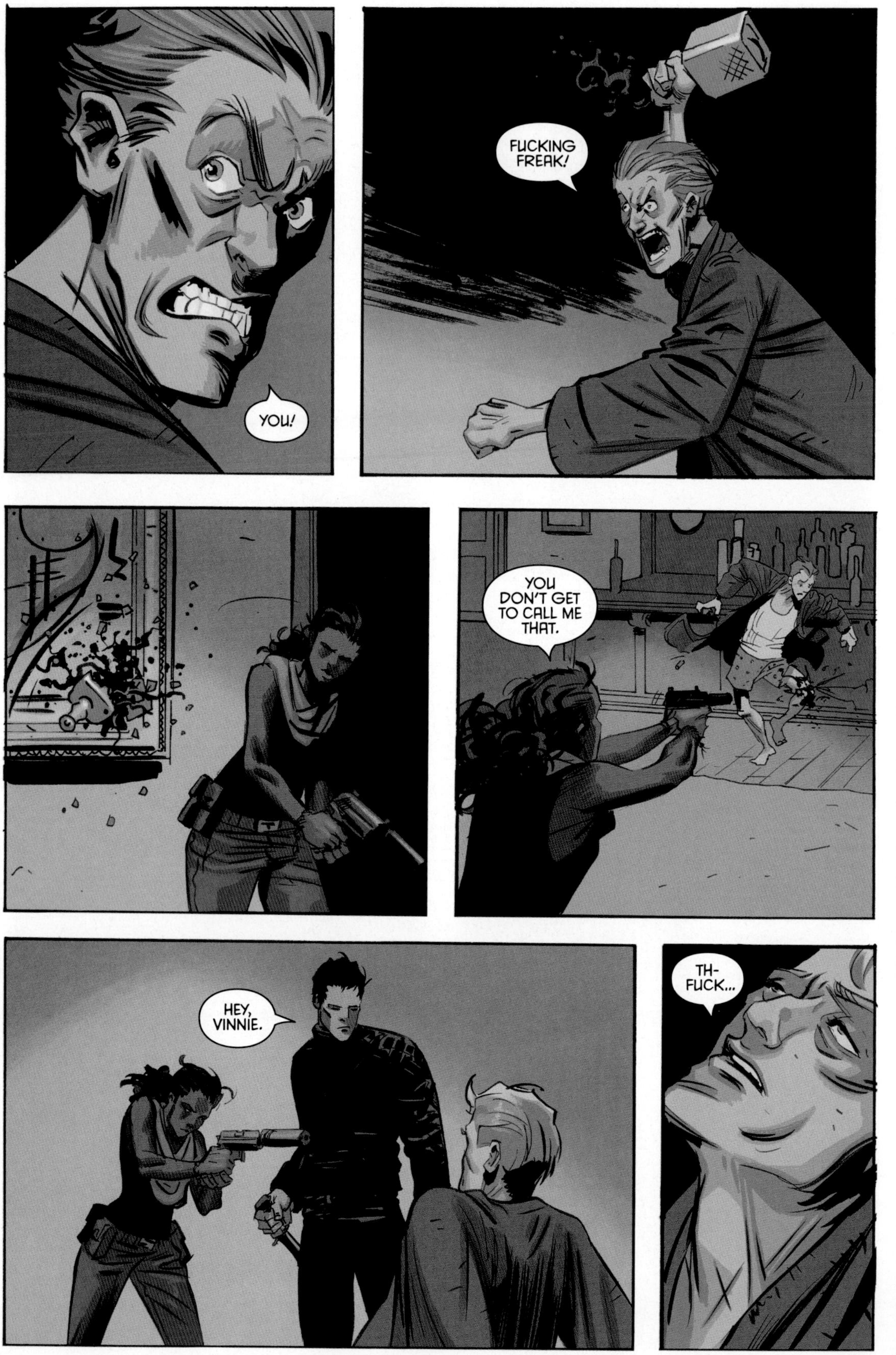
YOU!
FUCKING FREAK!
YOU DON'T GET TO CALL ME THAT.
HEY, VINNIE.
TH- FUCK...

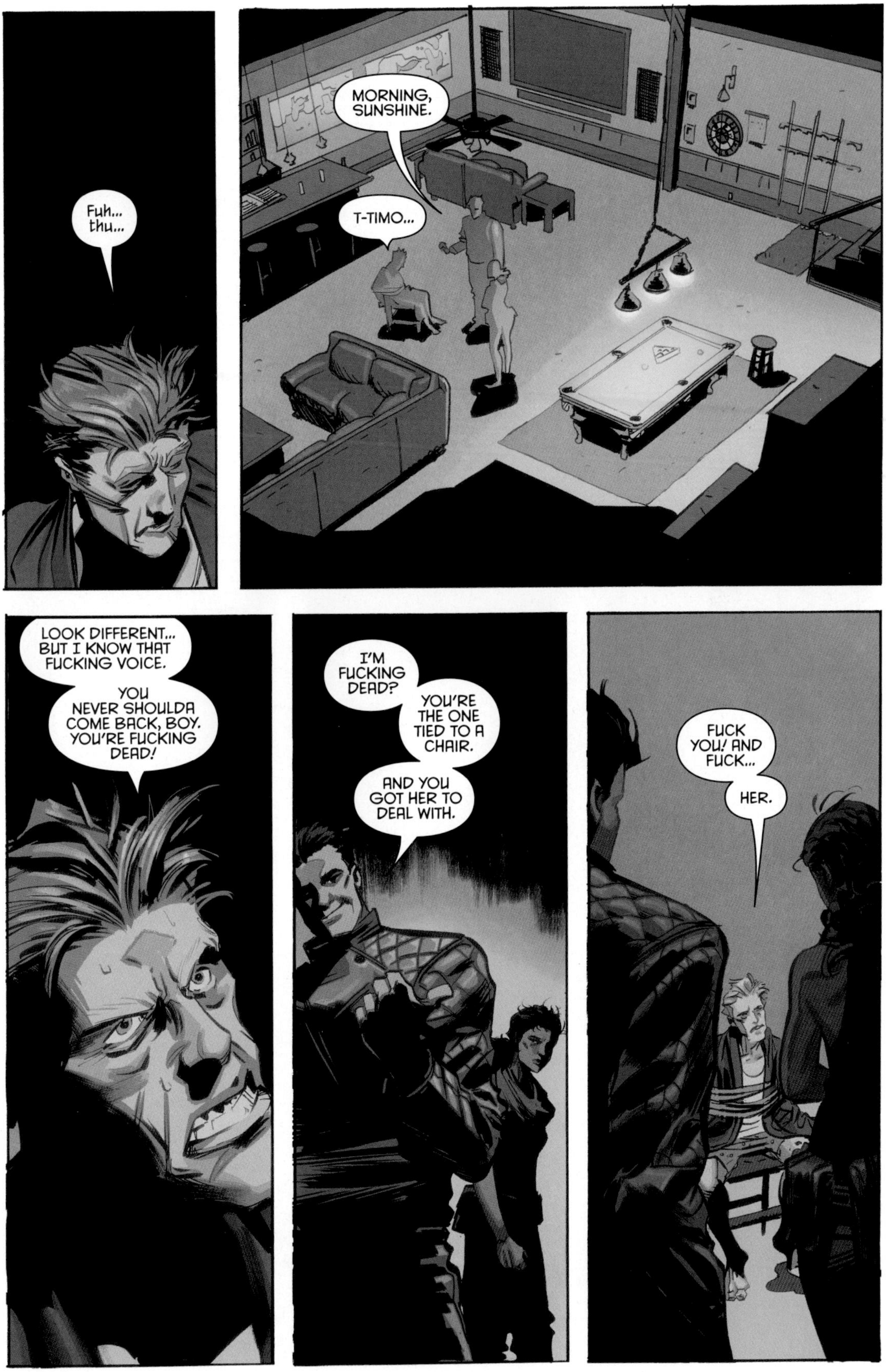
Fuh... thu...
MORNING, SUNSHINE.
T-TIMO...
LOOK DIFFERENT... BUT I KNOW THAT FUCKING VOICE.
YOU NEVER SHOULDA COME BACK, BOY. YOU'RE FUCKING DEAD!
I'M FUCKING DEAD?
YOU'RE THE ONE TIED TO A CHAIR.
AND YOU GOT HER TO DEAL WITH.
FUCK YOU! AND FUCK...
HER.

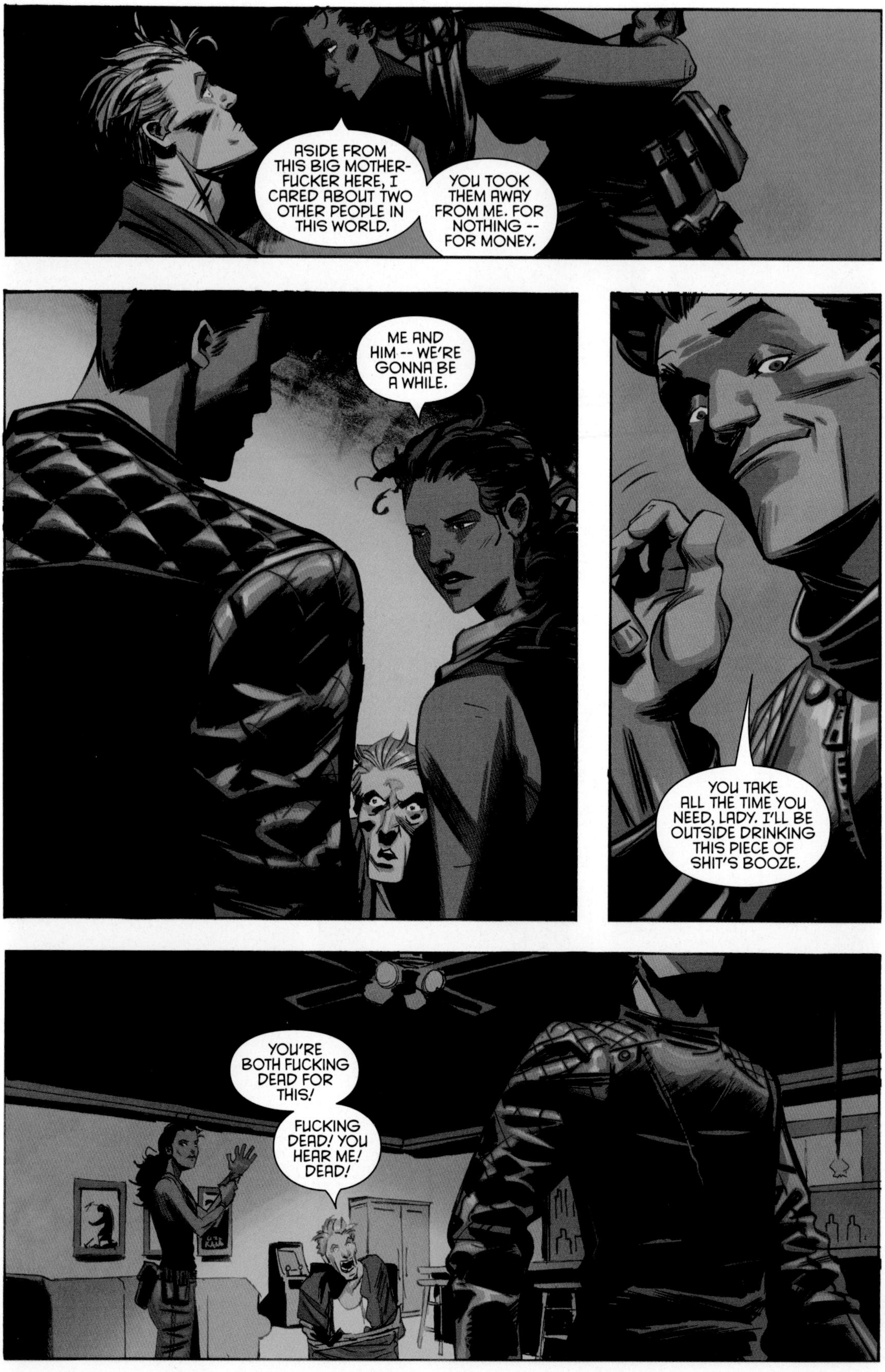
ASIDE FROM THIS BIG MOTHER-FUCKER HERE, I CARED ABOUT TWO OTHER PEOPLE IN THIS WORLD.
YOU TOOK THEM AWAY FROM ME. FOR NOTHING -- FOR MONEY.
ME AND HIM -- WE'RE GONNA BE A WHILE.
YOU TAKE ALL THE TIME YOU NEED, LADY. I'LL BE OUTSIDE DRINKING THIS PIECE OF SHIT'S BOOZE.
YOU'RE BOTH FUCKING DEAD FOR THIS!
FUCKING DEAD! YOU HEAR ME! DEAD!

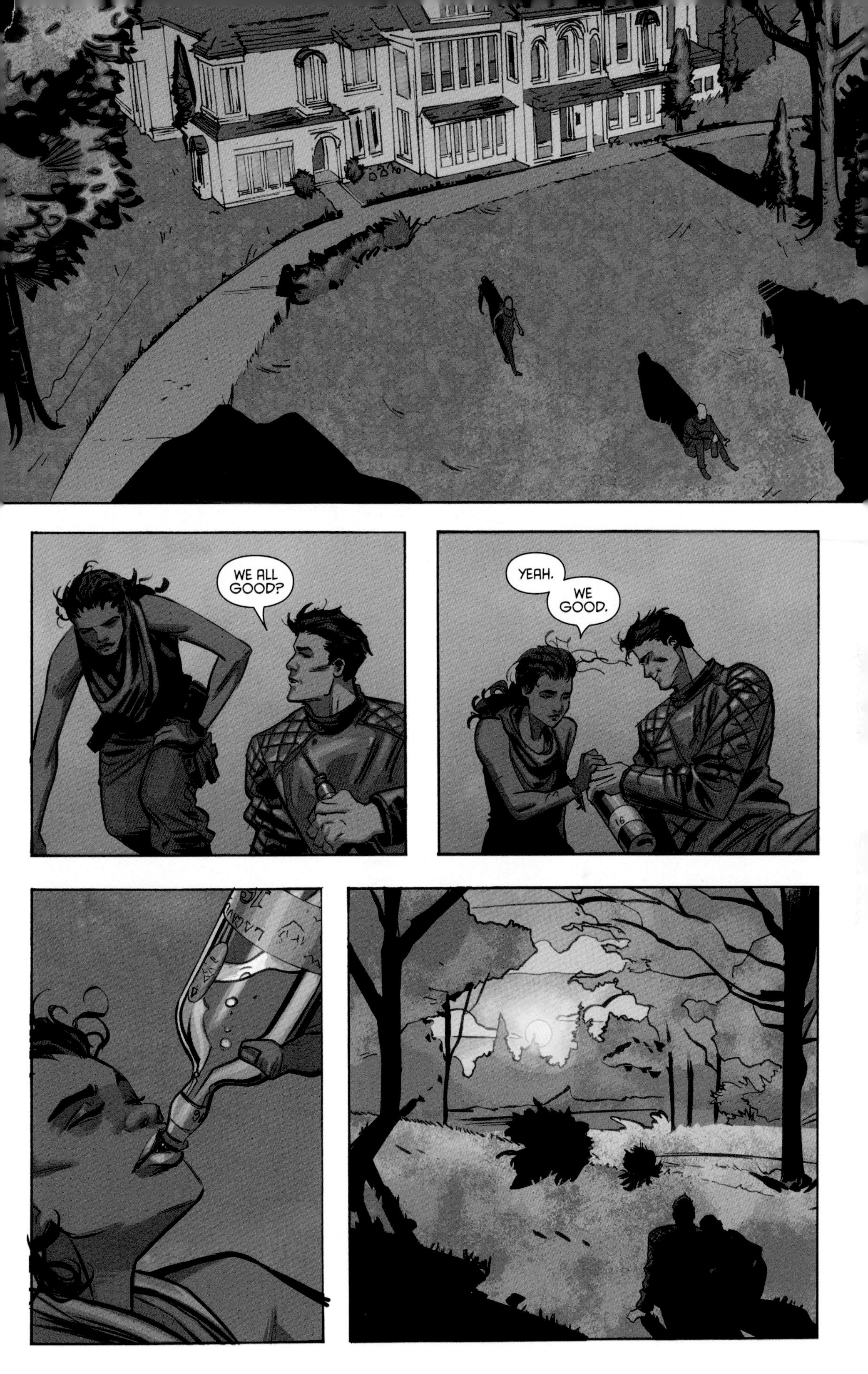
WE ALL GOOD?
YEAH.
WE GOOD.

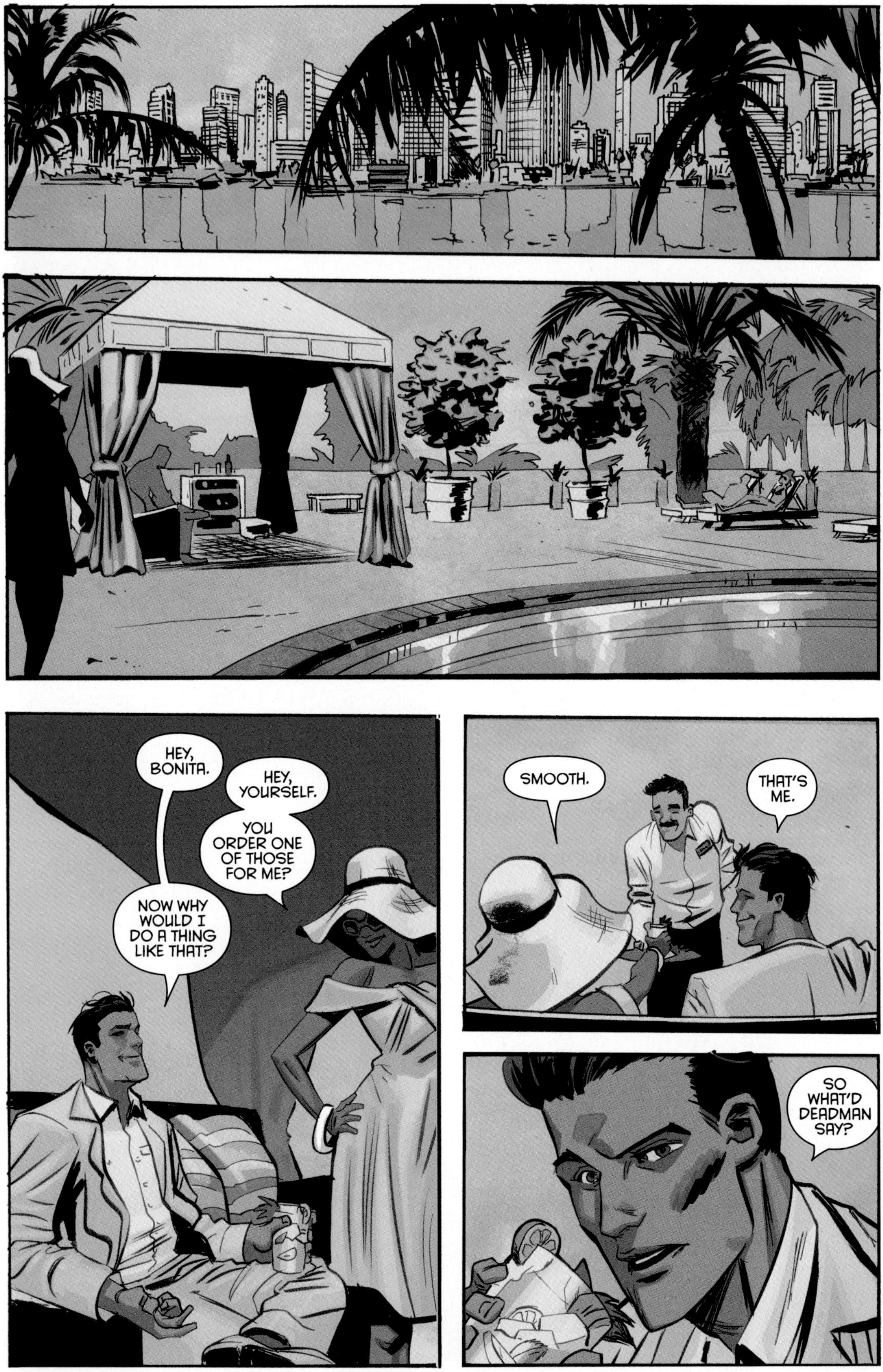
HEY, BONITA.
HEY, YOURSELF.
YOU ORDER ONE OF THOSE FOR ME?
NOW WHY WOULD I DO A THING LIKE THAT?
SMOOTH.
THAT'S ME.
SO WHAT'D DEADMAN SAY?

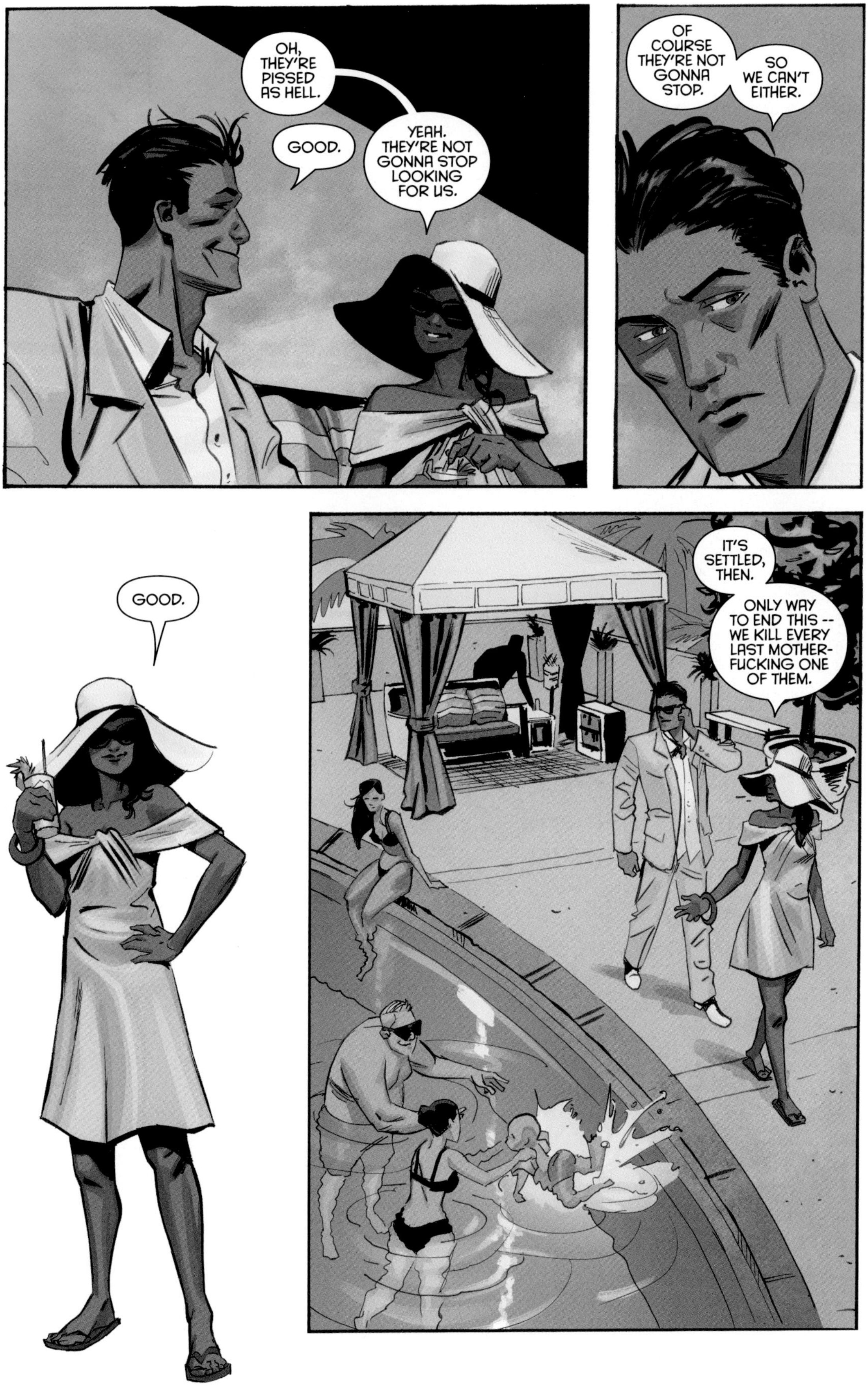
OH, THEY'RE PISSED AS HELL.
GOOD.
YEAH. THEY'RE NOT GONNA STOP LOOKING FOR US.
OF COURSE THEY'RE NOT GONNA STOP.
SO WE CAN'T EITHER.
GOOD.
IT'S SETTLED, THEN.
ONLY WAY TO END THIS -- WE KILL EVERY LAST MOTHER-FUCKING ONE OF THEM.

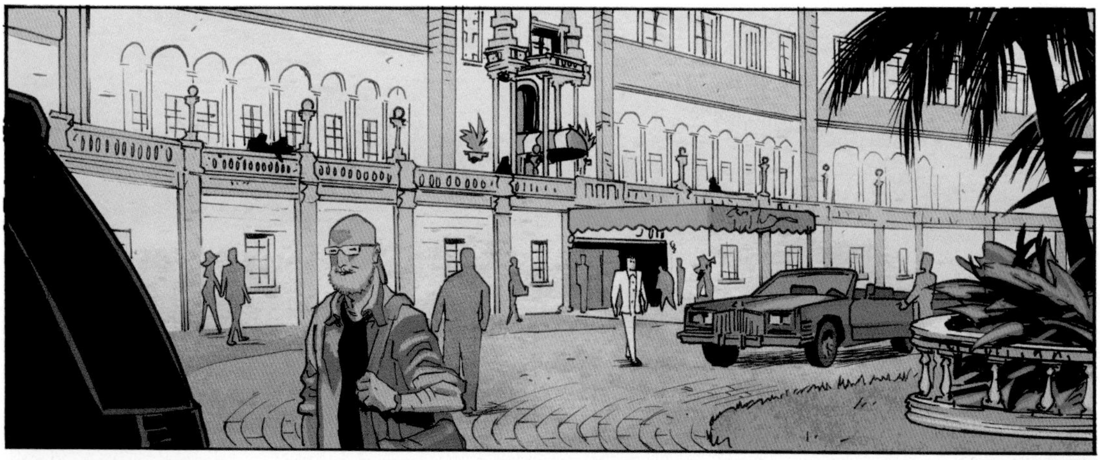

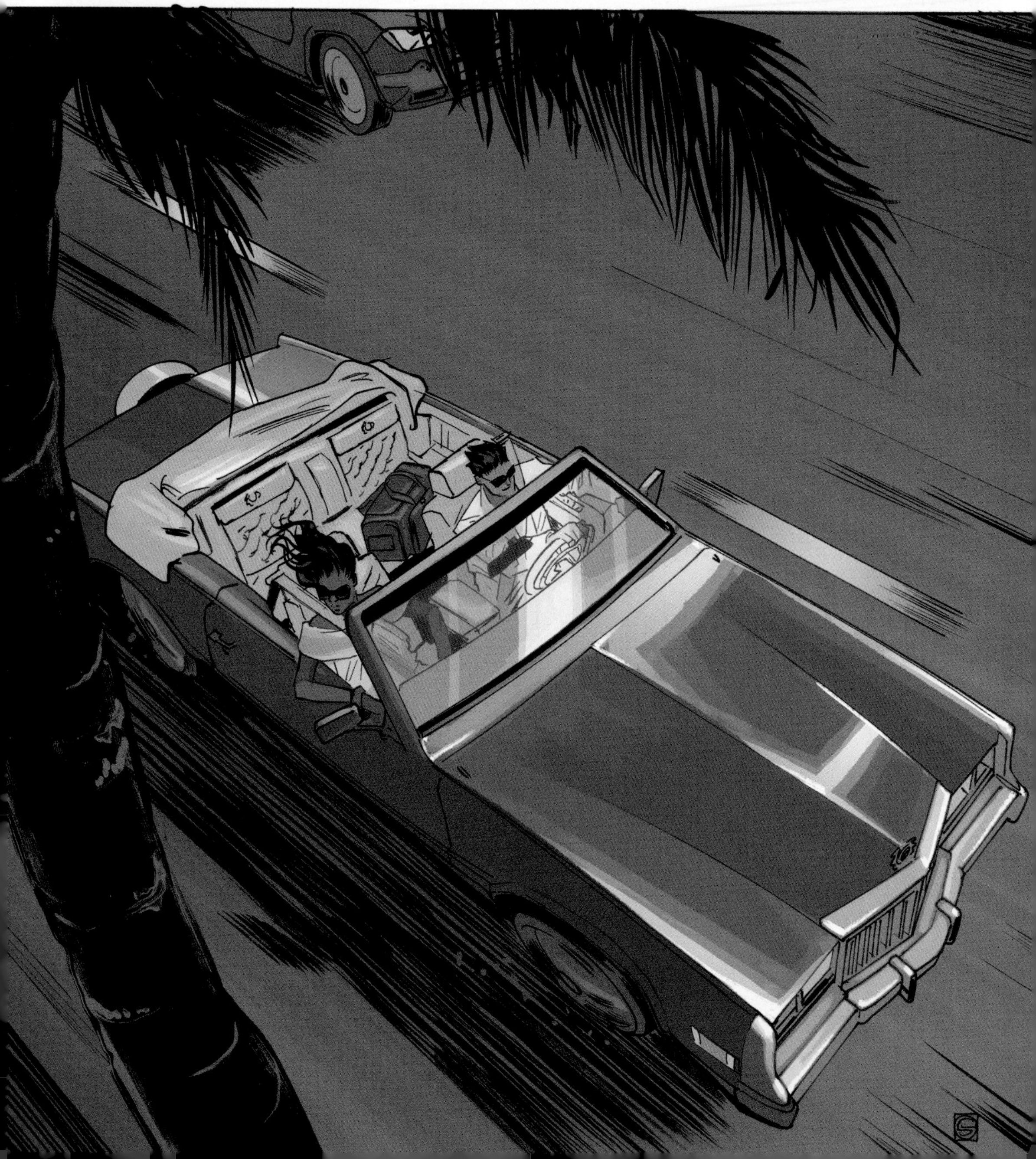

COVERS

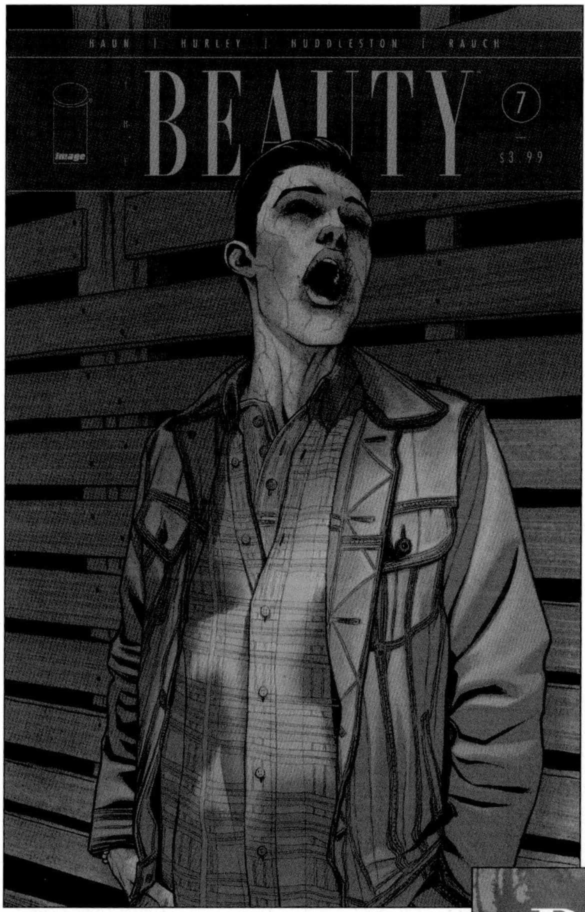

HAUN | HURLEY | HUDDLESTON | RAUCH
BEAUTY
7
$3.99

ISSUE #7
Cover A
Jeremy Haun
& John Rauch

ISSUE #7
Cover B
Brett Weldele

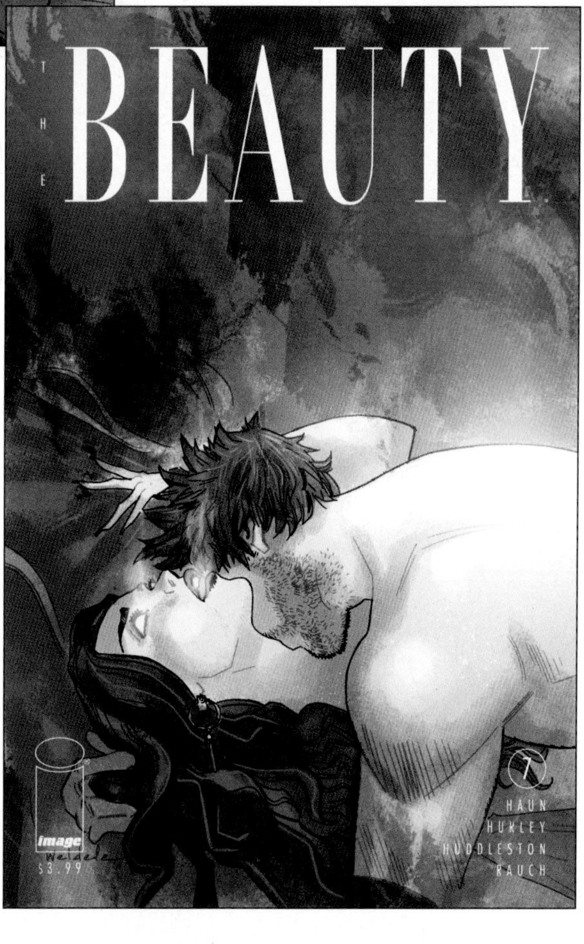

THE BEAUTY
7
HAUN
HURLEY
HUDDLESTON
RAUCH
$3.99

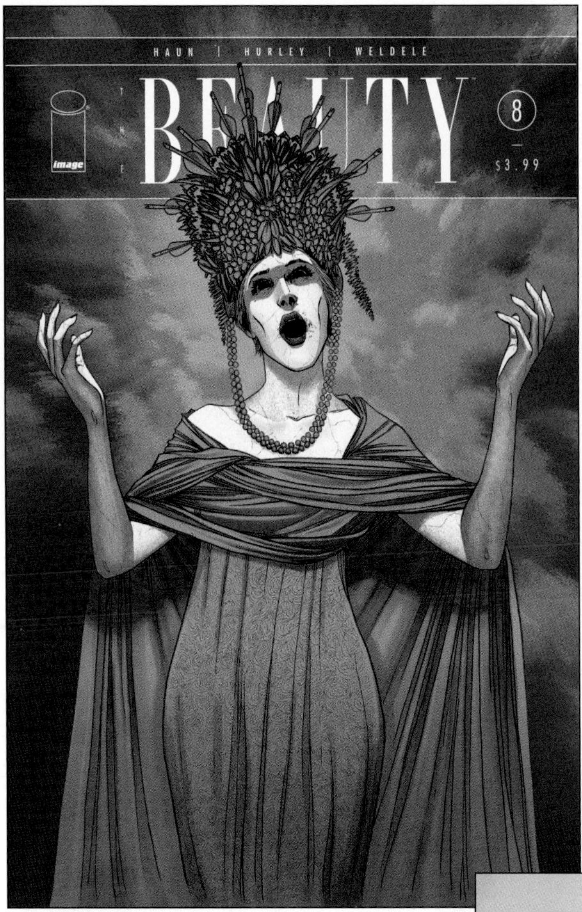
HAUN | HURLEY | WELDELE
THE
BEAUTY
8
$3.99
image

ISSUE #8
Cover A
Jeremy Haun
& John Rauch

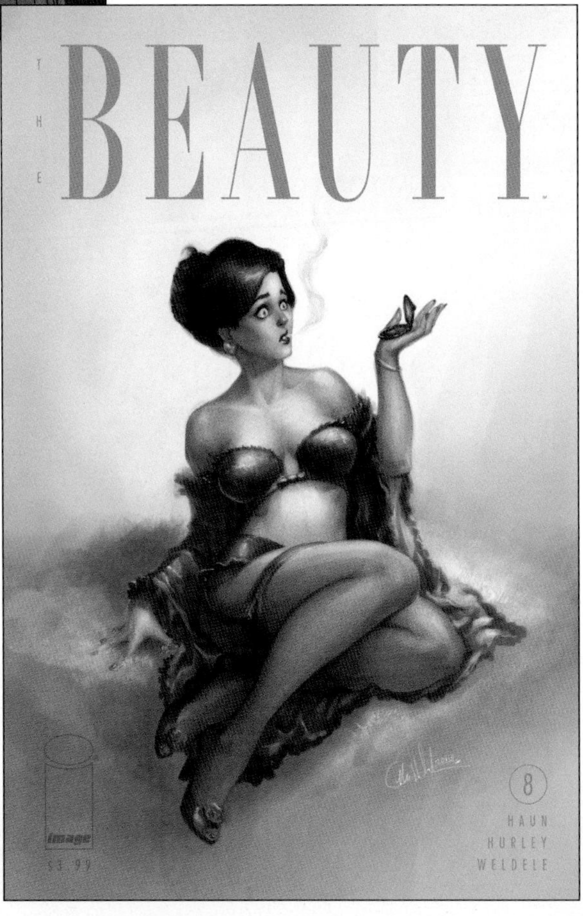
THE
BEAUTY
image
$3.99
8
HAUN
HURLEY
WELDELE

ISSUE #8
Cover B
Meghan Hetrick

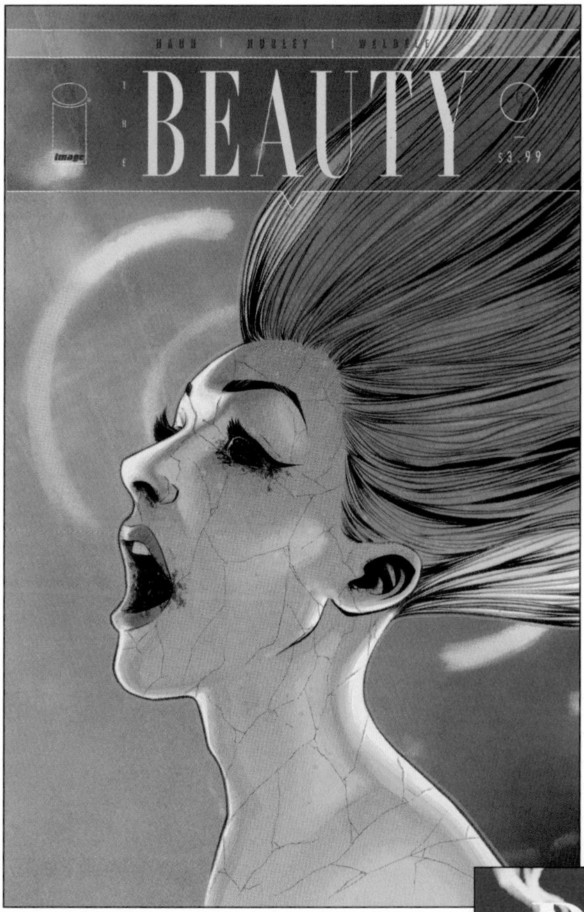
HAUN | HURLEY | WELDELE
THE BEAUTY
$3.99

ISSUE #9
Cover A
Jeremy Haun
& John Rauch

ISSUE #9
Cover B
Trungles

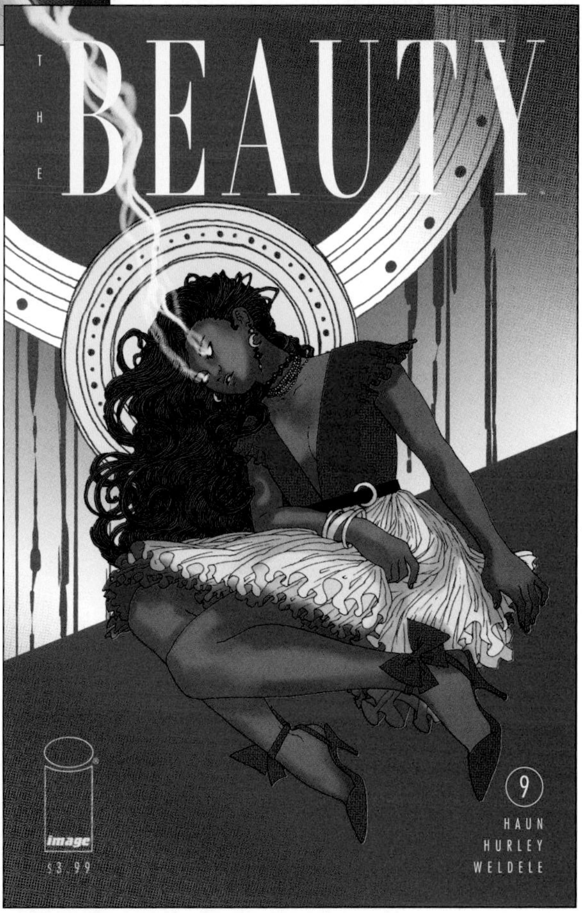
THE BEAUTY
9
HAUN
HURLEY
WELDELE
$3.99

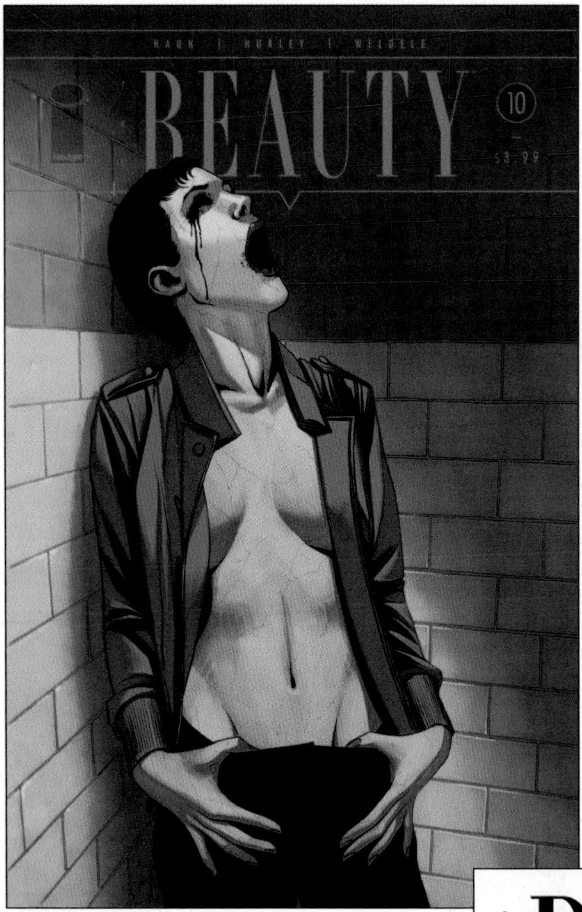
HAUN | HURLEY | WELDELE
THE BEAUTY
10
$3.99

ISSUE #10
Cover A
Jeremy Haun
& John Rauch

ISSUE #10
Cover B
Tigh Walker

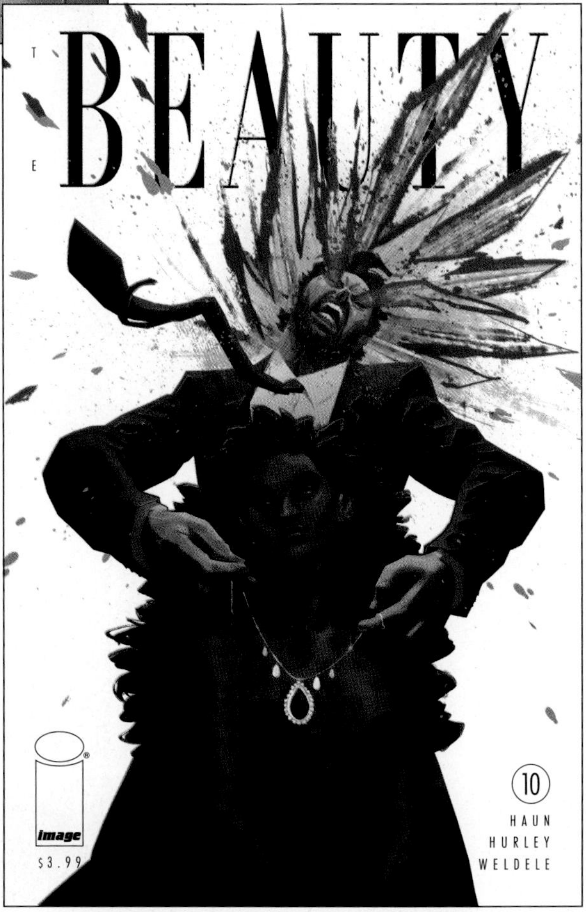
THE BEAUTY
image
$3.99
10
HAUN
HURLEY
WELDELE

BEAUTY
11

ISSUE #11
Cover A
Jeremy Haun
& John Rauch

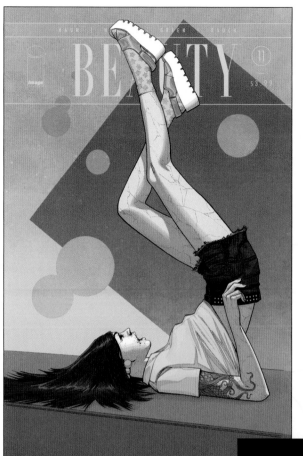

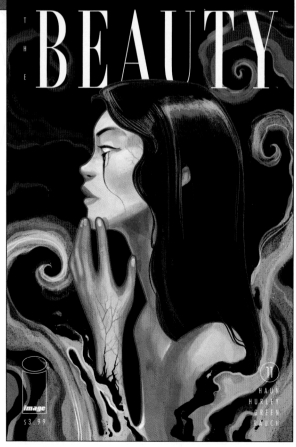

ISSUE #11
Cover B
Danielle Otrakji

THE BEAUTY
11
HAUN
HURLEY
GREEN
RAUCH
image
$3.99

BIOGRAPHIES

Jeremy Haun, co-writer, co-creator, and often artist of THE BEAUTY, has also worked on *Wolf Moon* from Vertigo, and *Constantine* and *Batwoman* from DC. Over the past decade plus, along with wearing calluses on his fingers doing work for DC, Marvel, Image, and others, he has created and written several projects. Some you might know are the graphic novel *Narcoleptic Sunday, The Leading Man,* and *Dino Day.* He is a part of the Bad Karma Creative group, whose *Bad Karma Volume One* debuted at NYCC 2013, thanks to Kickstarter funding.

Jeremy resides in a crumbling mansion in Joplin, Missouri, with his wife and two superheroes-in-training.

Jason A. Hurley has been in the comic book game for over fifteen years. However, none of you have ever heard of him because, until recently, he's been almost completely exclusive to the retail sector. In addition to comic books, he loves pro wrestling, bad horror movies, Freddy Mercury, hummingbirds, his parents, and pizza. While he's never actually tried it, he also thinks curling looks like a hell of a lot of fun. Hurley claims his personal heroes are Earl Bassett and Valentine McKee, because they live a life of adventure on their own terms. He also claims that he would brain anyone who showed even the most remote signs of becoming a cannibalistic undead bastard, including his own brother, without a second thought. He's lived in Joplin, Missouri, for most of his life, and never plans to leave.

Mike Huddleston is an American comic book artist who has worked on multiple DC, Marvel, and Image comics, as well as on Guillermo del Toro's *The Strain* for Dark Horse.

Brett Weldele is an Eisner-nominated comic book painter and *New York Times* best-selling author. He's probably best known for co-creating the hit comic book *The Surrogates,* which was adapted into the 2009 film starring Bruce Willis. His recent projects include working with *Shrek* producer Aron Warner on *Pariah* for Dark Horse Comics, *Vampirella 1969* for Dynamite, and *The Hammer Trinity* for The Arsht Center in Miami. Weldele also has a craft product line, The Art of Brett Weldele through Stampers Anonymous, which includes rubber stamps and stencils.

Stephen Green is an artist and animal hypnotist residing in historic Savannah, Georgia. His work can be found in THE LEGACY OF LUTHER STRODE, *Dark Horse Presents,* and *Hellboy and the B.P.R.D.: 1954.* He is represented by Felix Comic Art. He will be happy to sing at your funeral.

John Rauch is an American comic book colorist whose credits include: THE DARKNESS, INVINCIBLE, *Teen Titans: Year One, Patsy Walker: Hellcat,* and a bunch of other stuff not worth bragging about. He enjoys speaking about himself in the third person and pretending he is more talented and relevant than he really is to fight off bouts of depression.

Fonografiks The banner name for the comics work of designer Steven Finch, "Fonografiks" has provided lettering and design to a number of Image Comics titles, including NOWHERE MEN, INJECTION, TREES, WE STAND ON GUARD, the Eisner Award-winning anthology series POPGUN, and the multi-award winning SAGA.

Joel Enos is a writer and editor of comics and stories. Recent editing projects include the graphic novel THE RATTLER and the collected edition of THE SAVIORS, both published by Image Comics.